# The Queen's Governess

20.

# The Queen's Governess

## Karen Harper

W F HOWES LTD

This large print edition published in 2011 by
W F Howes Ltd
Unit 4, Rearsby Business Park, Gaddesby Lane,
Rearsby, Leicester LE7 4YH

1  3  5  7  9  10  8  6  4  2

First published in the United Kingdom in 2011
by Ebury Press

A CIP catalogue record for this book is available
from the British Library

ISBN 978 1 40748 881 3

Typeset by Palimpsest Book Production Limited,
Falkirk, Stirlingshire
Printed and bound in Great Britain
by MPG Books Ltd, Bodmin, Cornwall

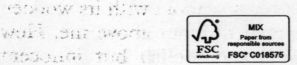

MIX
Paper from
responsible sources
FSC
www.fsc.org    FSC® C018575

# CHAPTER 1

## THE TOWER OF LONDON

*May 19, 1536*

I could not fathom they were going to kill the queen. Nor could I bear to witness Anne Boleyn's beheading. Still, I stepped off the barge on the choppy Thames and, with the other observers, entered the Tower through the water gate. I felt sick to my stomach and my very soul.

The spring sun and soft river breeze deserted us as we entered the Tower. All seemed dark and airless within the tall stone walls. We were shown our place at the back of the small, elite crowd. Thank the Lord, I did not have to stand close to the wooden scaffold that had been built for this dread deed. I had vowed to myself I would keep my eyes shut, and, standing back here, no one would know. Yet I stared straight ahead, taking it all in.

For, despite my distance of some twenty feet from it, the straw-strewn scaffold with its wooden stairs going up seemed to loom above me. How would Anne, brazen and foolish but innocent

1

Anne, stripped now of her title, her power, her daughter and husband, manage to get herself through this horror? She had always professed to be a woman of strong faith, so perhaps that would sustain her.

I yearned to bolt from the premises. I nearly lost my hard-won control. Tears blurred my vision, but I blinked them back.

The crowd hushed as the former queen came out into the sun, led by the Tower constable Sir William Kingston, with four ladies following. At least she had company at the end. Anne's almoner was with her; they both held prayer books. Her eyes up and straight ahead, her lips moved in silent prayer. I thought I read the words on them: '*Yea, though I walk through the valley of the shadow of death . . .*'

Before she reached the scaffold, others mounted it as if to greet her: the Lord Mayor of London, who had arranged her fine coronation flotilla but three years ago this very month, and several sheriffs in their scarlet robes. Then, too, the black-hooded French swordsman and his assistant, who had come from France. Anne's head jerked when she saw her executioner.

The woman who had been Queen of England hesitated but a moment at the bottom of the steps, then mounted. She wore a robe of black damask, cut low and trimmed with fur, and a crimson kirtle, the color of martyr's blood, I thought. She had gathered her luxuriant dark hair into a net but over it wore the style of headdress she had made fashionable, a half-moon shape trimmed with pearls.

I saw no paper in her hand, nor did she look down as her clear voice rang out words she had obviously memorized: 'Good Christian people, I am come hither to die according to law, therefore I will speak nothing against it. I am come hither to accuse no man, nor to speak anything of that whereof I am accused.'

I knew such contrition was part of her agreement with the king's henchman Cromwell. It was also the price she had to pay for having me here today. I could hardly bear it. Yet, for her, I stood straight, staring at her. Betrayed and abandoned, if she could face this, I could too.

'I come here,' Anne went on with a glance and a nod directly at me, though others might think it was but to emphasize her words, 'only to die, and thus to yield myself humbly unto the will of my lord the king.'

*Damn the king*, I vowed, however treasonous that mere thought. Men, not even the great Henry Tudor, had a right to cast off and execute a woman he had pursued and lusted for, had bred a child on, the little Elizabeth I knew and loved so well. The terrible charges against Anne had been trumped up, yet I dared not say so. I wanted to scream out my anger, to leap upon the scaffold and save her – but I stood silent as a stone, struck with awe and dread. But then, since no one stood

3

behind me, I dared to lift my hand to hold up the tiny treasure she had entrusted to me. Perhaps she could not see it; perhaps she would think I was waving farewell to her, but I did it anyway, then pulled my hand back down.

'I pray God to save the king,' she went on with another nod, which I prayed meant she had seen my gesture, 'and send him long to reign over you, for a gentler or more merciful prince was there never. To me he was ever a good and gentle sovereign lord.'

Shuffling feet nearby, nervous shifting in the crowd. A smothered snort. I was not the only one who knew this was a public sham and shame. No doubt, she said all that to protect her daughter's future, the slim possibility that, if the king had no legitimate son and Catholic Mary was not fully reinstated, Elizabeth could be returned to the line of succession – for the poor three-year-old was declared a bastard now. I swore silently I would ever serve Elizabeth well and protect her as best I could from such tyrannical rule by men. At least Anne Boleyn was going to a better place.

Again, I longed to close my eyes, but I could not. When had the terrible things I had borne in my life been halted or helped one whit by cowering or fleeing?

Anne spoke briefly to her ladies, and they removed her cape. She gave a necklace, earrings, a ring and her prayer book away to them, while I fingered the secret gift she had given me. She gave the swordsman a coin and, as was tradition, asked him to make his work quick and forgave him for what he was bound to do.

She knelt and rearranged her skirts. She even helped one of her trembling ladies to adjust a bandage tied over her eyes. Huddled off to the side, her women began to cry, but, beyond that, utter silence but the screech of a seagull flying free over the Thames. I realized I was holding my breath and let it out jerkily, as if I would fall to panting like a dog.

To bare her neck, Anne held her head erect as if she still wore St Edward's crown as she had in the Abbey on her coronation day. Then came her hurried, repeated words, 'O Lord God, have pity on my soul, O Lord God, have pity on my soul . . .'

I wondered if, in her last frenzied moments, she was picturing her little Elizabeth. I sucked in a sharp sob of regret that the child would never really remember her mother. At least I had known mine before she died – slain as surely as this so someone else might have her husband. That cast me back to my mother's death, vile and violent, too . . .'

'O Lord God, have pity on my soul, O Lord God, have pity on my—'

The swordsman lifted a long silver sword from the straw and struck in one swift swing. The crowd gave a common gasp, and someone screamed. As

Anne's slender body fell, spouting blood, the executioner held up her head with the lips still moving. Horror-struck, I imagined that, at the very end, she had meant to shout, 'O Lord God, have pity on my daughter!'

# CHAPTER 2

Near Dartington, Devon

*April 4, 1516*

G od have mercy on her soul. She's gone,'
my father told the two of us. 'Dear Lord
God, have pity on her soul.'

'Mother. Mother! Please, please wake up! Please
come back!' I screamed again and again, throwing
river water on her face, until my father shook me
hard by the shoulders.

'Leave off!' he demanded, his forehead furrowed,
his eyes glassy with unshed tears. We knelt in the
thick grass by the rushing River Dart where her
body had been laid out, covered by her friend
Maud Wicker's wet apron, for her own clothes had
nearly burned away. When I still shrieked as loudly
as the gulls on the river, he commanded, 'Enough,
Kat!' Unlike Mother, he had seldom used the pet
name I'd had since I couldn't pronounce my own
when I was still in leading strings. That sweet little
comfort almost steadied me until he added, 'You'll
learn to accept much more than this, so bear up,
girl!'

But I couldn't. I just couldn't and heaved great breaths in my frenzy. If only we had been here sooner! But by the time I returned home from keeping watch over Lord Barlow's daughter at Dartington Hall where Father kept his lordship's beehives, the local tinker had come to our house to fetch us. While seagulls wheeled and shrieked overhead as if in warning, Father and I hied ourselves across the cattle field, toward the river.

Now, my cheeks slick with tears, I finally sat in sullen silence. He patted Maud's shoulder, then squeezed her hand before he let it go and stood looking away, head down, leaning stiff-armed against a tree. Why did he seem only resigned, not more shaken? His wife, Cecily Champernowne, aged twenty-eight years, had hit the back of her head and bled into her brown hair. Her entire body was bruised and blackened, even her face mine so resembled.

[Years later, time and again, I tried to tell myself that stoic mourning was just the way with men, but even cruel King Henry piteously grieved the death of his third wife, Queen Jane, and William Cecil sobbed when his second son – not even his heir – died.]

'I – I am overthrown by it all,' Maud said, talking to me as much as to Father. 'She must have caught her skirts in the hearth fire.' Sitting on her heels, several feet away, she wrung her hands. Gray soot and brown river mud smeared her sopped petti-coats. Tears from her long-lashed blue eyes speckled her rosy cheeks. 'I was drawing nigh the house for a visit and heard her screams. She rushed out willy-nilly. I – I believe she struck her head on the hearthstones, trying to get the fire out. God as my judge, I tried to roll her on the ground to smother the flames. But in her pain and panic, she ran toward the river. The winds – they made it worse. But I . . . she jumped in the water. I think she died of drowning, not the flames, though I tried to pull her out in time, God rest her soul.'

Father muttered something about God's will. I swore silently that if I'd been there, I'd have put those flames out fast.

That day a part of me died too – my entire girl-hood, truth be told. I was ten years old. I was angry with God's will and even more furious that Father kept comforting Maud Wicker more than he did me.

In four months' time, Mistress Wicker became my stepmother. She was but eighteen, one of six daughters of the man who wove my father's beehives from stout wicker he soaked in the river to get it to bend. Maud had always brought the finished hives to father in a cart and had laughed at his silly stories that Mother only rolled her eyes at. The only good thing for me about their marriage was that the arguing my parents had done now became all honeyed words. Father never raised a hand to his second wife, though she had a temper hotter than my mother's.

And Maud had a shrewish side she showed only to me. As I grew older, festering under her orders – and pinches and slaps, when Father wasn't about the house – I sometimes took to wondering if my stepmother had been with my mother when her skirts caught the flames, instead of just coming toward the house, as she'd said. That day two new hives had been left out back, and fresh cart tracks marred the mud. But the cart had also left tracks as it was trundled across the field toward the river. When I asked her once why, since it was not the way she went home, she told me she was just dawdling about the area so her father would not give her another task. As I oft did such myself, I let it go. But I'd found a willow green ribbon when I swept the hearth the night Mother died, and Maud Wicker loved such fripperies for her yellow curls.

I kept that ribbon buried in my secret box of dried flowers, along with a sweet bag given me by Lady Barlow of Dartington Hall, else Maud would have taken it for her own. The sweet bag was a gift, Lady Barlow said, for my helping to care for her Sarah during tutoring sessions with her older brother, Percy. Poor Sarah went about in a wheeled chair at times, her tongue lolling from her mouth, her body shaking when she had her fits. I used to help hold her quill and form her words on paper. I held her book for her so she could read from it. But there was a keen brain inside her too, and – like me – she loved learning.

Also in the box, which I kept hidden in the thick hedge out back, were two smooth stones from the River Dart near where Mother died and clover from a pixie circle on the moors before they were chased off by one of the ghostly hellhounds. Everyone roundabout knew not to go out on the moors at night. Sometimes I wasn't sure if the cries of gulls in the creeping fogs weren't the shrieks of lost souls out on the moors. The box also used to hold my mother's garnet necklace, but Maud had wheedled it from my father when she bore their second child, a daughter this time. Her little Simon and Amelia were the loves of my life then, so innocent and angelic, until they began to act like their mother, throwing tantrums for things they must have.

Yet I did not mislike my half siblings as I did Maud. Things she did were not their fault. Rather, I pitied them even as I did my own father, who, like a dumb rutting ram had made his bed and obviously liked well to lie in it. Maud – whom I called Mistress instead of Mother, no matter how she fussed at me – would no doubt have made me toil for her all day had not the Barlows paid Father for my services to Sarah. They never knew I would have happily helped their child for nothing, as I learned to read and write while tending her.

Most important of all in my hidden treasure box, now that my necklace had as good as been stolen from me, I kept these pages of my story. Once I learned to write well, from the time I was about twelve years of age, when Sarah was taking her naps in her chamber, I borrowed pen and paper from her writing table and began this record of my life, hoping I would someday amount to something. Over the years, from time to time, I went back and amended it from a far wiser point of view. And, oh yes, in my treasure box, I also kept a list of hints I brooded over, hoping to prove Maud had something to do with my mother's accident, but who would credit it since it would be my word against hers?

Without my tasks at Dartington Hall and my walks to and from that fine gray stone manor each day, I would never have had time to hide these pages or to seize a moment to myself – *carpe diem*, my first snippet of Latin. Without the kindly Barlows, I would not have learned about the other world beyond our thatched longhouse built of moorstone with the attached shippon which housed our six cattle. I never would have known about fine needlework or Turkey carpets or tapestries or delicacies like squab pie instead of fat bacon or Latin, let alone English sentences. I never would have heard of the other English shires beyond remote Devon, a distant world where a king ruled his people from great palaces. Without my times at Dartington Hall, I would never have learned such or yearned much. But still, it was not enough, and I longed to escape to – to I knew not where.

★　★　★

'Unless her ladyship can find a lad in service for you to wed, you've managed to outprice yourself for the likes of most men round here,' Mistress Maud scolded me one day. 'Too much fancy learning makes you put on airs. Your speech apes the Barlows' and makes you stand out like a white duckling among the yellows. Besides, too many Champernownes live in these parts. They'd be the best prospects, but you're cousins to most of them. So mayhap like a nun, you should just stay to home.'

I was nearly nineteen then, but had kept myself so busy – and stayed so solitary when I could snatch some moments to myself – that I hadn't given marriage a thought. Besides, Maud had managed to subtly convince me I was not, as she put it once, 'fetching enough to fetch a good man.'

Even after two children and nine years wed, Maud was still comely and knew it well. Her blond curls and blue eyes made me feel a lesser being with my unruly bounty of auburn hair and what Lady Barlow had once called my 'tawny brown eyes.' I thought my face was fine enough with a straight nose and full, pert mouth, though my cheeks and nose were too oft tinged russet by the sun. But I was never one to study myself in the polished copper surface of a looking glass Maud had bought, and Lady Barlow kept such out of Sarah's chamber.

Then, too, Maud was slight and graceful, a far cry from my hourglass build. Lady Barlow was

13

graceful too. I loved to watch her ride sidesaddle round the walls of Dartington Hall with her husband and son while Sarah and I waved. Someday, I vowed silently, I would learn to ride like that. In faith, even if it meant living near Maud, I'd rather read or ride than be wed – unless my husband bought me a horse and took me to live in London, that is.

All these years, I was certain the good Lord would send me some sign that I was meant for better things than housemaid and nursemaid. I've since oft asked for forgiveness for this sinful thought, but then I thought the Great Creator of the world must owe me something for the loss of my mother so young. How was I to know what I deemed a gift from God for my deliverance must have come instead from the very gates of hottest hell?

The second day that was to change my life forever, the first being the day my mother died, was the day I saw a king's man, come clear from London. It was mid-October 1525, and the man was far more exciting than glimpses of Lord Barlow, who leased Dartington Hall from the Crown, even though it was the same fine manor that had once been owned by the Dukes of Exeter. But a man who worked for the king – or rather for King Henry's great and powerful Cardinal Wolsey – that was splendid, despite the way I discovered the poor man. As if it were indeed a heavenly omen,

I found him nearly in the same spot my mother had died, but nearer the road toward the old clapper bridge.

'Hey, there! Mistress!' a man called out to me. 'My master's been ill with a fever, and now his horse stepped in a hole and threw him. Perchance you can summon aid.'

I knew instantly they were not from Devon, for the man's speech was not broad and slow but clipped, sharper. I peered round a tree and saw the other man on the ground with the one who'd called out hovering over him. Two horses stood nearby, fetlock-deep in the brightly hued tumble of fallen leaves.

'I can't bring him round, but he's breathing,' the burly man said as I approached, wary at first of a trick. The man who had called out looked terrified. That and their fine mounts and the prone man's clothes made me think he must be someone important. And yes, he was sweated up with a fever, so it seemed someone had thrown river water on his face already.

While I kept back a bit, the man who'd called out asked, 'Pray, can you help me to waken him, then fetch help?'

My heart thudded like horses' hooves. Again I saw my mother's body laid out here, but I bent at the river's edge to fill my cupped hands with water and threw it on the unconscious man's face. A strong face, chiseled, with dark, straight eyebrows. He was clean shaven, but not a young man, mayhap in the midst of his third decade. He had a pronounced scar across his pointed chin as if he were a ruffian, but his hands were not those of a fighter or laborer. Long-fingered, he had a pronounced callus where he must have oft gripped a pen; ink circled the close-cut nails of his right hand like half-moons. Dressed in leather and brown wool, he wore a befurred cape spread out under him as if he had wings – like an angel, I thought, another celestial sign.

I got a second double handful of water and – unlike with my mother – brought him back to life, cursing and sputtering. But when he tried to shift his position, he muttered 'Araugh!' through gritted teeth.

'Master Cromwell, should I go for help?' his man asked. He was younger, burlier, more guard than secretary.

'Can't – move my shoulder – without pain – araugh!' he cried, clutching at it. The cords of his neck stood out; his face went red and more sweat popped out on his forehead. 'Mistress, do you live nearby? This fever's just from something I must have eaten – not the sweat or worse. We can pay for food and shelter, till – till my man here finds a place – ah, hell's gates, it might be broken and my writing arm, too!'

'I live with my father and his wife nearby in humble circumstances, just across that field,' I said, gesturing. 'But if you could make it a mile beyond, I'm sure the Barlows would take you in at Dartington Hall. I know the family. It's a grand place, once the seat of the Dukes of Exeter.'

'We were headed there – for the night. But no. Too far. Maybe on the morrow. I'll barely make it anywhere . . . and you speak well.'

I spoke well! My heart leaped with loyalty, even a sort of love for this stranger. So I led their horses, as sleek and well fed as those the Barlows rode, while Master Stephen – that was the only name I knew him by, even years later – assisted Master Cromwell across the field toward our house.

One look at the men and, with assurance the fever was not dangerous, Father lodged them in his bedroom, while the pregnant Maud took my tiny room where I usually slept with the two children. That night Father stayed on a pallet before the hearth and I on the thick horse blanket that had been under Mr Cromwell's saddle with his fine fur-lined cape spread over me. It smelled of wind and mist and pure adventure.

In his fever that first night, he ranted about making his way in the world. Father and I tended him, with his man's help. By candlelight, for hours, after Father went to look in on Maud, I wiped Master Cromwell's face with cool water and tipped a mug of ale to his parched lips. Once, when Master Stephen went into the shippon to see to their horses tethered amidst our cattle, Thomas Cromwell seized my wrist and called me wife.

'Wife, my time has come. Through Wolsey, I shall serve the king.'

'I'm Katherine Champernowne, Master Cromwell. Your horse threw you in Devon, and you have a fever.'

'All my work,' he went on as if I had not spoken. 'I couldn't see why at first he wanted me to survey the abbeys this far away, but now I do. He'll quietly close them; he'll use their riches for the schools he'll build in his name. His great legacy is not only ruling England for the king but his new colleges at Ipswich and Oxford.'

'Who is that, sir?'

'Wolsey. His Eminence, the Cardinal Wolsey!'

It was the first time it had occurred to me that the king might reign, yet did not rule England by himself. Without anyone else to hear, it was great fun to pretend I was this man's wife and lived in London and had a horse of my own to ride.

'I should like to see your Cardinal Wolsey,' I told him. I knew he wasn't hearing what I said in his delirium. How I'd like to beg him to take me with him when he went back to London. The privy desires of my heart went to my head as I told him, 'I should like to see London and the king and his Spanish queen and live there too!'

'Who would think it?' he raved on, thankfully not responding to my chatter. 'I must list the abbeys for him. But don't tell the king!'

'No, I won't.'

'Won't what?' he said, looking at me, puzzled. As if his fever had broken, he was even more drenched with sweat. Since he hadn't really heard a thing I'd said, I told him, 'I won't tell the king that you had to put up here in the likes of a cattle- and beekeeper's house in the depths of Devon, tended by a maid who longs to see the places you've been dreaming about.'

'Dreaming? Have I?' he said, releasing his strong grip on my wrist at last. 'Dreaming, I warrant, of a Devon lass. One with a quick wit. I was talking about Cardinal Wolsey's orders, was I not?'

I looked him straight in the eyes, eyes darker than my tawny brown ones and far deeper set, as if shadows lurked there, guarding whatever depths lay within.

'You did, Master Cromwell, but I know how to keep a secret and am of no account in this back- water place anyway.'

His eyes glittered with the remnants of delirium. Eagerly he drank from the cup of ale I offered him, then cleared his throat and said, 'I think your father told me you can read and write.'

'I tend the lord and lady's daughter at the Hall, so when she and her brother are tutored, I am too, silently, but I rehearse it all well later.'

'Clever girl. I'm exhausted now. Pain – debili- tating,' he said, though I recall I didn't know what that last word meant then and later asked Sarah. 'I need to sleep, and we will talk in the morning.'

'In the morning, if you wish, we can move you to Dartington Hall.'

He shook his sleek, dark head. 'Shoulder hurts too much. Maybe later, everything later . . .'

He seemed instantly to sleep. But with Thomas Cromwell, I learned later to my detriment, seeming was more important than being.

It's true and no mistake that Thomas Cromwell was secretary and councilor to the king's great and powerful Cardinal Wolsey. Cromwell had no broken shoulder but a severely wrenched one that had come out of its socket. Sadly, for me, he did move to Dartington Hall, where Lord Barlow's leech put it back in place and made him a sling and dosed him with pain-deadening herbs. Maud, fat as a woolsack in her third pregnancy, was ecstatic that he'd given Father a half crown for our tending of him. For several days, I caught only glimpses of Cromwell here and there about the manor grounds with Lord Barlow. I heard Cromwell had ordered his man Stephen on to Plymouth to send word to the cardinal about why he was delayed. Secretary Cromwell did, however, come to the schoolroom to speak privily to the tutor one day and nodded to me both when he entered and when he left.

Then, the third day after he'd departed from our house, I'd heard he'd soon be leaving. I longed to bid him farewell, but was told he had gone for a ride to test his arm. To my surprise and pleasure, he came upon me as I was walking home that day, scuffing through dry leaves, loath to leave the Hall for home. He slowed his big horse to a walk beside me.

Before I could inquire about his arm, he asked, 'Did you mean what you said, that you really long to go to London?'

A new-fledged hope bloomed in me. 'I – I didn't know you had heard that.'

'Then you must learn to be careful what you say, for even the walls have ears.'

I looked up at him. He was not smiling, but had that avid, almost hungry look that I later learned was a sign he was devouring facts, information, things he somehow stowed away in that fertile, many-chambered brain of his. When I said nothing, he added, 'Life is like climbing a ladder. I'm on a sturdy rung, but not one lofty enough by far. Do you catch my meaning, Mistress Champernowne?'

'I think I do, Master Cromwell. You are an ambitious man on your way up. You have plans.'

'Precise and pithy – I like that in you. And the fact you evidently have told no one of my babblings about visiting the monasteries hereabouts or why.'

'Such as Buckfast and Buckland?'

'Ah, even sharper than I thought,' he whispered, staring down at me with narrowed eyes. We had stopped. The crisp autumn wind tugged at our hair and cloaks.

'One is Benedictine and one Cistercian, you know,' I added.

'I do indeed. Mistress, I may rely upon your wit someday, but not in this current matter. To cut to the quick, I am building a circle of people I can trust and who trust me, people who will work for me.'

'And for the cardinal?'

His eyes widened again. His nostrils flared. 'Yes, of course, for the cardinal through me, and so – in essence for King Henry, whom we all serve.'

'I never thought of it that way, of serving the king. Not from here,' I admitted with a sweep of my hand at the lonely, copper-colored moors with seagulls soaring in pointless circles overhead.

'Mistress, heed me now. Your father tells me he is distantly related to Sir Philip Champernowne of Modbury, a bit to the south, second cousins or some such. As Sir Philip is a king's man, well-off with lands and men for the royal armies, I happen to know him and will be visiting him on my way back to London. As at Dartington Hall, Sir Philip educates his daughters with his sons and with a far finer tutor than is here.'

I didn't know what to say. I dared hope that he was telling me these things because it had something to do with my future, but that hope must be wide of the mark. When he dismounted – with difficulty, for I could tell his shoulder still pained him greatly – I blurted out, 'How fortunate those families are.'

'No rabbit trails now. I do not deal with ninnyhammers, so heed my words, Kat Champernowne.'

He knew my pet name. Had my father told him

that, as he had that I was literate? Rather, I could see Thomas Cromwell questioning my father, much as I'd seen him interrogate the Barlows' tutor.

'I have a proposal to make to you, a bargain, if you will agree,' he went on, his expression intent. I felt my face flush, but I looked him straight in the eyes. 'You are a gem, mistress, but only partly polished yet and in too rude a setting. If I see to your better placement, where tutoring both in studies and in becoming a gentlewoman – and in the new Lutheran religion – is offered, I would expect you to soak it all in. Because then, when I declare the time to be ripe, I will see that you are placed with a noble family of my choosing in London, not as a servant but as a companion, a gentlewoman-in-waiting, so to speak. And then, who knows what that waiting will be for, eh?'

For once, I had nothing to say. It was all too impossible, too wonderful. To go somewhere, to be someone – to escape Maud. To have in plain sight my box of treasures and to openly write my memories and hopes – and to serve someone deserving, someone who did not harm or kill others to climb life's ladder as Maud had, but who only helped and served others, like Master Cromwell!

'It is more, far more, than I could ever have hoped . . .' I stammered, so breathily that it didn't sound like sensible, solitary me at all. 'But – what is the rest of the bargain?'

23

He nodded curtly. 'The acquisition of information is essential for positions of power.'

'You mean, I would inquire things of the Champernownes or of the noble London family and then write or tell you?'

'In a way. A clever, beguiling, buxom and pretty girl with no dangerous family ties, who can read and write and move in circles of people both high and low, and – most of all – keep a confidence, is just what I will need.'

Beguiling? Pretty? Me? But Maud had said – And what did buxom mean? [I add this note now, later, in London: *buxom* can mean both pliant and agreeable, as in wedding vows when the bride promises 'to be buxom in both board and bed.' I suppose Cromwell could have meant that, but I later came to think he at least implied the second meaning, for I was full breasted above my supple waist and knew men's eyes oft moved from my face to my breasts, before darting guiltily or invitingly back up again. But Thomas Cromwell seemed all business.]

'Do we have a bargain then, mistress?'

I nodded fervently.

'Say it then.'

'We have a bargain, Master Cromwell.'

To my surprise, moving only his good arm, he took my hand – the one not holding the rolled-up pages of my story I had penned that day – and lifted it to his lips and kissed it. No man had done such before. He turned away and walked his horse to a tree stump he stepped on so he could mount easily, though he still grunted in pain.

'Be patient, Mistress Champernowne. I will care for the details.'

'How long will I be in Modbury before you summon me to London?'

'Time and events will tell,' he said, staying his horse one moment more. 'But the point is, whatever befalls, you will learn not to tell, not without my permission.' Without a backward glance, he wheeled his horse away.

I did not realize then how many times later that would be the case. He would listen to me avidly, use me for his gain – though oft for mine too – then turn tail and move on to his next task, the next rung up his life's ladder. I marveled at the aura of control and power that reeked from the man, but then, I hadn't yet met the Tudors.

The next morn I almost wondered if I had dreamed it all. But it was no dream that Maud flew into a fit of temper – despite another half crown from Cromwell's purse that sealed the bargain with my father – when she heard I was to be sent to Sir Philip Champernowne's household at Modbury, not as servant but as companion to his daughters.

Maud yanked her blond curls with both hands and screamed at my father, 'I don't care one whit if the Barlows give her leave to go. I need her here. I'm about to have another babe, and I'm not young anymore!'

Father frowned. 'We've been promised a half crown a year – a year! – while she's with my cousins, so you can hire a housemaid or nurse-maid.'

'In this wretched place while she goes to Modbury?' [She said that as if I were heading for Paris or already to London.] 'I won't trust just anyone with my children. I've done a lot for you, Hugh Champernowne, you know I have, and I need her here!'

Father looked stoic and sullen, just as he did when he used to argue with my mother. But he shouted, 'She's going! You two sort out when. There's even to be a horse for her to ride and an escort for her from the Hall.'

Did everyone dance so easily to Cromwell's tune? I was in utter awe.

'I never should have listened to your wild schemes!' Maud shrieked and threw a candlestick on the hearthstones while Simon and Amelia cowered in the corner. 'She has to help birth this child you've planted in my belly! You know about bees, don't you, Hugh? By hell's gates, I'm the queen bee here, and you're going to see more sting than honey if you let her go, bec—'

My father went out and slammed the door.

She turned to me, leveling her hand, pointing her finger like the Barlows' tutor when he was angry. 'I don't give a fig how many bribes that king's man sends, you're not going anywhere to learn to be a gentlewoman, not the likes of you.'

I was more angry and desperate than I'd ever been, though that predicament was naught compare to the tight places I got in once I really began to serve Cromwell and the Tudors, once I started to 'pay my dues,' as he reminded me once when I rebelled.

'Learn to be a lady?' I said, hands thrust on my hips as I faced her down. 'Yes, that would be lovely, and I shall wear green ribbons in my hair like this one. I shall amble about and ape you,' I taunted, producing from my bodice the ribbon I'd found years ago and was about to discard since I was going to be quit of her for good. 'I do regret, though, it is a bit soiled from the hearth – from a strange, sudden fire there once that caught my mother's skirts, when not a thing was spitted over it that might have caused her to get too close. And then, I warrant,' I added, as I dangled the ribbon before her, 'it is a bit burned because it was dropped in some sort of scuffle right here on the hearth when you claimed you were not even inside with her that day, the day I believe someone hit my mother hard on the back of her head. How fortunate that you were coming to visit then, especially since you'd already been here earlier to deliver the two beehives you left out back.'

She stared aghast at me, then at her sniveling children – perhaps to assure herself they had not taken my meaning. Wide-eyed, gasping air like a beached fish, she turned to gaze at me again.

'If I were you,' I went on, 'I'd be pleased to be

27

rid of someone who can produce other proofs about what really happened that day. As you yourself put it, 'I've done a lot for you, Hugh.' Mayhap since you've turned to such a shrew, if he sees I can prove what I can prove, he'll give evidence against you too.'

She looked so frightened I almost felt guilty, for I had no other proofs but only festering suspicions from long-smothered resentment. Evidently fearful of saying another word to me, she flounced off to her room, leaving me to tend her children for the last time. Maud was so distraught that she went into labor that night, and I helped deliver her of a puny baby girl, one she named Katherine after me, as if to mollify or bribe me. I cuddled and kissed the little mite that was my namesake, but nothing was keeping me there. Two days later, I turned my face to the south toward another, richer, more powerful family of Champernownes.

I didn't realize until years later, working first for Cromwell and then the Tudors, that the lies, the bluffs, the innuendos, the screws I had put to the woman who had been the bane of my existence, were the best practice I could have had for later life in London.

# CHAPTER 3

Bigbury-on-Sea, Devon

*July 19, 1526*

I cannot believe you have never seen the sea!'
Joan cried as, holding hands, we ran toward
the waves across the wide beach. We were barefoot and had our skirts belted up, baring our legs
below the knee. Though we could not take big
strides, the sand and surf felt delightful on bare
skin. Seagulls strutting on the sands screeched and
took flight before us as we ran as fast as our tied
thighs, holding up our skirt hems, would allow.

Joan spoke true, I thought. I am twenty years of
age and have never seen water wider than the
Dart. But after eight months in Modbury, I had
seen so much and – if Master Cromwell did not
forget me – I will see much more than even this
wonder of vast, rolling water.

'Wait until you see the tides come in and out!'
Joan told me. I thanked the Lord that she had
been my special guide and friend in my new life.
'We shall walk the tidal causeway to that island
out there, see?' she cried, pointing, her voice so

excited it was shrill. 'But we must return across the sand straits by a certain time or water will devour us like a sea monster!'

Joan was eleven that first summer I lived in Modbury with Sir Philip Champernowne's family, she was already betrothed to a landed neighbor, Robert Gamage, but at least she knew and liked him. An almost mirror image of her mother and two sisters, Joan was dark-haired with beautiful green eyes, eyebrows arched like ravens' wings, and an oval face with milky skin. To protect our complexions, we had our heads covered with floppy, woven hats tied with gay colored ribbons fluttering in the salty breeze.

Behind us, trying to keep up, came Elizabeth, called Bess, of thirteen years, pulling her sister Katherine, called Kate, eight years, the youngest of the Champernowne brood. Ahead of us raced the lads, John, the heir, just turned eighteen, and Arthur but a year younger, both tall and lanky. Arthur, as ever, kept turning back to look at me, his avid gaze on my heaving breasts beneath my tight bodice, but today also ogling my legs. That subtle feeling of unease set in, but, in faith, it was a day for freedom, a day not to fret about Arthur's smothered, forbidden feelings for me.

At a slower pace behind us all came Sir Philip and Lady Katherine, arm in arm, followed by servants with baskets of food. My mentors also looked excited on this day of their annual family visit to the southern shore, but a few hours ahorse from their manor house on the fringe of busy Modbury. Already, just last month, I had learned to swim with the girls in the four-foot-deep pond behind the house, though I'd hated it when minnows nibbled on my legs. I could not fathom what great sea creatures must live in the green-gray depths before us.

Even when the boys began to splash us, I looked about to try to take it all in, as if I could press this memory in my treasure box with dried roses from the gardens behind Modbury Manor. Here were dark cliffs half-hidden by humps of hills and the broad, pale sand shore studded by random clusters of black rocks as if a huge hand had strewn them amidst the sea grasses of Sedgewell Cove.

'Just think!' Joan cried, finally loosing my hand. 'This is the very spot where smugglers bring their goods ashore at night, fineries maybe clear from France!'

John doused us with another flung handful of water, but she just squealed and laughed. Had she been home, most likely she would have tat-taled on him to the girls' governess, Gertrude.

'Cutthroat pirates from the Scilly Isles put in here,' John said, trying to scare us as usual. 'Heard tell they abduct fair maids for ransom, so beware! I'd not pay a farthing for either of you, always picking at me to keep my nose in a book when the whole world waits out here!'

He rampaged off through the cresting waves,

kicking up spray, but Arthur lingered a moment. 'I'd raise the ransom somehow,' he said, turning red as a pippin. Poor Arthur, I thought, ever brooding over the fact he was the second son. He'd told me privily he would have been sent to be a priest in the old days before the new religious learning the family espoused and I eagerly studied. But Arthur had told me, too, that his sire had vowed to buy him a fine manor somewhere in Devon, so he would someday have even better prospects to wed well.

I shuddered, even as Arthur turned tail and chased after his brother. The last thing I needed was to have Sir Philip or Lady Katherine mistrusting me for leading Arthur on – which I had not – when I wanted a good report to Cromwell and no strings to hold me here when he summoned me to London. Besides, had I cared for Arthur that way, I was under no illusions that one of Sir Philip's sons would be allowed to wed a woman without lands or dowry.

'Let's find some pretty shells!' I cried, eager for something tangible to keep in my treasure box to mark this day. 'Oh, look at this!' I produced a corkscrew-shaped one from the sand at my feet. 'But I'll bet you can all find even better ones!'

Since I was older than the children, I tried to watch over them and bring out the best in Joan, Bess and little Kate. It was instinct in me from my earlier days, I guess, and the gratitude I owed my hosts, Sir Philip and Lady Katherine, for in bed and board and education, they treated me as one of their own.

'I can tell you are a green girl here!' Bess replied with a little shake of her head as she shouted into the wind. 'Newcomers always want to pick up shells, but I want to throw them in the waves and make them skip and skip until they disappear!'

*Skip and skip until they disappear* . . . That was the way my days and months with the Champernownes flew past, however much I chafed that I did not hear from Thomas Cromwell.


MODBURY, DEVON

To tell true, Cromwell was only mentioned twice in my hearing, if I don't count the time I over-heard the lord and lady discussing 'the troubles in London,' but I will record that in a bit. The first day I arrived at Modbury, Sir Philip had said, 'Master Cromwell holds out much hope for your future with our family or another in London someday.'

Someday – that seemed so vague, so far away, though his words lifted my heart.

'Will your family be going to London?' I had asked.

'I believe someday my daughters and their husbands will all serve the royal family there in some capacity. Perhaps you will go to court in one of their households. Time will tell.'

33

I was sad that he spoke not of such things after, though I thought perhaps Master Cromwell was testing me through Sir Philip. After all, Cromwell had told me, 'Time will tell,' so was that a coded message to me? He had said he valued one who could keep a confidence, and his final words to me were to learn *not* to tell things, not without his permission.

The other time I heard Cromwell's name was the day Sir Philip and Lady Katherine took me on horseback to see Modbury. I was learning to sit a horse sidesaddle quite well and reveled in the lofty view of things it gave me, I who had walked everywhere in the earlier years of my life. Also, that day I came to realize that these kin of mine were indeed the premier family of the area. Laborers doffed their hats and stood aside, sometimes with heads bowed a bit. Mothers pointed us out to their children. More than one woman on the street curtsied, a custom to honor one's betters, a skill I had recently learned from the family's dancing instructor, Master Martin. He had not only lived in London – I questioned him about that whenever I could manage – but had seen Her Grace Mary Tudor, Princess of Wales, pass by on the road with her huge entourage not once but twice on her way to Ludlow Castle in Wales. Hundreds of horses and carts, so he told me, and the princess herself riding in a fine litter.

Oh, yes, with Joan and Bess, for Kate was

deemed yet too young, I had learned what Master Martin called 'court dances': the stately pavane; the quick coranto; and my favorite, the charming, five-step galliard the French called the *cinquepace*. Because of our heights, I sometimes partnered John, but more often he danced with lanky Joan and I was with Arthur. That was the beginning of my troubles with him, I supposed, for he fell over his big feet in my presence, when I knew he wanted to please Master Martin and me too.

But on my introduction to Modbury by my mentors, I was in awe, and not just from seeing the high regard which they enjoyed among the local citizenry. That day, again, Master Cromwell was mentioned. His name came up in this wise. Modbury was a booming wool town with mills producing cloth, especially felt. All about, weavers' cottages had long windows to let the light in on their looms. Along the river stood fulling mills where huge mallets pounded the wetted wool into flat, smooth felt called 'tuckey,' to sell at home and abroad.

As we walked through one such mill Sir Philip owned, with the sounds of the rushing river and stamping of the mallets, Lady Katherine said to her husband, 'I hear Secretary Cromwell owns a fulling mill at Putney near London. Indeed, there is not much the man hasn't done.'

'A jack-of-all-trades but a master of one,' Sir Philip put in. 'His ultimate skill is not secretarial but managerial. He may manage his own business, but his genius lies in handling other, powerful people.'

'Quite a past but an even brighter future,' she said, turning to me with a little half smile that was so characteristic of her, as if she wanted to break into a grin but something always held her back. 'Tell Kat a bit about her patron, then,' she urged her husband as we walked outside to where two men held our horses.

'Though he comes from common stock and wed the daughter of a shearman, he's worked his way up with his wit and talents,' Sir Philip said. 'He tells me he had a rough beginning, was once a common soldier in Italy, and later saw how corrupt Pope Julius II and his lackeys were selling indulgences and such.'

I had more than once heard Sir Philip bemoaning the corruption of the Catholic Church, both in Rome and England. So had he imbibed that attitude from Cromwell? But I did not want to hear of the new religion, but more of Master Cromwell.

'So,' I dared to prompt him, 'he finally came back to England with new ideas?'

'Aye, and became a moneylender, lawyer and solicitor. You've seen his captivating manner and, I tell you, he has a memory like a trap of Spanish steel for names, numbers and faces—'

'And favors,' Lady Katherine added pointedly, so I hope she didn't mean that Cromwell owed them something because of me.

'He's now a member of Parliament,' Sir Philip said as he gave the horse boys each a groat and we mounted with their help. I hardly understood what Parliament was then, but I did not interrupt. 'He's a fine speaker there, became a member of Grey's Inn recently,' he added as we turned our mounts toward the manor and rode past the shambles where meat was sold and the Roofed Round House where both corn and yarn were bargained for. My horse must have sensed my mood, for she tossed her head and snorted. I was champing at my own bit to hear more, for I knew naught of Grey's Inn or any other in London.

Finally, I could not hold my tongue. I was desirous of any hint, however obscure, of when Secretary Cromwell might send for me. 'But he still works for Cardinal Wolsey, does he not?' I ventured.

With a sneer at the mere mention of the cardinal's name, Sir Philip nodded brusquely. 'Of course. He cares for all of Wolsey's affairs, for that corrupt prelate cares for all the king's affairs. That is where the power should lie, with our sovereign, not with one who owes obedience to the Pope in Rome.'

I had a hundred other questions, but I forced myself to silence. I had told Secretary Cromwell I could hold my tongue, so I would strive to do so. But it did warm me to hear the Champernownes praise the man they had called my patron and who

I prayed would be my deliverer from Devon, however beautiful it was here.

My home to the north had seemed so isolated and hemmed in by Dartmoor's hedges and tall, stunted oaks; ancient stone walls; high, turf-topped banks and deep-cut lanes. By comparison, this area of Devon, called the South Hams, lay more welcoming. Though Modbury was sheltered by three hills, the land opened to wide vistas with fertile farms and pinkish soil producing barley, wheat and rye. It was a far cry from the tough plowing through turf and thick grass at home. Like the southern sea, it was a new, rich world in many ways, and, as my patron had commanded me, I soaked up every bit of it I could.

I was dismayed one winter night when chill crept up the staircase and I hurried down it, to find my way blocked by Arthur. 'Oh, you gave me a fright!' I told him, and gathered my skirts tighter to go around him. The family was roasting chestnuts downstairs, and all of us had been reciting parts from our lessons in geography and mathematics and displaying examples of our prayers in our best handwriting. They were prayers addressed directly to the Lord Jesus, not to the Virgin Mary or the saints, since the new religion did not accept such mediators to our Lord. My flowing, steady script had been especially praised; I knew I wrote a good hand, one I hoped a busy secretary would appreciate should I ever have an opportunity to write to him. For some reason, had Cromwell decided to leave me here?

'Wait – I pray you,' Arthur said, putting out a long arm to block my way downstairs. 'I – I've been sent up to fetch my astronomy drawings, but I – Father says my written hand is dreadful, and I beg you to help me with it.'

'Oh,' I said, not looking directly in his wide eyes, soft and pleading like those of a deer in the manor's small hunt park. 'If we have permission from your parents and Master Martin, then all right.'

He snatched my hand and planted a wet kiss on my palm, not a steady, assured touch of the lips as Cromwell had done nigh on two years before. Of course, I liked the feeling of power over this young man. I was glad to prove Maud wrong, that I was not fetching enough to fetch attention from a lad worth the while. But I could not afford to displease his parents. Yet if they and Master Martin gave their permission, I would gladly help.

A few days later, as we huddled at a schoolroom table over a single piece of parchment, Arthur asked, 'Can you not place your hand over mine to guide it when I form my letters?'

'I believe it best you watch and copy my movements.'

We were briefly alone, but I could hear Master Martin's voice droning on to someone in the hall. Arthur pressed his thigh tighter against my skirts and shifted his foot against mine. I moved farther away.

'I do watch your movements, all of them,' Arthur whispered, his eyes narrowed. He breathed through his mouth, which made it seem he was panting. 'Please, dear Kat, I adore—'

'No, I cannot adore your handwriting unless you improve it greatly,' I cut him off, and bounced up to move my stool farther yet from his.

'Kat, listen to me,' he pleaded. He looked so desperate – so besotted – my heart wrenched, but I was coming to fear him. Not that he would leap at me, though I sensed he longed to, but that he would endanger my own dreams and desires.

'Stop and copy that last line!' I clipped out, with a voice so stern it surprised even me. I hadn't used such a tone since I'd told Maud I suspected her of my mother's murder.

'Kat,' he breathed out, his eyes darting from my face to my bodice and back again, 'do not flee. I swear to you, I will not so much as touch you, but I must tell you my prospects. Though I am not the heir, Father is talking to the Crown through a man named Thomas Cromwell, who is close to the seat of power, about buying Dartington Hall for me, near where you used to live. I shall move there, rear my family there, and would you not like to return to that place, to be Lady Champernowne, when I am knighted someday for my service to the king?'

I stared at him utterly aghast. Dartington Hall?

But Cromwell had been hosted by the Barlows there, and they had been not only kind to me but to him. They had saved me by letting me tend poor Sarah, and what would she do without the home she knew and loved? Oh, yes, I knew the Barlows had leased the place from the Crown, that it was not theirs by birthright, inheritance or service, but surely the Thomas Cromwell I knew would not backstab them by seeing that their home went to another. Or – please, no, dear Lord – by his helping Sir Philip take the Hall from the Barlows because that was part of the bargain of my living here these years.

'I can tell you are overthrown,' Arthur said. 'You have no words yet, but unlike my silly sisters, you are a rational woman, brighter than all, save mayhap John. In our lessons, you excel. You have outstripped us even in Latin grammar and rhetoric, I heard Master Martin say. You could teach much of it yourself, he told my mother.'

Ordinarily, I could have danced a jig at such praise, but my thoughts were snagged on the Barlows losing Dartington Hall.

'Can you even give me the faintest hope that you will think on my offer?' Arthur whispered, leaning closer to me across the table. 'Before Master Martin comes back in to see how we are getting on, can you not vow at the very least you will think on it? My parents would accept it – a love match. We are but third cousins, 'tis done time to time hereabouts. And for you to go back to Dartington in triumph – Kat, you look pale. You will not faint? Say something.'

Should I finally write Cromwell and beg him not to let the Hall slip from the Barlows? But who would take such a privy message to him? Should I tell Arthur if he cared a fig for me that he should dissuade his father from this double-dealing? Cromwell tumbled off the pedestal of my hopes that day, for I saw now he must be one of those who helped others only if it helped himself. Yes, yes, I had seen that before in what he told me. And now, if I wanted to mount that ladder of life he had spoken of, was I tied to him?

Not for one moment did I allow Arthur to believe I would consider his pleas or promises. I would not go back home as his wife, even to live in the Hall, for that would devastate people I cared for deeply. I had to go to London. I must at least glimpse the Tudors and their palaces and power.

'Tell no one you have told me all this, please,' I said to Arthur as I rose from the table on shaky feet. 'It must go no further.'

'I – I can keep a secret, but can I dare to hope? Of course, if you have your heart set on London, we could visit there. When I earn my way, we could even get a house there . . .'

'Arthur,' I said, turning back toward him at the door to the corridor from which I could still hear Master Martin's voice. From here, I could tell he was speaking to young Kate. 'I can promise nothing. It would not be fair to you or to your parents. Dartington Hall is already the home to a fine family, folk who have been kind to me, even as your family has. I – cannot say more now, but I have other plans.'

I felt crushed by what he had told me today. That things had gotten stickier with Arthur grieved me, yes. But more than that, I mourned because I saw now my shining savior Cromwell had feet of clay.

Within a fortnight, Arthur had been sent to the household of Sir Philip's brother who lived near Exeter. I was not told until he was gone, though Joan handed me a fervent farewell letter from him, hidden in the palm of her hand. The foolish boy had told his parents of his love for me. It was unrequited only, he was sure, because of my loyalty to them. I read his tortured promises and burned the letter. I was guilt-ridden. Since his thwarted, hopeless love for me had been discovered, should I not be the one sent away?

I felt I walked on eggshells, fearful the Champernownes would blame me for enticing him. But soon John, too, was sent away, to the Earl of Warwick's house, no less. I could only pray that, direct or indirect, it would not be my fault if Cromwell's influence took Dartington Hall from the Barlows.

In the first month of 1528, after I had resided at Modbury Manor for over two years and Arthur had been gone for five weeks, Sir Philip suddenly summoned me to his privy chamber. Lady Katherine sat beside him across a small round table strewn with papers, a sanding box, an inkwell and a brace of quills. I rather feared I was to be either chastised or banished, and my heartbeat kicked up even harder.

'Sit, please, Kat,' Sir Philip said, gesturing to the short bench facing them.

I sat, wanting to stare at my knees but keeping my head up as I had been taught by the girls' governess. I warranted I had learned good graces in my time here, but what if I was no longer in the Champernownes' good graces?

'A message has come for you from London, from Secretary Cromwell, though it is addressed to me,' he told me, picking up a piece of parchment from his pile of them.

Despite my disillusionment about Secretary Cromwell, I longed to lunge across the table and snatch the missive from his hand. Finally? He had not forgotten me? Was the time ripe, as he had said once? And was I a vile betrayer of the Barlows to still want to serve the man who would take their home away, if that was still in the offing? How I longed to be in London, where I was sure I could speak my mind, make my own way – with Cromwell's help and sponsorship, of course.

'He says,' Sir Philip went on, maddeningly slow, 'he is well pleased to hear of your academic and mannerly achievements in this household and may soon have a place for you at court.'

'At court?' I burst out. 'At *court*?'

'Thrilling, isn't it?' Lady Katherine said with that wistful smile. 'God willing, some of my daughters will hear those words someday.'

'Does he say when?' I asked, trying to keep my voice from trembling. I clenched my hands so tightly in my lap, my fingers went numb. Since they knew full well I could read, why not hand it to me – or was there something written of Dartington Hall, their price for keeping me these years?

'He says soon,' Sir Philip told me, 'now that the world is changing.'

'With the new learning and religion?' I floundered.

'As you may well have observed, even here in our own household,' Sir Philip said, 'the will of a woman can be powerful, and I speak not of my lovely lady wife. We are grateful that you, ah – handled Arthur's foolish fancies properly. His wishes were entirely unreasonable. Clever woman that you are, you saw that.'

At least they didn't not blame me, were even grateful. Or was Cromwell's power over them my shield and buckler for that too? 'Yes, my lord, my lady,' I said only.

'But as for the when of this – soon, is all it says,' he repeated, lifting the paper closer to his face and running his gaze over it again. 'I warrant it will be when the Lady Anne Boleyn goes to court and manages to completely dislodge the queen in the king's affections. Ah, the troubles in London.'

My mouth fell open. I knew none of this, though I had avidly learned the lists of England's kings and families, even of present events such as how King Henry must balance the foreign powers of France and Spain, not to mention the Holy Roman Emperor Charles, who was his Spanish queen's nephew. I could recite dates and outcomes of the battles of the so-called War of the Roses wherein the current king's father had won his crown – but who was the Lady Anne Boleyn?

'You mean, I might serve this lady?' I asked.

'We all might, if she does not agree to be His Grace's mistress soon and not keep dangling him,' Sir Philip muttered, and Lady Katherine shook her head. 'As her family are upstarts and climbers – even if ones well-versed in the new learning – it may cause chaos at court. Well, that is all for now, Kat. We will most certainly keep you apprised of events. By the way, Arthur is to be betrothed to a lady from Kent, and after he earns his spurs, so to speak, they will reside not far from where you grew up, in a fine hall, where I believe you were once a servant.'

For the first time since I had known him, Sir Philip had a cutting edge to his voice, especially on that last word, *servant*. Was it my imagination that her ladyship looked down her nose at me and narrowed her eyes? Did I feel their disdain now because they deemed I was not worthy of the care they had taken for me, even if it had gotten them Dartington Hall for Arthur and his future bride? Or because their son had dared to want someone beneath his station? Or could it even be because of the interest shown in me by Cromwell, the man who had a ruffian beginning, as they had said once? If anyone was an upstart and a climber, it was he, though I did not feel contempt but kinship for that.

I rose, curtsied and left the chamber, but I also left the door ajar and paused in the hall, leaning my back against the oaken wainscoting. It surely wasn't my fault if the Barlows were to be displaced, I tried to buck myself up. But to go to court! Not just to London, but to court and perhaps to the household of a woman the king favored – but at the cost of his lawful queen and his marriage? This Anne Boleyn must be a powerful woman, one worth knowing and studying. Was that what I must do now to pay back and please Thomas Cromwell – study her at close range and then tell him all about it?

I was relieved no servant or child was in the hall, for the words within floated clearly to me. 'This Boleyn matter is outrageous! Insane!' Sir Philip cried. 'His Grace has bedded the others without breaking down the order of things. Her Grace has managed to look askance since she bears him only dead sons and one living daughter. But the gall of this Boleyn whore does boggle the mind!'

'She isn't a whore if she doesn't lie with him,' Lady Katherine protested meekly.

'Not yet, but he'll have her. Who would dare to gainsay the king?'

I realized then I had much more to learn. I had longed – yes, lusted, even as poor Arthur had for me – for lovely London, but now, I was not so sure.

# CHAPTER 4

## MODBURY TO LONDON

Finally, London loomed on my horizon, but not as soon as I had hoped and expected. It was a gloriously sunny day in late September 1528, and I had gone nigh mad waiting yet seven months more before the actual summons came for me to bid my Modbury hosts – for they were never quite my family – fare-thee-well and turn my face toward the desire of my dreams.

With a good-bye letter to my father, sent through the Barlows, I had planned to leave Devon as soon as the roads cleared of snow and winter mud. But warm weather had brought much rain and worse. The sweating sickness, that oft fatal summer slayer of hundreds – which was, at least, far different from the fever Master Cromwell had suffered from – nearly carried off Mistress Boleyn, in whose household I was to live at court. No doubt, I was as relieved as her royal suitor that she had survived.

I traveled toward London well protected by a band of twelve new-fledged Devon-born soldiers, sent by Sir Philip to serve the king. Four of the men had their wives with them, so I slept in inns or houses on the way with one of those women sharing my bed and the others on floor pallets. Much of those seven nights, as exhausted and saddle sore as I was, I lay awake, listening to whispers, sighs or snores. I was beside myself with excitement, too wild in hopes and heart to sleep.

As we approached the great city of London through Southwark, thatched, timbered houses, three or four stories high, jutted out over us, shouldering the sky. I shuddered with excitement as we rode through the shadow of a great cathedral. How I wished I had someone with me who could name each street, each church, to tell me what the crudely painted pictures on the hanging signs indicated lay within. A tongue thrust out with a pill on the tip of it, I knew, for there was an apothecary shop in Modbury, but what were these other wonders? I had so much to learn of my new world.

But familiar sights and smells assailed me too. Sheep and cattle being driven to market shoved folks aside. The stench from nearby slaughterhouses, tanneries and the garbage in the streets' center gutters filled our nostrils, so that we breathed through our mouths. Hawkers elbowed each other for space while carters cursed. Would the jostling for positions at court be even more daunting and dangerous? Despite my rural companions and those bustling past, I felt so alone.

The hubbub grew thicker as we approached the curving, silver serpent that was the River Thames. It made the Dart shrink to naught in my regard. On the Thames, scores of boats wended their ways, wherries and barges, some of the latter with ornate carvings, gildings and livery-clad oarsmen. One long bridge with houses and shops crammed cheek by jowl upon it spanned the river. Across that busy thoroughfare lay the hulking royal fortress called the Tower, a palace and a prison, I had learned in our history lessons. Above all soared seagulls, reminding me of home, but I longed only to be here.

At the base of London Bridge, water rushed through the supports, especially at high tide, we heard, but it looked quite calm now. Amidst the watermen with boats for hire shouting 'Oars east!' or 'Oars west!' two soldiers, their wives and I boarded a barge and were rowed downstream toward Westminster Palace. It greatly cheered me to see fields along the way and grander homes than I had beheld in Southwark. I thought we must surely be to the king's Westminster Palace when, after the curve in the river, we approached a magnificent edifice, and I blurted out, 'There it is!'

'That be Cardinal Wolsey's York Place,' the boatman told me. 'Wi' his power and wealth, he been abuilding it for years, finer than the king's Westminster by far.'

As we passed gleaming glass windows, expanses of slate rooftops with ornate brick chimneys and weather vanes, water stairs and iron gates with glimpses into gardens, we Devoners were agog. So I had my first lesson in the true might of the man who employed Thomas Cromwell and, therefore, me.

When we arrived at the smaller and older Westminster Palace, I was to meet with disappointment, and not just for its less handsome facade. Rather than my being greeted by Cromwell or sent to the Lady Anne's apartments, I was met by Master Stephen, the man who had been at Cromwell's side in Devon.

'King and court's off to Hampton Court, the newest royal palace, a gift from Cardinal Wolsey,' he told me as one of Sir Philip's soldiers hefted my single trunk and fell in behind us. Cromwell's man led us from the worn water stairs toward the palace. 'You are to be sent there on the morrow via river. His Majesty goes much from place to place, especially,' he added, lowering his voice and bending slightly toward me, 'to escape the presence of his wife so that he can disport more with his future wife, the Lady Anne.'

'He really will marry her?' I asked.

His mouth tipped in a stiff grin. 'Ah, you have much to learn,' he told me with a look that took me in from head to toe. 'You must be weary, but Secretary Cromwell will see you now afore he leaves on his master's business to York Place, then on to Hampton Court.'

'His master, the cardinal?'

'Actually, his master, Henry Rex. We hear you

excel in Latin and have some Greek and a bit of French,' he said as if to change the subject. 'We have all come a long way, have we not? And, as my master, Cromwell, says, much more to go.'

Leaving the man with my trunk outside a door on the first floor of the vast, old palace near the great cathedral of the same name, Master Stephen led me into a large room, well lit from sconces, candles, and late afternoon light slanting through mullioned windows set ajar. I knew that Lady Barlow and Lady Katherine would have deplored the fact I was not well chaperoned, but I soon saw the chamber was filled with secretaries or clerks bent over their work. Yet, when Cromwell looked up, with a single clap and wave of his hands, he quickly cleared the area of all but Stephen and me.

He came around his big desk, covered with stacks of neatly aligned papers. Putting his hands on my shoulders, he stood me back a bit, looking me over. 'Now a polished gem,' he declared, and kissed me lightly on each check, as was, I had learned, the French fashion. Lady Katherine had told me – warned me, as she put it – that the English courtiers' greeting was a kiss directly on the mouth.

I had rehearsed words to ask him to be certain the Barlows had a suitable place to live when they gave up Dartington Hall, but that and much else flew right out of my head. Even with king and court away, this place and this man reeked of purpose and power.

'Come sit, and I'll send for malmsey wine, a hearty venison pie and some sugar bread with currants – one of my favorite sweets.' He looked behind me at Stephen, who evidently took that hint and went out to order the food, leaving us alone. 'Sit, sit,' he said again, choosing the chair next to mine, 'and I will explain how things are here – or wherever His Grace, the king, goes these days. Then we shall see you get some rest before joining the Lady Anne's household. I'll put you on a supply barge to Hampton Court – it's a ways out in the country – and see you there myself in a few days. Now, to business . . .'

And business it was. I was to be a circumspect, clever observer of what Cromwell called the lay of the land. That is, how the Lady Anne Boleyn and the king were getting on, anything I overheard or observed that was not common court knowledge. I was especially to be aware of anything that lady might say to her father or to her brother, George, who were much about the court and rode high in the king's favor.

'So you are working for the cardinal or the king?'

'I believe you asked me that once before, Mistress Champernowne,' he said with a hint of a smile. 'Both, of course. Both, until the wind somehow shifts.'

'I will do my best,' I promised him. 'And I will do my best to not think of myself as spying for my bread and butter.'

His ink-stained fingers tapped the arm of his chair.

'You are not to think or say such. You are merely informing and, thereby, helping to keep the great wheel that is the court and the country rotating in perfect harmony. Now for the most important part.'

I frowned at him, confused. Had he not told me all?

'You see,' he went on, turning even more toward me in his chair, then glancing behind us to be certain that, I take it, neither Stephen nor his clerks had come back in, 'the Lady Anne does not get on with my master, the cardinal. Both she and His Majesty bear him some ill will that His Eminence has not obtained the king's divorce yet. Well, of course, as fond lovers, they are impatient.'

'I hear she is of the new learning and, obviously, the cardinal is not.'

'Astute but not the key thing here. Now harken to this: the Lady Anne especially dislikes the cardinal because he once rescinded her covert and willful betrothal to Henry Percy, heir to the earldom of Northumberland. Then later the cardinal said in her hearing that she was a foolish girl of no account to hope to wed so high.'

*Of no account* – those words poked at me. How I had feared the same. Yes, I dared to think that the king's beloved Anne Boleyn and I had something, at least, in common. I had not been good enough even for Arthur, the second son of Sir Philip, and how I had feared I would be of no account if I were to be left marooned in Dartington. Anne, too, came from the countryside; Anne, too, had ambitions; Anne, too, resented those who would hold her back. I dared to think I almost understood her.

'Are you listening, mistress?'

'Yes. Yes, I am. Say on.'

'That Percy flap is all water over the mill dam now, since he's wed to an earl's daughter and the Boleyn will wed His Majesty. But my point is that there is bad blood between Anne Boleyn and the cardinal, so she doesn't trust him.' He took a little breath. 'But she does trust me.'

My eyes widened. I leaned toward him to know what he would say more.

'You see,' he said, looking a bit smug, 'I have done favors for her father, Viscount Rochford, for her brother, George, Lord Rochford, too, so I naturally came to her attention.'

'Naturally.'

He bit back a smile. 'But the thing is – the thing that concerns you – is that neither the cardinal nor the king know that I am finding ways to champion her cause beyond what the cardinal yet deems to do. The lady and I correspond privily from time to time, and that has been difficult. But with you living there with her and in her favor—'

'In her favor? But—'

'Because she knows that not only Sir Philip of Modbury is your sponsor – which everyone will know – but that I am your privy sponsor, too, and that you are sworn to help her cause, through me. Is that not so?'

I sat up straighter. 'It is, Master Cromwell. I believe it means you have a bit of a balancing act, holding up the interests of both Lady Anne and the cardinal – and ever, of course, the king – but I shall put my trust in you.'

I felt a bit like a traitor to the Barlows, throwing my lot so completely in with Cromwell. But I, too, had come so far so fast, and there was no way in Christendom I could or would turn back. I owed this man a great deal. True, I'd seen hints that he was devious, but he also seemed devoted to his masters and the Lady Anne and, of course, to himself – but weren't we all? I jolted alert, for he was lecturing me again.

'On the shirttail – or, should I say, petticoat hem – of the Boleyns and their kin the Howards, many are coming to court who will wield influence. Like it or not,' I recall he muttered later that night before a link boy lit me to my chamber, 'Anne Boleyn is the king's and this kingdom's future, and we must hitch our wagon to her star.'

I knew not then what a shining star – and then a falling one – she would be in the vast firmament I had just found.

LONDON TO HAMPTON COURT

The next morning, without seeing Cromwell again, I was off to Hampton Court on a royal barge, one stripped of its hangings, crests and seat cushions, though loaded with wooden boxes tied down with straps. I intended to see the countryside sights all the way, but a companion – a young, handsome man who leaped on at the last moment in the most brave style – took much of my attention.

'Mistress,' he greeted me in a rich voice, and doffed his flat leather cap in a half bow as the barge was rowed away from the landing and turned westward against the stiff current. 'As I see you have no protector with you but the oarsmen, I will have to do. Tom Seymour of Wolf Hall in Wiltshire at your service.' As we set out into the choppy river, he bent over my hand and kissed it, which made my skin tingle clear up to my shoulder.

I felt my insides cartwheel, and my face heated – and not from the warm September sun. Tom of Wolf Hall was tall – later I learned few but the king were taller – and dark-haired, with brown eyes that seemed to look right through me, or at least through my clothing. He sported a quick white smile that flashed from his face. I gave him the story of my life that Cromwell and I had discussed about being reared with Sir Philip Champernowne's family in Devon and coming to court in service to the Lady Anne. I told him I had been an only child but Sir Philip's brood were like my own siblings.

'An only child – you and the Princess Mary both,' he said, frowning at some privy thought and putting his packet of papers down at his booted feet. I feared they'd get wet from the spray, but it seemed not to worry him. Meanwhile, the oarsmen labored against wind and waves, though the man closest to us, right in my line of vision, was obviously amused by Tom's bravado. Though bent over his oar, he looked up with a grin and a roll of his eyes before he winked at me. I ignored him as well as the pretty villages and fields we passed and concentrated on my charming fellow traveler.

'Sometimes, I get so vexed with my older brother Edward,' he said, frowning and shaking his head. 'Hell's gates, let's just say I wouldn't mind being the only son. Now, my sisters are a different story. Jane's the one I really miss since I've come to court in Sir Francis Bryan's household. She's sweet, quiet, pretty – quite blond, with blue eyes – while the rest of us are darker. But as for the king's Princess Mary, His Grace has sent her to live at Richmond Palace in her own household – not unusual, of course, but I think he's done it to put the screws even more to her doting mother. Mary's as good as exiled from court, and, I warrant, the queen shall be next.'

I soon learned Tom Seymour could dart from topic to topic at will. Yet he knew how to look one in the eye and listen intently with a penetrating gaze, though I later learned his thoughts might well be elsewhere. He had a habit that was both disconcerting and delicious of looking me over. The man, young as he was then at age twenty, was the first who ever made me aware of my body in a new way. Before, the heated looks of men had made me want to turn away, but that devil made me want to flaunt myself, toss my head, pull in my stomach and thrust out my breasts. He was a great teaser and masterful flirt too. He cast a sort of devil-may-care spell that made one – made me – want to give him and tell him all.

It was only when the barge approached a cluster of eddies and small rapids that my surroundings seemed real again.

'High tide and rough waters ahead,' Tom told me, as if I could not see or hear the white water. The oarsmen not only rowed now, but they braced the barge to keep it from spinning. 'Fear not, fair maiden,' Tom yelled to me over the men's shouted orders and gurgling of the waters, 'the royal oarsmen are skilled. They know we can't keep the king – or now the Lady Anne – waiting!'

We began to spin, but they shot us through. Too much rain lately, I thought. Yet all this was exciting and seemed to heartily please my companion. We slanted up, down. I squealed and, despite trying to hold on to my nailed-down bench, was thrown toward Tom. He seized me and held me close as we bumped and turned, just missed a large rock, then burst free of the foam.

It was only later, when the waters and my heart-beat calmed, I realized he'd held me much too tight, one hand hard on my bottom right through my spray-damp skirts and the other cupping my left heaving breast.

For years after, anytime I was near Tom, it was just like that thrilling, bumpy ride.

I thought Hampton Court was the most glorious, grand place I had ever beheld. Tom gave me a running commentary on it. 'Cardinal Wolsey presented it to His Majesty three years ago when it became obvious to the king that His Eminence was living better than the sovereign. Quite a bribe to stay in favor, eh? I swear, York Place in London will be his next gift to the king if he doesn't ram this damned divorce through soon.'

For once I was speechless, but Tom made up for that. 'One thousand rooms here – about the same number as courtiers – and two-hundred eighty beds, they say, so I am sure we will find one that suits us.'

When I glared at him and turned away, much embarrassed, he went on as if naught were amiss, pointing in various directions, 'Acres of tiltyards with observation towers, vast parklands, two massive courtyards, ponds and knot gardens. And, oh yes, a hornbeam maze perfect for lovers' rendezvous. The king's given the lady apartments next to his, despite the fact the queen still lives here too, but rumors are His Grace will send her away soon.'

I wanted to remain cold to him for his crude innuendo I might bed with him, yet curiosity and excitement got the best of me. 'But how does the queen abide the Lady Anne when they are both here?' I asked, tearing my gaze away from the rosy-hued brick buildings that seemed to go on forever. We walked the quay toward the water gate, though I did not let him take my arm. I had been promised my trunk would be delivered. We had both dried out from our brief, rough passage, buffeted by the gentle autumn breeze the rest of the way. I tried to push my wayward tresses back under my gabled hood. Again, I was enthralled by all I saw. As in London, people darted here and there, streaming in or out of the palace, some ahorse. Cromwell had said I would be met here. Were none of these people looking for me?

'Ah, about the queen,' Tom said. I had nearly forgotten what I had asked him. 'As you may have heard, she is stubborn and stoic about it all – that her king declares himself to be a bachelor since they were never legally wed, but to be certain, His Majesty plans to have their marriage annulled. Their Majesties will face off in court over that soon, at Blackfriars in London with Cardinal Campeggio sent from the Vatican to hear evidence and give his ruling.'

'One can indeed pity her.'

'But His Majesty cites much evidence for the annulment or divorce, including the fact that but one of their several children have lived, and that a girl – a clear sign that God does not approve of the union, he claims. For now, Queen Catherine mostly stays to her apartments and pretends to ignore the situation of the Lady Anne as best she can, hoping her husband returns to her royal bed.'

'Which, I warrant, he will never do if he has annoyed and defied the Pope and her nephew the Holy Roman Emperor to have the Lady Anne.'

'I knew there was a good mind inside those pretty wrappings,' he declared, making me blush again as we crossed the moat. As thrilled as I was to be here and despite the brash comment he had made to me earlier, I must admit I was loath to part with him. To my surprise he kissed me on the mouth, quick but hard.

'Fear not, fair maiden,' he said, sweeping his cap off with a grin and a mock salute of his hand pressed to his heart, 'for I shall find you again in this great pile.'

With a laugh and a wave, he was off at a good clip across the huge base court we had entered. I looked around me, suddenly feeling dizzy, as if I still rode the barge in the rapids. Three stories with glittering windows glared down at me. Clots of clouds, racing overhead, made it seem the buildings would topple and crush me to the paving stones. For one moment, I couldn't breathe. What was I doing here, Kat Champernowne from the small stone house near the moors where the wind blew cold and harsh?

People continued to scurry past. I wished Cromwell's Master Stephen would materialize from one of the doorways or the next court I could see through an inner gateway beyond.

'Mistress Katherine Champernowne?' a voice called from behind me. I turned to see a smiling, petite, pert-faced woman. 'Word had been sent you would arrive late midday, so I was watching for you.' She seemed to draw herself stiffly to her full height as she said, 'I am Viscountess Rochford, wife of Lady Anne's brother George, attendant on the Lady Anne, but you may address me as Lady Jane. I'm sure your things will be sent up to the chamber you'll be sharing with two others. I hope your river trip was pleasant. Come this way.'

I believe, as kindly couched as she put that, it was the first of thousands of commands and orders I was to follow in my new life at one of many Tudor courts.

Anne Boleyn. Mistress Boleyn. The Lady Anne. Or often, most simply, the lady. Her name was on everyone's lips. When I first went to court, everything revolved around the king's beloved, and for the first time in my life, I glimpsed the true power a woman could wield.

After I had rested and washed, settling into a small but pleasant chamber with two others of her ladies, the maidservant assigned to us unpacked my trunk while I was summoned by Lady Jane to meet my new mistress. Names and titles and connections already bombarded me: Lady Jane, Viscountess Rochford; the other two ladies in my chamber, Dorothy Cobham, Lord Sheffield's daughter from Derbyshire, and Mary Talbot, the Earl of Shrewsbury's youngest daughter – and the wife of Anne's Boleyn's former love, Henry Percy, no less! Thanks to the lady and Cromwell, I was instantly living in heady company.

I soon learned the Percy marriage was an unhappy one and they were much estranged, though Percy, heir to the earldom of Northumberland, was about the court in the king's service, having previously served Cardinal Wolsey. [As many years and as many Tudor sovereigns as I knew, relationships both formal and informal, marital and political, did boggle the mind. Especially when my dear Elizabeth finally mounted the throne and advanced men of ability as well as nobility, it was a veritable spiderweb.]

I had to remind myself to breathe as I was led through a series of beautifully decorated chambers, each one with fewer curious and staring people in them, until we reached a small, empty but ornately appointed sitting room. Lady Jane knocked on a carved door, listened for a reply with her ear to the wood, then stuck her head in.

'Milady, the new gentlewoman from Devon, Mistress Katherine Champernowne, is here as you asked.'

The voice that answered was mellifluous but authoritative. 'Send her in and close the door when you leave.' I could tell Lady Jane was not pleased, for she flounced out and closed the door a bit too loudly.

I saw the chamber I entered was a fairyland of woven tapestries, Turkey carpets on the table and a massive bed draped with red-gold silken curtains. It was said that Anne Boleyn had told the king she would not be his mistress but only his wife, yet here was a bed fit for royalty. Yet it was not the furbishings but the lady herself who commanded my interest.

This woman of twenty-seven years, who was the cause of 'the king's great matter,' also called by some 'the troubles,' looked delicate and graceful. Her hair was raven black; she had dark doe eyes with a tilt to them that made her seem she would smile or flirt. I had expected her to be a ravishing beauty, but she was not. Yet there was something so inherently elegant and vivacious – something superior too – about her manner, the tilt of her head, the way she carried herself as she came away from looking out the window and turned toward me.

She wore a half-moon-shaped French headdress studded with pearls, which made my old-fashioned gabled hood feel heavy on my head. Like my stepmother, Maud, she seemed to float as she moved, which made me once again feel earthbound. About her slender neck, she had a strand of pearls from which hung an ornate, golden *B* with three oblong pearls dangling. She wore blue that day, shimmering peacock blue velvet with long sculpted brocade ivory satin inner sleeves, which hid most of her hands. I was soon to learn that the long-sleeved fashion was partly to cover a tiny sixth finger on her left hand, something used against her later, as was a mark on her neck, to accuse her of witchcraft.

I was grateful I knew to curtsy long and low. As I rose, she kindly held out her right hand to raise me, then indicated I might sit on a needlepoint stool while she took the chair. I saw she had been reading a book, a New Testament, and in English rather than the approved Latin. How much she dared, I thought, even then, for the king had been declared Defender of the Catholic Faith before all this came to a boil.

'I am pleased to have about me those who will be loyal, those from many shires of the kingdom,' Anne told me. 'Devon is quite wild, is it not?'

'It is remote, my lady. It stretches from the lonely moors in the north to the cliffs overlooking the sea in the south, but there are many civilized places in between, I assure you.'

She asked me about my education and my faith. I told her the truth about Sir Philip's household's belief in the new learning and mostly the truth about everything else she asked. Since we were alone, would she not mention that I was to be her go-between to Cromwell when needed? But I learned then that she already knew what he had told me years ago, that the very walls might have ears. For, toying with her sweet-scented filigreed pomander, she rose in a rustle of skirts and summoned me with a graceful gesture over to a window she had flung wide. We stood in it, looking out over a pond and lovely, late-blooming garden.

Her bell-clear voice now dropped to a whisper. 'I must tell you that here at Hampton Court, which once belonged to the pompous 'pope' of England, Cardinal Wolsey, and at York Palace in London are several secret staircases and passageways connecting the king's chambers with others and to the courtyard or gardens outside – exits for times of need or desire. I tell you that not so that you will use them – for they are for the monarch only – but so that you know why, even in such a chamber as this, someone might overhear.'

'Yes, my lady.'

'And since you will be privy to some of my business, you must also realize that the king does not use those passages to visit me secretly, for I have told him that cannot be. But cleverness and care – that is what I expect of you. I believe you understand,' she went on, 'that I will at times have need of you to carry a message for me to our mutual friend and perhaps return such from him, quietly and circumspectly.'

'I do, my lady.'

'It is all for a righteous cause, and those who stay with me to the end will reap rewards.'

'Yes, my lady. I shall serve you loyally.'

How many times later I recalled her words to me when we first parted: *those who stay with me to the end.* That day she dismissed me, I left her standing there at the window, suddenly silent, frowning and brooding. I quietly approached the outer door to not disturb her thoughts. When I opened it, Lady Jane, who must have been leaning tight against it, nearly fell into the room.

# CHAPTER 5

HAMPTON COURT

*September 1528*

Come one and all, ladies!' Mary Talbot summoned us on my fifth day in Anne Boleyn's household. Mary clapped her hands as if we were the lap spaniels the ladies loved so much, though Anne herself stood out from the rest by favoring a sleek greyhound at her heels. 'Bowling on the green today with the king's coterie. Though,' Mary went on, rolling her eyes at me, probably because she believed I was so new and unconnected that it didn't matter a fig what I saw or heard, 'I wish he would not bring my helpmeet with him, damn the man – not the king, of course, but Percy.'

At age seventeen, Henry Percy, after his secret betrothal to Anne Boleyn had been crushed by the king and Wolsey, had been ordered to wed Mary. Their union had been agony for both. Mary would fall flat on the floor if she knew that Cromwell had told me all that. After two years of wedlock, with Percy yearning for his lost love,

70

moping about, oft falling ill, Mary had left him. Yet both served at court these five years later, he as esquire of the body for the king, she first with Queen Catherine and now with Anne. The Percys tolerated each other – barely. It was, I thought, a fair warning about forced marriage. But my parents had chosen each other, and they fought far too much. And then there was the Tudor royal marriage, or rather, the ruin of it.

Her fourteen ladies fell in behind Anne, some-what in pecking order, which put me in the last pair beside the pretty Madge Shelton, whom I was helping to learn to write a better hand. She read poorly too, but my tending to that would have to wait. I vow, I had never studied geography, history or Latin verb conjugations harder than I studied the customs and courtiers of the king. The do's and do not's of the Tudor court astounded me.

I had to learn titles and duties – for example, an esquire of the body, like Henry Percy, was in charge of everything above and below stairs while the king slept at night. I became familiar with proper allotments in the bouche; that is, the amount and selections of food, drink, candles and fuel for each position at court. My bouche included a few coins monthly, too, but I learned I must save that to go toward His Grace's – and mayhap this year, the Lady Anne's – Christmas gifts. I realized I might be dependent on Cromwell for extra money, since there had been no mention of such from Sir Philip.

At first I had little to report to Cromwell, nor did the Lady Anne send me to him with missives, until this fifth day at Hampton Court when so much happened at once that I struggle to recall and record it all.

First, I must note that, although the Lady Anne I saw in my brief initial interview had then seemed reserved, polite and pensive in private, she was quite the opposite when in public. She knew her allure and how to use it, and, I must admit, I studied that. I saw now why heads, especially men's heads, turned her way when she passed, and it wasn't all just reflected glow from the king's presence. She exuded enjoyment and excitement. From her time at the French court, she had evidently learned to bestow a daily *bon mot* on most courtiers and a tease for her king; her laughter trilled; she knew everyone's name and, some said, their secrets.

This was the first day she whispered to me in passing, though her smile did not fade and she laughed to throw others off her purpose: 'Mistress, there is a note for our friend pinned on the bottom of the stool in which you sat the day we met.' I smiled back at her as if she had made a pleasant jest.

With everyone trooping outside in order, I would have to find a solitary moment to go back to her chamber to fetch the note. I knew Cromwell and his army of clerks were ensconced near where Cardinal Wolsey still kept some privy chambers.

But, oh yes, before I recount the events of this day, I must record that Henry Tudor at age thirty-seven was a giant bestriding his world. Tall, robust, with a reddish sheen to his hair and beard and a golden sheen to his entire person, no one could best King Henry. He could out-eat, out-joust, out-dance, out-hunt, out-reason anyone. All the air seemed to suck toward him when he entered a room. His booming voice, his exuberant, hail-fellow-well-met greetings – though he could terrify one by glowering or even pouting – filled our lives. As his power spilled over onto Anne, most of his *bonhomie spilled over onto us, that is, unless someone called the Spanish Catherine his queen. That is, unless someone did not show the proper demeanor to or delight in his dear Anne. That is, unless someone seemed too familiar with his sweetheart, which is what happened that day.*

So her ladies followed Anne outside to the bowling green near the many acres of tiltyards. Along the gravel pathways, on tall posts, stood the king's beasts, staring down at us as they did in the gardens and gates of the palace: the lion rampant, the red dragon of Wales, antlered deer, griffins and unicorns and all manner of ornately carved, painted and gilded creatures.

I had heard of the game of bowls but had never seen it played, so I hoped no one would ask me to take part. At dancing, I had been included. I had been nervous, then delighted when I found myself paired for a pavane with Tom Seymour, whom I had not seen in the crowd. He had asked me to meet him out by the fishpond in the gardens that night. I might have been entranced enough to do so, but the Lady Anne had retired early that evening with pain from her monthly menses and had taken her coterie of ladies with her.

Today I saw Tom standing back on the opposite side of the bowling green, as if he felt not quite part of things either. Before I knew it, as the king and some of his favorites took turns casting the round bowl or jack, Tom appeared at my side.

'Would you pleasure me with a stroll in the maze while they are all at their own play?' he whispered and shot me a hopeful grin. He was as charming and well favored as I remembered him; my pulse pounded.

'I am busy, attached to the Lady Anne,' I told him, hoping he did not see me as an easy conquest.

'I'd like for us to be attached – very.'

'You are a rogue, Tom Seymour.'

'So, if not now, will you dare to slip away tonight? Meanwhile, we shall watch this rogues' gallery of gallants, eh?' he asked and pinched my bum right through my layers of skirts. I jumped. I still had my old wardrobe, which made me stand out like an unshorn sheep among those with fine, clipped coats. But I was waiting for my allotted three kirtles, four sets of sleeves, two bodices and other items made through the Lady Anne's – actually, His Majesty's – bottomless purse.

Tom and I could almost talk full voice now, for the laughter and wild bets – the courtiers wagered at everything – rent the air. 'Rub! Rub! I'll place half a crown on my next cast!' Henry Percy shouted as his bowl headed for the wooden mark. But he was eliminated, so that left only the king and a man I did not know. Courtiers pressed closer, cheering, urging them on. His Majesty's opponent was classically handsome with a Roman nose, close-clipped beard and curly hair. He reminded me of the stone carvings of the emperors' heads which adorned the outer walls of this palace.

'No cutting out!' someone shouted. 'I'll wager my inheritance on His Grace's cast!'

'And I'll wager my poems and masques on myself!' a clarion voice called out. I saw it was the man who opposed the king.

'Who is that?' I asked Tom.

'Handsome, isn't he? Thomas Wyatt, and he's wed, so don't get your hopes up.'

'I would not presume.'

'But I believe you do presume, my sweet – at least as much as the rest of us just waiting for our chance, eh? Wyatt's an old friend of the Lady Anne from way back – farther back than Percy. First loves are oft not forgotten, and Wyatt's much enamored of her still.'

'How unwise of him. But then – why would His Grace allow him here?'

'He's useful. Poet, playwright, lutenist, deviser of masques – and, if he knows what's good for him, loser at bowls. But he has a stubborn streak, a man after my own heart. See that thin gold ring His Grace wears on his little finger?'

'He took it from Lady Anne in jest as a love token yesterday – as if he needed such, but I think it was so romantic.'

'Romantic? Hell's gates, you sound as silly as the rest of them,' he muttered, frowning. 'But see that locket on the chain Wyatt's wearing? It was Anne's too. He's had it for years, dares to wear it about his neck, the lackbrain. And, what the deuce,' he said with a snicker and shake of his head, 'but it looks as if he's actually out to best the king. If he can't have the lady, at least he'll have this little victory.'

I, too, stared at the position where both bowls had landed.

'I win,' the king declared, hands on hips. 'Mine's slightly closer to the mark.'

'I'm not so certain,' Wyatt declared. 'Here, let me measure to be sure.' He unclasped the very locket Tom had just mentioned and, stretching it out end to end, measured that his bowl was nearer to the mark than the king's. His Majesty's snort and dour look threw a damper on all the noise and movement. It was as if everyone had frozen in position in a game of statue like Sir Philip's children used to play. Even the impeccably controlled Lady Anne looked as if she'd swallowed something dreadful.

Crooking his little finger with Anne's ring at her – perhaps at us all – Henry Tudor announced,

'I prefer to be shooting at the butts today anyway. Poet Wyatt, I leave you to your own games, but beware putting that locket back on your neck. Lockets and necks can be delicate things . . .'

Perhaps he swore or muttered else, I know not. I only knew that I had something to tell as well as take to Cromwell at last, not that it was privy information, but that it had ramifications. The king was still jealous of Anne's past suitor Wyatt, mayhap of Henry Percy, too.

'Devil take Wyatt, we'll all suffer from the king's bad temper for that foolish affront,' Tom groused. 'Tonight then,' he said in my ear, heating its shell and lobe with his warm breath, 'when the moon is full, during the dancing. I will be at the very start of the maze so you won't get lost within – it is I who am lost in admiration for you, mistress.'

I knew full well his pretty words were mere bombast, but I treasured them anyway. I was glad to see him dart away with the others, for I had my own business – Cromwell and my lady's business – to attend to.

As I hurried back to the Lady Anne's apartments, I rehearsed what I would tell the guards at her door: that she had sent me to fetch a handkerchief she'd left within. But no one stood watch. Her bedchamber door was unlocked and, surprised at that, I darted in. Perhaps those guards who trailed her today had come from here. The yeomen looked alike to me in their caps and red and gold garb, especially standing behind their big halberds that were half lance and half battle-ax.

I noted for the first time that the embroidered stool on which I had sat was adorned with the white falcon and tree stump of Anne's badge. I knelt and felt underneath, pricking my hand with one of the pins that held the note in place. I pulled the missive out and squeezed a drop of blood from my finger. Anne was a fine seamstress, so could she not be more careful with pins?

'Blast it!' I clipped out, doubly angry with myself. Not only had I gotten a blot of blood on the note, but I was beginning to take up the courtiers' custom of swearing. My mother had hated cursing, and I tried to honor her memory by avoiding it.

I decided to put the missive, which was sealed with wax, down my bodice, but I noticed that the twice-folded parchment had a single scribbled line on the outside: *For the hind of my heart*, it read.

I frowned, staring at that. A hind was a female deer. Surely, I could not have taken the wrong note. I had no intention of making a mistake and annoying the lady or Cromwell. Without breaking the seal, I squeezed the folds of the note so it belled open and I could read the signature. I turned toward the window light and read the last few lines of what appeared to be a poem, a sonnet, which was all the rage for courtiers to write to their ladyloves:

*. . . graven with diamonds in letters plain*
*There is written, her fair neck round about,*
*'Noli me tangere, for Caesar's I am,*
*And wild for to hold, though I seem tame.'*

It was signed simply but boldly TW.

Thomas Wyatt? He was leaving her love sonnets in her bed-chamber? Was he mad? And now I knew a dangerous secret.

I reread the lines I could see. *Noli me tangere* meant 'Do not touch me' in Latin, and it was obvious that Caesar was the king. Were Wyatt and Anne playing an even more dangerous game than his flaunting her old locket and winning at bowls? Could he have been sneaking up those secret stairways from outside she had mentioned?

Panicked now, I got on my knees, put one ear clear into the rush mat and saw another letter pinned on the far side, one more neatly placed. I put Wyatt's back and took the other. I was shaking to think of the power I held now – knowledge that could harm Anne, however much in thrall she seemed to hold the king, knowledge that could change a poet's life and maybe mine. It was something I should tell Cromwell, but would I? Maybe if he knew this, he could warn her to be more careful, but then she could deduce I had found the poem. Or I could just take it and destroy it. No, no, I would do only what the king's lady had ordered me to do and be the first to tell Cromwell about what happened on the bowling green. That would be enough to tip him off that Wyatt was playing a dangerous game.

A dangerous game, that's what I knew I was playing with Tom Seymour that night too. I had done what Cromwell said, sent a note to Master Stephen and then met Cromwell on the back stairs when he came down. He had taken Anne's note and listened avidly to my rendition of the royal explosion on the bowling green. He'd said, 'The Tudors keep those they do not trust either in prison for interrogation or at their elbow for observation. You have done well, Kat, or is it Mistress Katherine Champernowne here?'

'I have asked Mary Percy and Dorothy Cobham to call me Kat, but the others do not.'

'Back to your new life,' he'd said and turned away, reading the lady's note as he climbed the stairs. But now, even as gaming went on in the king's apartments after dancing, I had slipped away to meet Tom Seymour at the maze. I wasn't going into it with him, I'd vowed to myself. From the second – story windows, the huge hornbeam maze could be seen in the distance, tall, thick and daunting.

Tom emerged instantly from the dark mouth of the maze when I ventured toward it. He pulled me inside, directly into his arms for a long kiss, one in which he slanted his head, then moved it so his lips caressed mine, coaxing them open so his tongue could plunder my mouth. I had never been kissed like that and I liked it immensely. His hands were busy on my waist and hips, but that felt reassuring as well as arousing. His cheek pressed to mine, he whispered, 'Kat, Kat, I have dreamed of this, such a sweet kiss.'

Perhaps Wyatt wasn't the only poet on the premises, I thought. When the next kiss finally ended and we were both breathing raggedly, I tugged back a bit to restore my control. 'But you are so young,' I blurted foolishly.

'Which means I have no experience at this?' he countered with a low laugh that sent my stomach into even faster cartwheels. 'Have you not heard of country matters, sweet, coupling in the hay and such? Wolf Hall in Wiltshire, I warrant, is as fine a place for such schooling as is your Devon.'

'You're teasing me.'

'No, you're teasing me – your face, so calm which hides such unleashed passion, your beautiful body. Kat, more kisses . . .'

While he kissed me again, however tightly I was laced in back, he managed to tug my low, square bodice off my shoulders and down to bare my breasts. While I gasped and fought to calm my trembling knees, he used his wicked fingers, then his tongue to awaken them and me. I became aware of myself in a whole new way. The world spun; the hedge seemed to swallow us. He actually had me on the ground under him and was ruffling up my petticoats when we heard voices close by.

We froze. Sanity smacked me. I was not such a green girl I did not know where my tumble with Tom could take me – to the heights of joy but also to the depths of shame, censure and banishment from all I'd worked so hard for, especially if I caught a child from him. And I knew whose voices those were just one width of hedge away. Jane Rochford was arguing with her husband, George, Anne's brother.

'I followed you!' she said, hardly keeping her voice down. I pulled away from Tom and sat up, tugging my bodice back in place.

'If I favor a solitary walk in the moonlight, I don't need you about!' he countered.

'Meeting someone for a tryst?' she hissed. My face flamed. As much as I was attracted to Tom, I could not let my passions rule me.

'And if I am?'

'If you are, I warrant it is another man. Married to a sodomite, I am, now wouldn't your father and the king, too, like to know that? I swear, the only woman you ever loved was your precious, spoiled sister Anne!'

Their voices were beginning to fade. At least they weren't coming in here, where they could see us or force us to retreat farther into the maze. More secrets of the Boleyns, I thought. Secrets on secrets, all dangerous, even for someone simply to know.

'Leave Anne out of this!' George demanded. I had to strain now to hear their words over the rustle of my gown as I got to my feet. 'How do I know you're not out here, playing the doxy, meeting someone?' he ranted on. 'No wonder I could not get you with child when we Boleyns are prolific, our Howard kin too!'

'George, blast you, you can't get a woman with child unless you lie with her, and you haven't been in my bed for . . .'

They were gone. Before the brazen Seymour could seize me again, I started away. 'Kat,' he said, still sitting on the ground but snatching at my ankle to hold me there a moment more, 'I know where there is a room not being used, clear up under the eaves on the north side. And it has a truckle bed.'

'I can't,' I told him.

'I'll let you know when the coast is clear,' he said as I pulled my ankle loose. 'I adore you, sweet, and want to prove it in every way.'

I almost made a wrong turn, but I saw lights from the palace through the leafy wall and fled.

What saved me from being seduced to lie with Tom, on the grass, no less – and loving every moment of it, I suppose – was his being called home from court when his youngest brother died: not the eldest one, the heir whom he had wished did not exist. After that, either his father or Sir Francis Bryan sent him to the Continent, so he was gone for nigh on two years, and I admit I missed him sorely and feared he'd die abroad.

I learned Cromwell's wife had died; perhaps that was another reason besides his raw ambition that his work consumed him: he became the king's chief secretary and took on more duties than ever.

Yet thirteen months after I first arrived at court, the divorce dilemma dragged on. The Campeggio proceedings at Blackfriars, which the king thought would free him, were challenged by Queen Catherine's dramatic appearance and pleas. The king finally banished her from court, sending her to various distant old castles and forbidding her to see her beloved daughter, the Princess Mary. In October of 1529, Wolsey was stripped of his powers, leaving the Boleyns and their kin, the powerful Howard clan, especially the Duke of Norfolk, greatly in control of the court, and they thought, the king. Wolsey was arrested for treason – Henry Percy was sent by the king to do the deed, no less – and was heading to London for trial when he died in October 1530. His Majesty quickly took York Place that I had so admired in London for his own, began massive renovations and renamed the wondrous building Whitehall Palace.

But perhaps, most amazing of all that happened in my early years at court, Cromwell suggested to the king that, if the Pope would not grant him an annulment or divorce, he should become head of the church in his kingdom and declare himself free to wed the Lady Anne. It might mean his excommunication from the Holy Mother Church he had once championed, it might mean religious rebellion in his kingdom, but the king would not be denied Anne at any price.

People were stunned and, depending on their religious leanings, were either gladdened or horrified, especially by the charges that the great abbeys, monasteries and nunneries of the land were corrupt and must be rooted out, with their vast properties and funds going to the king and those he favored. I must say that was a clever move, for it kept many nobles quiet in the purge of those who opposed the king. How could they argue with all that while they were building their new manors on former church lands? But the king's daring move hardly surprised me: I had seen where Secretary Cromwell got that idea years before. It had been set in place by His Eminence Cardinal Wolsey when he had Cromwell close a few small rural monasteries so he could take the money to dedicate two colleges to himself.

What shocked and saddened me was that I, who never took ill, was laid low with a fever and could not go to France in the large entourage that met with the French king, Francis, in Calais; His Grace took Anne and her ladies with him. I was so downhearted, especially because everyone said it was a great success in many ways – including that, for some reason, the Lady Anne had at last decided the king needed an extra fill-up to keep him totally in thrall and had finally let him share her bed.

'I have a passion for eating apples!' she crowed

to a crowd of us in late autumn when the court was back in London. 'His Majesty needs me and he needs a son, and I shall see to both!'

I seldom carried messages between her and Cromwell anymore, for the Boleyns had so inserted themselves into the politics of the land that she oft summoned Cromwell to her as if she were England's ruler. Cromwell was rising farther and faster: he was named Privy Councillor to the king, on equal footing with Anne's father and uncle.

Still, I was bound to report to Cromwell – usually now through Master Stephen – when I found something new about the Boleyns, whom he yet thought bore watching. But today, when Master Stephen came down the back stairs at Whitehall where I used to meet with Cromwell, I said, somewhat petulantly, 'I suppose he knows the lady is with child, but he might want to know she's flaunting it, and those about the court who detest the Boleyns for being climbers are seething.'

'The first, he knows; the second, he assumes, but will care for,' Stephen told me with a tight smile. He was so much like his master. Both spoke quickly and concisely almost without moving their mouths. 'So, how are you getting on after several years here and wherever the court progresses, mistress? You know, our mutual master was greatly impressed that you did not get snared by that young cub Seymour when you first arrived at court.'

I gaped at him. I had learned to assume certain facial expressions to dissemble my true feelings as well as the next courtier, but his mention of Tom – and that he knew of us – took me off guard. When I just stared at him, he added, 'As young as Seymour is, he has a reputation as a bed swerver, so let that be a word to the wise, because he's coming back to court; his older brother Edward too.'

'So, our mutual master, as you said, spies on his spies?'

Stephen only smiled, waved and started back upstairs. 'Oh,' he called to me, and came back down, 'I forgot to tell you the biggest surprise of all – though not to those who are as watchful as you. Of course, you know the Lady Anne is with child. His Grace desperately wants their son to be born legitimate, so he intends to wed her privily, and soon. Keep an eye out for signs of that, lest we miss it somehow.'

Astounded at all I had heard, I leaned against the stairwell wall until my legs steadied, then went back out into the biting winter wind blowing off the Thames.

# CHAPTER 6

GREENWICH PALACE, NEAR LONDON

*May 31, 1533*

Look, a boat with a moving dragon, one belching smoke and fire!' Queen Anne called to her ladies. Before us, coming up the Thames toward Greenwich Palace, where we stood waiting at the water stairs, were at least fifty boats decorated by the merchant guilds of London. In her royal barge, Anne, accompanied by her ladies, was to be escorted by the flotilla into the city. Tonight, as was tradition, we would stay at the palace within the Tower walls to prepare for her coronation parade the next day before her crowning in Westminster Abbey.

Music flowed around us as we set off in the queen's barge, which had hastily been stripped of Queen Catherine's crests and colors and replaced with Anne's. Gay tunes from sackbuts and crumhorns, trumpets and drums, serenaded us from various watercraft. The Lord Mayor of London, Sir Stephen Peacock, had outdone himself for this first part of the great public play in which the new queen would enter London and be shown to all the people.

It was a wonderful time to serve her, and I felt so excited that I could have flown. Granted, Their Majesties had arguments at times, some over his attentions to other ladies while Anne was six months gone with child. Last week, when she had dared to scold him in public for his roving eye, he had turned on her and spewed out, 'You had best wink at such things, madam, and put up with them, as your betters have before you!'

Though she dared not answer, I warrant his calling other queens her betters set her back, for Anne was on a crusade to outdo her predecessor. For a while after that she seemed to coddle the king. If she threw a tantrum, in light of her condition, the king forgave her. After all, sooth-sayers and astrologers alike had promised His Majesty the babe would be a boy. Mostly, with plans for her coronation, they had been cooing doves.

My life was better too, for no more did I carry notes between Anne and Cromwell. The king's chief secretary was now Master of the Jewels, a symbolic position of power, and Chancellor of the Exchequer, a real position of power. If Anne dared to send billets-doux to Wyatt or even to Percy, I, thank the Lord, was not involved.

But I cannot say the same for my woman's heart: for the first time in my life, it was involved. Though Tom Seymour was seldom at court, for he was yet oft sent on errands both in England and to the Continent, when he was about I took a page from Anne Boleyn's book and kept him at bay. Kisses, yes. Caresses I craved, but I refused to be alone with him. It was working wonders. The idea of romance he once mocked now kept him on his toes: he brought me gifts from France, he even wrote me very bad sonnets, but I treasured them, and wrote him love letters back. I had no title, but neither did he. At least I was one of the queen's court, so perhaps I could wed him someday and then I would deny him nothing. Yes, I looked to the queen for my inspiration on how to deal with men.

For besides Tom Seymour, I had a new man in my life, one of those who had swelled Her Majesty's entourage after the king secretly wed her at Whitehall in January. Even as I watched and was part of the parade of boats, the sounds and sights of my first meeting with John Ashley floated through my mind again.

It was at a joust in the tiltyard at Hampton Court in late March, a sunny but windy day after much rain. In the third pass at the tilt rail, His Majesty had bested his challenger but dropped his lance, a new one that had replaced the one he'd splintered. Apparently winded, he was immediately helped off his horse. At age forty-one, he had waited for Anne for eight years. During their honeymoon period, he had seemed like a youth again, dancing and gaming till all hours. But lately his jowls had widened, and his girth even more. His appetite had increased. He sweated harder and breathed heavier.

People in the stands and higher in the painted and beflagged observation towers murmured as he was helped off toward the tiring tents with his armor clanking. 'Kat,' the queen called to me – most called me Kat now – 'take my handkerchief to His Grace so that his squire may wipe his brow. And pass on the message that, if his queen were not so heavy with his son, I would run down to care for him myself and hope to see him privily soon.'

I took the heavily embroidered square of linen and made my way out of the stands. Before I descended the stairs toward the tents, I noted that a man I did not know, big shouldered with finely muscled legs, rode out onto the tiltyard on a beautiful chestnut horse. At quite a gallop, without reining in to dismount, he snatched off his hat so he wouldn't lose it, leaned down from his saddle and retrieved His Majesty's dropped lance in one smooth grasp. As he put his hat back on, many in the stands applauded. I yearned to, but not wanting to muss the queen's handkerchief, holding up my skirts to pick my way along the boards laid over the mud, I hurried toward the tiring tent where the jousters' pieces of armor were strapped on or taken off.

The man who had retrieved the lance rode up beside me. Still holding it, he dismounted. I must admit I had never seen anyone – titled, noble, even royal – handle or sit a horse like he.

'Mistress Champernowne,' he said, and swept off his hat again, 'it is muddy back here, and there are horse droppings. May I be of service?'

'You know my name, so you have me at a disadvantage, I'm afraid. I'm to take this token to His Majesty from the queen.'

'Best I put you up on my mount to save your slippers and skirts – with your permission,' he said, with a nod toward his horse. 'This is Brill, short for Brilliant, for he is that in the sheen of his coat and his loyalty and obedience, aren't you, my boy?' He patted Brill's flank.

I swear, that animal nodded as if he agreed. I had never been introduced to a horse, especially before hearing its master's name. It was as if the steed were a person – a friend of its rider. But this intriguing man was speaking to me again.

'I know the tent where you will find His Majesty. I am John Ashley, new come to court as senior gentleman to the queen. I am distantly related to her and now find myself assigned to work with her Master of the Horse, William Coffin. I love horses and hope to write a book about riding someday,' he added, reaching up to stroke Brill's sturdy neck. 'I miss my home but am honored to serve. May I lift you up, then?'

I had to tilt my head to look up at him, for he was a bit taller than Tom. For some reason, suddenly shy at his smooth speech and fine face and form, I nodded. He leaned the lance against the side of the stands. Then, by my waist, as if I weighed naught, he lifted me up on Brill's saddle and, as I held to the pommel with one hand, he led the steed back through the mud and mess toward the tents.

My thoughts were jumbled. Master Ashley had left the king's lance behind. He was obviously literate, bright and ambitious to speak of writing a book. And had not the queen realized it was mud and mire back here? It seemed either her new lofty position or her pregnancy had made her so sure of herself that she had become less thoughtful of others.

'If I may ask, Master Ashley, in what way are you related to Her Grace?'

'Ah, yes, connections are the keys to the kingdom here at court. My mother, Anne Wood, was a niece of the queen's mother, Elizabeth Boleyn, who was born a Howard. I grew up in East Burnham in Norfolk.'

'Yes, the Howards, headed by the Duke of Norfolk. He and the queen's father are the king's closest advisers with Secretary Cromwell.'

'Exactly. Then, on my father's side, I am descended from Lord Ashley, Baron of Ashley Castle in Warwickshire. But I won't inherit as my mother was my father's second wife, and he has a son by his first marriage, so I am here to make my own way. And you, Mistress Champernowne?'

'I was the ward of Sir Philip Champernowne of

Modbury in Devon, cousins of my father. I have been at court in the queen's household for four and a half years now.'

'Ah, a lifetime for surviving in favor here, but please tell no one I said that.'

He had slowed Brill, perhaps to give us more time to talk. Mud stuck to his highly polished boots. He was my own knight errant, I fancied, for I loved the old stories of chivalrous days, especially the tales of long-lost Camelot. Perhaps, like Sir Lancelot himself, John Ashley was dressed all in rich-smelling black leather; his skin was sunstruck, a bit darker than most pale Englishmen in springtime. He was rugged-looking with a straight nose, thick eyebrows framing sky blue eyes and a closely clipped beard. His eyelashes were sinfully thick for a man's. Strangely, his deep voice sent shivers through me. I guessed he was about my age or slightly older, and I longed to know if he was wed.

'Have you left behind a family in Norfolk?' I asked as he halted the horse before a large tent where squires and pages darted in and out. In faith, I had nearly forgotten my mission and saw I had wadded the queen's handkerchief in my sweating palm.

'Only my stepmother, father and elder half brother, both horse breeders,' he said, making me for the first time in months think about my family. Unlike Tom or other courtiers I knew, something wise and serious about this man made one think and feel deeply. 'Here,' he said, 'you can hardly go inside, and I warrant His Grace is resting. May I take that for you and then I'll walk Brill back to the stands for you. Was there a message?'

Staring down into his intent gaze, I nodded as if I had suddenly gone speechless, then blurted a nervous, jumpy rendition of what the queen had said: 'With love from his love, and she hopes to see him privily soon.'

He smiled up at me, and our fingers touched when he took it. Tom would have made some tease or double entendre over what I had said, but John told me only, 'A lovely thought for the most fortunate of men.'

'Oh, look at those wild men!' Madge Shelton shrieked next to me, jolting me from my reverie. She pointed at the barge with the dragon, which was being rowed directly beside us with the Tower and London Bridge in view. All around the dragon had suddenly emerged men dressed as monsters with long hair, wearing ragged animal skins and cavorting with screams and cries while people lining the riverbanks clapped and huzzahed. Anne and her ladies shouted and laughed to see such a display.

I stood there among them, joining in the fun but thinking again of John Ashley, imagining not only that he or I were mounted on his beautiful steed but that both of us were in his saddle together.

★　★　★

95

Some whispered that the king was giving Anne such a glorious flotilla, parade, coronation and banquet to make up for the ignominy of a secret wedding. Others said he'd worked so hard to have her that only a splendid effort would be appropriate. Yet some whispered he needed such pomp to establish her as queen with his subjects, many of whom were still loyal to Queen Catherine. The cast-off wife was now stripped of most of her staff and living in backwater, rural manors such as Buckden and Kimbolton. The Princess Mary, who also refused to recognize the new queen – Anne Boleyn was lately obsessed with humbling Mary – likewise lived exiled from court and her father.

The day of Anne's grand entry into London, I was thrilled to be in the coronation parade that made its way from the palace within the Tower to Westminster Palace. From there Anne would set out to be crowned in the Abbey on the morrow.

Madge Shelton and I shared a chariot driven by one of His Majesty's squires. We were so proud of our new red and gold velvet coronation gowns, for which we'd been allotted the exact yardage of material. Best of all, just ahead, I could not only see the queens' ornate litter but had a fine view of John Ashley's broad back and bouncing buttocks on his prancing steed.

It was Anne Boleyn's triumphant day, but I felt it was also mine. Without having to do Cromwell's bidding lately, I was still among the queen's ladies and privy to all the benefits that brought. I had escaped a life with a stepmother I could not abide and had – thanks to Cromwell – managed to obtain a good education, which I sought to further when I could. With the queen's permission, I tutored women at court who did not write or read well. She was a champion of women's educations, including religious ones. I read the Bible myself instead of having priests interpret it for me. Queen Anne was one of the first to promote Tyndale's Bible in English, rather than reading in Latin. I was honored to discuss religion with the queen and even with Archbishop Cranmer, Anne's spiritual adviser. He was steeped in the new learning, which the Catholics who detested it called Lutheranism.

Though six months pregnant, today Anne Boleyn was gloriously arrayed in a cloth-of-gold gown and jewels that glittered in the sun. The cavalcade wound its way through the narrow streets, newly graveled for this day. All around and above us, Londoners hung from windows, cheering – or, I noted, jeering.

Occasionally we heard sporadic cries of 'God Save Queen Catherine!' or the rumbling of muted boos. More than once, we stopped so that Anne could enjoy a street-side tableau or masque prepared for her. One was a costly pageant sponsored by the merchants of the steelyard, with a backdrop full of classical gods and goddesses designed by the German artist Hans Holbein, who was becoming a favorite for portraits of courtiers.

But over the music in her honor, I heard from deep within the crowd: 'King's wench! Concubine!' And once, so clearly, 'Whore!' John Ashley and some others rode over to push such naysayers back from the queen's hearing.

Then too, more than once along the way, I noted people laughing. At first, I thought they dared mock Anne herself. Though she was obviously pregnant, her garments were draped to obscure her growing belly. But I soon saw some folk in the crowd pointed at the painted, linked initials of Henry and Anne adorning her little, pennants and even our chariot: *HA, HA, HA*.

At Anne's banquet in old Westminster Hall in London, the king had given orders to elevate her above all others. The same had been done in the coronation ceremony itself in the Abbey earlier today. She had been crowned – unlike Queen Catherine – in St Edward's Chair, which heretofore had been used only for monarchs. Nor had King Henry's first queen been crowned with St Edward's Crown, worn only by rulers but not their wives. At least that part of the grand events went better than the parade, for no one inside dared to make a peep against their queen. Now, at the banquet, special favors for her abounded again.

Nary a soul was permitted near Anne, unless to serve her food or drink. The king, everyone knew, was watching events from a side room, for this was Anne's day, Anne's banquet. She sat on her husband's marble throne with her fringed and gilded cloth of estate on poles over her like a lofty second crown. Archbishop Cranmer was at her table, but at a goodly distance. Two countesses stood beside her, and two gentlewomen – I was glad I had not been selected – crouched under her table in an old rite. She sent them on errands from time to time, or spit food she did not care for into the linen cloths they held. And all this was on a dais, twelve stairs elevated and railed off from us mere mortals.

That was fine with me. The food was plentiful and excellent, and imported wine – not diluted or sweetened for once – flowed like water with no small beer or ale in sight. Then too, without turning my head, at other tables I could see both Tom Seymour and John Ashley. That warmed me even more than the malmsey and Rhenish I alternated in my crystal Venetian goblet. Tom was sitting with Sir Francis and Lady Elizabeth Bryan; John was with William Coffin, Master of the Horse, at a more distant table. Tom's elder brother Edward he did not trust or like – though in all his fussing he never quite said why – sat at a more forward table, probably because he served Archbishop Cranmer in those days. Secretary Cromwell, who nodded briefly to me in passing, seemed to be everywhere, trailed by a train of secretaries or lackeys of some sort.

I soon lost count of the kinds of delicacies that

came in great waves and seemed to go so well with the delicious wine. Why, before tonight, had I never noticed that wine tasted better in glass goblets than pewter cups? As at all royal meals, we had three courses: first, cold food; second course, hot; and third, sweets, though we had never seen such selections or abundance as this day. The parade of food brought in silver tureens or on platters almost made me dizzy.

The cold course consisted of artichokes, cabbage and cowcumbers, perch in jelly, cream of almonds, Colchester oysters, lovely cheese tarts and much more. The hot dishes included swan, capon, baked venison, porpoise in mustard sauce, larded pheasants and peacocks with lighted tapers in their beaks. Finally, the dulcets, or sweet dishes, arrived, and how beautifully they went down with sips of wine. Though I had been careful not to stuff myself should there be dancing back at Whitehall later – how I hoped John Ashley knew how to dance – I did taste one or two of these selections: almond tarts, jelly fritters, cinnamon custard, bread puddings, currant cake, quince pie and suckets, those delicious oranges hollowed out, chopped and put back in their rinds with wine and sugar. And my favorite, which I concentrated on, wardens, that is, imported pears served with cinnamon and mace and colored blue with mulberries.

Of course, everyone had their best manners on display. Holding one's little finger up, we used only our left hands to touch common dishes and our right hands to handle our personal knives and spoons. Servants called sewers passed along the twelve-foot tables covered by white linen with clean napkins and bowls of rosewater to wash one's hands between each course or to remove empty dishes. Salt from huge, gilt cellars had to be lifted with the point of a clean knife and laid upon one's trencher. I was cleaning my knife with a slice of manchet bread to put it back in a pocket up my sleeve when John Ashley suddenly appeared over my shoulder. I jumped so, I almost cut myself.

Hoping my lips were not blue from the mulberries, I tipped my head back to smile up at him. He helped me stand and step out over the long bench. It was a good thing his hands held me, for on my feet I still felt rocky – whether from too much wine or his presence, I knew not.

'Quite a day,' he said. His breath smelled deliciously of cloves. 'And more to come when we all get back to Whitehall.'

'I hope I don't sink the barge, for I have eaten far too much.'

'I like a lass with a bit of flesh on her bones,' he said with a slightly crooked smile that made my insides flip-flop.

John was the first man I could recall who looked deeply into my eyes without blatantly ogling the rest of me. Somehow that made me warmer than those who leered at my breasts or hips. Though I'd been a courtier long enough to know how to

101

dissemble or hide my feelings, I blushed hot and giggled like a milkmaid.

'Well,' he said, his hands still steadying me, one on my elbow and one on my shoulder before he pulled back, 'I should talk. I put away a yeoman's dinner tonight, including about a barrel of bread pudding. My mother used to make such, and I haven't had the like for years.'

'My mother made dishes I miss,' I told him. 'It was so different when my stepmother Maud came to live with us.' He nodded. I blinked back tears. In faith, was I going to cry? Why did this man make me so emotional with memories tumbling back?

Whenever I was near him, I also felt a delicious uncoiling of something taut in the pit of my belly. It took Tom's skilled touch to make me tingle, but this man could send me into shivers without a touch. I could almost sway right into him in the middle of this busy, noisy crowd.

'I won't be going back by barge,' he told me, taking what appeared to be a reluctant step farther away. 'Sir William and I are overseeing the return of horses from here to Whitehall, but if there is dancing or gaming tonight, and you are not busy with others . . .' I thought for a moment he might ask me to meet him in the maze as Tom had or to save a dance for him, but he went on, '. . . perhaps we can speak again. This is a day we will all remember, Mistress Champernowne—'

'Kat. My name is really Katherine but my friends call me Kat.'

'A day I will remember, Kat, for being able to watch you for all hours of this banquet. So close and yet so far.'

He was not jesting or teasing but looked utterly serious. He bowed to me, though he had no need since my rank was equal to his. As I watched him walk away, I realized that I had my legs pressed tight together, mayhap to stem my desire for him but especially because I realized I needed the jakes and fast. I'd had far too much wine.

I tried to walk quickly but carefully – it seemed my feet floated – between the long tables toward the door to the side corridor. Surely, the jakes or a room with extra close stools was down this way.

The buzz of voices grew more distant. 'S blood, I knew I'd had a good deal of wine, but I'd thought the amount of food would cover it. Yet, except for my beautiful blue dessert, I had to admit I had only tasted various dishes but had really drunk the wine.

The corridor was lit by sconces, but all the doors were closed. Should I have gone out another door into another corridor? This old palace was a web of halls and rooms, and I had lived here so seldom that I did not know my way.

Then I saw Madge come out a door and head toward me. 'Oh, good,' I told her. 'The jakes – down this way?'

'Just around the corner, then one turn,' she cried, and flew past me back toward the banquet.

I found it to my great relief. Surprisingly, it was deserted, so I had evidently come to the wrong one. There must be a place for the lords and ladies even closer. Like Madge, I started back at a good clip, but the entire corridor seemed to tilt, to turn into a tunnel. The buzz of distant voices made me think of a swarm of bees like my father tended. Wishing John were here to rescue me again, I put my hand to the wainscoted wall to steady myself. How glad I was to see Tom coming toward me – until I caught the expression on his face.

'I didn't know to go another way,' I began, 'so—'

'I actually expected to find you here with him in a hot embrace!' he told me, and grabbed my arms to give me a hard shake. My teeth almost rattled. 'Or lying flat on the floor with your skirts up. Do you think I'm such a country dolt that I don't know the trick of he goes one way, you the other, for an assignation? I know who he is, Kat.'

'He is a new friend, an acquaintance. L-let me go.'

'I saw how dazzled you were by him, and so did anyone else in the hall who cared to see you draped over him! So, how oft have you done that privily before – mayhap when I was writing you stupid poems or spending good coin for pretty presents?'

'You're demented. I did no such th—'

'Ashley's no more than a glorified stable hand, working in mud and mire. He stinks of horse droppings!'

'He does not. You've no right to—'

'Like a lackbrain, I've been waiting patiently, wooing you, dancing to your tune, and you—'

He was furious, livid. His spittle speckled my face. Perhaps he was in his cups too. I was so shaken, I wasn't certain whether I actually said to him that John had once pulled me from the mud and mire, but it finally dawned on me that Tom was dragging me down the hall away from the banquet.

I was dizzy with drink and furious but frightened, too. He was hurting me, almost pulling me off my feet. 'You owe me!' he muttered as he tried first one locked door and then another down a side hall, yanking me behind him. 'You'll not give that ripe body to another and think you have me on a leash. His Majesty waited much too long to tame the Boleyn tease, and I'll not have it!'

'Loose me! I'm going to be sick from the wine and from your touch!'

I opened my mouth to scream for help but his lips crushed mine in a brutal kiss, grinding the inside of my mouth against my teeth, pressing me so hard to the wall I could not breathe. He finally found a door that was open and pulled me in behind him, slamming it behind us. It was ill-lit by a single, closed window. The place smelled musty and dusty. Thank God, it had no bed, but that did not matter to him. He bent me backward over the table, hitting my head on it so hard I saw stars. He threw my skirts up nearly to my chin. I prayed I would be sick all over him, but the wine only seemed to make me dizzy, not nauseous.

'Leave off!' I cried, trying to kick him away as he seized and separated my ankles. 'Let me go, or I'll tell—'

'You'll tell no one, or I'll ruin you!' he shouted, bending over me, right in my face, as I heard him fumble with his points and shove his codpiece aside. He dragged me closer to him with my legs spread. 'You have nowhere to go, do you, Kat?' he goaded, his face a grotesque mask. 'The new queen is concerned only with herself, her damned, greedy family and her growing belly. Create a problem or scandal for our free-thinking little queen, and she'll drop you like a burning faggot.'

'Stop it! Get off me!'

'Afraid I'll find out you are not a virgin?'

'I am, and my maidenhead is not for the likes of you!'

He heeded nothing I said or did, but ranted on, 'You think Cromwell will take you in if Anne sends you away? Don't go running to him! He'll tell you to shut your mouth and get out of his busy way. You're of no account to him now.'

*No account*? I tried to scratch his eyes, his face, but only raked my nails across his neck.

'My family is on the rise,' he went on, 'even my flap-mouthed brother who has Archbishop Cranmer's ear. You have only your good reputation, little helper of those poor wenches who can't read, trustworthy servant of the queen. And, unless you tat-tale about our tryst here, I won't either to save your reputa—'

I screamed at the initial pain, but he muffled my cry with a sweating palm and thrust into me harder. What if I conceived a child from this – this brutal coupling I'd dreamed of so differently? He cared not a whit for me, for no one but himself. All my pretty plans, my long-tended love for him, twisted and died.

'So,' he muttered, 'at least I had you before your stable boy!'

Though it seemed to go on forever, I warrant it was over quickly.

Yet the pain and shame of what he had said and done – what he had ruined – had only begun.

I know not how I managed to take the barge back to Whitehall with the others chattering and laughing on board that night. Perhaps because they, too, had overindulged in food and drink, they paid no heed to my pained expression and faltering steps. As Anne's women prepared for bed, I mumbled some excuse to them and took the narrow back servants' stairs down and ran outside toward the river.

No, I would not drown myself, not face the

horror of that, as my poor mother had. I wanted to live. I wanted revenge. But right now I had to wash away Tom Seymour's brutality from my body, if not my mind. Perhaps the spouting fountain would do as well.

Then, blessedly, it began to rain. So common this time of year, but it seemed as if the Lord were comforting me with clean water from heaven. Heedless of who might pass by, I huddled against the wall of the deserted privy garden and stripped off my clothes, every stitch, though I had to twist and yank and tear the fine material without a maid to help me disrobe. If someone should come by, they would think me a lunatic, but I cared not. I sobbed myself breathless, cursing Tom, feeling not only ravaged and defiled by him but by some of the things I myself had done at court for Cromwell, things I had done to barter and bargain my way to where I was today. I was so out of breath and out of my mind that it took a nearby lightning bolt on one of the rooftop chimneys to jolt me to myself again.

Still, despite the storm, I stood with my bare back and bottom pressed against a rough brick wall I know not how long, in the driving rain, scrubbing myself all over with a sodden gold velvet sleeve from my precious gown, until it was quite ruined.

Ruined – my virginity, my hopes of a future with Tom, mayhap for any husband. Ruined. More than ever, my trust of men lay in tatters.

But, I told myself, hardening my heart, that could serve me well in terrible times yet to come in the Tudor court. Any woman, but especially a woman alone, was vulnerable in this world, and, God help me, I still wanted not only to survive but thrive.

# CHAPTER 7

Greenwich Palace, near London

*September 7, 1533*

I stood in the back of Queen Anne's birthing chamber and listened to her screams. Though I envied her a child, I was grateful I had not caught one from Tom's brutal rape. But why, I agonized again, if I was grateful for such a blessing, was I not to be angry with the Lord for allowing Tom to attack me in the first place? Ah, my deep talks with Her Majesty made me question everything at times – including her pain and terror now.

She was suffering not from labor pains, for those were past, and everyone said it had been an easy birth. But not easy to accept the result. Thank God, not a miscarriage or dead child, as Queen Catherine had oft suffered, but a girl. Another princess. After tearing the royal family apart, after rending religion limb from limb in England with worse to come, after alienating Spain, the Vatican and the Holy Roman Emperor and becoming the scandal of all Europe, His Majesty had only another daughter.

While the child was passed off to others to be washed and swaddled, the queen's mother tried to comfort Anne. Finally, when the baby wailed lustily, Anne's hysterics quieted to gasping sobs.

'Give her to me,' she commanded, and took the babe in her arms.

'His Majesty is coming,' her mother said, passing on what Jane Rochford had just darted in to announce. 'He must not see you like this.'

'Get me a comb and rice powder for my cheeks. I'll brazen it out, you'll see . . .' was the last I heard before those of us attending, though not assisting, were shuffled away from the birthing bed.

Princess Mary happily took her leave. She had been summoned to be present at the birth by the queen who had ruined her life. She now had a half sister who would soon take her former title of Princess of Wales. I had never met the seventeen-year-old princess before but was touched by how she carried herself, proudly but not haughtily. Her deep, almost mannish voice coming from such a petite body surprised me. Her face, framed by auburn hair, a heritage from both parents, gave away her inner torment. Already she had deep frown lines on her fair-complexioned forehead, caused not only by nearsightedness – she had to squint to see things at a distance – but her unhappiness. Most courtiers now treated the young woman, once the darling of everyone's eye, as if she had the plague.

The day she'd arrived, I'd put myself at her elbow

111

and quietly told her who stood across the with-drawing room as if I were her guide or translator. Let the others snub or scold me. If Cromwell was not pleased, I would tell him I was simply trying to learn what Mary said so that I could inform him.

Because – God forgive me, since so many of my friends felt hostile to Queen Catherine's girl – I sympathized from the first with a young woman who had a stepmother who wanted to hurt and humble her and a father who allowed and abetted that. I was glad for her sake that Mary was being permitted to return to Beaulieu, her house in Essex.

As we heard the king's voice boom in the distance, many of the queen's ladies fled, but I stayed where I was. At least the great Henry Rex would have to admit the child showed her Tudor heritage with her thatch of red hair, though her eyes were not pale blue but already dark, like her mother's. Cromwell had not given me an assignment for months, but he had expressly told me he wanted to know what passed between Their Graces when His Majesty first beheld the child.

'A daughter, my dear lord,' I heard Anne's voice ring out as he stomped to the side of the bed. 'See? Healthy and strong, a beautiful daughter with your hair and, I warrant, someday your hand-some nose.'

A good tactic, I thought, not to give him the first word. Perhaps Anne could brazen it through, despite the fact that announcements had already been written about the birth of a prince. Without turning my head, I slanted my gaze up from the far corner of the large room where I was helping Lady Margaret Bryan fold linen napkins for the child. Lady Margaret, who had been governess to Princess Mary, would no doubt tend the baby when she was given her own household away from court. She was the only other person I knew who had dared to welcome the king's older daughter to Greenwich. Now neither of us spoke. I don't think I so much as breathed.

The king still did not speak but bent over the big bed as Anne unwrapped the child for him to see. Although it was unhealthful for fresh air and much light to enter during confinement and labor, Anne had ordered one of the windows unboarded. Late afternoon sunlight slanted in to make the infant's head look gilded by a wispy red-gold crown, or so it had seemed to me when I had tiptoed close a while ago.

Perhaps His Majesty saw himself in the little mite as Anne suggested, for, before he went out again, he muttered, 'All right then. A girl now, a boy soon.'

That thought, I prayed, would keep Cromwell content, for I'd heard a dreadful thing as I waited outside his door when he'd summoned me last week about keeping an eye on the Princess Mary. I had no doubt my position here if not my very life would be forfeit if anyone knew what I had overheard him speak to Master Stephen: 'If the queen is not delivered of a living son, His Majesty has asked – just supposition now – for future reference – hypothetical, a mere rhetorical question – if he has any sensible, moral justification for putting Anne aside without having to return to the past queen . . .'

I had gasped, covered my mouth with both hands as I bent over in shock against the wall. Were Cromwell and the king both raving mad? I had not felt sicker or more furious when Tom Seymour attacked me the day the queen was crowned.

After that, I both detested and feared Henry Tudor. For the Princess Mary of whom Lady Margaret spoke so fondly. For Anne, of course, and now for her precious child. And for myself, who knew from dealing with both Cromwell and Tom Seymour how cruel a man could be, especially one with power. Here I was, tied to them both, and since I knew far too much, dangerous to them both.

Thank God, Tom was not much at court, but when he was, he held the threat of his cesspool lies over my head. He swore I would do as he wished in the future, or he would ruin my reputation, for yes, he was right: my good name was all I had as my shield and buckler. I had no powerful family, no fortune, no lands, no title, no champion. Granted, I had helped other women learn to read and write, and many were grateful.

The queen trusted me, but would a new queen simply dismiss me, if Anne did not bear him a son and he found a way to divorce her?

My foolish dreams of Tom Seymour in my future had died that night three months ago. At least, John, my dear friend, demanded naught of me but gave me his care and friendship. With a heavy heart and no explanation, I now avoided him so Tom would not erupt again and hurt us both. I was deeply ashamed of how poorly I had treated John to keep him at bay. Though in many ways John and I were both estranged and strangers yet, I feared if he knew what Tom had done, he would throw down the gauntlet for a fight, and then what would become of him and me?

Three days after her birth, the daughter of Henry Tudor and Anne Boleyn was regally christened in the Chapel Royal at Greenwich as Princess Elizabeth, named after both of her grandmothers. I was not at the ceremony, but they say she did not cry, even when dipped thrice in the baptismal water. She was five days old when I first held her in my arms and she looked up at me with – I vow this is true – curiosity and intelligence.

I felt I lived in limbo the next months leading toward the annual Yuletide celebration. The king was back in his wife's bed upon occasion, but everyone knew certain court ladies were in his. Elizabeth had been declared Princess of Wales, which meant Mary Tudor was disinherited and demoted to being called simply Lady Mary. The former princess had balked at being bastardized, which had sent Anne into another absolute rage, with mutterings she would box Mary's ears or worse.

Then came the summons from Cromwell that was to change my life as surely as had his promises to me so long ago in Devon.

'You asked to see me, Master Secretary?' I inquired as he met me on a back staircase at Hampton Court. I was surprised to see him instead of Master Stephen for once.

'Yes, Kat. I have an important and fortuitous assignment I am certain will please you.'

My stomach clenched. I trusted him not now.

'It will play to many of your strengths. You have shown your skills in helping others, and Lady Margaret Bryan favors you. You are quite well educated and enjoy learning and teaching, and the queen trusts you.'

'I am glad you are looking out for Her Majesty's welfare,' I said, leveling a look at him, heedless of the danger that now reeked from this man, my mentor. 'In a way, you have risen to power with her.'

'Ah, to quote the wise King Solomon, 'There is nothing new under the sun,' yet, Kat, knowing our King Henry as I do, I say, everything changes. But to this new duty for you. It does entail leaving court for a while,' he plunged on, 'but I thought, in light of things, you might not mind that.'

Our gazes locked and held. His eyes gleamed

dark and flat, like an adder's. Was this man all-knowing, all-seeing? Was he referring to my hatred of Tom or my thwarting feelings for John?

'In short,' he said, putting a hand on my shoulder I longed to shake off, 'you will be a companion and aide to Lady Bryan when the Princess Elizabeth's household is established at Hatfield House in Hertfordshire next week. Her title is Mistress and Governess of the princess. 'Tis custom, you know, that royal heirs have their own establishments, and I trust you will be a fine addition to that. You will receive a fair wage, too.'

'And?' I asked. I was pleased with what he had said, for escape from the tensions of the court suited me right now. I would greatly miss glimpses of John Ashley as he rode here and there, oft in the presence of the king, but not much else. Besides, I admired Lady Bryan and adored the pretty little princess.

'And what?' he demanded, frowning. 'I like not your tone nor that look.'

'I have learned that there is always more, Master Secretary.'

'Yes, well, you always were too bright for a woman. The Lady Mary is being sent to Hatfield too, without her retinue, by queen's command, to be in subjection and attendance on the Princess of Wales.'

'Poor lady.'

Now he looked as annoyed as I felt. 'Just be sure that is the way you address her. She is the Lady

117

Mary now and quite belligerent and wayward to defy Their Majesties, even as her mother does. But as for Hatfield, it is but twenty miles to the north, so either Stephen or I will be visiting from time to time, with or without Their Majesties. For once, put your reports to me in writing – without any address or signature – and slip them to us lest we have no time to talk during a visit. Do you understand me?'

'Yes. More and more.'

He glared at me. 'Do not be overly clever, Kat. The queen is that, and it doesn't become her or bode well for her. I do regret that your love for young Seymour made you so forward with him – and now bitter – but of course he had to tell you there was no hope for a future with him. Just do not throw yourself at the next promising young man.'

I could not breathe. Tom had told Cromwell that? If so, what else had he said of me? At that moment, I could have strangled Seymour – Cromwell too – with my bare hands, but here was my chance to escape all this, to find refuge and purpose at some rural place called Hatfield. I would be as happy to leave this court of scorpions and demons as I had been to enter it.


HATFIELD HOUSE, HERTFORDSHIRE

My heart ached for her the next two years. Not for the darling little Princess Elizabeth, but for

118

her older half sister. Mary Tudor was given the dampest, smallest bedchamber in vast Hatfield – or Hunsdon or Eltham, when we moved off and on – and had but one servant, a doltish chambermaid. Mary Tudor was the one treated much like a maid under Queen Anne's stringent orders as she tried to break the young woman's defiance and spirit. But, like her mother, Mary was indomitable. For one thing, she refused to curtsey to the little Elizabeth, though the child didn't know or care about that anyway.

I admired Mary because she was ever kind to the red-haired toddler in leading strings. Like me, Mary loved children. I can yet see in my mind's eye the elder sister holding the younger on a pony's back and walking her in a circle before the main entrance of the palace, though Queen Anne might have flown into a rage at such. Mary's face lit up when the child lifted her arms to be held or babbled her baby rendition of her name, 'Mar-mar.' I silently took great pride in the fact that the child always clearly called me 'Kat.'

As carefully as I could, I gave the Lady Mary my tacit support, and I knew she was silently grateful. Yet I saw her wasting away, losing weight with dark shadows under her eyes. Her headaches she called megrims were agony, and her sporadic menses pained her greatly. She spent hours on her knees in her bedchamber in prayer, perhaps her only real solace. It rankled me that the doting Queen Anne continually sent or brought pretty new clothes for her child, but that Mary seemed to go about in the same black gown, like a harbinger of doom. And, yes, as much as I had aped Queen Anne at times and admired her, too, I grieved sore for a young woman who had such a cruel stepmother – one she could not abide and did not want to acknowledge.

My ambitions to be at court cooled greatly, and I came to see the sweet countryside as a refuge from the trials of public life. Hatfield, once a manor house of the Bishop of Ely, was a lovely red brick edifice built around a quadrangle. Knot gardens and orchards lay to the south, and we had a vast lawn with ancient oaks to take our exercise in.

Inside the manor was a great hall, which we seldom used in lieu of a pleasant solarium with tall oriel windows; it included a walking gallery that was available in wet weather. The bedchambers in the upper stories were small but adequate with pretty views.

Outside our world, which revolved around the precocious, fast-growing little Elizabeth, the times were darkening. Acts of Parliament, at the bequest of the king and rammed through by Cromwell, formally declared Mary illegitimate and Elizabeth the heir. Also, Parliament passed a law demanding an Oath of Allegiance to the king as supreme head of the Church of England. Failure to sign meant a charge of treason with its horrible penalties of hanging, drawing and quartering. The king was so determined to bend everyone to his will that he allowed anyone who defied him, from his dear longtime friend Sir Thomas More to a lowly nun in Kent, to go to their deaths. At Hatfield, we all meekly signed the oath. I was glad enough to see the Catholic Church weakened, but the way it was done turned bitter in my mouth. The power of king – and Cromwell – was now boundless.

I adored little Elizabeth, but feared for Mary. Oh, she signed the oath and was finally cowed into accepting her reduced status, but she was fading before our eyes. She ate little; I knew Mary, like her mother, was fearful of being poisoned. She took to her bed in such peril of life that Lady Bryan sent for the king's own physician, fearful that if his daughter died in a household she oversaw, we could be blamed for her death.

Cromwell had told me more than once, through Master Stephen, that he did not like the slant of my reports to him. Since I was kind to the Lady Mary – I never knew who his other spies in the household were – I was told it had better be so that I could watch her closer to catch her in some sort of treason against king or country. But if Mary was covertly communicating with her mother, who was also gravely ill, or with the Spanish ambassador, I knew it not. At any rate, Master Stephen made it clear that I was to watch Mary like a hawk and find some slipup that Cromwell could use to allow the queen or her father to lock her up in the Tower of London.

That day came when the royal physician arrived at Hatfield and went directly in to see her.

Orders had been given long ago that Mary was never to be left alone with any outside visitors, lest she try to contact her mother or their Spanish allies. I was the one she asked for that day, but two others of the household were in the room too, farther back than I. I stood at the foot of the bed, holding on to the bedpost and wishing I could help.

The king's physician, despite his ride from London, was garbed in the traditional long gown with fur-trimmed wide sleeves. I knew from my time of illness that had made me miss a trip to France that the more fur on the gown, the more learned the man, so this was a skilled physician indeed. A neck ruff echoed the ruffles at his wrists – much dust stained – and he wore a close-fitting cap with ear flaps. He bled Mary, inquired of her astrological signs, then bathed her forehead in distilled water of lavender to refresh her from her megrim.

'Dear lady,' I heard him say after he had treated her with other herbs and possets – one, he'd said, containing crushed pearls, a curative to also relieve headaches – 'I believe the source of your disease may come partly from your circumstances.'

My eyes widened and my ears pricked up. Was the royal physician fishing for some sort of dangerous reply from her, or was his sympathy – and subtle criticism of her treatment here – sincere?

Tears filled her eyes; I saw her nod and grasp his hand. I knew she was desperate for any kindness and care. 'Doctor, before you go,' she said, 'would you mind if I practiced my Latin a bit? It has been a long time, and I fear it grows rusty.'

He adjusted his hood and nodded. 'You may, my lady.'

She spoke quickly, desperately, I thought. My Latin was a bit rusty too, but I caught the tenor of her words. Using perfect pronunciation, she begged the doctor to tell the Spanish ambassador in London, Eustace Chapuys, that she was being terribly treated here in her sister's household, at the command of the king's wife. King's wife – *uxor regis* – that's what she called the queen, and I had to admire her pluck. 'And, please, I beg you, tell no one but Chapuys,' she hurried on in Latin, gripping his wrist, even as Lady Bryan entered the small chamber to see how she was doing, 'that the king is threatening me with execution for my continued resistance, but it is the fault of that woman who has bewitched him!'

'Ah, my lady,' the doctor said in English, standing hastily and patting her shoulder, 'I shall pray for the best for you. And your Latin does need a bit of work.' But he nodded to her and pressed his hand to hers before he went below, for he was not to be permitted to remain the night. [I add a note here. Years later, I learned that the brave royal physician had indeed informed the Spanish ambassador of her deplorable treatment, but had begged him not to remonstrate with the king or she would be even more imperiled.]

Tears ran from the corners of Mary's eyes when he was gone. She blinked them back and looked straight at me, silent but pleading. She knew full well my Latin was good, for we had spoken it together before we'd been admonished by the house steward to speak the king's English in the English princess's household. So Mary was trusting me not to betray her.

That night, I sat over a piece of paper with my pen poised, realizing I now had the very thing Cromwell, and certainly the queen, desired: proof to put Mary away in the Tower, if not worse. Cromwell had done so much for me, and my future greatly depended on his goodwill. Anne Boleyn had befriended me and trusted me near her precious daughter, whom I loved and wanted to protect.

But I crumpled up the blank paper and sailed it into my low-burning fire, where it caught and flamed to ash. When the king's steward, Lord Shelton, my friend Madge's father, asked me the next day if I had overheard what the Lady Mary had said to the doctor in Latin, I told him she was reciting parts from Caesar's conquest of Gaul, but was also referring to her father as the

Caesar of England, who had conquered the hearts of his people.

I admit I had now learned to lie, even under fear and threat of duress, even if it meant defiance of the powers in the kingdom. That skill was to serve me well later as I continued to serve the Tudors.

The king was coming. Cromwell was coming. The household was in chaos.

The queen had visited rather often, once with His Majesty, but this was a visit on his own to see his little daughter. But would he see his older daughter?

Poor Mary, despite all she'd been through, had hopes. I could understand that now. Though her father had betrayed her and her mother, she loved him yet and wanted his goodwill, not only so she would not be completely cast aside from the line of succession, but because something instinctively made daughters love their fathers, even bad ones. Yes, I knew that.

Still weak from her illness, Mary waited in her small chamber, praying she would be summoned while the king dandled Elizabeth on his knee and carried her about downstairs, remarking how she looked Tudor through and through. Still, I must admit, Elizabeth had her mother's eyes and graceful, long-fingered hands. Though she was not yet two years old, she had inherited her mother's love of finery and tendency to primp and preen. Oh, yes, and she had both the Tudor and the Boleyn tempers, a volatile combination.

But Cromwell was the only visitor who called on Mary that day. As I passed in the hall, I could hear him berating her for still being so stubborn toward the queen, for not knowing her place as bastard, not heir. When he left her room, I ducked into another so he would not know I was hovering. He had already scolded me for not giving him what 'cannon fodder' he needed to deal with Mary Tudor once and for all. But he had urged me to stay in the little princess's affections, for the future lay in her.

While everyone was down in the great hall with the king, I knocked on the closed door of Mary's room. 'Who?' came her distinctive low voice.

'Kat, my lady.'

'Enter.'

She sat at her table before a small mirror, with a handkerchief crumpled in her hands as if she'd collapsed there after her interview with Cromwell. Her eyes and nose were red.

'I shall tell you plain in English and not Latin, Kat,' she said. 'I loathe him but love him and long to see him.'

I knew who she meant.

'But I am not to be summoned. I have not seen him for years, and he cannot even bid me good day or fare-thee-well. I wish I were dead!'

'No, no,' I said, and began to cry too. I knelt by

her stool – let anyone who came upon us think I was bowing the knee to her. 'My lady, you have too much to live for. Your heritage, your mother . . .'

'Yes, yes,' she said, pressing her clasped hands to her mouth. 'Tell no one of my despair. I would show my father I am his indeed, strong and regal . . .' She shook her head and blew her nose.

'You could wave him farewell.'

'They will not let me near him.'

'I know a place on the rooftop from which you could wave at him in the courtyard as he mounts, but you would have to climb many stairs in the tower turret – up on the battlements.'

Her head lifted. 'I could wage my own war on the battlements,' she said, nodding. 'He may not see me, but I shall see him, even if from afar, but I am still so weak from my affliction. Will you help me?'

*Devil take it – take them all*, I fumed silently, but said, 'I will, but we must go now.'

She struggled up the twisting staircase, out of breath. I dared to touch her royal person with my hands right on her waist and arm to help her climb. We emerged into a stiff breeze and startling sunlight, perhaps just in time, for we could hear horses stamping and snorting in the courtyard below amidst the murmurs of many voices.

'I must do this alone,' she told me, squeezing my hand. 'They must not know of your help to me. Go down now. Be seen among them all.'

'Yes, Your Grace,' I told her, using the forbidden form of address.

'Dear Kat, I shall not forget your kindnesses. Go!' she commanded, and pushed at me feebly.

I, too, was out of breath and sweating when I ran out a side door into the courtyard and mingled with the small crowd from the household encircling the royal party. Crowded toward the back of the cobbled courtyard were clusters of manor workers, no doubt thrilled to see their king. Everyone was prepared to bid His Majesty farewell. I glanced up and saw Mary above, leaning on the crenellations, waving.

Others noticed too. Necks craned. People gasped. The king had mounted before he noticed the lifted faces and looked up.

Silence fell. Only the creak of a saddle and shifting of a horseshoe on a cobble sounded.

Mary stepped even closer to the edge. Adjusting her skirts, she knelt in obeisance to her father and king. I gasped as I recalled her words to me that she would like to die. Surely, she would not cast herself off in protest! I would be to blame, for this ploy was my idea.

Still ahorse, the king bowed to her, sweeping off his plumed velvet hat in a broad and graceful arc. 'Good day and good health to you, daughter!' he called out, then turned and led his entourage from the courtyard through the cheering, waving crowd.

It was a good thing he was soon outside the

walls, heading down the gravel road, or he might have noted that the commoners, if not their betters, kept cheering when he was long gone, not for their king but for their once-upon-a-time, half-Spanish Catholic Princess of Wales.

# CHAPTER 8

*November 26, 1535*

Dearest Kat, I'm so happy we're together again!'

I was thrilled to see my old friend Joan Champernowne, now a twenty-two-year-old bride, Lady Denny. She had previously been widowed, when it was often the women who died in childbirth to leave young husbands behind. Still, I was not happy to be summoned back to court by the queen. In my nearly two-year absence from public life, Lady Joan Denny had arrived with her husband, who was much in favor with the king. Sir Anthony Denny had received rich lands in the full-scale dissolution of the monasteries and had been appointed to the office of king's remembrancer, or keeper of his personal records. And, truth be told, Sir Anthony kept accounts of who received or purchased former church lands. That royal largesse was still a powerful enticement to keep subjects in line who might balk at the king's increasing control of church and state. Joan's appointment as one of the queen's ladies swelled that number to nearly twenty. But, as delighted as I was to be reunited with her, I was torn about the reunion with Queen Anne I was awaiting as we stood in her privy chamber at Whitehall. The only relief I felt – though it pained me deeply too – was that I would not have to face John Ashley after how I had avoided him and left court without so much as a farewell. Because his father was ill, he had gone home for several months to help his half brother with their horse-breeding concerns.

I listened to Joan's excited words about court life in a melancholy humor, for I had once felt the same as she did now. At least she had a well-placed protector in her husband. Unfortunately for me, I learned that the Seymours had continued their rise: not only had Tom's favorite sister Jane come to court and caught the king's eye, but Edward Seymour had been appointed a gentleman of the king's privy chamber. Tom was soon to return from one of his glorified errands abroad, and I dreaded seeing the wretch again.

Though Joan pointed Jane Seymour out to me, I could have picked her out myself, perhaps because Tom's face was branded in my mind forever. As different as was Mistress Jane's coloring from that of her brothers, she had the Seymour nose and mouth, and Tom had told me she was blond with blue eyes. While Joan regaled me with stories of her own family, I cast glances at the Seymour woman, who seemed quite the opposite from her gregarious, aggressive brothers. She was also as day is to night from the bold, enticing, dark-haired and dark-eyed royal mistress she served. Anne was all for the new religion, but Joan said that Jane was still as Catholic as they come. If I had to sum up Tom's sister from watching her for that quarter of an hour, I would say she was sweet, shy and demure. *King's roving eye or not, she won't last long at court,* I thought.

I was also surprised to see quite a number of king's men – including the poet, Thomas Wyatt – in this chamber immediately adjacent to the queen's bedroom. In Anne's early days here, the approach to that ultimate sanctuary through a series of rooms was well controlled. From the presence chamber where most courtiers were permitted, the withdrawing chamber winnowed out all but those closest to the queen before the even more limited access to the Privy Chamber and then the very private bedchamber. How things had grown lax around Anne in the years I'd been away.

Now heads turned and elbows poked ribs; we slowly hushed as raised voices sounded through the door of Anne's inner sanctum. Quite clearly she cried, 'George, I am sick to death of it all! She's ill, so why can't she just die?'

I mouthed my words to Joan: 'The Queen Dowager or the Lady Mary?'

'She could mean either,' she whispered back.

Anne plunged recklessly on: 'Catherine took the motto 'Humble and loyal,' so why isn't she? She is overly proud and pompous to defy the king!'

'But to her way of thinking, she is yet ever loyal to him,' George Boleyn's voice came to us.

'You sound as if you are on her side! And here I have the motto 'Most happy' on my badges, and I am miserable! Mis—'

'Keep your voice down.'

'I shall not. Do not gainsay me. I am queen here.'

Thankfully, the argument became more muted. The latch on the door rattled and people turned away. A few began idle chatter; I saw some just roll their eyes as if to say, *The usual Boleyn behavior.* One thing I had learned quickly upon my return to court was that, even though Anne had been queen these last years, the 'climber Boleyns' still deeply rankled the nobility. I could not help but wonder if people resented Cromwell for his climb too.

Were things so dreadful between the king and queen here, and we at Hatfield had not heard? Perhaps Catherine, the former queen, was better off in exile from court, but my thoughts went to her dear daughter, Mary, ill herself with anguish and grief.

George Boleyn, Lord Rochford, looking flushed and harried, strode from Anne's chamber, looking neither right nor left. Either he or she had mussed his hair and pulled his doublet awry. I wondered if they'd even had a tussle. Without a word, even to his wife, he stormed through the room and out. Although the queen had summoned me to await her pleasure, I was tempted to flee also, for I had no stomach for facing Anne's choler. I would concoct some story of exhaustion or illness from my cold-weather journey yesterday.

I turned to make an excuse to Joan and found myself staring into the handsome, almost pretty face of a man holding a lute. His auburn hair was curled in ringlets, and he was finely garbed.

'Mistress Champernowne,' he said in a mellifluous voice, 'Her Grace will see you now.'

'We have not met,' I told him as the chatter in the room picked up again, that sound of buzzing bees from my father's hives.

'Mark Smeaton, the queen's lutenist, at your service,' he said, and swept me a fancy bow with a flourish of his willow green tasseled cap.

I glanced at Joan, who nodded. Indeed, what was Anne's court coming to, I thought, for her to have such a *contretemps* with her brother and for visitors to be summoned by a musician, one who seemed to dance his way back in her door and then close it behind me?

Inside Anne's spacious bedchamber, the scent of heavy perfume almost staggered me. As I curtsied, I noted silk and satin pillows strewn on the floor rushes as if that is where people sat now instead of on chairs or stools. To my amazement, Mark Smeaton went over to sit cross-legged on the bed and began to strum a slow melody, one I did not know.

'Dear Kat,' Anne called to me, sounding as if she had not a care in the world, 'what news of Elizabeth?' She gestured me over to a small parquet-topped table beneath a frost-blighted window while the wind howled outside. Such quicksilver moods, I thought, ones that seemed to match the tenor of tunes Smeaton played, for already he romped through a gay galliard. 'Tell me all the latest of my sweetling, even the smallest detail!' the queen insisted as we sat close, with only a corner of the table between us.

I regaled her for nearly a half an hour with minutiae about her poppet. I was heartened to see her face brighten and a smile tilt the tips of her eyes and lips. I was appalled at how she had aged, even since her latest visit to Hatfield in October. Dark half-moons hung under her eyes, her skin was sallow and she looked gaunt. Despite her welcome, she seemed to have a hectic in the blood, for her long fingers never stopped darting here and there. So distressed was she that she forgot to cover her left hand with that strange vestige of a sixth finger. All that time, Smeaton's skilled fingers danced from tune to tune as Anne listened avidly to my tales of Elizabeth's antics and more new words and favorite toys.

'Well, I must buck myself up,' she said finally, downing some wine I, too, had been drinking. I never drank to excess anymore after that terrible night of Anne's coronation, but all my talk made my throat dry. 'Our little princess is coming to court for Yule,' Anne said. 'I plan to have someone known as 'the lady' gone by then, so I shall have a happy time – time to conceive another child, a brother for my sweetling.'

I knew that Anne had suffered a miscarriage several months after Elizabeth was born, and had thought she was pregnant once when she was not. From what she said, I assumed she and the king were still bedding together, at least from time to time. I was perversely amused she referred to Jane Seymour as 'the lady,' for people used to call Anne that when I first came to court. As Cromwell had said once, 'There is nothing new under the sun, yet knowing King Henry, everything changes.'

Suddenly, leaning close to me across the corner of the table, she seized my wrist and said, 'I brought you back to court, not Cromwell. We argued over it, and I told him I would have his head if he keeps trying to naysay me. I trust you and want you to keep a good eye on Mistress Jane Seymour for me. The king has not made a move yet, I think, but is circling her as a hunter does a doe.'

I stared speechless at her as thoughts assailed me – anyone but the Seymours. So, Anne was jealous of the lady. Jane was a danger to her just as she had been to Queen Catherine. For this task she was desperate enough to take me away from her beloved child. How fortune's wheel had turned. But I sympathized with her hatred and fear of a Seymour. I actually yearned to put my arms around her and commiserate, but I simply nodded and said, 'I will do what I can.'

Yuletide came and went, a happy time for the Tudors; true to her word, the queen was pregnant again, and the king was ecstatic with hope. I was thrilled when Lady Bryan brought Elizabeth to court for the festivities; she remembered me and put out her little arms to be lifted up and held by her Kat. I vow but that child was precocious even then, but not, thank God, as things turned out, old enough to understand or recall what came next in that new year of 1536.

On January 8, word arrived that Catherine of Aragon had died the previous day at Kimbolton Castle. I became sick to my stomach at the celebrations that went on over that. The king, in canary yellow, hardly the hue of white for mourning, carried little Elizabeth about in his arms all day, rejoicing while Anne cavorted in her chambers. Her thoughtless, oft reckless behavior seemed to say that nothing could harm her now. The more the king flattered and flirted with Mistress Seymour, the more Anne flaunted her charms with male members of his court.

'What is good for the gander is good for the goose!' I heard her twist the old saying as she held wild parties in her chambers, often with the king's own comrades in attendance. With a new woman in favor, though one who, like Anne, was surprisingly clever at holding the king's avid attentions at bay, he, too, was acting as if he were invincible, with masques and dances, hunts and tournaments. In mid-January, he had an accident riding in the lists at Greenwich; thrown and partly crushed by his horse, he was unconscious for over two hours before slowly recovering. But he had sores on one leg and limped after that.

It wasn't until January 29 that Catherine of Aragon was buried at Peterborough Abbey, attended by professional mourners – and, we heard later, many of her former English subjects lining the road to show their respect. That was something Anne had never had from her subjects except in a few Protestant pockets and her home shire of Kent.

That was also the very day that the task to which Anne had assigned me ended with a bang. I had attached myself to Mistress Seymour without much trouble, praying Tom would not come back to court. But one day, there he was, striding toward us down the long gallery where we walked in bad weather. He still wore riding boots and a mud-speckled cape that flapped around him, he came so quickly. With a wink at me – I would have liked to punch him in that eye – he hugged his sister hard, even swinging her about, to lift her slippered feet from the floor.

'I have missed you, brother,' Jane told him as he put her down. She brushed at the smudge marks he'd made on her gold brocade gown. 'Edward is a bore, and his wife criticizes all I do, but with you home, we'll have fun now.'

I was close enough to hear their next whispered words. Though I wanted to run away, for my duty to Anne I gritted my teeth and held my ground.

'Is His Grace not fun?' Tom inquired, his mouth so close to her temple that her ear bob bounced. Curse the wretch, but it was as if I could feel that hot breath against my own ear, feel him pressing me down.

'He wants to be,' she whispered back, 'but I am true to my vow of chastity.'

'You had better be!' he said before he stepped away from her and turned toward me. *What a hypocrite, the blackguard,* I thought.

'Jane, did Kat Champernowne tell you that she and I are friends from far back, when we both first came to court?'

'No, I did not know,' she said, shaking a scolding finger at me, but smiling. 'My dear Kat, you must tell me all about my naughty brother,' she said with a little laugh. 'Come on then. Tom, you need to wash off that mud, and I shall see you later.'

Ah, he was so good with the ladies, even his own sister. Since I'd been back at court, I had heard more than one pretty maid ask Jane when he would be back and heave a heartfelt sigh.

Jane took my hand. She was one for that, always patting or touching people she liked. But I felt I was going to throw up all over that gentle little hand. How dare that lickspittle Seymour taunt me when he had dared to attack me and then lie to Cromwell and who knows who else about my throwing myself at him!

'Come, come then, Kat,' Jane cried, and tugged me away from the others. She pulled me into an alcove where, no doubt, I was to be privily interrogated about my relationship with Tom. Perhaps, I thought, he had set this up as a test that I would not give out what he had done to me. But both Jane and I gasped, for there, peeking out from the velvet draperies, stood the king. Was I to be an unwilling chaperone for their planned tryst? But no – Jane looked completely surprised.

'Oh, Your Grace,' she cried, and managed a graceful curtsy before I could even react. It was obvious to me that he had been watching us, perhaps stalking Jane.

'Mistress Champernowne,' he said, kissing Jane's lips first, lingeringly, and then quickly mine, 'how nice to see you back at court. Lady Bryan speaks highly of your services to our Princess Elizabeth.'

'The princess is dear to me and certainly a compliment to Your Majesty.' I was tempted to add, *as is the Princess Mary,* but, even as besotted as he seemed, gazing at Jane and barely listening to me, I dared not.

'You may wait with the others,' he said to me while his eyes, so small in his broad, florid face, glittered possessively over Jane. 'And say naught of my presence here.'

I curtsied again and took my leave. No matter what His Majesty said, I would have to tell the queen that the king had been following Jane and requested time alone with her, else someone would inform her first, I was back to pacing down the way with the others when I heard a distinctive tap-tap of the cork-heeled slippers the queen had taken a fancy to lately. Yes, she was striding toward us and would surely come upon the king and Jane in the alcove.

All four of us turned to look at her, but only I knew Jane wasn't alone within. I almost called out, *Oh, look, ladies, here comes the queen!* as loudly as I could to warn Jane, but it was too late. And then came the blast.

Anne glanced into the alcove and scréeched, 'Get off his lap, you strumpet! Doxy!' To everyone's horror, she leaped into the alcove with her fist raised.

A slap resounded. Had she struck the king? But Jane came flying out, her hand to her cheek, her skirts tumbling down from where they must have been lifted, her bodice slightly awry.

'Madam!' the king roared. 'Leave off!'

'I'm carrying your prince, and you dare to dally!'

Anne shrieked. 'No wonder I suffer so, for want of you!'

Curses. Cries. The king's booming voice. When Jane scurried past us, I hurried after her, hoping she wasn't running straight for her damned brother Tom.

On the same day that Catherine of Aragon was interred, Anne, as I heard her own uncle Norfolk pointedly put it, 'miscarried of her savior.' The fifteen-week-old fetus was formed enough to show it had been a boy. Anne blamed the king for the shock to her heart and soul. She insisted she had suffered when he was knocked unconscious at the tournament and that it was devastating to her health to see another woman being fondled by the man she loved so much.

And His Majesty's reaction, so I heard from Madge and Joan: 'You have caused the loss of my boy, madam! You will have no more sons from me!'

Lady Joan also told me that His Majesty had declared he had been seduced into wedding Anne by sorcery. After all, she did have the mark of a witch, that sixth finger on her left hand. God's denying him a son was proof to him that their marriage was null and void.

'Null and void? And sorcery?' I repeated aghast to Joan. 'What demented, desperate claims.'

'My Lord Anthony believes he is desperate to be rid of her,' she whispered.

After two more months of tension at court, I asked the queen if I could not be sent back to Hatfield to help care for Elizabeth. She seized my hand so hard she hurt me and, looking not at me but beyond while Mark Smeaton strummed some frenzied music across the room, whispered, 'Not yet, not yet. I need those loyal about me.'

At least I managed to avoid Tom Seymour. The king had sent Jane from court to her family home of Wolf Hall in Wiltshire, and since Edward was needed at court, Tom was sent as her guardian. Wolf Hall, I thought. How appropriate a spawning place for that flap-mouthed lewdster, that wolf in sheep's clothing. But if Anne thought she'd won a victory by getting rid of Jane, she was much mistaken, for the king had only sent his beloved away to protect her from the dreadful coming events he and Cromwell were covertly hatching.

At the annual May Day tournament at Greenwich, the powder keg exploded, and it was only then that we learned the trap for the queen had long been laid. I was not present that day, for I had the green sickness and was nauseous. [As I looked back on my absence years later, I thought it was perhaps for the best. From her formative years, Elizabeth privily pestered me for any memories of her mother, and it was hard to hold things back. But I had not seen her mother's arrest, so had an excuse for not telling her of that dreadful day. As for other terrible times to come, I lied to my sweet girl that I had not been there, for I could not bear for her to know the things I had been privy to.]

Anne was arrested at the May Day tournament and taken immediately by barge to the Tower, where at least she was lodged in the royal apartments and not in some wretched cell. The charges included witchcraft, treason and adultery with four of the king's closest men – yes, he was willing to sacrifice his boon companions – including her own brother George, which meant a charge of incest.

My stomach churns even now to recall the explicit accusations: that Anne and George did put their tongues in each other's mouth in the lewd French fashion, et cetera. Cromwell had taken and tortured Mark Smeaton until he admitted to carnal relations with the queen, while the other four men denied such to the death. The poet and courtier Thomas Wyatt was in the Tower too, but evidently for questioning, as he was not charged. I thought again of the passionate poem I'd seen from him to Anne years ago, and wondered if she had lain with him or Percy in her youth, though I could not fathom she'd be unfaithful with any of the others.

Cromwell's clever, bloodstained handwriting was on the wall, but I blamed the king even more. Sorcery and witchcraft indeed! As unwise and heedless of danger as Anne had been, I never believed one word of the worst charges. The entire thing made me vomit all the harder and longer, until I was so weak I could hardly stand.

Unfortunately, Cromwell summoned me to meet him in the rose garden to the east of the palace. Awaiting me was almost as great a shock as all else: John Ashley stood there, holding three horses, one of them Brill, the large chestnut horse he had ridden the day we met. I was so surprised that my legs almost buckled. I stepped back into the roses and snagged my skirts and cloak on the thorns.

'I did not mean to startle you,' he said with that deep, resonant and strangely comforting voice I hadn't heard for so long but had yearned to. 'Did not Lord Cromwell tell you of our mission? Here, I've brought you a favorite horse of mine to ride – Ginger,' he went on in a rush, patting the reddish mare next to the two larger mounts. 'She's Brill's favorite, too, and bore him a foal last summer.'

I nodded, then blurted, 'I did not know you were back!' Wondering if he meant some message in telling me that I would ride Brill's mate, I tried to unhook myself from several especially nasty canes. 'I assumed with the fall of the Boleyns, you would not return.'

He came close now, bending to unsnag my petticoat and, to my further amazement, cut a red rose for me, which I took in my trembling hand. 'My father is better, and I could not stay away now,' he explained. 'I returned in honor of my mother's Howard kin and to help our queen, though she's obviously beyond help now. They will hold her trial at the Tower, and Cromwell says she's doomed.'

'He ought to know,' I said, unable to keep the contempt from my voice. But I instinctively trusted this man not to betray me. Though I had felt ill and weak for nearly a fortnight, energy and excitement poured through my veins to be near him. 'But what mission do you speak of that concerns Cromwell and us?' I asked.

'Ah, did I hear my name?' The man who was, no doubt, the mastermind behind Anne's fall – anything at the king's bidding – emerged from behind the horses. 'Good, you have a hood on that cloak,' he said to me in way of greeting. 'Pull it up, and I'll explain to both of you on the way.'

I stood my ground. 'I need to know where I am going first,' I dared.

He and John had pulled hoods up too. Surely the May wind, even on the river, was not so cold. As John gave Cromwell a boost up on the third horse, the older man said down at me, 'I believe you, like Ashley here, still care for Anne Boleyn in all this, do you not? We go to do her a favor, that is all, so come along. We are not taking a royal barge where we might be noted, but riding to the bridge and then across, just three travelers ahorse, that is us, so keep up, Kat, and hold your tongue.'

★　★　★

The windy journey, including the first time I had ever ridden across busy London Bridge, passed in a blur. The queen had asked to see me, and Cromwell must have made some sort of bargain with her. That is all I really knew. I was frightened to enter the portals of the Tower, to ride across the moat and dismount in the place where three years ago Anne and her women had so happily awaited her parade and coronation.

Once we were inside the massive walls and had dismounted, Cromwell spoke with the Tower constable, Master Kingston, tall and somber, then led the way with me following, next John and the constable. I was grateful John took my elbow, because my legs shook, and not from the long ride. We climbed to the second story, then traversed a maze of corridors, silent, dusty and dim with closed draperies and cloth-shrouded furniture. Yes, these were the very chambers where we had so happily awaited the parade into London and Anne's coronation.

'Have her women been sent out?' Cromwell asked the guard at a door.

'Yes, my lord,' he said, and stepped aside to open it, his eyes wary as they went over us. So, I thought, Cromwell was a familiar visitor here, and the guards knew how to address him correctly. The king had named Cromwell Vicar General so that he could carry out punishments for those who had refused to sign the Oath of Allegiance; he had also been named to the important post of Lord Privy

147

Seal, and it was whispered he would soon be elevated to the peerage.

I still had my hood up over my head, but cast it back when we stepped inside what looked to be an empty chamber. It appeared familiar with its paneled walls and stone hearth, though there was no fire and a certain chill clung to the slightly stale air. A canopied bed stood in one corner. There was even a view toward the Thames out the narrow window. Had she gazed outside much onto that watery gray road to freedom? Yes, no doubt, for she emerged from the shadows there.

'Thank you, Cromwell,' she said, omitting his proper address and coming forward to pull me toward her with both hands holding mine. Her skin was cold and clammy. She nodded to John over my shoulder, then bent her head toward me. 'Kat, I—'

Cromwell interrupted, 'We have a bargain, Your Grace, and a bargain has two sides, two parts.'

She turned her head to look at him. I was amazed she seemed so in control. 'I told you,' she said, 'I will speak my own careful version of your words. Give the speech to me, then.' She snatched a paper from his hand and turned back to me. 'John,' she said, 'do you have the ring for her?'

'I do, Your Grace.'

For one tottering, insane moment, I thought – I wished – that for some strange reason she had brought John and me here for a trothplight or even a marriage. John stepped forward and handed her a small blue satin box, which she opened eagerly. It held a locket ring, for she opened the hinged ruby top of it and I saw inside, painted in miniature, a double portrait. The exterior of the ring was crafted with ivory, gems and beaten gold. When she held it up to the wan window light, I saw one painted head-and-shoulders miniature was of the little Elizabeth, the other facing portrait a charming one of Anne herself. A tear fell on the painting of her daughter, but she shook it off.

Cromwell crowded close to look at it, but Anne snapped it shut. 'It is lovely,' she told John, shouldering Cromwell out. 'Katherine Champernowne,' she said, putting it on the ring finger of my right hand, 'I give you this in trust for my daughter. For her, when she is older, so she won't lose it – so she understands and so she can know that I loved her. Cromwell, you swear to me again that Kat will be sent wherever Elizabeth goes, at least until her majority – you vowed it.'

'I did, Your Grace.'

'And since I cannot see my girl' – I could not help but think that she had kept Queen Catherine from her daughter – 'you will have Kat and that ring there at the end, Cromwell.'

'It is part of our bargain.'

Shivers shot through me. I was honored but horrified. Did she mean I was to be present if she was executed? And wearing this ring? I wanted to ask, but Anne was talking again. 'I still intend to proclaim my innocence at the trial, however trumped-up the charges are. You understand that, Cromwell? I am innocent and will say so.'

'Your speech there is your concern – within reason.'

'Reason!' she said with a bitter laugh. 'Begone now, before I lose control. I must not – cannot – lose control.'

I thought sadly that her entire life had now gone from her control. At the last moment, when I squeezed her hand and started to turn away, she reached out, pulled me to her and hugged me hard. 'For my precious, bright girl over the years, Kat,' she whispered, and kissed my cheek.

'Yes, Your Majesty. I vow I will be a good teacher and friend to her always.'

Cromwell hustled us out. I heard a sharp sniff before the door closed behind us and wondered if Anne would collapse in tears.

'So that speech you gave her is not for her trial, my lord?' John asked as we remounted in the courtyard.

Even the sharp cry of a gull from the river could not cloak Cromwell's muttered words. 'No. For the scaffold.'

After what I considered to be a sham of a trial [I heard later that during it, one of her judges, her first love, Henry Percy, now Duke of Northumberland, fainted and had to be carried out], Anne was convicted of all charges. The men with whom she was accused were sentenced to die on Tower Hill outside the walls and Anne on Tower Green within. To avoid both possible protests and gawkers, Cromwell kept the day and timing of her death vague, but because of his bargain with Anne, I was ordered to attend. How often I prayed no one would ever tell Elizabeth that I had been present to see her mother die.

John was a great comfort and strength to me. I was grateful Cromwell let him accompany me to the Tower that May 19. We rode on one of the barges from Whitehall, which held those who were to witness the queen's beheading, for the king had shown her a sort of mercy at the end. Though he could have had her burned to death for adultery and treason, he had commuted that to beheading – the first woman ever to face that. And when she requested a French swordsman instead of an ax man, he had allowed that too.

I knew that Cromwell would be there, of course, and we had heard some civic dignitaries as well as Lord Chancellor Audley, the Duke of Suffolk, would be in attendance as well as the Duke of Richmond, the king's illegitimate son by his former mistress Bessie Blount.

None of the queen's remaining family was allowed, not her parents nor her sister Mary, who

151

had been the king's mistress before he knew Anne. Mary Boleyn, now Mary Stafford, was now safely ensconced in the countryside with a husband she had dared to choose for herself. I heaved a huge sigh at the mere thought of that. How I wished that I were so fortunate, away from the cruel court with a husband I loved, though I would be loath to leave Elizabeth.

We had been told, too, that today the king himself was on the other side of the city, waiting to hear the Tower cannons boom to tell him he was free – free to become betrothed to Jane Seymour the very next day. The Seymours at least showed the good taste not to attend and gloat, but they were all busy playing broker between Henry and his next queen.

I felt the spring sun and soft river breeze as we went into the Tower through the water gate, but it seemed dark and airless within the walls. We waited a long time; it was nearly noon. I recalled a poem by Anne that was being surreptitiously circulated at court, smuggled out of the Tower by someone unnamed. I hoped that vile Cromwell would not think me the messenger, if he heard it. Some of the lines were '*Defiled is my name, full sore, through cruel spite and false report . . . O Death, rock me asleep, Bring me to quiet rest . . .* I prayed desperately that day that Anne would not lose control as she had feared when I saw her last.

And she did not. She managed to parrot the

speech Cromwell had given her in their bargain that day John and I went to the Tower. I dared, for we stood in the last row, to hold up my hand that wore the portrait ring and saw her nod at me in recognition and thanks. Poor Elizabeth, like her half sister before her, had now been declared a bastard, so Anne took that to her grave too. That dreadful day, I vowed silently to serve Elizabeth well, to protect her as best I could from such tyrannical rule by men. At least Anne Boleyn was going to a better place.

# CHAPTER 9

HATFIELD HOUSE

*October 13, 1537*

T he king has a son! King Henry and Queen Jane have a son! Born yesterday at Hampton Court Palace, named Edward. Prince Edward, heir to the throne, born yester—'

The messenger who had ridden in was evidently standing at the bottom of the main staircase to call out his glad tidings. His voice was distant to us upstairs in Elizabeth's schoolroom, but Margaret – Lady Bryan and I called each other by our given names now – rose and hurried out. I was teaching our just-turned-four-year-old charge, who was already reading too, to write her name in script instead of block letters and was amazed that she insisted on elaborate flourishes for it. She did not budge from her fierce concentration at her task. No doubt she did not grasp what the news meant for her – for all of us.

She was merely the Lady Elizabeth now, His Majesty's bastard child, living in this very house where her half sister, Mary, had once suffered. As

Mary had been, Elizabeth was in dire need of new clothes. Everything changes and there is nothing new under the sun, as King Solomon and Cromwell had said.

When Lady Bryan had tried to explain her new title to Elizabeth, our pert little mistress, hands on hips, had demanded, 'What means it that before I was Princess Elizabeth but now Lady Elizabeth?' Her backbone and wit for such a young child continually surprised me, but considering who her parents were, I should have expected such. She had a temper but managed patience and concentration when it suited her. Thank God, I was the only one to see she did not jump up and give thanks for the news about England's prince.

'Edward, Prince of Wales, born to King Henry and Queen Jane!' the muted messenger's voice droned on. I have learned that what one is looking at when momentous news arrives is oft burned into one's brain. So, yet to this day when I think of Prince Edward's birth, I see Anne Boleyn's girl bent over her work, laboriously, defiantly scribbling the word *P-r-i-n-c-e-s-s* in front of her name.

I should have snatched the pen and paper, blotted out that word and scolded her, but I only folded it when Margaret ran back into the chamber, clapping and smiling. Of course, all subjects rejoiced at news of a prince, for that meant the fruition of our sovereign's heartfelt desire and the future stability of the realm. But it shoved my sweet girl one more step down the ladder of possibilities, so I had to force myself to smile.

Elizabeth, though, once she understood, was all excitement to have a brother. I was ecstatic, too, when I learned there was good news in the birth for me. The same messenger who later told us the rest – that Queen Jane had labored terribly three days to bear the king's son and that Lady Bryan was summoned to court forthwith to take over the prince's household and governance – finally informed me that I was the Lady Elizabeth's new governess. So it was a great and grand day in my life after all.

Besides, it pleased me to know that that Cromwell, who fancied himself a great religious reformer in his destruction of the Catholic Church, must be greatly distressed by Catholic-leaning Jane's influence on the king. [He had wed her only eleven days after Anne's death!] God's truth, I too hated the rise of the Seymours and not only for their religious orthodoxy. It made Tom all the more dangerous. But to see Cromwell bested, ah, there was something in that!

From that day forward, more than ever, I protected my royal charge with fierce devotion, ever praying I would be worthy of her care and tutelage.

Elizabeth Tudor was a slim but sturdy child

with an oval face and pointed chin, an inheritance from her mother, as were her gray-black eyes and olive-hued complexion. But her glowing red hair branded her a Tudor, make no mistake – a gift from God, I warrant – for parents with hair as dark as Anne's oft passed that on. The child's teeth had all come in with pain, but her thin-lipped smile displayed them prettily. She had beautiful hands and was already quite aware of her charms. How sad that her garments were oft made over and out of style, for she adored pretty things, including my ruby ring, which I dared not let off my finger for fear of losing it. How long, I thought, before the time would be right to give it to her.

Despite her moodiness and occasional flares of the Tudor temper, I scolded Elizabeth when I needed to, but I encouraged and cuddled her, too, more than Margaret had, I admit that. Above all, I was ever newly astounded by her appetite for learning and sought to bring her along in her reading and writing skills as well as in the geography of England and Europe, and the names of kings and queens [which were about to become more confusing, as her father took three more wives in the next ten years]. Of course, she eventually also studied the seven liberal arts, including Latin grammar, rhetoric and logic as well as arithmetic, geometry, astronomy and music, though she was never the musician her father was. She studied many languages and had a talent for them. In her later adolescent studies, she outstripped me in French and taught me Spanish and Italian when she mastered those tongues.

As is suggested here, lest it slips past me later with all the upheaval and dangers we faced, I must admit that several years later my knowledge was not enough for her quick mind. I was grateful that she had a series of excellent male tutors and, blessedly, received a fine, if sporadic, education with her brother in his schoolroom, when her various stepmothers and the moods of the king allowed such.

Though I mean not to be sacrilegious in saying this, when it came to Elizabeth's sometimes obscure, mostly rural upbringing, I oft thought of the passage from the Bible which described the hidden years of our Savior's rearing and education: 'And Jesus increased in wisdom and stature, and in favor with God and man.' Of course, Elizabeth, poor girl, spent a great deal of time out of favor with the godlike Tudor men – and one woman – who ruled England before her. Yet as the Lord Jesus was Savior of all mankind, I saw Elizabeth Tudor as savior of all England, but that, indeed, comes later in this rendering of my life.

After Elizabeth was finally asleep that night we heard of her brother's birth, I saw Margaret was packing and went in to speak with her. 'I dared not believe it could fall to me again,' she said, clasping her hands to her breasts and gazing toward the ceiling. 'First to help rear Mary, then Elizabeth – but now the heir, though the king and his Seymour uncles will take him away from his women soon enough to turn him into a prince who will be our next king.'

The idea of Tom Seymour having any say over the upbringing of an innocent child sickened me, but I only nodded as she placed garments in her traveling trunk and chattered on. 'By the way, did you hear that Cromwell managed to have his heir Gregory wed another of the Seymour sisters, Elizabeth her name is too, not to mention 'tis said Cromwell's to become a Knight of the Garter, no less. They call him the blacksmith's son, you know, but I heard they also owned a fulling mill,' she added with a disdainful sniff.

'Yes,' I said as my mind spun back through the years, 'I heard that too.'

'To think His Majesty has seen fit to raise him to the peerage as Baron Cromwell of Oakham – well, I never! What will it be next?'

I could only shake my head at Cromwell's daring. A letter from Princess Mary had told me that she had been given but a pittance from her mother's estate and possessions, including a small gold cross and chain. My heart went out to her again as I recalled my mother's garnet necklace Maud had taken from me. Mary claimed that things of value from her mother had gone to Cromwell. The one-time clerk to

Cardinal Wolsey now stood at the pinnacle of the realm in service to the king. He could do what he willed and could hardly climb higher. But then, poor Anne had thought she was secure at her lofty height. I thanked God that Cromwell seemed content to leave me near Elizabeth and make no more demands on me as one of his spies.

'Both Edward and Thomas Seymour are to be elevated, Tom to be knighted,' Margaret went on. 'Will wonders never cease for those who began life as plain gentry and far from court?'

We spoke late into the night, but my thoughts clung to her last question. The daughter of the beekeeper from the far fringe of Devon's barren moors was now governess and – truth be told – foster mother to the king's daughter. Yet, since my parting with John Ashley so many months ago, I sometimes yearned to be just the country wife of a husband who bred and trained horses and had a child of her own. I had seen what power, pride and raw ambition could do to people, and it terrified me for myself and for the child for whom I kept the ruby ring.

Cromwell was king! Well, not king, but he acted as such and no doubt thought so. He was caring for all the business of the kingdom while His Majesty was in seclusion and deepest mourning. For once, it was not a newborn infant he had lost but Queen Jane, dead of childbed fever twelve days after giving birth.

We wore white, all but Elizabeth, who had nothing that would serve, because she was growing so fast and had been greatly ignored since Anne's death. Though I wanted naught to do with Cromwell, I humbled myself to write him a letter, begging, as Margaret had done before me, for a better allowance to clothe the king's daughter:

*To the Esteemed Baron Cromwell, G.K.:*

*His Majesty and you, my lord, would indeed be proud of the Lady Elizabeth. Each day she more resembles her sire in appearance and learning. She is healthy and fast-growing, and so her wardrobe is in sore need of replenishment. I thank you for reporting well of her to the king. I am loath to beg for moneys from my own father, who has as much to do with the little living he has as any man.*

*In your wisdom and wealth, I beseech you to send funds for her raiment, for she is in dire need of gowns, kirtles, bodices, sleeves, petticoats, linen smocks, nightgowns and nightcaps, slippers and boots.*

*Your longtime servant and the Lady Elizabeth's loving governess,*

*Katherine Champernowne*

There! I thought. I had reminded him of my service and implied that I am so desperate for garments for the king's girl that I had even considered asking my poor beekeeper father. [Only twice in the eleven years since I had left my father's house had I received news of him, once through the Barlows before they left Dartington Hall and once through Sir Philip. I assumed I would have heard from someone if my father were not alive.]

More than once over the next years, I wrote Cromwell such groveling letters; more than once he sent coin or bolts of cloth with a reminder that my present position was his doing and that he knew I would be willing to serve him in the future. Sometimes, I felt I had sold my soul to the very devil, but it was worth it to see Elizabeth had shoes and boots that fit and boned bodices that did not pinch her ribs.

What pains of heart and soul the motherless, bastardized young girl suffered from being oft ignored by her father, and I wished I could soothe those as well.

## GREENWICH PALACE

*June 1540*

When Elizabeth was nearly seven, we were summoned to court. That had occurred before but not in such tenuous times. Elizabeth was ecstatic, but I was terrified. I was even sent for to face the king himself, when that had never happened. Wishing with all my heart it was John Ashley I was going to see, anyone but the king – or Tom Seymour, now Sir Thomas Seymour, yet unwed, but quite a favorite with the ladies, so I heard – I left Elizabeth with her other tenders and set off.

Things were rocky at court and in the country now, for the religious schism had widened and several bad harvests had caused widespread discontent. Unrest in the north and tensions abroad kept courtiers on edge. At the center of our universe His Majesty detested his fourth wife, the German princess Anne of Cleves, chosen sight unseen for him except for a flattering Holbein portrait. Cromwell had arranged the painting and the match to secure a Protestant ally on the Continent.

It was common rumor that the king would soon have the Cleves marriage – unconsummated, he swore – annulled. After his disposing of two other queens, I had merely nodded when I heard that news. It was said His Majesty had announced of the German Anne, 'I like her not,' 'She has the face of a horse and smells worse' and 'I cannot abide her ugly breasts and belly.' As twice before, he had ordered Cromwell to amend the situation. But one thing I'd heard whispered shocked me: the king blamed Cromwell for the crude, plain wife he'd been maneuvered into wedding, and the man who had recently been given the title Earl of Essex was in deep trouble.

163

However, the current royal marital woes did not discourage the king from courting a new lady, Catherine Howard, pretty, young and vivacious – and one who could speak the king's English – a cousin to Anne Boleyn, no less. After my erroneously thinking that Jane Seymour would not keep the king's attention enough for him to wed her, I predicted that the Howard girl would hold out for wife instead of mistress. It did seem to me that each time the king considered a new wife, he chose one quite the opposite from the one he was replacing, but they all had learned to use the same tactics.

For this interview, I had dressed carefully but circumspectly in a simple dark-hued gown. My thick hair was pulled back under a borrowed gabled hood which His Majesty's still-mourned Queen Jane had brought back into fashion. Trembling, I waited in the presence chamber until my name was announced; one of the yeomen guards at the withdrawing room door swept it open for me.

'Your Majesty,' I said as I curtsied before him as deeply as I could manage and yet look graceful.

I stayed down a moment because I feared my face would show shock or alarm. How greatly the red-haired Adonis, the once athletic, virile man, had changed. Henry Tudor, who would have his forty-ninth birthday later this month of June 1540, not only filled the chair upon which he sat but overspilled it. His eyes, now beady like a trapped animal's, seemed to have sunk into his florid face. His auburn hair had grayed and thinned. And I could see from the vantage point of my curtsy, before he indicated I should rise, that his right leg was wrapped with a big, seeping bandage under his bulging silk stockings. And this was the man now courting a nineteen-year-old girl who loved to dance? At least, I prayed silently, let him be in a good humor.

'Cromwell, Earl of Essex, brought you to court years ago,' he said without so much as inquiring about Elizabeth's progress, though the child had spent some time with him the day before and was thrilled to have had even a few minutes of his attention.

*Dear Lord in heaven*, I thought, *he is going to dismiss me from my duties. Cromwell will pull me down with him.*

I struggled to strengthen my backbone and my voice. 'That is correct, Your Grace. I must admit that Master Cromwell, as he was then called, was impressed with my diligent learning and my desire to serve Your Majesty, which I have done these years with great pride and purpose.'

'Ah. Yes,' he said, stroking his salt-and-red-pepper beard and regarding me through narrowed eyes. 'At any rate, the child cares deeply for you, and you seem to have done a good service to her, but for her misliking needlework, which all women should favor.'

'Yes, Your Majesty. But she rides beautifully,

though she could never sit a horse as well as you.'

He merely nodded. I recalled that no compliment could possibly overreach with this man who was so used to being praised. 'Mistress Kat,' he said. 'She calls you Kat.'

'Yes, Your Grace.'

'And tells me you have a pet name for her: lovey.'

'She is a lovely child, a great honor to Your Majesty in her learning and her looks.'

'True. She has a sharp, busy little mind. Hair as crimson as my sister's – the Tudor rose, they called her. But to business.'

Cromwell's chant, I thought: to business. Always to business. I had to force myself to breathe. What would happen to the man who had been for a time another Wolsey, as powerful in this realm as the king? What would become of me if this man sent me away from his daughter? What if he had learned that I had abetted his stubborn daughter Mary's defiance years ago? Worse, what if Tom Seymour, who yet rode high in his regard as his heir's uncle, had told him dreadful lies about my character?

'I like someone solid and sober and staid around that child,' he said, tapping his beringed fingers on the carved arm of his chair. They had grown as puffy as sausages. 'I know you have a rural upbringing and favor the new learning and reformed religion.'

'Yes, Your Grace.'

'And have an impeccable reputation.'

Thank God, neither Tom Seymour nor Cromwell had told him different. Or was he baiting me?

'Yes, Sire, though to live at court off and on is to invite rumors, some of which are most unfair to reputations.'

'Very true. But, mistress, my point is this, so heed me well. Because Elizabeth carries her wanton mother's blood, she must be closely watched. She must not be encouraged to be frivolous or fanciful – or, later, flirty. She must be encouraged to follow my ruling and not to inquire of or romanticize her mother. Unlike the Boleyn, her cousin Catherine Howard is virtue personified. Elizabeth's mother did not set a good example for the girl, and she must needs be reminded of that.'

The ring I wore almost burned my finger, stoking anger in me. If I tried to fight him in any way, I knew I would lose Elizabeth, lose the opportunity to help her at least be near her brother's throne someday.

'I understand completely what you are saying, Your Majesty,' I managed, then actually bit my tongue to keep from declaring *but I believe you are completely wrong.*

'Good. I like a reasonable woman. Then we are agreed.'

I know not why, but a rebellious, rapturous thought rose within me, one I prayed would not cause harm if pursued.

'Your Grace, I was hoping I could make a request – about the Lady Elizabeth's riding. I can certainly work with her to develop her needlework, and I vow to have proof of that in your hands soon, but she could benefit from a riding instructor – to improve her already inherent talents that have come from you.'

'*Hm*, yes, I suppose I can spare a man. Or was there someone in the countryside you recommend?'

*Ha, Cromwell,* I thought perversely. *Your vaunted power with the king is slipping, but he is asking me for advice.*

'I know not, Your Grace, and would leave such judgments to you, of course,' I said, deciding to try to get my way by a feminine wile and not to stand up to him as I longed to do. My words came in a rush. 'But I do know that I have seen only one man who rides as smoothly as you do, and that is John Ashley, who I have heard serves with your Master of the Horse here at court.'

I was afraid again. What if John had become ambitious in my absence and no longer wanted to escape the hothouse of the court? What if he would curse me for having him assigned to rural places in service to the daughter of the disgraced Anne Boleyn? No, John had cared deeply for the Boleyn heritage. Surely, I could pay him back for his kindnesses to me this way. I prayed he had not formed an attachment to another woman. How deeply I longed to see him.

'I'll arrange it forthwith and look forward to a pretty piece of needlework from your lovey,' the king told me with a dismissive wave.

I thanked him, curtsied and backed a few steps away before turning toward the door. My love for my royal charge – and, yes, fear for my own well-being – had kept my contempt for this man from my face and voice. Yet now I understood how Anne Boleyn had stomached saying the words on the scaffold to praise the cruel and brutal king who had ruined her and could ruin any of us, even my Elizabeth.

That very evening, after Elizabeth fell asleep while a maid slept in a truckle bed nearby, I stepped out into the corridor at Greenwich. I was instantly on edge, for it was dim and deserted. Ever since Tom had attacked me when I was alone in the hall at Westminster Palace, I was wary of such situations. But my chamber was just next door so I hastened toward it, hearing only the swish of my own skirts and footsteps and – 'Kat! Kat!'

I nearly bolted, until I recognized that voice. My hand to the door latch, I hesitated. 'John?'

He appeared at the top of the servants' staircase and gestured to me. I quickly recalled what I had rehearsed all day since my interview with the king. If John was pleased with his new assignment, I would be modest, or if he did not know I had put his name forth, I would not mention how it came about. If he was unhappy, I would apologize and beg his forgiveness. If—

As I stepped closer, in the shadows between the top balustrade and the wall, he pulled me into his arms and kissed me.

Any words, any thoughts, went sailing into the wild blue. His hands anchored me to him breast to chest, soft thighs to his rockhard ones. His codpiece thrust my petticoats against the bottom of my belly. I was quickly so dizzy I thought I must be tumbling down the stairs with him. It went on and on until we both came up for air, breathing in unison.

'Did the king ask you?' I gasped out.

'Told me, more like, and told me who suggested it.'

'Yes, I thought—'

He was kissing me again, his hands roving my waist and back, then tipping my head to possess my mouth fully again. I tilted into him, any will of my own gone as yielding as water.

When we finally broke the next kiss, he whispered, 'The king is in a roaring good mood because of the young girl he's enamored with – his next wife, no doubt – but he's not my concern. Kat, I've waited for some real sign from you that you cared for me, especially after you avoided me when I first pursued you. So you had not a bit of self-interest in getting me appointed to the same household you are in?' Laughter mellowed his deep voice. 'You did it only for the

Lady Elizabeth, of course.' Holding my chin in his big callused hand, he looked deep into my eyes, demanding the truth and all I longed to give him.

'Why, what could there be in it for me?' I teased back, my voice shaky. As much as I wanted John Ashley, his passion almost frightened me – or, rather, my own did. I wanted to lie with him here and now, whoever came upon us be damned. 'I did it for Hatfield's horses, which are in dire need of care,' I told him with a low laugh. 'Besides, you told me you want to write a book about the art of riding, and I am writing a book about my life, so late into the evenings, we can write side by side, that is all.'

He chuckled, then sobered when we heard voices echo down the hall. 'We will serve Elizabeth well together, Kat,' he whispered hotly against my ear. 'And I pray there will be fewer people about in the country to catch us together, sunny days outside away from prying eyes, for do you not need riding lessons too?' he asked with a crooked grin and a soft double-bump against my hips.

Even though I felt so warm, I blushed. At the age of thirty-four, I was blushing! But I had been so busy that suitors of any sort – a plague on Tom Seymour – had not been part of my experience. Yet I could not allow our banter and heady feelings to cloak reality. 'Jesting aside, I've no doubt Cromwell still has spies in rural houses too,' I insisted.

'Soon, I think, he'll have no more need of spies,' he said, looking right, then left, as if the walls had ears. I recall once, in Devon, Cromwell had said that very thing. 'I scent it in the air,' John added, standing me back a bit as the voices of at least two women came closer. 'I hear Humpty Dumpty is heading for a fall, and all the king's horses and all the king's men will never put him back together again – or want to. Even his so-called friends hate Cromwell for climbing too far. I must go now, sweetheart.'

*Sweetheart!* No one had ever called me that, nor had a pet name been so precious. He kissed me yet again, quickly, hard, and was halfway down the first flight of stairs when Lady Joan and a chambermaid passed in the corridor. I heard them open then close a door. Silence again.

Touching my sweetly bruised, tingling lips with two fingertips, I was almost brazen enough to call down the staircase to John that the coast was clear now. But I did not want him to think I was an easy mark, however much I might have acted like one just now. Strangely, as ever, despite initially being seduced to desire Tom years ago, my feelings for John were not only wilder but deeper than that. Yes, he and I would flee this world and rear Elizabeth safely in the country, almost as if she were our own.

Shortly thereafter, before we were allowed to leave London, word came that Cromwell had been arrested for treason – bribes, dispensing heretical books, and nefarious plans to wed Mary Tudor and become king. It was like the charges against Anne all over again, I thought, everything thrown in to besmirch the accused and assure conviction. Well, for all I knew, he was guilty. Selfish as I was, I prayed continually that he would not be forced to give up the names of those who had spied for him. Seven weeks in the Tower, who knew what he would say?

I feared, too, from what John had said, that Cromwell had somehow recruited him, so he could be named too. Why were we not released forthwith to return to Hatfield? Was everything at a standstill now that the king's fourth marriage had been annulled and he was prepared to wed Catherine Howard, his 'virtue personified,' as he'd put it?

He married her on July 28, 1540, and rode off on a long honeymoon progress beginning at his rural palace of Oatlands. In His Majesty's usual exquisite timing, it was the very day that, on Tower Hill where had died the men accused of treason with Queen Anne, Cromwell was beheaded.

I went through the motions of the normal agenda with Elizabeth that day, listening to her chatter, sitting in on her lessons with her tutor, William Grindal, then rehearsing Latin and French with her, even pretending I was happy for her when she was allowed to visit her three-year-old brother, who was also visiting at court with his protective uncles, Edward and Tom. I was sure the Seymour brothers were elated about – perhaps even the cause of – Cromwell's shameful, grisly fate. Although Cromwell had manipulated me as if I were a puppet, he had saved me from obscurity and obtained my initial placement at court, so I was sad for his dreadful demise.

Late in the day, morose and exhausted, I sat on a turf bench overlooking the Thames flowing past Greenwich Palace and watched John work with Elizabeth on a graveled circle as she sat proudly on her pony, elegant and serious for her nearly seven years. I wished he would not let her make too much progress lest the king keep him here when we departed, for John had told me that His Majesty's Master of the Horse was loath to let him go. He had left John in charge of the royal stables here because he had gone to Oatlands with the king.

I heard a hissing sound behind me and turned. Surely, not a snake! No, a disembodied voice whispered, 'Mistress! Mistress!'

From behind a hedge, Master Stephen, Cromwell's man, gestured to me. My first impulse was to shake my head and walk closer to John. Could this man, who had never quite risen above being a loyal lackey to Cromwell, plan to take over for him? I stood and moved closer, though not around the corner of the hornbeam hedge. In my quick glimpse of him, I thought he looked harried and hounded.

'Have they a hue and cry out for you?' I asked.

'They released me after rough questioning. I'm heading home – to York. But I swore to my lord I would deliver messages to some. They let me see him briefly yesterday.'

'A message for me?'

Suddenly, the man was racked with huge, gasping sobs. His balled fists propped on his knees, he bent over, looking as if he would be ill on the ground. I took a step closer, around the hedge, and touched his shoulder.

'Were you there today?' I asked.

'It was awful,' he choked out without looking up at me. 'Bungled, too many blows – inept axman or intended, I know not. I kept thinking, *Cromwell never could stand incompetence of any sort.*'

He straightened and brushed his sleeve across his face to wipe away mucus and tears. 'He said – tell you that, when we met that first day in Devon – even if he knew what fate lay in store for him – ruination and a shameful death' – he sniffed again – 'that he would not have turned back. That it was worth it.'

'Yes. That sounds like him. Each one of us must decide what is worth great risk,' I whispered, turning the ring on my finger around and around with my thumb.

'If there's more to tell, I can't recall. He said so much in the little time they gave us, and I – I was terrified they wouldn't let me leave, but – they only wanted him.'

'Yes, that is so. I hear his son will even inherit

his father's old title of baron, but then he is wed to a Seymour.' My knees were shaking; my stomach clenched. As much as I had detested and feared Cromwell over many of the fifteen years I had known him, I grieved for him and this man. Once again, I wanted to flee this place and its rulers, not only my dear little charge's father she adored but Sir Thomas Seymour. I had not seen him for years, but did not want to.

'Go with God, Stephen,' I called to Cromwell's faithful man as he turned and strode away. Then I mouthed silently, 'Go with God, because devils still reign here.'

But my heart lifted when I saw John striding toward me, holding on to Elizabeth's pony's bridle while she held the reins. 'Some good news and some ill,' he told me, gesturing behind him at a man walking back toward the palace who must have brought him information.

I clasped my hands between my breasts. 'We can go to Hatfield?'

'I will tell my Kat, Master Ashley,' Elizabeth declared. 'I and my household are to leave on the morrow, but Master Ashley is not to join us until my father and the new queen return from their progress, mayhap in the autumn. That is because the Master of the Horse is with my father and so Master Ashley is needed here to oversee all in his absence.'

I nodded and blinked back tears, not only in my disappointment that John would be held here longer. Not only because I was moved by how logically and regally the child had relayed that information. It had finally hit me hard how careful John and I must be not to be caught together in compromising positions – that is, situations – including by my beloved little mistress. Perhaps my long years of keeping Cromwell's secrets would now be useful, for one sniff of the things His Majesty had warned me about could ruin our relationship with Elizabeth – if and when John ever came to live with us at all.

# CHAPTER 10

HAMPTON COURT

*July 12, 1543*

I stood in the back of the chapel, listening to the wedding vows of King Henry and his sixth wife, Katherine Parr, Lady Latimer. Craning her neck to see, Elizabeth perched next to her sister in the second pew, directly behind Prince Edward and his uncle, Edward Seymour. I could only pray that my talk to the nine-year-old about sober, calm decorum had sunk into that bright brain, for at times she was a highly excitable child.

Yesterday, I had been forced to chase her and young Edward Tudor through some of the dusty privy passages connecting the king's suite to the outside. They had somehow discovered the privy door from the clock courtyard and, shrieking like banshees, had played tag on the stairs within the dark walls. Servants could hear their voices but not locate them, for few knew the secret. [I would not have known either, but Queen Anne had told me of the hidden stairs and narrow passages years ago, and I had more than once

178

peeked behind the arras to note the outlines of their small doors.]

So I deduced how the two clever children had given their little entourage the slip. Holding a lantern aloft, trying not to trip on my skirts, out of breath, I pursued them up two flights of twisting stairs to the king's – thank the Lord – empty bedchamber and retrieved them there, running madly about, all sweaty and dusty and as happy as two young children could ever be.

Today Elizabeth was nearly beside herself with joy to be near her father, to be treated kindly by his new wife and to be attending her first wedding. Besides, although the three Tudor children had been with their sire from time to time since Queen Jane's death, Elizabeth was also thrilled to be with Mary, now twenty-seven, and Edward, now five. Mary made a show of fussing over her, so Elizabeth had never quite yet grasped the fact her older sister deeply resented her. Despite my love for my royal charge and the little family of her intimate servants we had gathered about her in the country, she ached for affection from her royal family and longed to please them.

'I vow to be buxom in bed and board,' the bride was saying. Her voice trembled slightly. 'In sickness and in health, to love, cherish, and to obey, till death us do part . . .'

It had been a challenging three years. The king's previous young wife, his 'virtue personified,' had lied to cover up her licentious past. Worse, abetted by George Boleyn's widow, Jane Rochford, who had been the first person to greet me when I arrived at court, Catherine Howard had taken a lover behind her besotted royal husband's back. Like her cousin Anne, she had died on the block in the Tower shortly after her lovers – actually guilty ones, unlike with Anne – had been hanged, drawn and quartered. Though I had not known His Majesty's fifth queen nor had I attended her execution, all that had brought back to me the horror of Elizabeth's mother's death.

How grateful I was that my little charge and I were not living at court then, for, to tell true, Catherine Howard's trial for adultery and death brought back memories of losing Elizabeth's mother as well as memories of how I could not help but admire Anne Boleyn. Ah, how I used to study her way with men, her cleverness and, indeed, her love for her daughter. My little lovey had lost her mother so young, and I could fully sympathize with how she longed for her and was passionate to know about her.

'Did you know my mother well?' she had asked me recently.

'She was kind to me, and I did favors for her too. She was a lovely and well-read woman, just as you shall be if you concentrate on your studies. Now read me that passage again,' I had said, pointing to the page, 'because you must learn how to pronounce several of the words – Plan-*tag*-e-net, see here?'

'But if she was so lovely and learned, why did my father put her away and then she died?'

'You know your sire, lovey. He – they disagreed on some things, and one must not disagree with a king.'

'But she was a queen and that's second best. I heard he had her head chopped off, just like Catherine Howard's!'

'Who told you such things? You come to me if you have questions like that!'

'But, my Kat, that is what I am doing!'

More than once we had gone in such circles. Despite my rehearsing what to say, conversations about her mother always went awry, and I agonized about how to best frame my answers. Should I tell her exactly what happened but, of course, lay no blame? I, too, had come from a bitter past where my young mother died tragically, even amidst my suspicions of murder. I knew precisely how it felt to have a stepmother, half siblings and an indifferent father.

I had to be so careful, for in truth I did blame the king for Anne's loss, though she had been foolish too. But things like adultery, incest – witchcraft and sorcery? I feared that, however intelligent Elizabeth was, she was not yet prepared to hear any of that. So I concentrated on telling her of happy times her mother had, of her firm belief in the new religion and how, while her parents were wed and she was born, they loved each other. Each time, I came closer to the

181

truth, closer to giving her Anne's ring, but I held back.

'Your Majesty, please repeat after me,' Bishop Gardiner intoned, dragging me back from my agonizing to the joyous occasion at hand. 'With this ring I thee wed, with my body I thee worship and with all my worldly goods I thee endow . . .'

The king's voice droned on. John Ashley had been with us for nearly two years at Hatfield, and we were desperately in love. But with the increased household staff – Elizabeth's retainers in and about Hatfield or the other rural homes we stayed in now numbered nearly one hundred twenty – it was difficult for us to be unseen alone, though we managed at times. It was a dangerous courtship but a wholesome one, lest we be discovered and chastised or dismissed, or lest I find myself with child. But how badly we wanted a bed of our own, a marriage of our own, so that . . .

The king was kissing his blushing bride, loudly, soundly. They turned and walked toward the back of the chapel, he beaming, she looking dazed and even apprehensive, and why not?

I had heard the twice-widowed heiress had told the king she would willingly be his mistress – quite a change from the way Anne, Jane and Catherine had played their cards. Henry Tudor was a dangerous husband, and Katherine Parr had wit enough to know it. A bit of doggerel had been going around that I hoped Elizabeth had not heard: 'The king's poor wives: divorced, beheaded, died, divorced, beheaded – that's five!' But now there were six, and what would be the fate of this lovely woman?

It was said the king had wed Katherine Parr partly because he needed a nurse for his old age, but it was also said that he was going to amend the Act of Succession to include any children they might have. What an optimist he was at his age, and the lady – now queen – had not caught a child in her other marriages. But if only it could be true that, after Edward and any future offspring, His Majesty might reinstate Mary and Elizabeth in line to rule the kingdom. It was my daily prayer, among all the twisted webs of rumors, that one might come true.

As we all followed out to where the bridal supper was laid in the great hall, I studied Katherine Parr, now age thirty-one but still in the flush of youthful good looks. She had reddish hair and warm hazel eyes. Though not a raving beauty, she seemed to glow from within, radiating warmth that had already drawn the king's three motherless children to her. But I studied her especially because it was common knowledge that she had been swept away in love by Sir Thomas Seymour before she caught the king's eye.

After being wed to and widowed by two men, the wealthy woman was thrilled to be courted by the handsome, dashing rake – yes, I admit he still was, for I had seen him from afar. Five years ago, it was said, Tom had turned down the Duke of

Norfolk's offer of marriage to his only daughter, the widowed Duchess of Richmond, a fine catch, because he was 'aiming higher.' How much higher? I wondered. And since he belonged to one of England's premier families and now boasted titles such as Baron Sudeley and Admiral of the Fleet and possessed great estates, why did he need a wealthy widow?

At any rate, the moment King Henry had turned his attentions to the widow Parr, she had accepted her fate to wed him, and Tom had quickly gone abroad as Ambassador to Belgium on top of his sea duties. He could stay away forever as far as I was concerned, the power-hungry, poxy wretch. He no doubt had a mistress in every port, and his paths at home and abroad were littered with trodden-down, longing women – but not me.

Early that autumn, when Their Majesties returned from their progress, we were all together at the rural palace of Ashridge in Hertfordshire. The king and queen seemed devoted to each other, and Her Majesty proved to be a loving stepmother Elizabeth adored, though it fretted me greatly that the girl had turned a bit testy around her father. I knew why. Just the week before we were summoned here, Elizabeth had grown so demanding about her mother that I had taken her for a walk alone – with two guards trailing us at a distance, that is – in the park at Hatfield where the tall oaks, beeches and sycamores shaded our way.

'So, you said my mother used to send me all sorts of pretty clothes?' she asked. Always questions about her mother. It was so simple to get to the topic I wanted to broach.

'Yes, and I kept some of them for you – perhaps for your own child someday.'

'Oh, I shall never wed, especially not to a king who might take my head as well as my maidenhead.'

'My lady, again I say, whom have you been talking to? You have sharp ears and a sharper tongue. Take your maidenhead, indeed! You know not whereof you speak and are too young to be bandying about such things,' I protested as we sat together on a wooden bench under a massive oak. Now and then an early acorn dropped on us, and the girl began to randomly throw ones she picked up.

'If I only had something from her as a keepsake,' she groused, 'not some old baby clothes. My sister says she at least got a gold cross and chain from her mother's things. I know she blames my mother for what happened to her, but I warrant she should blame the king – but I didn't say so, Kat, so don't scold me.'

I could not help but nod, tears in my eyes. So Elizabeth was carrying the extra burden that Mary resented her as well as the knowledge of why she did. If she could bear that, perhaps she was ready for the rest.

'If it means anything,' I said, trying to steady

185

my voice, 'my mother had a garnet necklace that came to me when she died but my stepmother took it away. Lovey, look,' I plunged on, turning toward her, 'in some ways you are older than your years so I do have something to tell you and give you. But what it is and means must be our secret. Can you keep a secret?'

Her lips pressed tightly together, she turned those dark eyes to me and nodded solemnly.

'I had planned to wait until you were older – how old, I know not. You see, when your mother was in prison in the Tower before her death—'

'It wasn't fair!' she burst out. 'You said they loved each other when they met and when I was born!'

'Yes, yes!' I cried, pulling her closer so I could put my arm around her shoulders. I saw the guards were not only standing back at a distance but had the decency to be looking out at some deer that ran through the trees. Neither they nor anyone must know of what I was about to say and do – only, maybe, John, for I unburdened myself of much to him. 'My dear girl, never forget or doubt you are a child of love, but sometimes love does not last.'

'Not with my father, but didn't it last for her?'

'Yes, and she gave a speech before she died that showed she still loved and respected him.' *Dear God, please*, I prayed, help me find *the right words here*. 'And you must respect him, too, no matter what he does or says, not only because he is your father, but even more so because he is our king. Now listen to me. If I give you something very, very special from your mother, I want your solemn vow that you will tell no one of it, especially your father, for he would not understand. It is a secret gift your mother gave me for you.'

'Then why did you not?' she asked, pulling slightly away.

'Because she made me promise I would wait until you were old enough that you would not lose it and old enough to accept the gift with gratitude and love and keep it a secret.'

To my utter amazement, as if she already knew, she looked down at the ring. What a bright girl, my Elizabeth. Slowly, I took the ruby and gold piece I had worn so faithfully from my finger. 'Look, lovey,' I whispered, blinking back tears, 'you press this stone and a tiny spring opens it to show portraits of you and her, face-to-face.'

She gasped as I opened the top and handed her the ring. Unspeaking, long she gazed at the portrait of her mother. 'So we are yet together, always, in a way,' she finally whispered.

'Yes. Yes, she loved you very much, even as your father does, but in a different way.'

'That is the thing about men and women, isn't it? They love in a different way? Oh, Kat, thank you, thank you,' she cried, hugging me hard. 'I shall keep it always on a chain around my neck until I can grow into it.'

'We can have it fitted for your finger.'

'No, I can't let it out of my sight, can't have it changed from the very way she gave it to you. And, Kat, I love you dearly, now even more so because you knew her and she trusted you, just like I do!'

We sat there that day, both sobbing like babies with our backs to the guards as she held the ring and I hugged her to me. When we finally walked back toward the palace, hand in hand, and a white falcon swooped over us in the sky, I was sure that was my sign that Anne's spirit was finally free.

But that gift of the ring, even hidden beneath Elizabeth's bodice, backfired with a huge bang. At Ashridge the next month, she presented the king with a beautifully hand-worked pillow with embroidered Tudor roses. He had looked at me standing off to the side with Margaret Bryan and winked. But then everything went wrong.

On the lawn outside the walls, Elizabeth was playing at bowls with Prince Edward, whose Uncle Edward, now the Earl of Hertford, the brother Tom could not abide, was nearby too, always watchful of his royal nephew's well-being. The king, bless him and his wonderful wife, had promised earlier today he would be sending Parliament a new order of succession, including Mary and Elizabeth, so even Mary managed a smile that day. Like all three Tudor heirs, she greatly favored her new stepmother.

But Edward of a sudden stopped and said in his

piercing six-year-old voice, 'Why do you have a ring on a chain, sister? It popped out of your bodice, see? Oh, it's come open! It has two pictures inside. Let me see!'

My heart careened to my feet. Anything Edward wanted, he got.

'No, it's just privy pictures, my lord,' Elizabeth protested with a sharp laugh as she tried to tug it back from him.

'I want to see it! Uncle!' The boy pouted, turning to Edward Seymour instead of the king. 'Make her show me!'

'Stop all that!' the king bellowed. Everyone grew silent. He had been on edge lately because his sore on his leg was infected. It had been cauterized and gave him much pain, despite the royal physician, Dr Butts, and the queen's tending it and his sitting in a chair with it propped up. 'Come over here, both of you.'

Like whipped puppies, they went. My heart was thundering in my chest. How I wished John were here – any ally. My knees almost buckled as the king lifted Elizabeth's ring yet on its chain and squinted closely at the portraits within, pulling his frightened daughter close to him.

Doomed, I thought. I would be dismissed. It was almost as if my entire life – especially that last interview with Anne in the Tower and the memory of her head, severed at the neck, her lips yet moving, flashed through my mind.

'Who gave you this!' the king roared, and yanked

189

the chain from her neck. 'This is the Boleyn's portrait!'

'My mother left it for me,' Elizabeth spoke back, now sounding strong, almost angry, hardly cowed. 'Some well – wisher gave it to me, I know not who,' she lied smoothly, even so near the lion's mouth.

'I'll not have it!'

'No, Your Majesty, for it is mine.'

'That's not what I meant. Did you mean to sass me? Ah, her daughter indeed! You will choose your loyalty, and if you choose her, it is because you are like her. You want to moon over this ring, I shall let you take it with you and go – and not write to me begging to come back – and just when I was about to put you in the line of succession!'

Shaking her head, Mary Tudor came closer, peering over the king's shoulder at the ring, then, nearsighted as she was, squinting and frowning at it.

'Your Grace,' Elizabeth went on, 'I love and respect you above all.' Good, I thought, words I had preached to her, despite my own feelings. 'But may I not have this single remembrance of her?'

'You need no remembrance of her. You have a fine new mother now who does not deceive people. But I see you have the making of a willful woman. Kat Champernowne,' he roared, 'I'll not have a willful woman! Take your charge and begone and teach her better wisdom, or I shall hold you responsible!'

Fearful Elizabeth would fly to my defense, or that, on second thought, he would dismiss me, I moved. Rushing forward, I took Elizabeth by the arm and pulled her into a curtsy beside me. 'Yes, Your Majesty,' I said, squeezing her hard enough that she winced. 'Apologize to your sovereign and father,' I ordered her.

'Your Grace, I regret th—' she got out, but he threw the ring at her.

'No, my love,' he told the queen, who stood by, wringing her hands, 'stay out of this, for I see her belligerent Boleyn blood is up. Get you gone, both of you!'

I snatched the ring from the grass, yet on its broken chain, and tugged Elizabeth away. The last thing I recalled was seeing the Princess Mary's smirking face. We were packed and in a curtained litter heading home to Hatfield before Elizabeth's pale, stunned countenance crumbled and she threw herself against me and sobbed wretchedly. 'He – he might as well cut off m-my h-head, too,' she choked out, 'for now I have the mark of the chain on my neck right where my mother lost her head!'

There was a red line where he had yanked the chain – as he yanked all the chains by which we were bound. The swaying of the litter almost made me ill. Again I saw Anne's bloody neck, her body fall into the straw, her head . . . and held Elizabeth to me all the harder while we cried together.

It took the king over a year to work himself up

to put Mary and Elizabeth back in line to mount the throne behind their brother and his future heirs, but at least he included my brave, sweet girl. [Whenever she was at court, until the day she became queen, Elizabeth wore her mother's ring on a leather thong tied about her waist. Once the throne was hers, despite the fact she had many beautiful rings to adorn those long, slender fingers of which she was so proud, that ring never left her right hand.]

But, sadly, what the king's daughter learned from being exiled from the court and her newly united family for a bitter year when she was ten – even forbidden to write to her father – was not only a lesson about the power of kings.

It was simply this: 'I see it is not good to express one's true feelings straightaway, especially to strong men,' she said after a week of intermittent sobbing and sulking. 'There must be ways of dealing with them besides giving in. There must be, and, with your help, my Kat, I shall find them.'

That, at age ten, so was it any wonder that later in life she acted as she did, both untouchable goddess and terrible tease, wary yet wanting, and 'wild for to hold,' as the poet Wyatt who had loved her mother once wrote? But the tough times of our year in exile was only one small step in the making of Elizabeth Tudor.

'Is she asleep?' John asked me as I met him by moonlight in the knot garden to the south of

Hatfield House two years after the king had banished us. Whenever the weather was good, we stole time together here or in the privy gardens by the west side of the palace. At other times, we had to make do with furtive kisses and caresses in dim corridors or even the back stairs.

'One never knows with her, as she is likely to lie awake, thinking her thoughts and dreaming dreams half the night. At least she is much calmer now that she is back in Their Majesties' good graces and has been to court off and on.'

'I tired her out as best I could on our ride this morning. Kat, I have nothing else to teach her about riding. At age twelve, she rides better than men twice her age.'

Business done, we kissed, then he just held me against him, my head tucked under his chin. 'It's an old cliché,' he whispered, 'but we cannot keep meeting like this.'

'But she's included you in our evening discussions. Tutor Grindal was surprised to find her horseman so well-read, a thinker and fine conversationalist.'

'It's why I told you nearly in my first breath the day we met that I was writing a book,' he said. 'I didn't want you to think I could only talk to horses.' With our arms about each other, we began to stroll the twisting gravel paths through the shadowed garden. How sweet the mingled scents of the gillyflowers and roses on this summer night. I *shall always recall this moment and every single one with this man*, I thought.

'My love,' I whispered, 'I knew a man who spoke as well as you was good for more than mucking out royal stables.'

'What am I good for to you, sweetheart? We've been parted too much and face being separated again at the king's whim. We have hidden our love from even Elizabeth, when, if she could, she would champion us. You, like she, are back in the king's good graces. It is past time to ask for permission to wed.'

I turned sharply toward him and caught my toe in my skirt, but he had a good hold of me. 'It sounds like a business deal.'

'Far from it, but if I take you around the other side of the hedge, we will not speak at all, for you will be at my mercy – and I cannot wait to have for you in my bed any more than I can manage to continually pretend we are simply acquaintances or friends or companionable fellow servants. Kat,' he went on, talking quicker now and pressing my hands in his, 'we are both people who use words well enough, but I want more. I want you for my wife, lover and mistress. Beyond that, words just won't do!'

'Then I shall only say 'yes!' I told him, and kissed him hard and was soon lost in his love.

The next morn, when we requested to speak with Elizabeth – and then when she knew our plight – her face lit up. She clapped her hands, jumped from her chair to hug both of us and cried, 'I would love to go to another wedding, and we shall have a fine one here in the hall – if, that is, we can obtain royal permission. At least His Majesty is not angry with either of us anymore, Kat, and he and the queen have liked the needlework we've sent them, and they were proud of my translation of *Mirror of the Sinful Soul*.' She began to pace as she always did when she was planning something.

'We are so grateful to you, Your Grace,' John told her.

'Well,' she said with a sigh and a roll of her eyes, 'I have seen you kissing outside in the moonlight more than once. It looked like great fun, but only with someone you really like. I vow, if I am betrothed to some foreign ruler as they say, I shall not like it if he is too old or cruel or wants to set me aside for another. So, then,' she said as she stopped her pacing so quickly that her skirts belled out, 'let's write the letter, and I warrant we can find some stable lad under your care, Master John, to ride to London with it. We must not wait until we all go to be with them next month. The only thing is, Kat, if you have a child, you must not leave me.' She stopped by her writing table, hands on hips, frowning now.

'No, my dearest Elizabeth,' I assured her, pulling away from John's hand and walking over to take hers. 'If I have any say in the matter, I will never leave you for any reason.'

'I, too,' John promised.

'Then let us write so we can plan a wedding. I

am sure my father will favor a married couple with me – more stability, and he knows you both. Though, if I can help it, I will never wed myself, I do so love weddings!'

She gestured John to us and took both our hands, then brought them together. 'And you,' the exuberant girl said, 'will be my country family even though I owe allegiance to the king and queen.'

She tugged me close, even, I thought, as I had often done her. It was the summer of 1545, and in all my days, I had never been happier or felt safer. You'd think I would have learned something from the fates of Anne and Cromwell, more fool I.

Our wedding day a fortnight later was crisp and clear. A local curate read our service in the Hatfield church just to the west of the palace, and we had a lovely bridal dinner in the solar, followed by dancing to the music of two lutenists and a drummer. I must admit, it was the first time I knew my husband – how strange that word sounded – could dance. He partnered me and then our twelve-year-old benefactress, who was having the time of her life overseeing everything.

Her other ladies prepared me for bed; Elizabeth herself had insisted we have a larger chamber down the hall from my old one. John came in, half dressed, teased and mussed by some of the male servants and our house steward. With fewer ribald jests than usual, since Elizabeth still stood wide-eyed in the hall, they shoved us into bed together and went back to their party downstairs.

That night, for the first time in my life, I surrendered myself to someone else, without worry, without qualms. I had struggled to be strong for so long, but now here was someone to trust and love, someone to tend to me as I did him. Oh, he knew the ways to pleasure a woman, my beloved John, but I had ever been a quick learner. He evoked a passion in me I had never fathomed and had foolishly thought I could control.

'Riding lessons, indeed,' I whispered as we were somehow wrapped together naked, tangled in bedsheets and my loosed hair.

'One lesson is never enough,' he murmured, looking sleepy-eyed with a lazy grin as he fondled my full breasts, which used to embarrass me so.

But with John, everything was perfect. There had been no pain of head or heart or maidenhead as when I had been ravished by the Seymour wretch. Everything was hot and wonderful, and I wanted more. I had fretted that John would ask me why I was not a virgin, but he had evidently been so intent he had not noticed.

'Then,' I said, lifting my knee over his leg to rub my thigh against his, 'how do I request another lesson and what will be its price?'

He reached for me and the short, short night spun away to dust us too soon with the dawn.

★　　★　　★

We were all back and forth to court for the next two years, until January of 1547 when the king took ill. Elizabeth's education had proceeded apace and was greatly strengthened by her being permitted to sit in with Prince Edward's tutors and nobly born schoolfellows from time to time. She especially formed a friendship with Robert Dudley, one of Edward's boon companions. They were close enough that they called each other Robin and Bess. But at Yule that year, the king took a turn for the worse, and all three children were sent to their respective rural households.

'The queen will nurse him back to health,' Elizabeth told us more than once. 'I am so glad they are reconciled. How dare others try to tell the king she had heretical books and so was dangerous.'

I nodded, and my eyes met John's as the three of us rode toward Hatfield House during our daily exercise. He and I had several of those same books in our possession, hardly heretical – books about the new religion, Protestantism, called so because its adherents protested the rigid practices of the popish Church.

Behind us came a rider at full gallop. John turned and lifted in his saddle. He rode a black stallion called Commander, and I was on Ginger's filly, Meadow. Elizabeth rode the three-year-old Regal, a horse John had let her name. The passing of Brill and Ginger, as well as the loss of people I had known, made me realize how much time had passed.

'It's Jamie, from court,' John said, his breath visible in the frosty air. 'Perhaps His Majesty has rallied, and we are summoned back again.'

Jamie, one of the men who had worked for John, reined in and nodded to Elizabeth, who sat between the two of us. 'Your Grace' – he addressed her as such since she was back in the royal line of succession as princess – 'you are ordered to Enfield to await the arrival of your brother.'

'My father's health?' she asked.

'Tenuous, but as ever, he is determined and strong.'

As we went into the house to pack, for the first time I tried to imagine what England would be like without the king. I had known no other, for he had inherited the throne in 1509 when I was but three. Despite his gross weight and painful leg, I knew that he would recover. But I did wonder how much the messenger had not told us. After all, it was high treason not only to plot the death of the king but to mention it or imagine it, as if someone besides the Lord High God could know one's thoughts. So, in effect, all my agonizing over this was illegal!

'Back to Enfield,' John whispered to me as he brought round our horses as we set out the next gray-sky morn.

'Yes, there is that,' I said, and smiled.

We both loved Enfield Palace in Middlesex, even more than we favored Hatfield. Called Enfield Chase by some for its large hunt park, it was a reddish brick, moated manor house, not a sprawling place, but charming and livable. Still, it had an impressive gatehouse and an approaching avenue lined with lime trees. The outer court bustled with domestic activities, but the cobbled inner court around which were built the privy apartments had a fountain where splashing water echoed pleasantly in the chambers about. Enfield boasted a chapel, a covered bowling green and conduits bringing in fresh water from up the hill. Two lakes teemed with fish, and the water gardens offered exquisite moonlight strolls. A bridge over Maidens Brook connected lush orchards to the enclosed deer park where John had led visitors and Elizabeth herself to the hunt. In short, it was John's and my favorite place.

But when we reached Enfield late that afternoon, it looked frozen in place and time. We had not seen it in the winter. The moat was iced, frost etched the windows and fresh snow sat pure upon the ground. We were greeted by the household steward and told that a message had already arrived that the prince and his entourage, headed by Edward Seymour, the Earl of Hertford, would be here soon. We had barely eaten and changed clothes when the royal party, with many more guards than I had ever seen, some in Tudor and some in Seymour livery, clattered into the inner courtyard and dismounted around the fountain.

From a second-story window, I watched John take charge of their horses. Elizabeth hurried out to greet her brother with a curtsy and a hug. Hand in hand – for they were yet children – they disappeared under my window, and I rushed down to greet them. The earl, Prince Edward's uncle and Tom's brother, dominated the scene. He had a more pointed face than Tom and a long, dark beard. His features seemed sharp, accented by an aquiline nose; his stance and attitude were ever aloof. To my dismay, he immediately ushered Elizabeth and Edward into the old medieval hall and closed the door on us all.

'How does the King's Majesty?' I asked one of the earl's men.

'Not well' was all he said.

And then came shrill cries, even a scream from Elizabeth. Instinct took over. I bolted for the door and pulled it open before one of the earl's men could stop me. The two royal children stood in the wash of late light before the bank of windows, holding tightly to each other and wailing while Seymour stood there, just watching.

*The king is dead*, I thought. On this cold, late January day in the new year of 1547, the king is dead! And before me stood the new king, a thin boy of nine, and my thirteen-year-old Elizabeth, now but two lives from the throne.

'I have not summoned you!' the earl shouted at

me as I held both children to me and Elizabeth locked her arms around my waist.

'She is my charge!' I challenged him.

'Then both of you can unhand and kneel to your new sovereign,' he ordered.

And so we did, soon backed by the others, all on our knees before one very frightened boy – frightened, I believed, as much by his uncle as by his father's loss and his new lofty place.

Just when I thought Thomas Seymour was out of my life for good, I found I was mistaken. I was outraged at him because, immediately after the king's death in the winter of 1547, he secretly made marital advances to the Princess Mary, then to Anne of Cleves, no less, and – the blackguard – even to Elizabeth! I had overseen her written refusal to him, though, I admit, I would have worded it more strongly. But ever since the king had sent her from court four years before, my princess had managed to get her way with powerful men more by honey than by vinegar. I recall parts of her reply to Seymour yet:

> . . . *I confess to you that your letter, charming as it is, has greatly surprised me, since, aside from the fact that I have neither the age nor the inclination to think of marriage, I should never have expected to find myself asked to a wedding at a time when I can only weep for the death of my father.*

*Therefore, my Lord Admiral, permit me to say frankly that . . . I shall make it my greatest pleasure to remain*

*Your servitor and friend,*

*ELIZABETH*

CHELSEA HOUSE, VILLAGE OF CHELSEA ON THE THAMES, NEAR LONDON

*April 1547*

Once again, I thought we were safe from Tom when, shortly after the old king's funeral and the new king's coronation, a command came to us from the Privy Council, now headed by Edward Seymour who had been named Lord Protector of the king and kingdom during the boy's minority. They were ordering the Princess Elizabeth into the care and household of the Queen Dowager, Katherine, at her new home in Chelsea on the Thames just southwest of London.

We were ecstatic, for we had feared a far worse situation. Elizabeth was very fond of her stepmother, and she could keep her household. We were close to London and so the seat of power. She had thought she would see her brother more, but the Lord Protector was keeping him very isolated. At first all went well in the lovely house, gardens and orchards at Chelsea until John was summoned back to Whitehall to help the Master of the Horse, who had hated to lose his talents in the first place. As a result, we were separated by nearly an hour ahorse or a quarter-hour trip by boat. John managed to visit twice a week, early morning, most often by boat since he had struck a deal with some oarsmen.

But one day, as the sun was just coming up, and I met him by the water stairs, his first words were not *I love you* or *I miss you.*

'I'm not the only one coming here to meet a beautiful woman,' he told me with a quick kiss.

'What?'

'I learned late night that the Lord Admiral, Thomas Seymour, has been riding to Chelsea secretly for months and is being let in the back gate by the fields. He takes a steed from the stable nearly in the middle of the night and returns it before dawn each day.'

'What? Surely, he's not hoping to see Eliza—'

He shook his head. 'His groom was drunk last night and told me that he has been secretly wed to the Queen Dowager since five weeks after King Henry died.'

My gasp nearly drowned out his next words, and not because they had wed in such indecent haste.

'They're going to announce it publicly soon,' he went on, 'and all hell is going to break loose from the Privy Council and Seymour's brother. So keep your and Elizabeth's heads down, because Sir

Thomas will soon be lord here. Kat. Kat! Did you hear what I just told you?' he said, giving me a little shake.

I know not what my expression was, but it must have been horrified. I had never breathed one word to John about my past with Tom. And Tom had threatened me if I told anyone, he would ruin me. I could not stomach being near him now, and under his command – no!

'I – I did hear you,' I stammered. 'I must get Elizabeth out of here. After that proposal of his to her – what if Katherine learns of it – that she was second – or fourth place? I heard he is charming and always looking to entice someone higher – and who is higher than the Queen Dowager but Elizabeth? She will be in his household, under his aegis – all of us. I am going to write a letter begging the Princess Mary to take her in.'

'You know they do not get on. Mary likes you, but she and Elizabeth will be like cats and dogs. Besides, you would be much farther away from me.'

But to my dismay, for the first time I could recall, Elizabeth gainsaid my suggestion we leave. 'How romantic!' she cried, jumping up from her writing desk and clapping her hands. 'A secret courtship and wedding after all that time they had to be apart! Remember, Kat, he was courting her before he probably thought he had to propose to others ere he could follow his heart back to her.

I think that is so lovely, and he is handsome and, I hear, a brave fighter of pirates, to boot. No, I am not budging from here, especially not to live in the country with Mary. But why are you so overturned and adamant, especially when you would be forced to live farther from your own dear love? There is nothing wrong between the two of you, is there?'

I could only shake my head. Nothing wrong between John and me – yet. But everything was wrong with my living in a house Tom Seymour commanded, and one where the two most important women in it were all dreamy-eyed about the ravishing – in more ways than one – whoreson wretch.

# CHAPTER 11

CHELSEA HOUSE

*Summer 1548*

Our staying with the Queen Dowager became torment for me when Thomas Seymour came to live with us. What made it worse was that every other woman in whatever house we stayed in – Katherine's Chelsea or Hanford, Tom's properties of Seymour House in London or Sudeley Castle in the Cotswolds – was ecstatic to be near the man.

Queen Katherine plainly adored her new husband. She blushed at his hotly whispered remarks and turned misty-eyed when he left the room. Lady Jane Grey, a cousin of Elizabeth, who had also been in the household off and on, obviously thought her guardian was delightful company. Even serving women watched the exuberant, tall and handsome Lord Admiral with awed expressions.

At least his brother and the Privy Council, on which Tom, too, now served, were outraged at his daring to covertly marry the former king's new widow without permission and in such haste. The Council had reprimanded him soundly, though he had stood up to them and cursed them. In his own domain, only I avoided him like the plague.

About a fortnight after Tom had come to live openly with Katherine, I had started toward the manor house to fetch a book that Master Grindal, Elizabeth's tutor, needed. He, the princess and Lady Jane Grey – though Jane was shy and quiet, Elizabeth enjoyed having a friend near her own age – were sitting outside beyond the rose garden in deep debate. I had been sitting long enough anyway, so was glad for the excuse to stretch my legs. But on my way up to the house, in a shaded bower of plaited, arched rose canes, Tom stepped out ahead of me and blocked my path.

I spun to stride back toward the river, but his hands clamped onto my shoulders; he pulled me back so hard my skirt bushed out from his boots.

''S blood, and I had hoped absence all these years would make the heart grow fonder,' he said with a chuckle, turning me back toward him. He tipped his head to one side with a mocking, beseeching look.

'Unhand me, my lord.'

''S blood, do you not think others might notice your frosty demeanor when everyone else falls all over themselves to please me, especially our little princess or my wife? Or are you yet playing Anne

208

Boleyn's old game of *noli me tangere* just to get me hot for you again? You have told John Ashley that I was your first love, have you not?'

'Love!' I said as if it were a curse word. I spit, just missing him. I shrugged his hands off and managed to take a big step back from him, though that put me head to hems in the rose thorns. 'I used to be a fool, but you cured me of that,' I told him, brushing myself off where he had touched me. 'As for your wife and Her Grace – Lady Jane, too – if you told them the sky was green, sad to say, they would agree with pleasure.'

'With pleasure' – a lovely motto.' He grinned but I only glared back. How he had changed from the young man I had first beheld on a barge to Hampton Court twenty years ago. He had filled out with meat and muscle. No longer clean shaven, he had a full beard, as was the fashion. His gaze still rudely assessed my body, but now white crow's-feet perched at the corner of each eye, and frown lines furrowed his high forehead.

His booming voice was much the same, but he swore even more stout sailors' oaths as if they made him more dashing or important. Most of his curses, it seemed to me, insulted the Maker of the Universe by trivializing His holy name with things like *'s wounds* or *'s teeth* or even *'s nightgown*. Sometimes he put in the word *God's* and sometimes not.

''S precious eyes, Kat, do not think I have

forgotten you. Why, I still have all the love letters you sent me back then, prettily written, too, and if you turn your back on me now . . .'

'I do not need your threats, indirect or blatant, or your brutal handling.'

'Brutal? Hell's gates, I had no brutality in mind, but just the opposite,' he said and dared to reach out to cup my chin. I hit his hand away. ''S precious soul, Kat, you've done well – risen high, even as I,' he said, trying another tactic. He hooked his thumbs in his wide belt and tilted back on his heels. 'You must admit we keep good company these days, eh? And did I not tell you once that you would never forget your first love? Here we are, together again. Have you not noticed how many secret, shady bowers abound for trysts on my properties?'

'Leave off, sir, and leave me. You insult me, your wife – even yourself, if that is possible.'

Bristling, he straightened to his full height. 'In a way you are my servant now, and they obey orders or are dismissed,' he clipped out. ''S bones, if that is the way you want to play it, let me lay my cards on the table. Do not gainsay me or get in my way here, and I will not tell the Council of your checkered past—'

'My past? That you brutally raped me during Elizabeth's mother's coronation feast?'

He seized my wrists so hard I felt my hands go numb; he leaned down to put his face near mine and gave me a single hard shake. 'Have you not noticed that I get my way now?' he demanded. 'The king adores his uncle Tom who gives him money and gifts while his cold uncle Edward keeps him isolated at his studies and runs the kingdom. That needs to change. Much needs to change. Do you want me to see to it that Elizabeth's governess is changed?'

His handsome face had contorted to a gargoyle mask, one I had seen only during that nightmare of a night he took my virginity. Was this the fun-loving, easygoing man who played cards with his wife and her guests, regaling them with stories of chasing pirates and the latest gossip and bawdy jests?

He finally loosed my wrists. 'If you are not for me, Mrs Ashley, you are against me. And if I see a sign of that, I swear—'

'Yes, you do swear. All the time.'

I thought he would strike me, but he plunged on. 'God as my judge, I swear I will have you dismissed by my wife or the Council, no matter what sordid tales you concoct about me. I have heard and seen that John Ashley is a good and moral man, so he does not need to learn he has wed cheap baggage who wrote those lusty letters and spread her legs for me off and on over the years.'

Lusty letters? He must have had them amended to suit his needs. Over the years? I was sure, thanks to his travels and my assignments, I could disprove that, but he could still do me irreparable damage.

As he swept me a mocking bow and left me standing there snagged in the thorns, I wanted to scream *Liar!* and every horrible name or curse I knew. But then I would be stooping to his level. *God as my judge*, indeed! I hoped this dreadful man would meet his fate and soon. I could summon no more words to tell him how much I hated him. But I feared him too. I would rather have had clever Cromwell back to threaten me. What if he besmirched my name so that my dear Elizabeth was taken from my charge? My only hope was that Tom would destroy himself – but would he take the princess and me down with him?

If I thought Tom's actions were bad then, soon the darker days began. I felt sick to my stomach to see him flirt with Elizabeth. Oh, not blatantly at first, but a special smile, a wink, a quick touch on her back or arm or shoulder, seducing her affections. Her cheeks blazed color when he was near, and she moped about when he was gone, no doubt reliving moments with him. Oh, yes, I knew well those signs. The girl actually seemed glad when Jane Grey was taken back by her family, as if she had been some sort of rival for Tom's attention.

I took to always referring to him as 'the Queen Dowager's husband,' though that seemed not to sink in. Finally, I said, 'Although you turned the Lord Admiral's marriage proposal down, he will think you are still interested.'

'Interested in him only as a friend and guardian, of course,' she said, intently regarding her hands as if she were looking for a chipped nail. Anne's ruby ring glinted in window light. 'I find him kind and cheerful, and I enjoy his company – his wife's, too, of course,' she assured me.

I could not help myself; I turned sarcastic [and did not know until much later that a clay-brained man supposedly in Tom's employ but evidently spying for his brother Edward was eavesdropping and took each word I said for gospel truth]. A hand on my hip, I said to Elizabeth, 'If the Lord Admiral was not wed and all the Council agreed, would you want him for yourself, for he would then be the highest, noblest unmarried man in the land?'

'No, Kat, no,' she whispered. 'Do not think such or say such!'

I leaned down to whisper in her ear, as harshly as I could manage, 'Then do not look as if you desire such! His lordship obviously would have no qualms about a hasty, secret marriage after a spouse's death, but it would ruin you! If you ever plight a secret troth or look like you would, you will regret it, my girl! We all will.'

She hugged me out of my vile mood, but I began to trust her not. Soon after, when I saw her and Tom walking in the gardens with his arm around her shoulders and hers around his waist, I pressed my knuckles against my lips and cried. The next morning, I told John what I saw happening. I almost told him all, but my stomach was tied in such knots I could not say more. What if he would believe Seymour's lies over my protestations of truth? My John was a reasonable man but very protective of me. I could not risk one of his honesty – and humble rank – taking on the deceitful Lord Admiral and royal uncle. So I told myself that in omitting my past with Tom, I was protecting him as well as myself.

'You must talk to the Queen Dowager,' he advised me after I met him on the riverbank and his oarsmen rowed away. 'Perhaps she can rein him in. And, if she throws you both out, that will settle things and you can go live with Princess Mary, or if not that, your foster sister, Joan Denny, at Cheshunt in Hertfordshire, for she is with child while Sir Anthony is at court.'

'Elizabeth would never forgive me.'

'You will never forgive yourself if he steps over the line with her.'

'But he is married to a beautiful, wealthy and high-ranking woman who adores him, a woman who has made him the second – or first, I do not know – man in the kingdom!'

'Sweetheart,' he said, pulling me close, 'this is not like you. Be your rational, calm self. Do not let them panic you. Perhaps you need to lay the law down a bit more to the princess or, as I said, even ask for support from the Queen Dowager.'

I nodded and thanked him, but I was prepared to do neither yet. Elizabeth had turned stubborn on this, and if I told Katherine, it would be like telling Tom and he might find a way to have me dismissed. But I thought, with his wife in the house and my keeping a sharp eye on Elizabeth – I took to trailing her day and night – surely nothing could accelerate.

Then one morning, the door to our bedchamber, for I slept in a truckle bed myself at her feet now, banged open. Groggy with lack of sleep from worrying all night, I rolled over but saw only two big, bare male feet and hairy lower legs beneath a nightshirt hem. Was I dreaming or were we at Hatfield and John had come to spend the night? I blinked and saw no one then.

Perhaps Elizabeth had waked me up, for she was giggling at something, then she squealed. I heard a smack as I clambered to my feet, nearly tripping on my night rail. Tom was bending over between the parted bed hangings, leaning far in, saying, 'Get up, get up slugabed. Get up or I will have to tickle and even spank you!'

'My lord, for shame!' I cried. 'Get out – out!'

'Ah, two lovely ladies in *dishabille*, nectar to my sore eyes!'

'This is most unseemly, and you know it!' I told him, and pointed at the door. 'Take your leave now, my lord.'

My fourteen-year-old charge had dived under the covers and was still giggling. He dared to swat at her bottom, then, roaring with laughter, made for the door. He winked at me, swept one or both of us a bow and was gone with a slam of the door and a loud guffaw.

That morning, I asked for a word with Katherine. Her chaplain, Miles Coverdale, was just leaving after leading her through her morning devotions. 'Yes, Kat,' she said, indicating a seat on the window bench where she sat. 'You must forgive me if I yawn, for my lord keeps me up till all hours.' Her cheeks colored as if she, too, were but fourteen.

That hardly helped me get a good start with this. But John was right. I must stay rational, not emotional. What was going on behind this woman's back, which Elizabeth, bright as she was, could not cope with emotionally, must be handled with kid gloves.

'Your Grace, the princess and I are so grateful for your sharing your home with us, but she is just an impressionable girl yet and the Lord Admiral is such a dynamic man that I fear she is becoming too fond of him.'

'Oh, he is so easy to love,' she agreed cheerily. 'I can certainly understand how she might dream of having a man like that someday.'

'He loves pranks overmuch and is such a strong person she may not understand,' I stumbled on, praying the words I had rehearsed would be of some use here. 'I fear she will misconstrue his coming into her bedchamber to wake her up, especially since neither of them is yet dressed.'

'Oh!' she said, obviously surprised. A frown line appeared between her arched brows. 'Yes, my husband's tomfoolery can get out of hand, but he loves life so, loves me, too, and I am yet amazed we are together after – after everything. Such a blessing. Dear Kat, do not fret, for he means naught by it. I will not say a word to him, but will accompany him if he does such again, so Elizabeth will see it is all in fun and play.'

I was much relieved, both that she would not tell Tom what I had said and that her presence would put an end to what she so aptly termed tomfoolery. But it did not end. It all got worse.

Not only did Elizabeth's stepmother actually partake in these morning raids – coming in with Tom and pulling the covers from the princess, who protested loudly yet loved it all – but there was an incident I could not ignore or forgive.

We were at Katherine's mansion at Hanworth near Hampton Court in the summer of 1548, picnicking. What began as a combined game of hide-and-seek and tag soon began to worry me, for Tom was 'it,' and supposedly searching for all of us. He and Elizabeth had been gone quite a while, but things were just too quiet. I left my hiding place and began to search for Elizabeth myself. Then I heard her shrieks. Curse it, delighted ones again, I could tell.

I rounded a clipped yew hedge and gasped. Katherine was holding Elizabeth's arms to her sides and Tom was slicing her skirts into a hundred ribbons with a dagger. Once, twice, before I reached them, I saw him surreptitiously thrust a hand through the long cuts he'd made and fondle her inner thighs – something Katherine could not see from her vantage point.

'My Lord Admiral!' I shouted. 'Stop, stop, my lord!'

'Just retribution for a saucy wench who called me a cutup. Didn't she, my sweet?' he asked Katherine.

She nodded, laughing. 'I will buy her a new gown,' she assured me, loosing Elizabeth at last. 'It was all in good fun.'

I was appalled, especially at this woman's abetting her husband's rank behavior. Besides, in King Henry's days, no one dared draw a sword or dagger in the presence of any member of the royal family. I feared where this would all end and, once in our chamber, scolded Elizabeth soundly. Still, that night I clearly heard her heave huge sighs upon her bed and not only, I warrant, because she thought I was a stuffy watchdog. I feared the sighs were because she was yearning for more than Tom Seymour's hand upon her bare thigh.

Finally, it happened, the thing that put Katherine on my side. She, who was barren in her two previous marriages, had told us she with child. She was elated, though she became much more emotional. I planned to try to talk to her again, this time asking her if she would write to Edward Seymour to ask if the princess' household would be permitted to

218

visit Hatfield for the rest of the summer and autumn so that the princess could be assured her principal residence was being well tended.

Katherine seemed amenable and went down the hall to her husband's office to ask him what he thought. I believed her asking Tom would doom us – maybe me for certain – but I tagged along. Elizabeth's departure from here must be accomplished at any cost.

The scene that met us made me recall the time Anne Boleyn had seen her husband caressing and kissing Jane Seymour. The door stood barely ajar and Katherine swung it open. She gasped, and I peeked around her shoulder, just in time to see Elizabeth, straightening her bodice and shaking out her skirts, jump away from a huge desk against which Tom leaned. The pomade color she had on her lips was smeared on her and him.

'Thomas!' Katherine cried, and slapped at the door instead of him.

'It is not as it looks, so –' he began, but his wife fled and there I stood.

'This is your fault,' he accused, pointing his finger at me. 'You brought her here to –'

'I did not,' I cried, 'for I still could not fathom even you sinking so low! How dare you seduce or force any woman – servant or gentry, noble or royal! Your Grace, come with me, for I think we are leaving.'

'I did not mean to hurt Katherine,' Elizabeth said in the hall as I hustled her upstairs as if she were a little child. 'I do not know how it happened, Kat.'

'It happened because you did not heed my warnings and are a mere innocent at this, especially with a man of his ilk. I only pray the Council does not get wind of it and assume you let him go further than a kiss, because that is where he was heading. You know, Your Grace, when Anne of Cleves wed your father, she thought pregnancies were caused by kissing, and everyone laughed and mocked her, but reputations are as fragile as that.'

'It was only our second kiss and nothing else happened, really. And what do you mean, 'of his ilk'? A dashing man? A buccaneer?'

I amazed myself then, for I blurted out, 'A ravisher of trust and dreams and young women's bodies. I know for a fact that if he cannot seduce and yet desires, he forcibly takes.'

She gasped and stared wide-eyed at me. 'Someone you knew – He hurt – forced someone you knew?'

I nodded jerkily, not looking at her so fiercely now, but turning my eyes away, peering into my own past, my own soul. How much must I – dare I – tell her?

She began to cry, soundlessly. I waited an endless moment for her to ask who it was Tom forced, or even tell me she knew that it was I. Perhaps she was too caught up in her own shock and shame, or else she could not fathom that her strict, stern

Kat was ever in such a situation with the very devil. But she only nodded and clung to the bedpost.

I, too, turned away and began to pack, trying to calm myself, for my heart was nearly pounding out of my chest as I forced my thoughts back to this current predicament. I might value my reputation, but Elizabeth's was of utter, utmost importance and in some peril again, thanks to the bastard we must now flee.

At least the fact she had admitted it was the second kiss from Tom comforted me, for she could have lied it was the first. Still, she had always been smarter than me. But, when it came to that sugary, self-serving, seducing whoreson Tom Seymour, not smart enough.

At first, we were permitted to stay with my dear friend Joan Denny at Cheshunt from which place Elizabeth sent the Queen Dowager an apologetic letter signed *Your Humble Daughter Elizabeth*. Katherine wrote her a gracious letter in return. The fact that Joan was about to give birth made Elizabeth feel even guiltier for being sent away shamefully from her pregnant stepmother. But what bothered me was that Sir Anthony Denny quickly came home and kept asking me and Elizabeth questions, framed kindly enough, about how we had gotten on with the Lord Admiral. I could tell he was pressing for details, some of which, I feared, someone else had already told him. We both managed to remain vague and non-committal.

While we were at Cheshunt, Tom Seymour seemed to go on an increasingly dangerous rampage against his brother, something I had seen coming for years. Sir Anthony told us that Tom, who also had the title of Master of the Ordinance and Warden of Wales, was boasting that he was so popular in the western counties he could raise ten thousand armed troops. Rumors said he even stored gunpowder in his London mansion, Seymour House. When Anne Stanhope, Edward Seymour's pompous wife, argued that she should take precedence over Katherine at court affairs, Tom publicly insulted her and his brother. Tom's name was on everyone's lips, and I could only rejoice his lips were long gone from me and my princess.

At the behest of the Privy Council, we moved to Hatfield House. Except for missing Joan and her new son, I was delighted we were home again. John himself rode in from London with the news that the Seymours were now parents, for at Sudeley Castle, where Tom was no doubt hoping his heir would be born, on August 29, Katherine had been delivered of a baby girl, named Mary. The old adage that history repeated itself was never more true, I thought, and I mourned Anne Boleyn not producing the king's heir to preserve her own life all over again. Still, if she had borne the son King Henry coveted, the world might not have had Elizabeth.

'I wish we could have been with Katherine,' Elizabeth bemoaned as she, John and I sat over a late supper the day he rode in. 'I wish I could see her child.'

'I am sure you will,' I said, and took her hand across the corner of the table. 'Someday, when the Lord High Admiral is chasing pirates at sea, we shall go to see Katherine's child.'

John, frowning, cleared his throat and said, 'They say he has taken bribes from pirates to permit them to ply the seas around the Scilly Isles, and that he's used the money to buy more weapons.'

'He had best beware,' Elizabeth observed, 'else his brother will think he is raising an army against him and the Council – even against my royal brother.'

'Exactly, Your Grace,' John said. 'It is important to see not only the strengths in people but their weaknesses too.'

After we had played but one hand of primero, she insisted we walk outside without her. John had only this night before he would be heading back to his duties, and the moon threw silver light on the shadowy paths before us. I was surprised he did not sweep me off to bed at once, as he had been wont to do, but I sensed he had something on his mind.

'Can you not convince them to let you come to serve here?' I asked, leaning my head on his shoulder as we walked.

'I believe that is in sight. I was told today that

the fact I had stayed in touch with the princess through my wife while you were living with the Queen Dowager showed my loyalty to the princess.'

'Oh, John!' I threw my arms around him.

'But there is one thing,' he said, not returning my embrace but merely standing within it. Foreboding sat hard on my heart.

'What? I don't care about anything if we can be a family again!'

'One of the oarsmen who always rowed me to Chelsea used to be a bargeman for King Henry.'

'And?'

'Marley, the grizzle-headed one. He said he thought he recognized you from when you came down to the water stairs to greet me each time at Chelsea, but he could not place you at first.'

'Place me how?'

'He says when he saw Tom Seymour one morning getting on a royal barge to go upriver, he recalled that you and Tom met on his barge twenty years ago. And that he thought you were a 'pretty couple' and so kept an eye out over the next years and heard the two of you were fond lovers.'

He had said all that so calmly – typical of my John – but a fierce tenor underlay his words. How long had he harbored this knowledge, perhaps biding his time until I would tell him all that on my own? I longed to scream my denial, my hatred of Seymour. I had told my husband all the details of what had passed between Elizabeth and Tom but none of what had passed between me and Tom.

I sank onto a wooden bench in deepest moon shadow. For a moment, I thought he would continue to stand, towering over me, but he sat too, giving me a bit of space. He leaned forward his elbows on his knees, not looking at me, and waited.

'I wanted to pretend it never happened. I detest him,' I said.

'I would not like to think you are protesting overmuch. He was – your first love? You never mentioned him that way. It makes me think there was something between you still.'

I almost burst into tears. *Stay calm and rational,* I told myself. *That is what John counseled you to do when Tom tried to ruin Elizabeth's life.* 'That is precisely what he told me he would tell you if I was not his ally with the princess.'

'And would it have been true? I have seen how he works, how women adore him.'

'No!' I turned to face him before I realized that I was already crying, tears streaking my face, making my cheeks icy in the breeze. I was getting cold all over, shivering. 'It would have been another of his foul lies,' I plunged on. 'I thought if you knew, you would go after him, forsake me – oh, I do not know what I thought, but that he would ruin me and Elizabeth!'

He turned toward me, took my hands and pressed them in my lap. I was grateful; I needed something to prop me up, for I wanted to throw myself at him or upon the ground and scream and cry. 'And were you lovers – physically too? Kat, I trusted you, thought I knew you so well when we were wed that I waited months, years, to possess you and, when I did, gave no thought to the fact you were not a virgin. It is well-known among those who teach riding that, even if a woman rides sidesaddle, she can break the hymen.'

'Oh, I am so sorry, so sorry, my love.'

'I too. That you did not trust me to tell me.'

'He – it was only once. I know that sounds lame. It was the evening of Anne's coronation banquet at Westminster and—'

'Spare me the details at least. You know, I would like to take on the braggart, bastard cockscomb, even with my bare hands, but I am trusting him to ruin himself the way he has others.'

'Including me? Including me ruined for you now?'

'I did not say that. I need some time. You did not trust me enough to tell me, and that pains me sore, so—'

We both jolted as a man – it was Thomas Parry, who kept the princess's books – called out in a frenzied voice, 'John! Kat! Another messenger has ridden in from London. You are to come at once!'

Unspeaking now, not touching, we both hurried in. I swiped at my tears; John looked like a thundercloud. Elizabeth stood at the bottom of the steps to greet us. 'I see you already heard,' she said with one look at us as she threw herself into my arms. 'My dear stepmother Katherine is dead of childbed fever, just like Queen Jane! And they say the Lord Admiral is so heartbroken he has ridden back to London and left the little child with her wet nurse.'

She tugged me upstairs, where we sat for a good hour, both crying, both bearing the burden of unspoken guilt. When I finally coaxed her into bed and went to find John, for I knew I must tell him the rest of my sordid Seymour story, Tom Parry told me John had set out for London with the other messenger, even in the dark.

Thus began that awful autumn and the worst winter of our lives. I wrote a letter to John that Her Grace had given me permission to come to him in London to talk. I had no answer from him, though I tried to tell myself that such hand-carried missives sometimes went astray. I longed to tell him the rest, that Tom had raped me that night.

I agonized over the fact it seemed John did not need me, but Elizabeth did. More than once she wakened from nightmares about her dead stepmother accusing her of perfidy and betrayal. I knew those fears had been awakened by the terrible news about Katherine's death. Racked by puerperal fever, in her delirium, we heard that she had accused Tom of wanting her death, even of poisoning her, so he could wed Elizabeth. Although he lay down with his wife and held her on her sweat-soaked bed, she said she feared him. Perhaps it was only the fever talking, but my girl suffered so from it. And all that fed the London gossip mills and made the Privy Council, so we heard later, begin to gather evidence against Tom.

And through all this mental, moral torment, I wondered if poor, dead Queen Katherine – like Anne, another victim of Elizabeth's dreadful father – had spoken her fear and hatred of Tom Seymour from mere delirium, or like me, had she finally seen the man for what he was?

'Lovey,' I said to Elizabeth when I could not bear John's not knowing the whole truth about Tom and me, 'I know you need me right now, but I must beg you to give me a day or two in London to find John and speak with him. You see, we had a falling-out that night before he left.'

'Oh, Kat! I did not know. Shall I write to him for you?'

'Just give me a few days in London, where I can stay with Lady Berkley in Fleet Street and then go to find him.'

'Yes, yes, all right, but I shall miss you sorely. For years we have not been parted.'

'And I vowed I would not leave you unless I had no choice. Please, Your Grace, I need to talk to my husband.'

And so I rode to London, setting out from Hatfield at the break of dawn three weeks before Christmas, accompanied by a messenger returning to court. But a dreadful sleet storm made us put up in a house on the way. It was midafternoon the next day, with the winter sun plunging, when the man left me at the narrow three-story house of the now retired Lady Berkley, who had served Queen Anne. Though I learned to my dismay that she was in Sussex, visiting a daughter, her servants took me in with much goodwill.

I was there but a quarter of an hour before I set out on my weary horse for Charing Cross, for there lay the royal mews. For obvious reasons, hundreds of horses were not stabled near the palace itself. Whitehall and its outbuildings sprawled over twenty-four acres along the Thames, and the mews were at the northeastern reach of it, near Charing Cross.

Other buildings crowded around a central area where an aqueduct brought in water, which poured out of huge brass taps shaped like leopards' heads. John had said the maze of buildings also included dovecots to provide food for the royal falcons housed here and kennels for hunting dogs. If John was not here in this busy place, at least some of his fellows would know where to find him, I told myself.

As I approached the vast stable blocks and riding rings, my heart beat so hard I fancied I must be shaking my mount. I, who had ridden into nearly all the palaces and castles of the Tudors, into most of their country estates and manors, was terrified to ride toward the royal mews.

'Madam,' one man ahorse called out to me, 'may we be of help or you be lost?'

I prayed that all was not lost between my beloved John and me but said only, 'I am Mrs Ashley, looking for my husband John.'

'Indispensable,' he said with a gap-toothed grin, 'that he is. Talks to horses, you know, and they obey him. But I warrant, he's gone by now to his house just down the way, but you know where. Been away, then?'

'I serve the Princess Elizabeth in the country.'

'Oh, that right? Is it true she's wi' child by the Lord Admiral?'

I gasped and jerked the reins so hard my horse almost reared. 'That is a bold-faced lie, sirrah, and see you tell everyone so!'

I was appalled. London rumors! But it made me realize I must hurry back to my princess. She must show herself, she must disprove such lies or all could be lost in her efforts even to be near her brother's throne.

I hurried to John's house, actually the sprawling top story above an apothecary, and rode around in back where the crooked outside stairs twisted up. I gave a neighbor boy a groat to guard my horse, lifted my skirts and hurried up the slightly slippery steps. In the fading light, made dimmer by the shadows cast by other tiled or thatch-roofed houses, I could see John through a back window bent over a writing table lit by four fat candles.

I prayed he was writing to me. Suddenly shy and afraid, for I knew I could not do without him, even to help Her Grace get along in life, I screwed up my courage and tapped my fingernail on the thick pane of glass.

He looked up and jumped up. 'Kat!' he cried, and hurried to the door.

I did not wait to see if he would spurn me but threw myself into his arms, clamping my own arms hard around his narrow waist and turning my head against his chest where I could hear the thudding of his heart. Thank God, this time he returned the embrace.

'John, please, I cannot bear life without you,' I said in a rush as my tears started. 'I love you, only you. I swear to you on my mother's grave I lay with the Seymour wretch only once and by force. Please, I—'

He drew me inside and sat down, pulling me into his lap, but not before I saw he was writing his riding book, sketches of horses and all. 'I started to tell you that night,' I rushed on, fearful if I stopped that he would turn cold again, 'but then everything happened at the worse moment, and I wrote to you that there was more to tell. That night of Anne's coronation he attacked me after he saw us talking at my table and followed me out into the hall, thinking I had planned a tryst with you. I – as you may have seen, I had too much to drink. I was so dizzy, but I still fought back. I was afraid to tell you he had ravished me and that at Chelsea he tried to blackmail me into helping him get close to the princess, or he said he would tell you we had been lovers all these years. John, I never coupled with him, and avoided him for years – and then I found and loved you and realized what real love could be. That night he took me by force, he was raving jealous.'

'Raving jealous,' he repeated, gripping my upper arms and seeming to look through me, as if he saw it all. 'Yes, I, too, when I heard about you and him. I could kill Seymour, but now I may not have to.'

We both got very still. He cupped my face, wiped at my tears with his thumbs, then gently kissed my nose and mouth. It finally sank in what he had told me last. 'What else has he done besides try to ruin my life and Elizabeth's too?' I asked.

'First, we will not let him ruin yours, though he may try to bring her down in his fall. I heard but an hour ago – and rejoiced – that he has just been arrested. He had evidently hatched some mad plot to wrest control of the king from his brother, perhaps even declare himself king. Late last night he got past Edward's guards and into the boy's bedroom. When Edward's spaniel barked at him, he ran the dog through with a sword.'

Picturing that – the boy's horror – I gasped. 'Which,' I said, 'makes his drawn dagger slicing Elizabeth's skirts apart seem mere child's play. John, some man at the mews where I went to find you said there are rumors Elizabeth is carrying

Seymour's child. That is blasphemy. How have such things been noised about?'

'Can someone who worked with Cromwell so long ask that? The rise of one spymaster only breeds others, even if the first is dead. Besides the Lord Protector hating him, the bombast of Tom Seymour is its own trumpet of bad tidings.'

'My dear lord, I only want the princess safe and everything between you and me to be healed. After you left that night, I wrote you a letter—'

'You said you did. I pray it did not say what you just told me in it, for I never had it.'

'No, I just wrote that there was much more to tell of Seymour. But now I must get to the princess, warn her.'

'I will send you back in the morning and would go myself but the Lord Protector has summoned me to him. I have trained horses for him before. Maybe I will learn something that can help. But tonight, my love, I would say your time and body belong only to me.'

'And my heart. Always, my heart only for you.'

He stood me up, lifted me in his arms, and carried me straight away to his neatly made bed. Indeed, we mussed it up. He made dusty, tear-salted, windblown and shaken me feel like a queen, one who is beloved. With our eager bodies, even, I believe, our joined souls, we sealed again the marital pact between us. It was a second wedding night, only sweeter since he now knew all and still wanted me. After we had risen for wine and meat pies, we tumbled back in bed and loved so hard and long that no one else even existed.

But when cruel dawn came, he sent me home with his servant William; a man named Hornby, a yeoman of the chamber; and another friend, Will Russell, a gentleman of the chamber. I could not bear to be parted from him and sobbed silently halfway back. I would have surely been hysterical had I known that, when he reached the Lord Protector's Somerset House, John was detained and questioned about what he knew of my time at Chelsea.

But worse greeted me at Hatfield. I had barely changed my gown and told Elizabeth all was well between John and me. Before I could tell her that the Lord Admiral had been arrested and that vile rumors about her were abroad in London, a large contingent of men rode in, as if they had been at my heels.

Sir Robert Tyrwhitt, who was to be Elizabeth's examiner, informed us that, after refusing to answer the Privy Council's questions in his usual high-handed manner, Tom Seymour had been charged with treason and taken to the Tower. Though the Princess Elizabeth was only under house arrest here, some who had served her were to be taken away and interrogated about a possible plot of Seymour's to wed the princess and seize the throne.

If I had not been so terrified for Elizabeth – and yes, for myself and John – I would have done a dance that Tom was ruined. But those to be dragged off to the Tower included Thomas Parry, my husband and me. With a burly guard standing over me, I was given ten minutes to gather a saddlebag of clothes. I could hear Elizabeth below, protesting in a nervous, strident voice, 'We have done nothing wrong, nothing against His Majesty, my brother. Katherine Ashley is my appointed governess and cannot be taken away!'

She and I managed one quick hug and a few whispered words. The last thing I recall hearing as I was roughly boosted up on a horse was Tyrwhitt's voice informing Her Grace, 'The Lord Protector of the realm has appointed my wife, Lady Tyrwhitt, your new governess and, by all that is holy, you will tell one or the other of us all you know about this plot!'

# CHAPTER 12

THE TOWER OF LONDON

*January 28, 1549*

The sound of the key grating in the door of my cell pierced my soul. I had never been more frightened by what had been and what was yet to come.

'Ah, Mrs Ashley,' the man who was my examiner intoned as he peered into the dimly lit cell that had been my prison for nigh on six weeks. At first they had just let me sit and stew – and freeze in this wretched place. 'I give you good day and bid you to join us for a tour of the Tower. The Lord Lieutenant has told me that has made more than one pretty bird sing. And, I warrant, such a learned woman as to have been the Lady Elizabeth's governess and councilor all these years is no simpleton, but a keen and able learner.'

I thanked God for full petticoats, else my shaking knees would have betrayed me. *Betrayed me . . .* Her Grace had whispered, 'Don't betray me!' to her closest confidantes before we were taken from her at Hatfield House.

'This way,' Sir Thomas Smith went on, frowning. He beckoned me forward as if I would dare to gainsay his command.

Wrapped in a fur-lined cloak draped with his chain of office, he was the Privy Council's secretary, no doubt come to torment me again with endless questions I had refused to answer. Had the Lady Elizabeth encouraged Tom Seymour to gather forces to overthrow her brother, the king? Did she know aught of rumors that Seymour had poisoned his wife so that he could wed Elizabeth? Had she hoped to make Seymour king or at least Lord Protector in place of his brother? And had I, Katherine Ashley, as the closest friend, the substitute for the deceased mother of Her Grace, the Lady Elizabeth, promoted lewd enticements in Chelsea, even under the nose of Tom Seymour's wife, the widow of King Henry?

As I stepped into the corridor, I saw that Sir Thomas was not alone. The beef-witted turnkey Gib, who brought my daily sustenance, waited just down the hall to tag along as a guard. Also glowering at me, the big-shouldered Sir Leonard Chamberlain, Lord Lieutenant of the Tower, stood at the ready, as if one lone, hedged-in woman of forty-two years would dash for escape through these mazes of halls and corkscrew stairs in dim, damp Beauchamp Tower.

The Tower of London was not one but a series of towers. My place of imprisonment was a semi-circular structure of three stories with inscriptions of its many victims carved into the walls. Out my narrow, deep-set window I could see Tower Green to the east, the very place where Elizabeth's mother and King Henry's fifth queen, Catherine Howard, had been beheaded. It amazed me to think that I, Kat from rural Devon, had known those Tudor-bred, Tudor-wed, even the Tudor dead. But more than the loss of them all, I grieved my separation from my fifteen-year-old charge, whom I dearly loved and desperately feared for.

'Exactly where are we going?' I asked, trying to summon a steady voice. I had been arrested under orders that I be 'seriously examined,' which was coded talk for the Privy Council's permission to use torture to extract my confession. Though they had not yet done so, I was wary, forever teetering on the jagged edge of outright terror. Barely sleeping each night, I had wandered through memories, tormenting myself with sins of my past and shattered hopes for my future.

God save me, women were not exempt from torture here and, as the so-called weaker sex, were considered easy marks to talk. I knew the once bold Queen Anne when brought here babbled much out of fear for her life. Last week a guard had made a cruel jest that Queen Anne and, later, Queen Catherine Howard had 'talked their heads off' once they were enclosed within these walls. I fought such temptation every moment I was entombed here.

In faith, I knew far too much of the history of

this place. Now not just I but the only two men I had ever loved – may the one be cursed, the other blessed – were imprisoned somewhere here beside the misty, murky Thames.

The cold river wind slapped me as we walked the green toward the White Tower. The gray sky – all was gray upon gray in this wretched place – shuddered with sleet. When I blinked, my eyelashes were wet – from tears or the weather, I knew not. At least out here I could breathe fresh air and hear city sounds. The bells of several churches clanged the time – three of the clock. Carters and peddlers shouted their wares from across the moat and tall walls, much sweeter sounds than the rattle of keys, or worse, the echo of disembodied voices from the dungeons of this place.

How I wished for an omen I would soon be safe and free. But one of the black-as-night Tower ravens screeched at me. A fierce beast from the royal menagerie in the Lion Tower roared just before the iron portcullis at the end of the Middle Tower slammed its teeth into the pavement as if to keep me in and salvation out. When I stumbled on a crooked paving stone, Sir Thomas put his hand to my elbow and spoke.

'No more cobbled-up excuses. Time to tell true, and you know it, Mrs Ashley.' He squeezed my arm before he let loose. His eyes seemed to pierce through me. Whatever abilities had brought him to the young king's Privy Council, I knew what talents made him their examiner: the man's mere presence chilled one to the bone, and he could twist and record the merest sigh or slip of the tongue faster than summer lightning. I drew back; they pushed me on. I feared – I knew – they were taking me to torture. I would be maimed for life; I would never live through such; I would blurt out all.

Just ahead of us sat the stone church of St Peter in Chains, a name so perfect for this place. Under the paving stones within, Anne Boleyn's body lay yet today, stuffed in an old wooden chest for arrows because no one had thought to bring a coffin for her. St Peter's lay just across the now frost-blighted green where had stood the scaffold for beheadings.

Even now I could see the swing of the sword that cleaved Anne's head from her body. I felt the bile rise in my throat again. Though I had only served Anne off and on in my earliest years at court, I had felt a bond with her, for she had needed me and trusted me with her confidences, with the ring for her child – and with Elizabeth's well-being. That time she had ordered Cromwell to bring me to the Tower she had demanded the promise of him that I be sent where Elizabeth went, at least until her majority. Though Anne and Cromwell were long gone, I had taken Anne's wish as my passion to protect Elizabeth. I felt close to Anne because I had become the mother Elizabeth had lost. Oh, yes, Anne Boleyn had given Elizabeth Tudor life, but I had given her love.

And so, in my deepest dreams, I had somehow been haunted by Anne. Worries I would let her down kept me awake some nights, and I fancied she sometimes spoke to me in my sleep, desperately, passionately, even as she had that last moment when she hugged me farewell in her prison room here at the Tower and I vowed to be her girl's good teacher and friend always.

But what was to become of us now? Would my lovey's interrogators charge her and imprison her? What if I shared Anne's fate here in the place she died? For indeed, it was now my turn to face the terrors of the Tower, ones I could not escape even in sleep.

For, though Anne had died more than twelve years ago, in a dream last night, I had seen her again. She'd come into my cell, crying, 'I beg you, tend my girl. Red-haired, the hue of my martyr's blood spilled for her – see?' she'd cried, touching her neck, then holding out beseeching crimson hands to me. 'Innocent, I was innocent. I praised the king from the scaffold when I should have cursed him . . . all, all so he would not harm Elizabeth. Innocent . . . tell them you are innocent and she is, too . . . take care of my girl . . .'

I shook my head to clear it, so exhausted I was seeing apparitions even now. Light-headed, I was floating, barely putting one foot before the other.

We entered the White Tower, which stood in the very center of the walls, then down we went, down narrow, twisting stairs below the ancient chapel. I gasped when they swung open the small, creaking door of a fetid-smelling cell, small and dark as an arrow-box coffin. The short, narrow door had no grate; all was dark within. I expected to be shoved inside and ducked to avoid banging my head.

Behind me, the Lord Lieutenant's voice boomed out, 'We call it the Little Ease, so small no one can stand erect in it nor sit, and 'tis as black as the pit of hell down here. So easy for one to be forgotten . . .'

His words struck me hard. One of my worst fears, even long before I made a devil's bargain to be brought to court from distant Devon, long before I began to serve the magnificent and terrible Tudors, was that I would be of no account in this life. I was living my life on the fringes of Dartmoor, which I now longed for with all my heart. Its mists could hide one, its desolation, loneliness and hauntings were naught compared to this looming horror.

Instead of Anne Boleyn's singsong pleas in my head, I heard a voice chant words I used to sing as a child: *Devon, O Devon, in wind and rain, my heart returns to you again.* Was I going mad in this place?

To my shock and utter relief, they turned me about and led me up and away from the dungeon of Little Ease to another of the towers. There they showed me the rack, which pulled one's joints asunder, the very rack where they had broken the Protestant martyr Anne Askew before her death. In other soot-smoked chambers, they paraded past my wide eyes dreadful instruments they called thumbscrews, obscene-looking knives, pincers and pokers heating in a brazier full of glowing coals. I dry-heaved when they displayed for me the collection of gleaming teeth that had been extracted from hapless prisoners. I began to shake so hard my own teeth chattered.

Worse even were what they boasted would be best for a 'woman's tender mercies, for they are named for womankind.' The Scavenger's Daughter was an iron ring that brought the head and feet and hands together in a backward circle of wrenching bones and muscles. The Iron Maiden, a life-sized case hammered out in a female form, pierced the person with iron spikes until their screams echoed 'clear across the green to my very lodgings hard by the Bell Tower,' the Lord Lieutenant observed with a sad shake of his hoary head. I could hear the very Tower walls echo with silent screams of lost souls.

'I will brook no excuse, so I pray our guest takes these things to heart – a word to the wise, Sir Thomas,' the Lord Lieutenant said as if trying to keep a naughty child in line or as if I were not even present. How often had men treated me thus, speaking in my earshot as if what I thought was of no matter in the grand scheme of things. 'And,

243

no doubt,' he went on, 'the governess of a Tudor has learned to be wise, however dense they both have pretended to be of late.'

'Aye, appointed to the Lady Elizabeth by King Henry himself, weren't you, Katherine Champernowne Ashley?' Sir Thomas asked, using my whole name as if he were familiar with the entire record of my life. 'With a nod from clever Cromwell, I hear.'

Now I could only nod. That question I could answer with impunity, at least. Lord Cromwell's sharp visage floated before me, then Henry Tudor's florid face – even my father's, as if I were reviewing my life before my impending death. Why did men ever seem to rule my life, rule the world? From my first days it had been so, but I had fought it and had helped my sweet, strong Elizabeth learn to fight it too. Even the Lord Jesus valued women, for to whom did He first appear after His resurrection but a woman? And three women boldly kept a vigil near the cross as he was tortured and died . . . was tortured and died. . . .

I shook my head to clear it. I must cling to the vow we, Her Grace's loyal friends who had been her family in her cruel exile, had made. We would not answer their vile, accusatory interrogations. John, I knew, would hold to that, no matter what, so – through my death or his – I might lose him for good. Parry, Her Grace's treasurer, had sworn wild horses would pull him apart before he would divulge the goings-on he had seen between our royal charge and that blackguard Tom Seymour. And therein, in all that I knew about Tom, all I had buried deep within me – not only of him and Her Grace, but of him and me – lay my deepest terrors. What would I blurt out if they tortured me?

But again, to my utter shock and relief, they escorted me away, back to my own cell. Despite the dank straw I had stuffed in the cracks around the window in a vain attempt to keep out the cold, despite the moldy walls and reeking chamber pot, it had never looked so grand or welcoming. I assumed these men meant to give me one last chance before they used their horrid instruments upon my tender woman's body.

'Such a beautiful body, full breasts, lush hips and strong legs to ride a horse – or a man,' John had whispered once, when he was wooing me. Unlike John, Tom had always just taken what he wanted and never with pretty words, for he thought women on their backsides at his feet were his birthright. I could hurt him now for all he had done with but a few comments, yet then my Elizabeth might be pulled down even more into the mire, her slim prospects ever to sit England's throne forever gone.

'Sit,' Sir Thomas said, and shoved me onto one of the two stools in the room. He perched behind a portable desk that had not been there today, though he had brought it with him twice before. 'I believe you see what awaits you if you refuse to answer our queries. I would read this to you, but I hear you are not only a fast reader but a good one – one who reads from the heart, I heard Queen Mary herself say once. Do not think to so much as bend that paper, Mrs Ashley, for we have two copies already, one en route to the Lord Protector to share with the Council. Quick, now. I'll brook no more of your delays or clever bantering. Here is the confession.' He held out to me a piece of parchment, written top to bottom, and I took it from his hand.

*Whose confession?* I thought, fearful at first they had forged one for me to sign. Surely not one from Her Grace or my lord John. *No, Parry's signature was here at the end, his writing indeed, but shaky. Dear Lord, had they tortured Parry to get this confession, and now they will do the same to me?*

Despite the dim light, I skimmed the piece. Dictated, evidently to Sir Thomas, was line after line of incidents and snippets of conversation Parry claimed to have witnessed *between Her Grace, the Lady Elizabeth, and Sir Thomas Seymour, Baron Sudeley, in the Chelsea household of the Queen Dowager, Katherine Parr, widow of our gracious sovereign, King Henry VIII of recent memory, and then the wife of said Baron Sudeley.*

Some of it Parry had indeed seen; some was secondhand hearsay, just a bit off, tittle-tattle from others. Plenty of it implicated me for, as governess, I knew I should have stood up to Tom more than I did. Yet I had even gone to his wife, the king's widow. I had lectured Elizabeth and warned Tom away, but neither of them had heeded me. Should I not now at least tell them those things in my own defense? Parry had given up what he had vowed wild horses would not drag out of him, so I, too, was surely doomed.

My insides almost let loose. My heartbeat kicked up to a canter, then a wild gallop. My hands shook so hard, the piece of parchment rattled.

'The game is up,' Sir Thomas said as he dipped his quill in the inkwell and poised it over fresh paper. With his other hand, he pulled Parry's confession from me and set it beside his blank paper with a flourish. 'So,' he prompted, when I yet sat still as a stone, staring at nothing and everything before me, 'let us begin at the beginning and tell the truth, all of it. You have seen the torments that await liars and those who defy us!'

The Privy Council's examiner's words resounded in my ears and brain and soul. Another powerful man held sway over my life. How I wish I had found the courage to stand up to Cromwell, even to the king, and above all, to Tom Seymour. I know not what inner stamina then stoked my heart and head, but I decided then I must do my best to stand up to him, even in this fearsome place, for myself and for Elizabeth.

'That is mere hearsay and quite slanted,' I dared, with a nod at Parry's confession.

'Are you calling the princess's bookkeeper, Thomas Parry, a liar for this confession he has written out for us?' he demanded, waving it in my face. 'I warrant Elizabeth Tudor has confessed to all of this and more by now. It is obvious she was in collusion with the Lord Admiral to harm the king and overthrow the power of the Privy Council and the Lord Protector!'

'Is it you, Sir Thomas, who is giving testimony or me?' I spit back at him. As frightened as I was, his hectoring got my hackles up, especially his insinuating that my princess would admit to treason. 'Cease trying to put words in my mouth, and I will tell you what happened – none of it to be held against a fourteen-year-old girl who was in the care of the Queen Dowager – to whom the Council sent us – and her husband, the Lord Admiral, who was given his rank and estates by King Henry, or by King Edward, who then held him in high and fond regard, or by that very Council!'

He puffed out his cheeks and leaned back from the table. I held my breath, amazed I had come up with those words. 'Enough about the princess who is not my duty,' he insisted. 'Do *you* favor the Lord Admiral or his cause then, Mrs Ashley?'

That set me back, but I prayed he knew naught of my past with Tom. Even though John had ferreted it out, he surely would not tell these examiners, for that could doom me.

'Favor that blackguard in what way?' I challenged, stalling for more time to think.

'Once, while at Chelsea, you were overheard to

say to the princess that the Lord Admiral, if not wed, could be the highest ranking unmarried male in the kingdom – implying he could be a suitable husband for her.'

'More hearsay, obviously gathered by an eavesdropper who hoped to ingratiate himself with those who hired him. I was assuring myself she knew to keep clear of him, and she assured me at that time she would not want to wed him, even if he were free to do so. And if your spy was of any account, sir, he no doubt would have told you I warned her that any marriage she considered would need permission of the Council and the Lord Protector! Write that all down, sir, every word of it!'

'All right then, Mrs Ashley, take your time and tell me more in your own words. You are well spoken, madam, and no one's fool, and I respect that. I am ready if you are,' he said, and, after scribbling all that down, dipped and poised his pen again. When I just glared at him, he said, 'Let us go on to this, then. Master Parry says in his deposition—'

'A much better term than calling it a confession, sir.'

'He says you rode in great haste to London three or so weeks before Christmas after a hurried conversation with the princess. Did you seek out Thomas Seymour that day and discuss his plans to capture the person of the king or pass on information about his wedding Elizabeth Tudor?'

'I did not, sir, but I shall recount for your ears and pen – and any eavesdroppers you yet here employ – exactly what happened.'

*Examinations and Depositions of Katherine Ashley, Governess to Princess Elizabeth, Regarding Possibly Questionable Dealings with Thomas Seymour, Lord High Admiral. The answers of Mistress Ashley. What communication she had with my Lady Elizabeth's grace as touching the marriage with the Lord Admiral:*

*Mrs Ashley saith she came to London but only to speak with her husband Mr Ashley. There came home with her William, Mr Ashley's servant and his horse-keeper; and one Hornby, Yeoman of the Chamber; and William Russell, Gentleman. But indeed the very matter was because there had been a jar betwixt her husband and her, and he parted from her in a displeasure, as she thought, and therefore she could not be merry till she had spoken with him. For she had sent him a letter, but he had made no answer. And so she stayed for him, and he did tarry with her all that night. Her errand was done when her husband and she were agreed. She saith she did not speak at that time neither with the Lord Admiral nor no one of his men.*

'I must say, I understand marital quarrels, Mrs Ashley, but you yet insist you did not carry a message from or to the princess concerning the Lord Admiral?'

'I believe if you must ask that question again

after I have answered it, your ears need a good cleaning out, Sir Thomas.' [I must admit, at this point, I was becoming more emboldened. Even though I am recalling this dreadful day from memory, I assure you I am not telling more here than was truly said.] 'As I have oft done that for the princess when she was small, I could oblige you. Let me see what you have written, to be certain it is correct.'

'I am not your pupil, and you are to take orders from me.'

'Then move on to your next topic.'

'Very well. What was the argument between you and your husband about?'

My hard-won facade of bravado almost crumbled. For if he could pry that from me, I was doomed. All the Council needed was to hear I had been enamored of Tom Seymour years ago. Could Tom himself, interrogated here in the Tower or at his trial for treason, have even lied that our liaison was ongoing, as he had threatened to tell my John?

'Are you wed, Sir Thomas?' I countered. Lord help me, how my voice shook, despite my brazen plan.

'Many years, Mrs Ashley. But I need to know—'

'Then you fully realize how petty arguments can become large ones. It began as a trifle, but I was so emotional that I reacted over-much, and he stalked out and then we heard the news that the Queen Dowager had died, which greatly grieved

251

us both as well as the princess, and then he went off in a huff before I could explain . . .'

'Yes, yes, all right,' he said, starting to scribble all that, then just giving up. 'Mr Ashley said it was a petty squabble too.'

My head snapped up. They had asked John all this, trying to snare us in a trap. But, by the grace of God – and my John's bold spirit – he must have stood up to them too, and, even though he had said he was jealous of Tom, he did not give up on me. That was all I needed to give me even more courage – that and knowing my lovey was safe from these wretches.

'I ask you to record something, though, sir,' I said, my voice now more my own. He filled his pen again and sat alert. 'Put down that it is so cold here that I cannot sleep at night and have the chilblains, and it is so dark I cannot in the day see to read, for I must stop the window with straw – put that down, sir.'

He actually wrote my complaint down. 'And you may end with this,' I added. 'For if it were possible that I might be with Her Grace again, never would I speak of marriage to her – no, not to win all the world. As touching Parry's secondhand account of Thomas Seymour's boldness in the princess' bedchamber, the Lord I take as my witness, I spoke roughly to the Lord Admiral to get out of her chamber and leave off his untoward play. But he swore he would tell my lords of the Council, 'So what if I do? I would they all saw it!' At last

I told the queen of it, who made a small matter of it to me and said she could come with him herself, and so she did ever after. Do you have that all, sir, crossing the *t*'s and dotting each *i*?'

'Yes, yes, sign here then, for I weary of your denials of any guilt.'

'Denials? I have told you all the truth, and not a bit of it conflicts with Thomas Parry's words – or, I warrant, my husband John's!'

So I signed boldly in my best hand, *Katherine Ashley*, and prayed to be done with it – and that on Elizabeth's end, harried at Hatfield, Her Grace was holding up well.

*January 28, 1549*

*Princess Elizabeth to Edward Seymour, Duke of Somerset, Lord Protector:*

*To my Lord Protector's grace, My very good lord:*

*As concerning Kat Ashley, she never advised me unto marriage with your brother but said always (when any talked of my marriage) that she would never have me marry – neither in England nor out of England – without the consent of the king's majesty, Your Grace's and the Council's. Others have told me that there goeth rumors abroad which be greatly both against mine honor and honesty, which above*

253

*all other things I esteem: that I am with child by my Lord Admiral. My lord, these are shameful slanders, for the which, besides the great desire I have to see the King's Majesty, I most heartily desire Your Lordship that I may come to the court, that I may show myself there as I am. Written in haste from Hatfield this 28 of January.*

*Your assured friend to my little power, Elizabeth*

*March 7, 1549, to my very good lord, my Lord Protector:*

*As for Kat Ashley, I request that it would please Your Grace and the rest of the Council to be good unto her. First, because that she hath been with me a long time and many years, and hath taken great labor and pain in bringing of me up in learning and honesty. The second is because I think that whatsoever she hath done in my Lord Admiral's matter as concerning the marrying of me, she did it because, knowing him to be one of the Council, she thought he would not go about any such thing without he had the Council's consent. For I have heard her many times say that she would never have me marry in any place without Your Grace's and the Council's consent. The third cause is because that it shall and doth make men think that I am not clear of the deed myself, but that it is pardoned in me because of my youth, because that she I love so well is in such a place as the Tower.*

*Also if I may be so bold, not offending, I beseech Your Grace and the rest of the Council to be good to Master Ashley, her husband, which because he is my kinsman.*

*Your assured friend to my little power, Elizabeth*

[It was years after I suffered in the Tower that I found copies of my testimony and of the letters Elizabeth had written on my behalf, for she had them in her things, which I cared for. Without her pleas, despite my standing up for myself and John's saying nothing incriminating even in the face of Tom Parry's confession and threat of torture, I might have perished there. As it was, I spent weeks within, suffering not only from that cold, cruel place but from having been separated and dismissed from my lovely, bright girl, who – God help me, though I never told a soul then, though she was royal and I of lower rank – was like a daughter to me.]

# CHAPTER 13

**M**rs Ashley,' Sir Leonard Chamberlain, Lord Lieutenant of the Tower, informed me, poking only his head in the door of my cell, 'good news for you and Master Ashley, for word has come you are both to be released today.'

So great was my shock and relief, I gasped and broke into tears. 'And to be returned t-to Her G-grace's household?' I stammered. By my reckoning, this was the nineteenth of March, and I had been in this place for nigh on four months. I dashed tears from my face and waited for news of the second-most-desired dream, a reunion with Elizabeth.

'Hardly that,' he told me, 'but you are to be released into the custody of one William Cecil, privy secretary to Edward Seymour, the Lord Protector Somerset. I'll be back for you within the hour,' he added, and closed the door.

Freedom! A reunion with John, though not with Elizabeth. I must be grateful for this blessing, yet I cursed those who would keep me from my girl. Would John and I ever be permitted to serve her again?

I was tempted to leave all my worldly goods here, for I had worn out my three gowns, which now looked and smelled of this fetid place. But I had no idea whether John would be reinstated at his post either. We might be forced to go north to beg bread and board from his stepbrother. So I rolled up my soiled, tattered garments and tucked them under my arm. I washed my face in my drinking water, since it was the only clean I had. I spit on the floor and, when the Lord Lieutenant came for me, followed him out with my head held high.

Ah, to breathe fresh air again. But where was John and in what condition would I find him?

'Kat, sweetheart,' came his voice behind me, and I turned to see him – thinner than he had been but even taller than I remembered – hurrying toward me. He looked unkempt with ragged beard and shaggy hair, but I would not have cared one whit had he turned blue. He hugged me hard, then set me back at once, turning to Lord Lieutenant Chamberlain and the turnkey Gib. 'I warrant,' John said, glaring at them, 'I was in a cell just above hers these months and never knew it. But I felt you close, my Kat. If you have no objection,' he told them, 'let us be going.'

We walked past the green where Queen Anne had met her fate. I had a hundred questions about Tom Seymour's treason trial, about why we were released now, and the well-being of my princess, but I said naught. I knew Tom had been convicted, and that the penalty for the charges was beheading.

As we traversed the central cobbled courtyard, I shivered with excitement, though it was a mild weather day, so different from the ones I'd suffered within these cold stone walls. Moving only my eyes, I glanced up and around, vowing I would never be in this vile place again, unless I came here before her crowning should my Elizabeth ever mount the throne.

And then I saw him.

At first, I thought it must be a ghost or a trick of the noontide light, but a gaunt, bearded face peered from a narrow window three floors up, in a different tower from the one where John and I had been held. Tom Seymour! I stubbed my toe on a cobblestone, but John held me up. The Lord Lieutenant, then John, evidently saw Tom too, but no one so much as paused.

'He's to die a traitor's death tomorrow on Tower Hill,' Master Chamberlain said. 'So sad that the king's uncle betrayed him.'

Neither of us said a word. I tried to summon up some sympathy – after all, Tom must have not betrayed us in his trial. But whatever I had once felt for him lay already dead, beheaded and bled out. Truth be told, I detested the man I once thought I had loved. And more than that, though revenge was not a Christian virtue, after all I had suffered from him, I could have suddenly danced beneath his prison window. I had to stop myself from cheering he was finally getting what he deserved, from jeering at him for his lies and pompousness – and for his brutal rape of me so long ago.

But I feared this might be a trap, to see what we would say or do when we heard of his coming demise and caught a last glimpse of the man. Nor could I budge to so much as quickly thumb my nose at Tom, for John grappled me tighter to his side, and we walked out through the gate toward the street without breaking stride. At least, I thought with nearly as much relief as in leaving the hellhole that was the Tower, Elizabeth and I and this kingdom were rid of Tom Seymour forever.

I gasped when the two guards there lowered their pikes to stop us. John's body tensed as if he would spring at them, but the Lord Lieutenant nodded to them and, pointing, said, 'They may pass. Over there, William Cecil to see that you are well tended.'

'I am sick to death of being well tended,' John whispered out of the side of his mouth, but he greeted the young man who strode toward us with a strong handshake.

William Cecil was young, at least by my standards, late in his second decade mayhap, though he sported a short, shovel-shaped beard, which made him look a bit grave. His sharp eyes were alert in his face, such intelligent, lively eyes, not flat, like Cromwell's. Yet I was done with trusting men who owed their souls to the great powers of this kingdom, and this man served Edward Seymour, the cold, cruel Lord Protector I had seen at far too close range, a man who ruled the young king and was evidently content to see his brother Tom go to his death.

Still, the wooden coach to which Cecil showed us looked so inviting, as did the mugs of ale one of his two men – guards? – offered us. I warned myself that the ale might be drugged, but John drank it straight down while he patted the closest of the four horses harnessed to the coach.

Once we were inside, I saw a repast of bread and cheese laid out for us on a tray, but I was too excited and upset to eat. Master Cecil climbed in behind us, then called out, 'To the Great South Road!'

As the coach lurched forward, I could bear the suspense no longer. 'I pray your orders are not to take us to exile, Master Cecil.'

'I swear to you both by all that's holy, you are in good hands. Not only those of my master the Lord Protector, but I vow you can count me among the future protectors of the woman you both served. Here,' he muttered, digging in his leather purse, 'my formal introduction. I am also the newly appointed land accounts manager for the Princess Elizabeth – the estates her father left her, including Hatfield, Woodstock and Enfield Chase. I assure you that took some doing with the Protector. I have a letter from her here, sadly not a personal one to you, for she was afraid to risk that, but one which beseeches me to do all in my power to see you were freed and cared for. Hence, we are off to my country house at Wimbledon, where my wife awaits her guests with a chamber and hot meal.'

My hands shook as hard as the coach rattling down the graveled street. I opened the first of two letters and recognized Elizabeth's hand-writing, asking her 'recorder of the rents, the trustworthy William Cecil,' to see that two unnamed prisoners were well cared for. I sighed and leaned back into John's embrace against the hard leather seat.

'Thank you, Master Cecil. Thank you that I know she is well,' I cried, and pressed to my breasts her signature I knew intimately, for I had taught her to write it.

CECIL'S HOUSE AT WIMBLEDON, NEAR LONDON

So that was my introduction to the man who would become my princess's and my queen's most important and loyal adviser, though I hardly knew that then. Still, hints of William Cecil's fierce loyalty and ambition for himself – but also for England and Elizabeth – abounded, so I decided he was a far different sort of man than Thomas Cromwell had been.

That evening, after we had bathed, Cecil and his wife, Mildred, dined with us and told us all

261

they knew of Tom's trial. He had been obstinate and insulting to the end. But, though Elizabeth was still under house arrest, Cecil said she had admitted to no wrongdoing and so had saved us all.

'Elizabeth of England may be young and yet untried,' he told us, 'but she has her father's mettle and, I pray, the morals of a good Christian, something that seemed to slip from His Majesty's grasp the more power he claimed for himself. Poor Prince Edward is so controlled by the Lord Protector, he can hardly be himself. And the Princess Mary – should she ever mount the throne, I fear that England will be turned topsy-turvy in religious matters once again.'

John and I slept the clock round that night and were only awakened by Cecil's seven-year-old son by his first marriage, calling to his dogs in the gardens behind the house. After making certain there was no trouble outside, we fell back into the bed in each other's arms and held tight. With my back pressed to John's chest as though I sat in his lap, we were yet unable to believe we were together and free. I thought we had talked ourselves out last night, sharing all that had happened to us during our time in the Tower, but John said, 'He dies today, the third person you have known well whose life is forfeit as a traitor.'

'But the difference is Queen Anne was innocent, and, like the charges against her, that devil

262

Cromwell's charges were overblown. But Tom Seymour has made his own bed, and – I did not mean it that way.'

'To hell with the wretched past. You and I have made our bed, my love, and will lie in it together.'

He turned me to him and so it was that we were one again.

You might know that demented Tom Seymour fought his captors on the scaffold and had to be hacked down. Just before that horrid scene, so Cecil said, the wretch had the gall to tell one of his servants, 'Remember the charge I gave you!'

The servant was questioned, and two letters in crude, scribbled code were found in the man's shoe, one to each of the king's royal sisters, urging them to press on against the Lord Protector, the brother Tom had always hated.

And speaking of hatred, the entire thing made me sick to my stomach. Picturing the scene of Tom's death appalled me, for, as different as it was from Anne Boleyn's execution, it brought all that back to haunt me. I wished I could forgive Tom for his wretched treatment of me and Elizabeth – I prayed I could – but I could not, even though he'd paid the ultimate price.

I lay abed for several days while John tended to Cecil's horses and I longed to tend Elizabeth. I felt both better and worse when John said Cecil had reported that, upon hearing of Seymour's death, Elizabeth had shown no emotion to those watching her closely and had said only, 'Today died a man of much wit and little judgment.'

However clever and strong she sounded, I knew she was yet tormented, not for the loss of Tom Seymour, but of her reputation and whatever shreds of safety and privacy she had once enjoyed. And when I learned that the Lady Tyrwhitt, the governess who had replaced me, was Katherine Parr's stepdaughter, I knew how Elizabeth must yet be suffering in lonely, desperate silence, fearful she had lost a future.

John and I desperately needed an income, and I hesitated to rely on the Cecils' goodwill much longer. So Cecil arranged for John to work at the Lord Protector's stables at Somerset House in London. It was then, when Mildred saw my despair, that she proposed a possible plan for me to receive permission to return to the princess.

Mildred had become a fast friend and support to me, especially after John left for London. Indeed, we had acquaintances in common, for she had been tutored by Roger Ascham, who had also tutored Elizabeth. Like me, she valued learning, however different her family and past were from mine.

And, truth be told, Mildred longed for children of her own. Cecil's boy was her stepson, and one obviously not interested in learned or serious pursuits, though he was the heir of brilliant and ambitious parents. I shared with Mildred how I, too, had longed for a child with John, but at my age I knew that was never to be. Like us, the Cecils had not been wed for many years, though Mildred was but twenty-three and I, forty-two. At least John seemed well enough content as we were. I told her that my childlessness made me yearn even more for the only child I had ever reared.

'I have an idea,' she said, 'but one fraught with risk – and it might mean you will have to eat crow.'

'Anything worth having is worth risking,' I told her. 'Besides, when my family was so poor when I was growing up, I might have already eaten crow.'

We smiled and nodded, almost in unison.

'Your idea just might work,' Cecil admitted that night after Mildred broached it to him at supper. 'When I see John in the city tomorrow, I will ask him what he thinks. Though it appears no one in the kingdom gainsays the Lord Protector, the exception to that is his wife, Anne. I swear but she is a shrewish harridan, willing to demean anyone to elevate herself. But you'd have to swallow your pride, Kat, take her scolding and, above all, find something in it for her. The woman's passion for power knows no bounds.'

'I am well acquainted with that ilk.'

Looking wise beyond his age, he nodded. 'No doubt, after years with the Tudors and those who try to climb into their favor. Kat Ashley, I pray for you and myself many more years of honest service for the good of the ruler and the realm.

Our rewards can be great, but the sacrifices greater.'

So it was that John agreed, and Cecil arranged that I should have an interview with the woman I recalled had insisted she take precedence over Katherine Parr, the widow of a king, no less. I had no illusions she would not abase and abuse me, but I had hopes she might put in a good word for me to return to Elizabeth's service. Besides, I had already survived the terrors and torments of the Tower.

## SOMERSET HOUSE, LONDON

*March 1549*

The day I had an interview with Anne Stanhope Seymour, the Duchess of Somerset, John seemed as nervous as I. When Cecil and I rode in to Somerset House, two great wings of which I was surprised to see still being built, John was waiting with a warm greeting but words of warning.

'Kat, I've seen her close up, and the word *shrew* doesn't do her justice,' he whispered to me, pulling me aside while Cecil spoke with others. 'She's a virago, a harpy. Nothing suits her. I swear, since the boy king is her nephew – by marriage only – she sees herself as queen!'

'Cecil says she and her husband have the queen's suite of rooms at Whitehall, so I'm glad to be summoned here instead. I could not bear

266

to see this 'Queen Anne' in Queen Anne's rooms. I have to dare this. I know you understand. And, if she's that way, can her husband or the Council abide her either? Perhaps if I grovel low enough, I can wheedle this favor from her.'

I kissed him again and was off to catch up to Cecil as he headed for the back door of massive Somerset House. As I said, it was still abuilding, and Cecil filled me in on how huge it would be when finished, and he added with a roll of his eyes, 'That western wing they are working on is made of stones from the demolition of the cloister and library at St Paul's Cathedral. The Seymours have a talent for pulling things down and trying to build anew their own way. Wait here, and I'll be certain you're announced.'

This was to be like a royal audience, I thought, when I was escorted into a vast chamber by a man in Somerset livery. He announced my name to the cavernous room and left me alone. As I approached the duchess, my footsteps echoed doubly from the marble floor and lofty ceiling, making it sound as if I were being stalked. The room was impressively furnished, and out the bank of windows behind the duchess I could see workmen's scaffolds and, through new-leafed trees, the busy Thames. Both within and without the vast mansion, I could hear sawing and hammering.

I curtsied low and stayed down, as I would for royalty.

'You may rise,' she said from her position on a

heavily carved chair that might as well have been a throne. Alive with swirling dust motes, the spring sun streamed in upon me. I had the urge to sneeze. With the light in my eyes, I could barely make out her features, so I sidestepped, and our gazes collided.

The woman who was, no doubt, the most powerful female in the realm had a high forehead and deep-set, cold, blue eyes. Since her mouth was pinched to a tight line, it was her classical Roman nose that seemed to dominate her face – a nose, Mildred had said, she stuck in her husband's business and that of everyone else. Suffice it to say she was richly garbed and laden with jewels, and in midday.

'I permit this interview,' she said, looking down that nose at me, 'because I feel you should be told that, despite your release from the Tower, you will be watched. Well, whatever are you staring at, woman?' she demanded, I suppose, because it was not polite to stare at one's betters.

'Forgive me, Your Grace,' I said, lowering my gaze, 'but I heard you are descended from the great Plantagenet rulers of the realm and, as a student of English history, I thought a glimpse of you would give me some notion of their appearances, the queens at least.'

She fluffed out her skirts, preening. I thanked the Lord that wording did its intended work. Daring to look her in the face again, I saw her countenance soften and blessed Cecil's advice:

Treat her like royalty and perhaps largesse will fall the way of the groveling underling.

'Well, yes, English royal history,' she said, clearing her throat. 'I hear you are well schooled and helped the Princess Elizabeth in her early days.'

'Despite the mistakes I have made, Your Grace, she and I are very close, and both of us would be eternally grateful to you if we might be reunited.'

'She has another governess now, one the Council and the Lord Protector approve of.'

'At her age and with her tutors, she is beyond needing a governess, but she does need loyal servants, especially ones who admire the strong Protestant leanings of the Lord Protector.'

'Ah, well, I must admit my husband thinks your husband's talent with horses is a bit wasted since he is well read in the new faith too.'

'I assure you, my lord John and I – and the princess – have ever been loyal to her brother, the king, and to his Council, despite what Tom Seymour said or did.'

'That wretch was a terrible influence on everyone, may his soul be rewarded for his earthly deeds!'

That, as I heard it, was a far cry from *May he rest in peace*, and I heartily agreed, though I held my tongue on that. Did I dare to hope this interview I had so dreaded was going well?

'Since you knew of my royal Plantagenet blood,' she told me, lifting her chin even higher, 'you may

269

also know that I once served Her Majesty, Queen Catherine of Aragon, as a lady-in-waiting. You – I believe – served the woman who stole the queen's affections, Elizabeth's mother, the Boleyn.'

My temper almost flared, but I beat it down. As in the Tower, I decided to say as little as possible to questions yet to assert myself. 'I did as I was assigned to do, perhaps as you yourself.'

Her eyes widened at the reply. 'My point is,' she said in an exasperated tone as if I were a dolt-head, 'that the princess I am fond of, despite her clinging to her mother's Spanish Catholicism, is the Princess Mary, who yet calls me her Nann for my early service to her mother.'

Doomed! This attempt to beg to be returned to Elizabeth was doomed, for the older they got, the less well Mary and Elizabeth seemed to get on. But, thank the Lord, I was reasoning wrong. Why had I not learned by now that surprises and shocks always surrounded the Tudors?

'So,' the duchess went on, popping a section of imported orange in her mouth and speaking while she chewed it, 'Princess Mary writes that you once did her a good deed, or perhaps two, protecting her when all could have been lost. She gave me no details but will when we next invite her to court, no doubt.'

'Yes, Your Grace. She and I were allies years ago at Hatfield House, and I yet feel great affection for her.'

'Though the Princess Elizabeth has asked my

husband and the Council to be good to you' – [that warmed me, for then I did not know this] –'I do so because the Princess Mary has asked me to be kind to you, though of your own accord, you deserve to be dismissed from royal service forever!'

I bowed my head as if her words had crushed me, but I held my breath, hoping to hear something good and thanks to Mary Tudor. Cecil had been right about this woman: She wanted to best even her husband and the king's Privy Council. She wanted to do things her own way for her own reasons.

'So – for the Princess Mary as well as our poor, misguided Elizabeth, who was nearly taken in by my deceased brother-in-law's seductive ploys,' the duchess droned on in her nasal voice, 'I will see what I can do with the Protector and thus the Council. But if I give you this favor, you and your lord John will be loyal to us – and, of course, to the king for whom my husband rules.'

'As I said, we are already so, Your Grace! I am so grateful.'

When she nodded dismissively and went back to eating orange sections, I curtsied again and backed away. My joy almost went to my head. I fought the urge to keep from skipping, from twirling toward the door, thinking I had not only survived but succeeded. I had bearded the lioness in her den, the woman John had whispered was now 'the power behind the power behind the throne.'

★　★　★

271

It took another month before we heard any word from the Privy Council. I had despaired of being returned to the princess's service and was trying to talk John into our riding to Hatfield, just to catch a glimpse of her. As anywhere he tended horses, he had become a favorite with the Lord Protector, so I marveled indeed when word came that we were both to be sent to Hatfield. Not only were we assigned there, but Thomas Parry too, who feared Elizabeth would never want him back keeping her books after his confession in the Tower. But I knew her – I knew we had all become her family in exile from her royal one.

When we arrived at Hatfield House on a bright, crisp spring evening in May, no one greeted us at first, and the windows were curtained. As if it had been long closed, the house wafted out musty coolness when we entered. No one bustled about. Even when Lord and Lady Tyrwhitt came from the great hall and greeted me coldly, I already felt chilled to the bone.

'Is the princess unwell?' I asked her, my voice quavering.

'She keeps much to her chamber and her bed.'

Even without their leave, I turned away and started up the staircase, lifting my skirts and taking two steps at a time.

'She's stricken with melancholia,' she called after me, coming to the banister, 'but we've had a physician out from London twice. She eats next to nothing. He says she's anemic, but 'tis guilt that racks her.'

I almost expected a guard at her door but saw none. The hall smelled dusty and still. If she was locked in . . .

She wasn't, and the familiar heavy latch lifted easily in my hand. Her withdrawing chamber and bedchamber beyond lay dark and still. Melancholia, anemia and guilt indeed! Elizabeth of England had survived the downfall of that bastard Seymour, and I had dealt with another Seymour devil to get back to her, so all must be well.

Pieces of clothing were strewn haphazardly about, anathema to her tidy habits. And each garment was black, as if a nun had stripped and gone to bed.

'Elizabeth! Lovey, your Kat is here,' I cried, and pulled the bed curtains a bit apart so I could see within.

At first, as my eyes adjusted to the darkness, I thought no one was there. But a slim form swathed in sheets moved slightly between two huge bolsters.

'Kat. Mm, Kat, am I dreaming?' came the muted words, not her voice. 'Oh, thank God, you are here.'

I sat on the side of the bed and leaned toward her. She smelled of sweat, camphor and some other dosing herbs, I know not. But I beheld a ghost of my girl with her greasy hair pulled straight back so it seemed I peered at a skull atop a wasted form.

'Lovey, what have they done to you?' I demanded, and lifted her thin body to me.

'Not them, Kat,' she whispered, her voice like wind through dried leaves. 'I've done it to myself.' And she burst into tears in my arms.

I did not scold anyone but took over with a vengeance. I hand-fed my girl hot broth and insisted she eat strawberries with cream. I aired out her rooms and let the light in. But by candlelight that very night I bathed her in water with lavender oil and washed and toweled her hair. I saw her mother's precious ring was neither on her fingers nor on a cord around her waist, and she'd stripped herself of all other jewelry she so loved to wear. The next day, I brought first John and then Tom Parry upstairs so she could welcome them back, but she seemed a phantom of the girl she had been, and they went from her disturbed and grieving.

'Shall I ride to London for a different physician?' John whispered to me in the hall.

'Yes, get one Cecil trusts and bring him back. But I must get her to talk. She insists she's done this to herself, so perhaps she can heal herself.'

Despite the Tyrwhitts' insistence I keep to my own room, I slept in a truckle bed at the foot of Elizabeth's. After my second night with her, dawn had barely dusted the mullioned windowpanes when she said, 'Kat, are you awake?'

'Yes, lovey, yes, I'm here.'

'I am so very, very sorry – so sorry!' she burst out in a voice that was finally hers and dissolved into tears. I was up and to her in an instant, holding her, rocking her as I had done many times when fear or pain or bugaboos had assailed her as a child.

'If you mean sorry about us in the Tower, we don't blame you,' I told her. 'It wasn't your fault, so—'

'Of course, it was. I adored him, trusted him, wanted him! I as good as killed Queen Katherine, who had been so good to m—'

'Stuff and nonsense. A childbed fever killed her.'

'But I had become like my mother. Flirty, wanton. Kat, I could have conceived a child out of wedlock as she did me. My father used to tell me to never be like her, and now my reputation – all I have but my royal blood – has been sullied for all England to see.'

'All England may go to hell in a handbasket if they think that of you. But,' I told her, rocking her again, holding her close, 'it is in your power to keep that from ever happening again, to become and remain pure in all eyes. I see you've renounced all sorts of pretty things.'

She nodded against my shoulder. 'Even my mother's ring.'

'Lovey, you will always be Anne Boleyn's girl, but you're Henry Rex's too. She made mistakes in her life but didn't have time to correct them

275

when she saw the error of her ways. But you do. You are young and bright and beautiful—'

'No more, Kat, no more, however much I want to be and want to have pleasant pastimes and be loved.'

'Now you listen to your friend Kat Ashley. When my lord and I walked out of the Tower, we held our heads high. We had been scared and shamed, but we held our heads high. If you must dress severely, do so, but no hiding or moping, or people will think their English Elizabeth is guilty and grieving what could have been.'

'Between Tom Seymour and me?'

'No, good riddance to him! They will think you are mourning what could have been for the future of their Princess Elizabeth!'

Though much changed, as if she had grown wiser and older during these cruel winter and spring months, Elizabeth Tudor emerged from her self-imposed prison to almost be her old – or should I say young? – self. She put her mother's ring back on a cord around her waist and managed to eat enough that she had hips to hold the cord up again. She accepted dosings from the physician John brought – especially a mint and borage elixir which helped to lift her melancholia and let her sleep. Despite the scoldings of the watchdog Tyrwhitts, she kept all her old servants close and relied on Cecil, too, for advice when he visited with the excuse of showing her the rural rent rolls she did not really need to see. But if 1549 was a better year than the last for Elizabeth of England, for England itself it was a terrible time.

Edward Seymour, the Lord Protector Somerset as we all called him now, turned out to be a disaster as a ruler. When protests arose against the new Book of Common Prayer, and pockets of Catholics – including in my home shire of Devon – rebelled, he ordered the rebellions brutally put down. Farmlands long leased by the lower classes were being enclosed to raise sheep, for the sale of wool lined the pockets of rich landowners, and vagrants by the hundreds streamed into the cities looking for food. The exchequer was empty, and Protector Somerset proved to be a claybrain about foreign affairs. For one thing, his miscalculations lost the future Scottish queen, Mary Stuart, to the Dauphin of France instead of her being betrothed to King Edward.

Though Somerset had been known as 'the good duke' by the common people, even some of them turned against him, and no wonder why. When chastised by the Council, he had fled with the king in tow, first to Hampton Court, then to Windsor Castle. He had even shouted, 'I shall not fall alone. If I am destroyed, the king will be destroyed. If I die, he shall die before me.' King Edward was scared and the Council was appalled, which made the rise to power of his chief rival, John Dudley, Earl of Warwick, smooth and fast. The once-popular Protector Somerset was arrested and lodged in the very Tower where he had sent his brother and John and me.

It was an entire year after that, as 1550 slid into 1551, that Elizabeth received an invitation to come to court for Christmas. She had been briefly back and forth to visit her brother before, but not for such a long time and such a festive occasion.

'Oh, Kat,' she said, her eyes shining as she showed me the parchment her royal brother had signed in his own hand, 'perhaps with the Earl of Warwick in control now, I can be with my family for more than brief visits!'

Though we would not leave for two days, she began to pack for herself the garments of somber blacks and grays she yet favored. She still wore her hair pulled straight back under a severe headpiece and then spilling down her back in maidenly fashion. Her long, graceful hands she so loved to adorn bore but one plain gold ring. Yet my heart thrilled to see her animated and happy. Some color had even come into her cheeks, and I knew the winter wind would burnish that hue even more.

I was thrilled too when I observed the warm, even wild reception she met with along the roads to London, then at the court when she was presented to her brother. [If I recall aright, Mary, though invited, preferred not to come for Yule that year, since she knew her brother would have insisted she attend all the Protestant services. I was disappointed, for I had hoped to thank her for her support of me to the Duchess of Somerset. Oh, yes, by the way, John Dudley, the new power behind King Edward's throne at court, had magnanimously pardoned Somerset and had him released to increase his own popularity with the people, though Cecil said he was just setting him up for another fall. At least the Somersets were not at court.]

But I must recount some of the hopeful things I heard amid huzzahs on the road and comments at court about Elizabeth: 'Is this plain girl the one they whispered was a strumpet like her mother?' 'Fie on such rumors, for look how humble she is.' 'Anne Boleyn's girl is pure English, the best of the reformed religion and the heritage of the Tudors.' 'I swear I never saw a purer-looking maiden! What rot about her and that blackguard Lord Admiral!'

My clever girl! It was, I reckon, the harbinger of her brilliance to later create herself in the pure, powerful image of the Virgin Queen – but there was much, much more to suffer first.


WHITEHALL PALACE

*Yuletide 1550–1551*

Like Elizabeth, I favored the darkly handsome, virile John Dudley, Earl of Warwick, over the cold, bloodless Edward Seymour, Duke of Somerset. Make no mistake, Warwick was as ambitious as they come, but he seemed somehow more human. He had five fine sons with whom he seemed to get on well, including Robert, the king and Elizabeth's old schoolmate she had so favored when they were younger, the one she still called Robin. Now that they were both seventeen, he was the one she blushed at whenever he teased her or called her Bess or even turned her way. Though I was wary of all comers after the Tom Seymour debacle, surely this was harmless. Warwick kept a fatherly eye on all his boys, and two of them – Robin included – were soon to be wed.

But most of all, both Elizabeth and I admired Warwick for the fatherly way he treated the thirteen-year-old king. He gave him duties to instruct him in the role of kingship and let him play instead of just study and work. He knew Edward loved pageantry, so sometimes Warwick staged a parade through the streets with the boy dressed in the rich fabrics and jewels he loved. No doubt, he spent more time with him than his Seymour uncles or even King Henry ever had, and Edward seemed to blossom into young manhood under his wing.

'But there is one thing that bothers me about the earl, Kat,' the princess told me when I came to her bedchamber to bid her good night on the Twelfth Day of the Christmas celebrations.

'What, my dear?' I asked, anxious to join my John down the hall for our own privy New Year's celebration.

'I see he's out to make my sister's life a horror again, since she won't relent on her strict Catholicism. I believe that there is only one Jesus Christ and all the rest is trifles. Why cannot we just come together in our Christian faith and not argue among ourselves? Each man should keep his own soul and conscience as long as he or she is loyal to the king.'

'No wonder the people see you as their figure-head for Protestantism, but if only the Catholics of our land would know they could too,' I told her, and kissed the top of her tousled head. 'That would be the best of all worlds. Perhaps, someday, you can make that world come true, by helping to support and advise your brother.'

I hugged her good night, grateful to feel her form was filling out even more with all the rich holiday food we'd had here at court. Yet it made me sad too, for I knew so many were cold and hungry in English cities and towns, and I yet grieved for the brutal way Lord Russell, under Somerset's orders, had put down the Prayer Book Rebellion in Devon. I prayed that my father and his family had not been involved or harmed. Strange, but the older I got, the longer I was away from Devon, the more I thought of him.

Elizabeth flopped back in bed with her hands over her head and sighed. 'If I had one whit of power, I'd advise the king and Warwick not to marry Robin off to that country girl, Amy Robsart. They say she brings him a few lands but not much else.'

'Perhaps it is a love match,' I blurted, my thoughts on my husband again, keeping our bed warm for me.

She snatched up and threw a pillow at me. 'Ah, well,' she said as she turned on her side and pulled the covers up, 'I shall never wed anyway – ever. I mean it, Kat.'

'Just because you dress like a nun lately, best not start thinking like one.'

'There are no nuns in the true faith, the new faith,' she told me, her eyelids heavy. 'My father and your old friend Cromwell sent them all away, and my black trappings are but play, and Robin likes me anyway, and that's all I have to say, but I could not do without you any day,' she rhymed, 'and that's that, Kat.'

It was the most lovely Christmas greeting I had ever had. As I snuffed out several candles and tiptoed out, I prayed for good, safe times to come for England and my Elizabeth in the future. But, I warrant, considering all that came soon after, the Lord God had his own plans for all of us.

# CHAPTER 14

Hatfield House

*October 1551*

Such a blustery day,' Elizabeth said with a shudder as we gathered in the solar. 'The chill is creeping inside the house and inside my bones.'

I put my palm on her forehead to see if she was feverish. No, normal as could be. 'Perhaps those winds shrieking like a banshee mean a cold winter, but we'll be safe and warm here – I pray we will,' I told her as we sat down in the usual chairs in our familiar circle.

Each late afternoon before supper, we gathered by the hearth and took turns reading aloud or discussing many things: Greek plays, English history or some new book on religion. Though I never said so but to John, our cozy little coterie lulled me into complacency. I oft pretended he and I were the parents, and Elizabeth – now just turned eighteen by one month – our daughter. Tom Parry seemed like an uncle, and Blanche Parry, her Welsh nurse from years ago, was like a

283

maiden aunt, though Tom and Blanche were only distantly related. Her tutor, Roger Ascham, seemed a sort of older brother who knew everything. And Cecil, now secretary of state, who owed his allegiance no longer to the once-again imprisoned Somerset but directly to the king and his adviser Warwick, was like a visiting cousin from time to time.

Unfortunately, the Tyrwhitts had not yet been recalled by the Privy Council. The two of them hovered, but we oft took no heed of them. We were doing naught amiss, at least openly. If Warwick kept them or others as spies – for I was certain they had been such for Somerset before he fell from power – I cared not. I finally felt safe and happy, despite the fact John sometimes sent and received Her Grace's secret messages to and from Cecil. Yet he sometimes came in person, supposedly just passing by while coming from or going to his ancestral home in Stamford, Northamptonshire, which he was then rebuilding.

On that windy day, I proudly listened to my girl espouse her ideas about why followers of the Lord Jesus should pray directly to Him and not to a panoply – yes, that was the very erudite word she used – a panoply of so-called saints and the Virgin Mary.

'Still, I can see why her image is venerated,' she admitted. 'All those idealized statues and paintings of her are powerful tools to sway people.'

At eighteen, Elizabeth Tudor was a striking young

woman, but still somewhat severe-looking, which was her choice. Even indoors at Hatfield, she dressed plainly and kept her bright red hair covered by modest caps. Her eyebrows and lashes were so pale that her penetrating Boleyn black-gray eyes dominated her face, along with her high-bridged nose she had inherited from her father. The child had finally become an adult; her body was catching up with her precocious mind.

It was, I recall, that very afternoon of October 18, 1551, that Cecil rode in with several men and changed my reverie of coming warm winter afternoons before our hearth to cold reality again.

'I shall go outside to greet him!' Elizabeth declared when a servant announced Cecil's arrival.

I rose also; unfortunately, Lady Tyrwhitt jumped to her feet too. 'But,' she protested, 'you just said, Your Grace, that you are chilled and glad to be inside. Let the chief secretary come in before us all with his news, for, heaven knows, we hear little of London here.'

'Shall I again write the Earl of Warwick that you yearn to be sent back there, then?' she parried as she wrapped her shawl tighter about her shoulders and nodded to me to follow her. John closed the book of maps he'd been perusing and came too. Lately he'd been much enamored with the idea of visiting Italy someday. But Her Grace could not spare him and I certainly could not. She had made him her privy secretary – more

285

privy than the Tyrwhitts knew. If they managed to read what formal correspondence passed between the princess and her royal brother or Cecil, they did not know that John sent messages to Cecil, and received others, secreted within saddles custom-made for particular horses. John oft acted as a guard for Her Grace's royal person, too, though we usually managed to make it look as if he were just with me and I were with her.

Despite the wind buffeting us, Elizabeth, John and I made it outside to Cecil just as he began to untie his saddlebags. 'My lord Cecil!' she greeted him as the Tyrwhitts scrambled to keep up, turning back only to tell a servant to fetch their cloaks. [Once, I recall, when Lady Tyrwhitt came out with a cloak, Elizabeth thanked her for her kindness and put it on herself, forcing the woman to run back inside for another while Elizabeth learned what privy news and advice Cecil brought.]

But on this day, he frightened the three of us, the only ones who could hear what he whispered in the whipping wind, especially as John managed to turn four horses into a snorting, stomping fence around us.

'Somerset is no doubt going to follow his brother Tom Seymour from the Tower to the block,' Cecil said without ado after he bowed to Elizabeth and she hastily raised him. 'I have just been knighted to keep me in line, and Warwick has convinced the king to elevate him to the title Duke of Northumberland.'

'He dares?' Elizabeth whispered. 'He dares to take the dukedom of the powerful Percys for his own? I feared his hail-fellow-well-met appearance was a guise, so I fear for my brother who admires him. Is treason against Somerset the charge?'

'Yes,' he said as the Tyrwhitts managed to finally work their way in among the horses. Elizabeth turned away from them, her arm now through Cecil's as she mimed showing him the bounty of fallen leaves they scuffed noisily through. 'But the thing is,' Cecil said, still speaking quickly as John and I fell in behind again to cut the Tyrwhitts off, 'he's elevated Jane Grey's father to a dukedom too, Duke of Suffolk. He's obviously planning more than Somerset's demise, and making certain that I am not privy to those plans. By the way, the charges against Somerset are not that he threatened the king's life months ago but that he was plotting to assassinate Warwick this time. Your Grace, whatever chance we have to talk today, keep this in mind. If Warw – I mean, if Northumberland summons you to London, lie low. Feign illness, find a way, but do not go! I fear he would like to get you and the Princess Mary in his clutches too.'

'I shall take that to heart, my friend Cecil, now Sir William Cecil,' she said, turning toward the Tyrwhitts as they hurried around John and me. 'Good news,' she told them, 'for I have just been informed that this is now Sir William Cecil, elevated for service to the king and to John

Dudley, the newly created Duke of Northumberland!'

'And more good news from the new duke, Your Grace,' Cecil said, falling right in with her playacting. 'Northumberland bids me inform you that he greatly regrets that Somerset took your London residence, Durham House your father left you, but he now offers you Seymour House instead, should you go to London soon.'

I feared Elizabeth's countenance would betray emotion at that. It had been Tom Seymour's house, and we had all spent time there together. Was some hidden message in that offer, other than a bribe to stay in her favor? For it was a fine, large house in the Strand, close to Whitehall Palace.

'How kind and generous of him!' she said only, smiling and clasping her hands together. 'You bring us naught but good news today, Sir William!'

She kept up that facade until long after dark, when I went in to bid her a good night.

'Cecil's right,' she told me, keeping her voice down. 'The former Earl of Warwick, now the vaunted Duke of Northumberland, is planning something, and he's buying us all off to favor him. But what could he have in mind, what higher honor and post than that historical dukedom and as favorite adviser to my brother? And why did he elevate Jane Grey's father to a dukedom too? Oh, I hope Robin and his brothers have no part in this, but something's coming. Those winds

288

battering this house today are winds of change, betrayal and death!'

I comforted her, even chided her, as I recall, that she was over-reading the signs. Which soon only proved to me, and probably to her, that, as educated and well read as was her Kat, I was sometimes still unlearned and stupid too. For within a fortnight, she received a letter from the imprisoned Somerset begging that she plead for him. Her reply, written to avoid angering Northumberland, whom we all now feared, read: *Being so young a woman, I have no power to do anything in your behalf.* Not only had Cecil taught her to avoid involvement, but she told the truth: the king's sister or not, she had no power but was yet a pawn on a chessboard with shifting rules.

'Twas bitter winter weather but with no snow upon the ground the day I heard I had a visitor. John looked up from writing a letter for Elizabeth as I said to the servant standing at our bedchamber door, 'You mean, Her Grace has a visitor, and I'm to come down too?'

'No, Mistress Ashley,' the kitchen lad said. 'The man come to the back door and says his last name in Champer . . . Champer – something.'

I gasped and dropped my needlework. I had not heard my maiden name spoken for years. Sir Philip Champernowne of Modbury had been dead nigh on six years, so had one of his sons come calling – perhaps Arthur, who had favored me once?

John and I went downstairs together. The moment I saw the man, whom they had put in the great hall by the hearth and, thank the Lord, had given a steaming mug of cider, I knew who it was. Older, stooped, gray-haired, it was my father.

'Father!' I choked out, and hurried to him.

'My Kat,' he said only, and banged his mug down so hard on a bench, some of the cider sloshed out. He hugged me hard and swept me off my feet for a spin. The years flew away; tears blurred my sight of him when we stepped apart to behold each other.

I introduced him to John, and they eyed each other before a hearty handshake. 'Is all well?' I asked him as we three huddled by the hearth. 'How are Maud and the children? It has been – let's see, nigh on twenty-six years now.'

'Aye. All of them wed, glad for you too, Kat,' he told me, with a nod at John. 'I'm a grandsire, seven times over. I had to see you afore I die.'

'You're not ill? You don't look ill.'

'No. Maud's dead.'

'Oh, I didn't know.'

'Course you didn't, living with the Tudors all these years.'

'When – how did she die?'

'A tumor inside her last summer. But she told me you'd accused her once of – of harming your mother.'

'I was young and bitter that you had married again so soon, and—'

'On her deathbed, she said it was true.'

Frozen in place, I stared at him. John's big hand reached out to squeeze my knee through my skirts. 'She – she,' I stammered with a voice not my own, 'hit her over the head, then drowned her, didn't she?'

He nodded. 'I shoulda knowed, maybe did, but we got on like cats and dogs, Cecily and me, and – God forgive me – I wanted Maud. Kat, I'm asking if you can forgive me. God as my judge, I'm glad you got away from Maud, from us. I can never make it up to you, but wanted you to have this.' He dug in the pouch he had belted to his waist and extended to me, dripping through his gnarled fingers, my mother's garnet necklace I had loved, her final gift to me before she died. Ninnyhammer that I was, I burst into tears again.

Both men let me cry. Finally, with a nod from my father, John clasped the necklace around my throat, and I thought again about the ruby ring I'd saved for Elizabeth from her mother, and the red ring of blood around Anne Boleyn's neck the day she died. The nightmare of her ghost had not haunted me for several years, but that night she was back, begging me to protect and tend her girl.

My father stayed that night. Her Grace kindly ordered a fine dinner for us in her withdrawing room and stopped by to meet him afterwards, shook his hand and even tried and praised the honey he had brought in pottery jars in his saddle-bags. Though she looked plain and pale, I could tell he was bedazzled by her. After she left, Father, John and I talked much of the night and, more than once, he told me he was proud of me. I assured him I forgave him for not knowing Maud was a murderess. The fact my mother had her life cruelly and unjustly taken made me feel even closer to Elizabeth.

She came back in to bid us good night and, the next morn, as I brushed her long hair, she said, 'Kat, you have come much farther in life than I.'

'But, lovey, you have much farther to go.'

'But I heard your father say he was proud of you.' Her voice broke. 'I vow I would have given anything in Christendom to have heard my father say that of me.'

When my father said he must leave, she gave him a gold sovereign, for he would not take anything from us. She insisted it was payment for the delicious honey, carried all those miles. A fine snow was falling when I waved good-bye to him, but John rode with him part of his long way home. And ever after, each time I fingered my mother's necklace about my throat, I thought how sad it is that some people leave the earth before their sins can be forgiven them and family amends can be made. Despite my father's humble life and his faults, I felt he was a far better man than Her Grace's royal sire had ever been.

The very next day, we had a message for everyone from Cecil that Somerset had been beheaded and all his properties forfeit. What would become of his proud duchess now? I wondered. No doubt, her many enemies they had lorded over rejoiced. She had lost everything and gone into exile in the country. Worse, that spring, we saw clearly what we had been dreading from the Duke of Northumberland. The king had fallen ill, but worse, he had for some unfathomable reason struck down his royal father's Act of Succession and disinherited both his sisters.

'I cannot believe it,' Elizabeth said over and over as she paced in her withdrawing chamber, flinging gestures. 'Edward loves both of us. I knew Northumberland was up to something! No sign of this from either him or His Majesty, and then a strike out of the blue! Out of the blue, that is, except I feared for all of us – including my cousin Jane, when I heard Northumberland had elevated her father then wed her to his own son Guildford Dudley, and she most unwilling! So what does the damned duke have in mind now?' she demanded of John and me, then answered herself. 'Will he declare Jane Grey as the king's sister in our stead and Edward's new heir? Blast him! My father would kill him for this, kill him with his bare hands!'

When I was a girl, there was an old wives' saying in Devon that deaths or tragedies come in scores. I warrant that was true, for in July of 1553, His Royal Highness Edward Tudor, but sixteen years old, died a dreadful, painful, scabrous death, whether of the French pox or some other malady, we did not know. Some even whispered it was from poisoning, but that was never openly charged. Northumberland summoned Elizabeth to London both before and after her brother's death, but she took to her bed, claiming to be ill as well as stricken with grief. She was careful, as Cecil had long counseled, not to fall into Northumberland's clutches – or even into Mary's, now that she would be declared queen.

But the last blow was that Northumberland produced a royal edict, signed and sealed by King Edward, naming the duke's own daughter-in-law Jane Grey, who had royal blood, as queen and his son, Robin's brother Guildford, King of England.

Mary, too, sent for Elizabeth to rally to her righteous cause, for many Englishmen rose in arms to defend her right to the throne. It was greatly the Protestants against the Catholics again, a short civil war, but Elizabeth managed not to be embroiled for the nine precarious days Jane Grey was queen.

But when the false king and queen were captured and imprisoned in the Tower – with Northumberland and two others of his sons, one being Elizabeth's friend Robin – she had no choice but to go to London for her sister's coronation, for the snub of a refusal would have been too much. At least, in the English people's rising to make Mary queen, Elizabeth was also temporarily swept back into the line of succession.

'I cannot go into the Tower, Kat, not even just to the palace there to await my sister's parade through London and her coronation, I don't care what royal tradition decrees,' Elizabeth declared as we made our final stop for sustenance in an inn before entering London. 'I thought I could manage going to the place my mother was as good as murdered, but now I know I cannot. I will enter London, but not go to join Mary at the palace in the Tower grounds as she commanded.'

'But royal tradition matters, and you know it. Your mother went there in triumph before her crowning, so the place holds good memories too. Besides, everyone's been cheering you,' I pressed on, taking her elbow and leaning close as we stood in the emptied-out common room of the inn. 'Do you think I want to put one foot in that place again? But I will if it returns you to Mary's good-will and brings you back permanently in the line of succession after all these difficult years.'

Pressing my other hand between hers, she bit her lower lip and nodded. 'But my cousin Jane is still imprisoned there, and Robin too. Perhaps they will even hear our merrymaking in the palace, poor souls.'

'You know, Your Grace,' I said, deciding not to coddle her as I longed to, 'I believe Elizabeth Tudor can do whatever she must for the good of England and for the possibility to someday claim England's throne.'

She looked at me hard, rather than staring out

through the October sunshine at the crowds of people waiting for her reappearance. 'She'll try to turn me to Catholicism, but I'll not bend on that,' she told me.

'My lord John and I are with you on that and all else.'

'My people,' she said with a decisive nod, and I knew not whether she was acknowledging that John and I were her people or the crowds outside. She kissed my cheek, squared her shoulders, lifted her chin and went out, waving and nodding to a roar of recognition.

'God save you, Princess!' 'Bess Tudor, English through and through!' I heard among huzzahs and cheers and clapping.

And so we went in triumph to meet Queen Mary at the palace in the Tower and await her coronation with high hopes for a good and kindly reign. At least we got a short one.

# CHAPTER 15

WHITEHALL PALACE

*October 1, 1553*

'So, the new queen, looking resplendent in her jewel-encrusted gown, asked her younger sister, 'what did you think of it all today? Wasn't it magnificent? At last, God's will be done.'

After the five-hour coronation at the abbey and the long banquet at Westminster Palace, we had just returned by barge to Whitehall. At the abbey, I had been one of many attendants following the new queen's sister, but here Elizabeth had asked only John and me to remain with her. We stood behind her in the chamber of state, where Queen Mary's retainers, priests and advisers still swarmed about her like the queen bee in one of my father's hives.

'A beautiful and impressive two days,' Elizabeth answered Mary. 'Those who helped to preserve Your Majesty's rightful throne are truly blessed.'

'And for that we must give thanks,' she said, with a little clap of her hands. 'Will you come to Mass with me, here, now in my own chapel?'

'Sister, as you have long asked to be allowed to follow the dictates of your conscience, will you not now allow the same for me?'

'But mine is the true faith, and everyone shall know it. I realize you have been long misled, but I cannot abide such a long face on this glorious day.' She patted Elizabeth's flushed cheek – more a little slap than a pat, I thought.

I, with John behind me, stood in a corner, hemmed in by the press of people. The chamber was crowded with furniture too. Mary had been queen since her brother's death in July, and this was the first day of October. In those three months she had much changed the look of palace rooms, for they were full of ornate old, heavy furniture. She must have rescued pieces from her mother's time from some storehouse; I prayed she would not also resurrect the painful past.

Yesterday, behind my princess in the parade from the Tower into the city, I had seen a subtle sign of the queen's desire to denigrate Elizabeth, I had ridden on a beautiful horse John had arranged for me. Just ahead of me, Elizabeth had been in a chariot, but not alone. She'd had to share it with the befuddled, elderly Anne of Cleves, who evidently thought the cheers for Mary's heir were all for her and waved broadly, her hand often flailing before Elizabeth's face. Had that been happenstance or by design? I wondered. If it was not arranged by Mary, I knew her advisers wanted to defame the great

298

hope of the English Protestants, the Princess Elizabeth.

Still, both Elizabeth and I had reveled in her welcome. And I was grateful to Queen Mary for one thing: she had ordered her sister to get out of her stark, dark garb and don a lovely gown of white and silver tissue cloth, at least for these two festive days.

Now I felt exhausted and, truth be told, a heaviness not only caused by the grueling ceremony and rituals. We dreaded the future for Elizabeth but for England too. The advisers Mary heeded were the Catholic hierarchy of the land, streaming back from foreign exile or emerging from hiding. Stephen Gardiner, Bishop of Winchester, and the Spanish Ambassador, Simon Renard, had Mary's ear as two of her chief advisers. She had packed her Council with those who were of her faith.

Sir William Cecil had hastily resigned from public life and retired to his country house in Stamford, but not before warning us that, if Mary, in honor of her mother's heritage, took a Spanish husband, as was rumored, England could become a colony of our greatest rival and enemy. But above all, I dreaded an argument between the royal sisters, and I could scent one coming at this very moment.

'Your Majesty,' Elizabeth replied, 'I will ever be your most loyal sister and subject, but I beg this one indulgence from you, that I may follow my own conscience in the way I worship. Of course, I will pray for you and your kingdom, but—'

'We will discuss this no more today. You will come to see the error of your ways, will she not, Kat Ashley?' she asked, turning toward me with her back to her sister.

'I am certain Her Grace will be ever loyal and grateful to you.'

Squinting, the queen took several steps closer to me. The near-sightedness that gave her a perpetual frown had incised deep lines on the forehead of the thirty-seven-year-old woman. The result – that and the mannish voice – could be quite unsettling when she turned her attention to one. I curtsied, but she took my hands and drew me up. Despite the heat of her words, her touch was icy cold.

'You too, my friend?' she challenged. 'You prevaricate and dance about the issue too? Ah, two clever women are more dangerous than one. I should have known you would both be stubborn. But for the debt I owe you, we will not argue either,' she said, and loosed her grip on me.

The powerful scent of the incense from the Catholic coronation service still seemed to waft out from her – that and the rank scent of raw power after all the years she'd been shunted off and denied affection.

'I shall not forget,' she said, her voice quiet now. People tried in vain to lean close to hear her words, but they dared not jostle her as she had backed us into a corner. 'You protected and advised me when I was sore ill and battered and friendless at Hatfield all those years ago. Then you helped me up to the battlements to call out to my father – and he doffed his hat and addressed me, do you remember?'

'I do, indeed, Your Majesty. And may I say your asking the Duchess of Somerset to plead for me to be reunited with my mistress makes me ever grateful to you.'

'Then see that you and your lord attend Mass each day and work to soften my sister's heart – her mother's heart, I fear,' she said with sudden vehemence. 'And this,' she added, turning to John, 'is Master Ashley?'

'Yes, Your Grace,' I told her. 'May I present to you my lord John, a loyal servant to Her Grace and to his new queen.'

He bowed low to her, his bum, I recall, bumping into the wall and nearly shooting him forward at her. Ordinarily, I would have laughed, but this suddenly seemed to me deadly serious business.

'A loving, strong marriage,' she said. 'Ah, I envy you. That is what I too seek and I will have. But as for my younger sister, see that you both keep her safe,' she said as others kept crowding close in an attempt to overhear her words. Her last warning came out almost as a hiss: 'Safe from those who would use her against me. See to it!'

'Yes, Your Majesty,' John and I said, almost in unison.

She hit her balled fist in her palm and almost

mouthed the words. 'Especially when my people hear I will wed the Spanish prince Philip, from my mother's beloved country, I want no rabble around my sister, using her, for I am certain she would not of her own accord gainsay my will.'

'No, she would not!' I declared, louder than I had meant to in the hush. John squeezed my elbow in warning, or else he was trying to steady himself, for the rumored Spanish liaison was what most Protestant Englishmen feared above all else.

But this Protestant Englishwoman, Katherine Champernowne Ashley, feared one thing more: that over the years to come Catherine of Aragon's daughter would take out her long-festering hatred of Anne Boleyn on my princess.

In the next four months, while Elizabeth and her household awaited news of the Spanish marriage, troubles tumbled upon us. Northumberland had been beheaded months ago, but in February, Elizabeth's young cousin Jane Grey and her husband, Guildford Dudley, were also executed. Jane was beheaded on the site where Anne Boleyn had lost her head. It brought back that dreadful day to me again, and I awakened to night terrors, comforted by John, and even by Elizabeth when I was with her one night when she felt ill, though I told her naught of my dream.

'Thank the Lord, the queen hasn't had Robin executed,' she told me more than once. 'He is not with his wife, but I pray he is somehow encouraged and comforted by his life being spared. He was only obeying his father when he tried to take Mary prisoner during the Jane Grey rebellion. He never would have done that on his own.'

It bothered me that she seemed pleased he wasn't with his wife, but worse was soon to come our way. Just as Mary had predicted, and as John and I had feared, a new rebellion was raised by a man who proclaimed Elizabeth as rightful queen. As she had done before when dangers lurked, Elizabeth took to her bed, though she truly was ailing from some malady that made her retain water and bloated. her thin body and narrow face.

Sadly, part of this upheaval arose in the west country again, Devon, my home shire, and Cornwall. But the major unrest was in the southern shire of Kent, from which a popular rebel led the revolt and the ragtag army that marched on London. Unfortunately, he was the son of the man who had loved Anne Boleyn from her youth to her death, and Mary knew it. His father was now dead, but Thomas Wyatt the younger was that man, and we were all to suffer greatly and unjustly for what came to be called the Wyatt Rebellion.

ASHRIDGE HOUSE, HERTFORDSHIRE

*February 10, 1554*

In the depths of our bed, I lay warm, but for once not feeling secure, in my husband's arms. It was nearly dawn, and light intruded through the crack in our bed curtains. We were not at Hatfield or even at Enfield, which John and I so dearly loved, but at Ashridge, one of Elizabeth's houses we visited from time to time. She preferred this one lately, for it was farther away from her sister.

We had heard that Wyatt's march on London had almost succeeded, for Queen Mary had no standing army and her advisers did not think the rabble army could come to much. But just as boldly as Mary had fought for her throne from those supporting Jane Grey, the queen had paraded through London with her guards to address citizens at the Guildhall. 'Pluck up your courage!' Cecil's letter had told us she had cried. 'Stand fast, fear not!' She had also, Cecil said, boldly lied to the people that she would make no foreign marriage when it was already agreed upon. At any rate, London had rallied for her, Wyatt has been arrested and taken to the Tower on February 3. We dreaded what the man might say, even under torture, about Elizabeth's inspiring or abetting his treason.

'Awake, my love?' John murmured, his lips caressing my naked shoulder. He stretched and yawned, so he had hardly been lying there, worrying. But I could not help it, for fear curled around me tight as his arms.

'I've been awake for a while. That way I won't have that vile nightmare again. It's as if Queen Anne keeps coming back from the grave to warn me.'

'About Queen Mary's hatred of Elizabeth?'

'In a way. She always begs me to tend to her girl and keep her safe. But I am so afraid I cannot protect her in these tenuous times.'

'Tougher to come, I fear,' he whispered and pulled me even closer to his muscular, hairy chest. We cuddled, spoon fashioned, he called it. 'I'm afraid the queen's going to give in to her advisers and start persecuting those she deems heretics, damn those popish Spanish lackeys pouring poison in her ears.'

'Heretics,' I whispered. 'By Mary's definition, that includes us, just because we do not bow to her popish Catholicism. Some of the books we have hidden in your rooms near the stables in the city and ones I left at Somerset House—'

'Yes, we'd best pull those out and hide them away from our property and the princess's chambers next time we're there. Maybe your nightmares have been triggered by word that, if the queen goes through with this Spanish marriage to Prince Philip, she'll annul the marriage of Elizabeth's parents. That would make her a bastard again, and no bastard can ascend the throne if something happens to Mary. But is she too old to bear children?'

'Like me, you mean?'

'No, my love. You are too tender on that subject. I meant I'm afraid this Wyatt mess might even goad Mary to move faster to disinherit Elizabeth.'

'What a fool to raise troops and march on

London in Elizabeth's name! He's hurting her, not helping her! I must get up and see how she's feeling this morning. That bloating worries me and I wonder if she has somehow caught the green sickness again. She's weak and so pale.'

'*Hm*, the so-called virgin's illness for our precious virgin. More like, her head and heart are making her ill. What I wouldn't give to spirit you and me off to sunny Italy, our princess too. Ah,' he said, his voice growing more resonant, as it always did when he espoused what I called his 'Italian dreams,' 'we would study there and have our talks and walks and rides in the sun. Mayhap I'd have time to write more of my book on riding. I must convince people that the best way to tame a horse is through patience and gentleness. We'd go to Padua, I think, with its fine old university.'

'You are such a dreamer.'

He squeezed me so hard my breath oofed out. 'Better to have dreams than nightmares, my Kat.'

But that very morning – I remember the date well, February 10, 1554 – not a nightmare of my mind but a real one clamped us all in its iron jaws.

That night, I first knew something was wrong when I heard running footsteps in the hall, for that sound never boded well. Could Elizabeth be poorly again and had she sent for help? But no, she would have also sent for me. Then voices – shouts – and a pounding on a distant door.

'Get a gown or robe on,' John told me, jumping

up and yanking on breeches and a shirt. 'Damn the Tyrwhitts if they let envoys in at this hour without telling me first.' His feet thrust in his leather mules, he ran out into the hall, banging the door closed behind him.

In the weak light of dawn, I tugged on the gown and sleeves I'd discarded like a wonton last night to fall into John's arms. I did not even try to lace the gown or shove my feet in shoes, but in the cold winter ran down the hall barefoot. Without my petticoats, my hems dragged and almost tripped me. I gasped to see outside Her Grace's door John in a shoving, shouting match with one man, and two other men in royal livery. Despite their raised voices, I heard someone scrape out a sword. Lady Tyrwhitt, who must have let them in, looked like a ghost in a white night rail and cap.

Then came Elizabeth's voice from inside her room: 'Stand off! I command you to leave my presence!'

Dear Lord in heaven, had these men breached her door?

'What means this affront to Her Majesty's sister?' I demanded, striding toward them just as John dared to yank the man with the naked sword back out into the hall.

A burly oaf I did not know thrust out both hands to stop the melee and bellowed, 'The queen summons the princess to London to answer for her part in the rebel Wyatt's plot! Since Her Grace did not want an excuse of illness, she has sent a physician here, Dr Huckson!' He jerked his thumb in the direction of a stout man who had gone into Elizabeth's chamber, then asked me, 'You be Mrs Ashley?'

'Yes, I—'

'We're to fetch you too. If Her Grace be well enough to refuse the royal physician, a half an hour now, that's all, and we'll be off with her and you in tow. We brought a litter and more men wait outside.'

'I *am* unwell and weak,' Elizabeth, still abed, insisted, 'but want my own physician!' The pale moon of her face peeked through the curtains of her bed. John had backed the men off and was now guarding her door. The physician, in his befurred robes and eared cap, looking most insulted, huffed out of the room. I edged past them all and went in, then tried in vain to close the door.

'No closed doors, for the Crown must have answer for the treason!' the burly one in charge yelled.

'There is no treason in this house!' I shouted back. I swear but I would have cuffed him, had I not been trying to keep my unlaced gown up on my shoulders so I would not bare my bosom. 'And how dare you tell the sister of the queen she cannot have a door closed while she prepares herself to answer your questions right here, for, as she said, she is weak and cannot go abroad in this raw weather! It is the green sickness at best and something far more dire at worst, perhaps even a contagion! And do you think either of us would just fly out these upstairs windows to escape?'

'We are not interrogators, mistress, but the messengers,' he insisted, but, with John's help, I closed the door on all their faces.

'If she does not present herself in the hall as I said, I have orders to drag her out!' came only slightly muffled through the oaken door. 'And this royal physician is to examine her!'

'Kat,' she cried in a low voice once we were alone, 'I will not go, cannot, for my monthlies are painful, and my swelling is worse. Cannot we convince them I can't be moved, stall for time?'

'I think he means it, so the queen must too,' I muttered, digging in her coffer for her warmest gown and cloak. Even if she could stall them, we must be prepared.

'She's been looking for an excuse. I kept to my bed, as during the upheaval over the Jane Grey rebellion, and I can't help it that madman Wyatt wrote me a letter. My answer was noncommittal to his cause.'

I had not told her of that 'madman's' father's love for her mother. Perhaps I should have, but I still had never admitted I was at Anne's beheading and saw him sobbing there. Besides, if my princess was to be questioned, best she truthfully say she had no ties to the Wyatts and did not even know the rebel's father had gone to the Tower because he loved her mother. Surely, his son's trying to put Anne Boleyn's daughter on the throne was partly caused by his father's old passion. The queen's hatred of Wyatt must be doublefold, since she still detested Anne Boleyn and anyone who had loved her. Why could people not let the past rest in peace?

'I don't want them dragging you out into the cold,' I told her, 'but we can hardly refuse. Those men are armed, and there's a goodly number of them.'

'Kat, I have cramps, I'm bleeding, weak and bloated and I hurt to my very teeth!'

I rounded on her, arms on my hips. 'Am I speaking to Princess Elizabeth of England?'

'Not anymore. Mary's going to bastardize me again when she annuls my parents' vows so she can wed that Spaniard. We're all doomed.'

'Get up. We will get you dressed and make a last stand here together. Let that physician of the queen see how poorly you look. Mayhap we can gainsay them, but, if not, I will be with you all the way, thank God, for she has told them to bring me too.'

Putting her head in her hands, then pulling at her hair, she cried, 'Oh, Kat, not this again, not questionings and suspicions and everyone at court staring at me with distrust and disdain!'

But the queen's men would not be refused. Despite how terrible Elizabeth looked, the royal physician said she could travel. At least they let John ride a horse behind our bouncing litter on the grueling journey to London, but even at the plodding pace of seven or eight miles a day, it was hellish for Her Grace, who began to vomit, mayhap from fear. She got worse, weaker, and looked more ashen pale and swollen.

At Highgate, a mere five miles from Whitehall, she collapsed completely and was bedridden for a week. I almost despaired for her life, despite three royal physicians attending her. On February 22, we went on. Though we had been told not to open the curtains of the litter wherein the two of us rode, she drew them back so the London crowds could see her hollow-eyed and white as a corpse. Even in her disease and despair, Elizabeth Tudor had learned to use high drama to promote her cause. People shouted out their blessings and some cursed the queen. When I heard that, fearful of even more retribution, I slapped the curtains closed.

My princess seemed to rally a bit when we neared Whitehall. 'At least,' she whispered, leaning back against a bolster, 'it isn't the Tower and we are together, all three of us.'

I almost said, 'Famous last words,' but I just nodded and blinked back my tears.

Elizabeth was immediately given over into the care of some of the queen's 'loyal ladies,' as it was put to me.

'No, Mistress Ashley stays with me,' Elizabeth protested. 'I must have her with me!'

At their refusal, it broke my heart that she clung

to my hand, even as we were roughly separated by guards. I tried to push one man aside to hug her, but they pulled me away. How I wished John were there to help us fight them, for they had sent him with the horses to the stables, and then he was to join us. But I did not even trust that now. The queen was baiting traps.

'All will be well, Your Grace!' I called to Elizabeth as her voice faded down the hall. 'All will be well because you are innocent of all vile charges and loyal to the queen!'

I was escorted to a small but well-appointed waiting room which I knew to be at the very edge of the queen's suite of rooms. The door was not only closed behind me but loudly locked.

I paced and prayed. *Dear Lord, am I to be imprisoned and interrogated again? Please, Lord, not the Tower, not any of us to the Tower! And please, don't let them take my John away too.*

I know not how long I waited for something to happen, someone to come. I ended up using a ewer of drinking water to wash road dust from my face and hands and then to squat over it for a chamber pot because I could hold my water no longer. Had I been forgotten? What was happening to my princess and my John?

Daylight began to wane. I saw no candles or lamps in the room. My stomach growled from hunger and twisted in terror. Sleet began to pepper the thick panes of the chamber's single window. Were they going to just leave me here until I broke and screamed for someone? In their desire to break Elizabeth, had they forgotten me? And, as during my dreadful days in the Tower, was John imprisoned somewhere nearby?

At last, voices in the hall! I was going to call out, but they came closer. Guards, then another man's low, commanding voice. No, not a man's. I knew that voice.

The lock rattled, the latch lifted. Queen Mary stood there, frowning.

# CHAPTER 16

WHITEHALL PALACE

*February 22, 1554*

I curtsied as the queen came in. Without further ado, she said, 'You did not obey me, to keep her from complications and disloyalties! Nor did you heed my words to go to Holy Mass, and, by implication, abandon your heretical ways.'

Spies! I knew Mary must have spies in Elizabeth's household. Perhaps that was my just retribution for having been one myself. 'I – Your Majesty, the princess is innocent of any disloyalty, and I too.'

'Bring the books,' she called over her shoulder. A guard came in with a stack of books – John's and mine we had read and discussed, Elizabeth's too – on the new religion. So, I assumed this meant that even if we were not even guilty of complicity in the Wyatt Rebellion, we were still in peril of life and limb – as heretics.

'Do not shame yourself by denying these are yours, Kat Ashley, for several bear your name and notations and several your lord John's. We were not searching for them at his chambers near

Charing Cross nor in your rooms at your mistress's Somerset House. We were looking for correspondence from Thomas Wyatt, who tried to overturn my righteous rule, with the Protestant princess's help and encouragement, no doubt. But,' she added, enunciating each word, '*we found these*. You have defied your queen and one who has done you good!'

'Your Majesty, you above all understand being true to one's beliefs. I honored and respected you for your strength in your darkest days, and supported you, did you good, too—'

'For which you have been repaid by a favor – a previous reunion with your mistress. However, you do not support me now but her.'

'Your Majesty, I fervently believe I can be true to you as my queen, yet chose to worship in another way so—'

'Say no more, for you only dig yourself in deeper!' She was shouting; spittle flecked her lips. 'You are ever loyal to my wayward, stubborn sister just as you were to her mother – as, evidently, are all the Thomas Wyatts of this land – and do not deny it! But now, I give you a choice – a gift, as it were. As soon as she stops puking, Elizabeth is going to the Tower for questioning—'

'No, not there! Please, she cannot abide—'

'She will abide it and bide there too, just as her mother did before her, the Boleyn whore! Would you like to go with her?' she taunted, her tone and expression ugly.

I knew I should show humility, even grovel as I had before the Duchess of Somerset five years ago, but I squared my shoulders. 'To be with her? Yes.'

'Ha, I knew it! Even there, the place you must hate. You'd follow her to fiery hell, would you not, and mayhap shall!'

At the flick of her wrist, the man with the books went back out, but several guards still blocked the door. I recalled it was whispered that Mary's advisers were insisting heretics be burned at the stake. Cecil had written that she was coming to see fiery public executions as the only way to save Catholicism in 'her' country. My knees almost buckled as she said, 'One of you – you or your lord John – are going not to the Tower but to the Fleet Prison. The other to exile, and the choice is yours alone, Kat Ashley.'

The Fleet! It was a noisome, old stone prison encompassed by a moat here in London, which held those committed by the monarch's personal decree as well as debtors and offenders of the royal courts. It also held minor political prisoners, which I feared I was in these terrible times with worse to come. But why was she giving me the choice? At any rate, I knew better than to try to bargain my way out of it, for veins pulsated in her temples and her hands were balled into fists.

Despite my horror, I tried to clear my mind. John, of course, would insist on going to prison while I fled to safety abroad, but I must stay near

Elizabeth, even though she would be in the Tower to the east of the city and I in a prison to the west. And mayhap John could go to Italy, his sunny Italy. I had let him down years before when I did not tell him about my past with Tom Seymour, so maybe I could make it up to him now.

'Well?' she said, folding her arms over her breasts. 'I know how much you love my sister, but how much do you love your husband?'

'You are torturing me, but I pray you will not torture your sister.'

'My half sister,' she spit out. 'May the sins of the mother be visited upon the daughter!'

I could have struck her. It was exactly what I had feared from her. The persecuted had become the persecutor. I saw why she gave me a choice now. She knew me well enough to know I would save my husband over myself. John was to be shoved out of the way so I had no support but myself – or my queen. She was making me choose not only between prison for John or me but between her and Elizabeth. *Anne*, I thought, as if addressing the ghost who haunted my dreams, *Anne, I will not let you or your daughter down*.

'I'll go to the Fleet,' I told her, staring straight into those narrowed eyes, 'for I know you will be fair and honest with both my husband and my mistress, for, like us all, even kings and queens answer to the Lord.'

She glared at me but turned away. No rejoinder to that but no pity or remorse either. Just power. And something even more frightening – a righteous belief in herself and her Catholic cause at all costs.

'Your Majesty, may I not bid him farewell?' I dared to ask her. After defying her so, choosing to stay near Elizabeth at great danger to myself, I knew she would say no, but I would humble myself for the chance at one farewell glimpse of him.

She turned back again. 'Yes, in honor of the love I shall owe my husband when he comes and we have a family, I shall grant you that, Kat Ashley. 'She lifted her right arm stiffly, pointing at me. 'You see, even heretics deserve time to get their souls right with God before He settles with them for all eternity.'

After she went out, I stood in that small chamber, waiting to bid farewell for a while – or for all eternity, I did not know – to my beloved John. And, in doing so, I would have to lie to him again, or he would never go.

'Sweetheart!' he cried, and hugged me hard, ignoring the guard in the room and the open door to the hall with even more guards. For all I knew, Mary hovered just outside, listening, suspecting we might say something incriminating to each other.

'Did they tell you?' I asked. In our mutual hug,

I whispered in his ear, 'They not only suspect us of collusion in the Wyatt plot but have our books.'

'They showed them to me. So I'm being exiled, and you are to stay here with Elizabeth.'

So that was what he had been told. Then I would not be lying to him directly. In a way, I was staying here with Elizabeth. But after he had forgiven me for not telling him all about the Tom Seymour mess years ago, I'd vowed to him – even without his prompting – that I would never lie to him again.

'Yes. Yes – so you get to see sunny Italy after all.'

'It won't be sunny without you. And how long I'll be away – they're taking me to the docks at first light – I don't know. I'll write you through Cecil, but if you're at the palace with the princess, I don't know if he can get news to you.'

So, to make him go, they had not told him Elizabeth was going to the Tower. 'How will you live?' I asked him, almost choking on my words.

He gave me a gentle shake, then clamped me to him again as we kept whispering. 'You know I can make my way anywhere there are horses. I will find a patron if I must, since many supporters of our cause have already fled abroad.'

Our cause. Yes, we were rebels now indeed, like poor Thomas Wyatt, captured and tormented ones. And now I was losing both the loves of my life and was going to a dreadful place while Elizabeth suffered in the Tower.

We kissed and held tight, whispering love words and promises. They had to drag us apart. For all I knew, I would never see him again, and if the queen began to burn heretics, I might be first in line. Damn the queen for her perverted sense of favors and justice, her overweening power and pride I had seen in her father too.

When they took John out and slammed and locked my door, I collapsed at last, holding nothing back, not trying to be strong for him or Elizabeth or even myself. I sat in the pool of my skirts on the floor and sobbed until I could barely breathe.

Bereft, devastated . . . I was a little girl losing my mother all over again, burned, battered and drowned as she was as I knelt by her body. It was seeing Anne Boleyn ripped from this life again, her lips moving in desperate prayers for her soul. My John and my girl – gone. And I alone and afraid, not only for myself but for them, the only ones I loved above all life in this brutal Tudor world.

THE FLEET PRISON, LONDON

*March 19, 1554*

It was bitter cold that winter, but, at first, I hardly noticed. I was devoid of all feeling but that of impending doom and death. I huddled under a threadbare blanket and my single cloak on the wooden cot in my solitary cell in the queen's ward of the Fleet Prison. The cell had a small fireplace with a coal grate, but that, like everything else in here, cost money. I hid my mother's garnet necklace in my bodice, but I would starve before I would sell it or trade it, even for food. I ate little, until the warden threatened to put me in ankle irons if I didn't eat. And so, hardly tasting how vile was the tepid beef broth with a bare bone in it, I ate, and drank some of the small beer I was allotted.

The place smelled to high heaven even in the winter, though the fetid moat into which refuse was dumped and sewers spewed, was partly frozen. The Fleet River, which emptied farther south into the Thames, the turnkey said, was frozen, too.

As was my heart. The worst was not knowing how John was faring – though I feared less for him than I did my princess. When I asked if she had been sent to the Tower, all I got was shrugs.

I lost weight and my skin dried; I picked at the cracks of my fingers and bit my nails. Somehow the first long hours and days passed and blurred. I wore my hair down, dragging in my face. I understood now how Elizabeth had made herself sick with grief. My two gowns they'd brought to my cell hung on me as if I were a scare-the-crow from fields at home. At home – Devon, *Devon in wind and rain, when will I see my loves again?* At home, with our little family around my lovey at Hatfield or better yet at John's and my beloved Enfield where we walked the gardens and kissed . . .

I sat bolt upright. The man with my food was not the usual turnkey.

'Good day, Mistress Ashley,' he bid me kindly. He did not slam the tray down on the floor and leave. He was a portly man, which looked odd in this place, where even the better folk with fees for extra food looked gaunt. He had a gentle voice. A scar marked his mouth, almost as if he had two half pairs of lips, and several front teeth were missing.

'You are not the same one,' was all I could manage at first. 'And – is that for me?'

It was not the usual greasy broth but a piece of capon and a thick hunk of bread with cheese and a pewter mug of what looked to be claret. Hell's gates – which was how I had come to think of this place – this new man was confused and this fare was not for me. My stomach growled so loud, it sounded like thunder from a coming storm.

'Yes, mistress,' he said, keeping his voice low and steady. 'Someone is now paying for coal, wash water and a chamber fee, too, for linens which will be coming soon.'

'But who?'

He shrugged as if he didn't know, but he also winked. Had John found a way to send money already? How did he learn I was here? Or was it Elizabeth? Or Queen Mary with a change of heart?

'My wife's name is Cecily,' he said. 'A nice name, is it not?'

'Yes, but—'

Cecily. Cecil? Could William Cecil and Mildred be behind this kindness? If he did not tell, I dared not ask. And Cecily had been my dear mother's name – a sign from God to trust this man?

'I am desperate, sir, for word of my mistress, the Princess Elizabeth.'

He shrugged again but, as he bent toward me to put the wooden tray of food and drink on my knees, whispered, 'Today is March 19. Yesterday, she was sent to the Tower after her health improved enough.'

'Dear Lord, protect her, for she is innocent!'

'Indeed she is. I will get you word when I can. Queen Mary is to formally wed Prince Philip of Spain next June, for she has already done so by proxy. And the burning of heretics is to start soon at Smithfield.'

'Right here in London? In the very heart of London?'

'Cecily and I fear the ground will be red with martyrs' blood and the air – well, even worse than it is here.'

He sounded to be a man of learning, well-spoken. Was he telling me about the coming martyrs just to inform me of the terrible times, or because he knew I would be one of them and needed time to prepare myself?

Money was the grease in the wheels of everything at the Fleet, so I came to see how my new turnkey,

Tiler, his name was, could replace the first one I had had. But in this world of lies and spies, I told myself at first not to tell him too much. I realized that my early deprivation here could have set me up to trust any kindness, and for all I knew he reported straight to Queen Mary or her advisers. After all, it was common knowledge in the Fleet that Bishop Gardiner had been a prisoner here during the reign of King Edward, so he would know all the ins and outs. Sadly, I had learned to trust no one.

Still, each time Tiler brought me food or coal or, every so often, fresh linens, he always told me something or other about his 'dear Cecily' including that she was born in Stamford, where Cecil was from and was living now, so in my desperate heart, I trusted him.

'Hold on,' he oft told me when he came back for my tray or emptied my slop bucket. Or sometimes 'Hold tight.' When I asked him if I could be on the list of martyrs to be burned, he simply said, 'Not if Cecily and I can help it. Elizabeth may be a state prisoner and is being questioned by the Council, but they know not to step over a line with the possible future queen.'

The possible future queen! My Elizabeth! But still, I had seen the worst of Mary, and with a powerful Catholic and Spanish husband coming soon to help her rule, I feared for my princess as well as myself.

★　★　★

Even with Tiler's care, I had trouble sleeping. But, as I drifted off, I saw her then again, like many nights, not Elizabeth but Anne, floating in through my window, despite the thick panes and the grate there. Imprisoned. I was in the Fleet, but she was in the grave, so we were both imprisoned. Another thing we shared . . . why did I always feel close to Queen Anne, even before I tended and loved her daughter?

'Take care of her for me. Keep as close as she keeps her ruby ring.'

It was Anne with a ruby stain around her slender neck, holding her hands out to me, beseeching me. How she had hated Mary, so now that she was queen, I knew Anne could not rest well. I wanted to comfort Anne, to tell her to hold on, to hold tight, but I was terrified to touch her. She was dead, dead, in her arrow-box coffin under the stones of St Peter in Chains in the Tower, near where my lovey was in prison.

I wanted to tell her I had tried to protect the princess, but I could not form the words. I tried to move back from her cold embrace, but my feet were leaden, dead. Did this visitation mean I would soon be dead too? Mary had ordered heretics burned at Smithfield in the heart of London, in . . . the . . . heart . . .

Anne embraced me, icy cold. 'Save her, help her . . .' When she pressed her temple to mine, her head tottered and fell and rolled . . .

I sat up and screamed. The shrill sound echoed in my cell, in my brain. John! Where was he, where was I? – and then it all rushed back to me. John gone, mayhap forever. Elizabeth in the Tower, near where her mother had died, in mortal danger of not only losing any path to the throne but her very life.

Half awake, half asleep, I tried to brush Anne's cold embrace away, but saw that I had shoved my sheet, blanket and cloak to the floor. Surely, that's why I'd had the dream she was so cold.

That spring it bucked me up to hear Elizabeth had been released from the Tower, though she was sent to house arrest to Woodstock, the only one of her country houses she could not abide. No doubt she had told that once to Mary. What did it matter? I thought. My girl had outlasted the Tower.

Woodstock was a small old royal house, most lately a mere hunt lodge, and Tiler said she was enclosed in the small gatehouse there and was most vehemently protesting. That made me smile, the first time I'd done so in months. Mary and all she had brought to bear had not broken that Tudor temper or Boleyn backbone. And I could not help but wonder if my lovey had seen her secret love, Robin Dudley, when she was in the Tower.

But a few weeks later I was removed from prison and given over into the care of a Sir Roger Cholmley's household in the country, a man and area I did not know. I was relieved to escape the Fleet, but I had lost my lifeline in Tiler and longed to know outside news. The Cholmley daughter, Meg, finally mentioned that the queen was to wed her Spanish prince at Winchester Cathedral in late July, and that all England rejoiced. That – and being forced to attend Mass in a chapel in the Cholmley house – reminded me of what I already knew, that my hosts were not to be trusted. I did pity Meg, though, for her face had been so horribly scarred and deeply pitted by the smallpox that it grieved me to look at her.

But my soft feelings for my hosts halted with that. What a lie that all England rejoiced over that marriage bond with Spain. Be hanged to Mary and her Spanish prince and English king! And here I was with naught but popish tracts to read in a backwater rural house where I might as well be a cloistered nun. Alack the day I ever helped Mary Tudor in any way!

Bored, bereft, terrified, traitorous . . . I passed much of my days playing word games in my head or writing imaginary epistles – to John, of course; to Elizabeth; to my father; to myself, though I was not permitted to have pen and paper. I was allowed to walk in a small walled garden, if I would say a rosary. I went so stir-crazy that I finally acquiesced, though I was skilled at saying, 'Hail, Mary, Mother of God, pray for us . . .' and thinking far other thoughts.

But then one day in crisp September 1554, true salvation arrived with a knock on the wooden gate of the garden, which the steward who served as my guard opened, still keeping a wary eye on me as if I would bolt.

Tiler stood there, holding two horses, and handed my gaolcr a letter with a large seal on it. My heartbeat kicked up; my eyes met Tiler's and held.

'I'll have her things fetched, then,' the steward told him. ''Tis but two gowns and her proper reading matter. Take that rosary now, too, Mistress Ashley.'

I couldn't hold back my tears as Tiler helped me up on the second horse, then stuffed my things in my saddlebags, except for the Catholic papers and rosary, which I held to me as he thrust them up with a dour face and a wink. I could hardly believe I was free, free at last.

'But where are we going?' I asked him as we pushed our horses from a walk to a trot.

'Your mistress – now disinherited to be only the Lady Elizabeth again – is free from Woodstock and has gone to Hatfield. We are stopping the night at the Cecil house in Wimbledon – ah, I believe you have heard of my dear wife Cecily, have you not? I can't promise yet you are to be returned to your mistress, but she is ranting and raving about it.'

'And John? Is there any news of my husband, John?'

'Safe and sound, in Padua, so I hear, and I think dear Cecily's seen to his room and board too. But, however much we all rejoice for our safety, there are good, common English folk being burned at the stake for believing as we do – and for our loyalty to England's hope during these dread times.'

England's hope – my Elizabeth. I had learned the hard way that life brought the bitter with the sweet. As my father used to say, 'The Lord giveth and the Lord taketh away.' Yet I could not help myself, but when we rode over a humpbacked bridge above a spring-swollen brook, I dropped my rosary into its depths and tossed the torn popish papers after them.

In the closed-up Cecil home in Wimbledon, Mildred and I picked up exactly where we had left off, as friends and supports to each other. It turned out that it was she who had come closer to London to be my hostess, while Cecil, ever wary of Mary's increasing net [though the Cecils, like many who wished to stay alive, had taken a Catholic oath], remained in rural Stamford.

'Tell me what else the princess has written to you,' Mildred prompted as she quickly worked her needle on a piece of crewel and I read a letter from Elizabeth aloud.

'That she vows she will have me back with her soon – but then, she's said that before. That I am not to worry about my lord John, "for he and his horses can fend for themselves anywhere."'

'And my lord said he is writing his book. Still, it seems our letters do not reach him so that he knows you are safe.'

That was what bothered me the most. Cecil had received only two letters from John, ones I had read to death until they were tattered. Was he no longer in Padua? Was he well? Or – God forbid – had he found a life more suited to his heart there – found someone else?

Although I was going to return with Mildred to Stamford far from London and far from Elizabeth at Hatfield, I had a wild scheme that as our entourage passed in that area, I would ride off to see her. But just as we were to set out for the north, I finally received good news, not of my beloved husband but from my girl.

'Oh, my,' Mildred said as she read the missive from her husband, then held it out to me. 'Queen Mary must be in a good mood from her marriage: 'tis said here she is head over heels for King Philip, though he seems bored with her and is buttering her up to get English troops and funds so he can go to war with France. But look, she grants Elizabeth her wish to have back her Lady Katherine Ashley!'

I seized the letter. 'I'm to go to Hatfield and then attend Elizabeth at court? Oh, why cannot we just stay at Hatfield, away from that beehive? But why is the queen letting us come back to court? You are not smiling. What is wrong?'

'Read on,' she said. 'She has relented toward you both, but I warrant it is because she wishes to do to you what Anne Boleyn once forced her to do. You were there then, were you not, when Anne

330

Boleyn demanded Mary come to court for Elizabeth's birth, which would displace her in the royal line and take away any hope Mary could ascend the throne? See there – at the bottom of the missive in my lord's smaller writing? You and the princess are to be summoned to court in the spring to attend the queen for the birth of her and King Philip's half-Spanish, all-Catholic heir.'

# CHAPTER 17

HATFIELD HOUSE

*October 1554*

'Kat! My Kat!'

We ran into each other's arms and held tight. It had been eight months since we had been dragged apart by Queen Marry's guards in London.

'You have lost weight!' she said, and hugged me harder.

'Better I than you! At least I did not lose you.'

'I cannot wait for you to scold me again and make me eat and tell me what to wear.'

We held each other at arm's length. We were both crying like green girls. 'I'm so sorry about John being sent away,' she gasped out, 'but we will have him back.'

'Not if he would be safer there. I pray he's writing his book and making his way by training the horses of his sunny Italy.'

'Ah,' she said as we wiped tears from our faces, 'would that we all could be spirited away from Mary's England. She's burning people for their faith, Kat. And when I was finally sent away from London, I glimpsed the quartered, headless bodies of some of Wyatt's men nailed up on gates and even along the wharfs. And all the way here, people cheered and cheered me. The queen should recognize the power of her people, for she is angering them with all this unjust bloodshed.'

'And, they say, King Philip is draining our treasury to raise an army of our men for a war against France.'

'Enough of terrible topics,' Elizabeth declared. 'You must wash and rest, then I'll see that you have all your favorite foods. And then we must catch up with each other, for there is so much to say.'

She linked her arm through mine and tugged me gently toward the main entrance to Hatfield, then kissed me on both cheeks and held me tight again. For once, I realized, she was comforting me and not the other way around.

Late that afternoon, as the sun sent its pale October rays across the great park beyond the palace, we walked arm in arm with four guards trailing at a distance. We sat in the same place we had the day I had given her the ruby ring from her mother nearly a dozen years ago. How could the time have fled so fast? And yet I prayed it would go even faster so that I could have John back, so that Mary might not rule and my girl could have the throne. Treasonous thoughts. I had once pitied Mary

Tudor, but now I was a rebel indeed to want her gone.

'I worried so while you were in the Tower,' I told her.

'When they took me in, I saw the scaffolding on which Jane Grey had died. Kat, they still had it up, and I was terrified it would be for me! Worse, I kept thinking it was where my mother died, and when they put me in the old palace my father had built not only for her coronation but for her imprisonment before her death—'

Despite the slant of sun, she shuddered. I reached over to cover her hand with mine. 'I know the place well,' I told her. 'I was there with her in the happy days leading to her parade and coronation. Three years later, when she was there again, they did not break her, no matter what befell. And I see full well they did not break you either.'

'Thanks not only to my own defiance of them but to two men.'

'The constable and Cecil?'

'Neither. I know Cecil saved you when I could not, but the constable nearly did me in, though not through a threat or intentional cruelty. Just before they let me go, he was ordered to raise a hundred men for the queen and he mustered them on the Tower grounds. Kat,' she cried, turning toward me and gripping both of my hands in hers, 'I was certain they were there to keep the crowds under control during my beheading!'

'Oh, my lovey.' I pulled her to me, with her head

on my shoulder, tucked under my chin just as when she was small and haunted by some night fear. 'Who were the men who helped you, then?'

'Thomas Wyatt, of course, when he dared to declare – even on the scaffold before they beheaded him – that I was innocent of any of his plans.'

'He owed you that. He had no right to raise his banners in your name! And the other man?'

She sat up straight, and I saw her countenance change as from night to day. 'Robin Dudley is still in the Tower. I glimpsed him up in a high window once, and he bowed his head and waved to me.'

Vividly, the memory of my glancing up at the doomed Tom Seymour as John and I left the Tower assailed me. But she was chattering on, her voice light now. 'And when I finally obtained permission to walk in the privy gardens, he once sent me flowers brought by a small child. It was just some trailing ivy I think he might have pulled off the stone walls outside his window, and a few daisies, but I kept them and they heartened me. I pressed every one of those flowers and leaves in my Bible!'

She sighed. Though she had said in our reunion she could not wait for me to scold her again, this was hardly the time to admonish her for yearning for a married man, especially one who was a traitor in the Tower. Instead, I said, 'I was never so proud of you as when I heard you had stood up to the Council's threats and badgering.'

'But, Kat,' she said, sitting up straight and pulling her hands back from mine, 'I was and am innocent of all conniving against my royal sister. I am happy that she will have an heir, and I am sewing an infant cap and gown for the child now. If ever anyone asks you, under duress or not, about my feelings toward my future royal niece or nephew, you must say I cannot wait for the child's safe arrival and long life.'

Her steady gaze held mine. Was she saying that to protect me or herself? Surely, she did not think I had been sent back to her on the condition that I spy. Yet could I blame her if she'd learned to trust no one?

'When I was interrogated by the Council,' she said, her voice hardening – yes, I knew her tones of speech that well to realize something dire was coming – 'one of them let slip that Thomas Wyatt the younger, the rebel, was the son of a man who had once loved my mother, a man of the same name. Why didn't you tell me? Did you know of it or know him? Should I be ashamed of my mother as my father wanted? Kat, I am not some child to be protected at all costs. I am one-and-twenty and a woman grown!'

'You are that, Your Grace, Elizabeth Tudor. Come on, then, let's walk and talk more,' I said, and rose to tug her to her feet.

We strolled under the ancient oaks on the grounds while I told her things I never thought I would. That Thomas Wyatt and her mother had loved each other in their green years before Anne was sent to France and later caught King Henry's eye. That they had exchanged secret notes and poems at Hampton Court while the king was courting her. That once her father had lost his temper at Wyatt, not as much for beating him in a game of bowls but for goading His Majesty by flaunting Anne's necklace. Nervously, I toyed with my mother's garnet necklace through all that, until I realized what I was doing and let loose of it.

'So, despite great Henry's passion for her, the seeds of distrust might have been planted early,' she reasoned, half to herself. We stopped at the edge of a weedy meadow where a rabbit warren full of holes and dens could mean a turned ankle for man or beast. 'Tell me the rest, Kat. I take it that Thomas Wyatt the elder was in the Tower with the other men she was accused with, but he was released. I gleaned that from the Council's questions too.'

I hesitated. Not only had I never told her that I saw her mother die but I had actually lied to her years ago, when she asked me if I had been there.

'If I were queen now, I would command you to tell me,' she said, almost pouting. 'You must tell me what you are thinking, what you know. If you love me, you will tell me – I know you loved her too!'

I put my arm around her shoulders, surprised anew she was taller than I by half a head. We leaned together, looking out over the blowing meadow with the guards a ways back. 'I believe she always loved Wyatt but was not untrue to your father with him, or surely they would have ferreted it out of Wyatt in her downfall. His sister was one of her attendants on the scaffold, and I saw Queen Anne give the woman something at the last minute – for him, I think.'

She gasped and turned to me, pulling away. 'You – but you said once you weren't there.'

'Only to keep from having to tell about it to a little girl who was not ready to hear it. Anne Boleyn was brave and beautiful that day, and resigned to her fate. She wanted me there – John went, too, and practically held me up – because she had given me the ring for you and wanted it there – your portrait. So I held it up to her, though too far for her to see it. But she was reminded of you just before the end, and I'm sure it gave her strength, her love for you. And I had vowed to her I would do all I could to take care of her little girl.'

She swayed on her feet; I held her tight to me again. The guards came closer, but I motioned them back. Amazingly, they stood away.

'You – you saw her die,' she whispered.

'And it's haunted me ever since.'

'But I'm so glad you were there. And, with the ring, in a way, I was too. Maybe now the sad dreams of her will stop. Kat, thank you for being loyal to her and to me all these years.' She threw her arms around me but did not cry.

'Sad dreams?' I asked, stroking her back. 'Bad dreams?'

'A sort of nightmare, but I didn't used to mind because that way I could see her. She looks just like the woman in the ring portrait, of course. She drifts in the window and watches me, hugs me with her icy arms and tells me she loves me, so it's not so very bad. I was afraid if I told anyone, the dream would stop and I wouldn't see her anymore.'

I began to shake. Nearly the same dream – or nightmare – I had suffered for years. Anne. Anne haunting us both. When would she be at rest?

'What is it?' she asked. 'You're trembling.'

'Since it seems we have no more secrets, I will tell you that is much the same dream I have had for years, where she asks me to care for you.'

She took a step away and turned to stare at me. Her head bobbed in surprise; her eyes widened before she blinked. She glanced at the guards, then whispered so silently I had to read her lips. 'She will rest when I am queen. She said so.'

'I pray so.'

'And that's why my sister's marriage and coming child do not sadden or frighten me. God willing, it must be true that I shall rule. That must be why I have escaped the lion's den in the damned Tower. Oh, I know I've been disinherited again, and I know my royal sister and her advisers hate and fear me, but I think it may be God's will that I have the throne someday.'

Still stunned, I nodded.

'Whatever happens,' she said, looking out over the meadow, 'I will always love you, Kat. You have been my other mother, the one of the real world. Yes, I will ever say that Anne Boleyn gave me life, but Kat Ashley gave me love.'

In May 1555, we were sent for to Hampton Court where the queen was lying in, awaiting the birth of her heir. For miles as we approached on horseback, we heard the distant tolling of bells and cannon shots from time to time. We could see celebration bonfires hastily being built on hills.

Trying desperately to cloak our alarm at the possible import of the ruckus – for that was the way royal births were announced – Elizabeth and I looked grimly at each other.

'The queen has been delivered of a prince!' someone along the road cried. Huzzahs followed, from the queen's guards in our entourage at least, though some along the road just shook their heads. But before we reached the Thames and the palace, the news was different. The birth of a royal son was a rumor which had somehow spread like wildfire. How shameful for Their Majesties, I thought, and what a blessing for Elizabeth, albeit a temporary one.

At the palace, we were greeted by more guards and led without ado to a small suite of guarded rooms far from the royal chambers. 'We have been sent for to see the queen,' Elizabeth protested before they closed the door on her and her four ladies. But it was not Elizabeth who received a royal summons the next afternoon but I.

My escort was Susan Clarencieux, the queen's Mistress of the Robes, a lofty position of intimacy and trust. 'How fares Her Majesty?' I dared to ask.

'It has been a difficult pregnancy, as you will see.'

'On the road, rumors were abroad she was already delivered of a son.'

'Unfortunate – the rumors, I mean,' the attractive woman, who looked quite hurried and harassed, said. 'Her Grace did not need that too. Speak softly in her presence, for she has splitting head pains.'

'Why has she sent for her sister if she will not see her?'

'Hers is to command and I to obey. I,' she said, putting undue emphasis on that word, 'do not meddle in my mistress's business.'

I said no more, but trod carefully with feet and tongue as we traversed a series of withdrawing rooms to the royal bedchamber. I found it not unusual that the room was dim. But it seemed dreary too – silent as a tomb, unlike what I recalled of Anne Boleyn's lying-in, at least before everyone knew the child was a girl. We had heard that Mary had chosen to have her heir here because the country air was salubrious, but this room was closed and the air stale. Yet through the shuttered windows I could hear the ever-present droning of the priests and bishops who walked in the courtyard below chanting their rosaries for the safe birth of the royal child. It reminded me of the buzz of bees behind our house when I was a girl.

Several women moved away from the huge canopied bed as Lady Susan brought me closer. The queen sat within, propped up by pillows. She, too, looked like a fat white pillow. Yes, far gone in a pregnancy indeed, but she seemed swollen all over.

'So, Kat Ashley,' she said in her deep voice as I curtsied to her, 'now I have a husband with me and you do not.'

I bit my lower lip, for I was tempted to say something tart and bitter, such was the taste this woman always left in my mouth and thoughts now.

'I am pleased,' I told her, 'you find such happiness in your marriage.' Though Elizabeth and her women had been cloistered here so far, that had not kept us from overhearing tittle-tattle from servants that Philip was bored with his dour, much older wife and anxious to get away from the country his Spanish companions thought of as 'barbarous.' And en route here, we had heard and seen that ridicule and derision against Mary and Philip ran rampant in English villages and towns.

'I sent for you,' Mary said, 'because I still cannot bear to greet my sister, not after that rebellion.'

'For which accusations your Council found her innocent. She wishes you well. She has worked diligently on a gift for your heir and hopes to be able to present it to you in person.'

'Yes, when I bear the babe, of course. Did you hear that my ladies showed me triplets born in London of a mother of my age, and that she is fine and out of danger? Three healthy babes for her, but, this time, I shall just bear one.'

She sounded on the edge of desperation, but I had seen that before in royal childbed. As my eyes adjusted to the dim light, I saw dark circles hung under Mary's eyes like half-moons; her skin looked grayish. She shifted her bulk and pointed to something behind me. I turned to behold a beautifully crafted cradle with a carved and gilded crown at its head.

'Read me the inscription, Kat,' she said, as if we were the best of friends after all she'd done to me and mine. 'I remember you always read things with measure and meaning, and the verse comforts me.'

I had to bend close to it in the wan light to see. I read to her, '"The child which through Mary, O Lord of Might, did send, / To England's joy, in health preserve, keep and defend."'

'God's will be done,' she intoned and clasped her hands across her distended belly. 'Tell my sister that.'

'I will, Your Majesty, for she believes that too. But will you not see her and tell her yourself?'

I thought she would be angry, but she said with a sigh, 'My beloved husband wishes to see her, so tell her he will call upon her in her withdrawing room in an hour or so. I am sending her a gown to wear, for I will not have her face the King of England in some unadorned, grim garb as if she were here for a funeral and not a birthing.'

'Yes, Your Majesty.'

'He fancies a foreign wedding for her, one in the true faith, of course.'

My insides cartwheeled. I almost retorted that my mistress fancied no such thing and would never have one foisted upon her, foreign or domestic, but I held my tongue on that. 'She will be honored to meet the king,' I managed, when I longed to say so much more. But when had standing up to Tudor queens or kings ever brought me anything but trouble?

'So do you think he is the puppet master behind the throne?' Elizabeth whispered to me after she was gowned and coiffed to meet the king. She still wore her hair long as she had for several years, in the style of a virgin or a bride. The others had left us, and I waited with her in the small withdrawing room which led to the corridor, where a guard ever stood.

'Yes, best to whisper. Someone told me once the very walls have ears, and I don't doubt it around here. I recall, too, that both this palace and Whitehall have secret passageways, like you and your brother rampaged through years ago. But anywhere the queen and king live, 'tis said that

His Majesty seems to know things he wouldn't unless he'd been peeping through keyholes or mouse holes or some such.'

She laughed. Such a change in mood, but then she was thrilled to be wearing the first new gown she'd had in two years and a beautiful one. She was excited to meet the king, I could tell, however much grief he and his Catholics had caused her and the country. She preened, twirling to watch the huge embroidered skirts of fine canary-hued brocade bell out. The natural vanity of my girl had been buried deep for years, but it was still there. I weighed whether or not to warn her that Philip might hope to marry her off for royal advantage, but she had faced such before with no result. Besides, a knock sounded on the door, and it swung open. Elizabeth turned slowly and feigned flustered surprise, then curtsied gracefully. I followed suit, then backed quickly from the room, though I left the door slightly ajar.

Philip entered alone and raised Elizabeth to her feet. I saw them in silhouette, like a shadow play, for light spilled in the door behind him. He kissed both her cheeks, then her mouth. The man was fingering her red-gold hair, I could tell that much!

'They say, dear sister,' he commented in heavily accented English, 'that King Henry had hair of flame too.'

'He did, indeed, Your Majesty. It is a great honor to meet you.'

'Time hangs heavy now – for the queen and for me too.'

'But soon your joy will be complete,' she replied, this time in Spanish.

'I heard you are as well educated as you are lovely,' he said, no doubt pleased to converse in his native tongue, which I had learned years ago, though his speed and different accent took me by storm. Surely, his presence was not affecting Elizabeth the same way. His soothing words sounded as if he wanted to seduce her. I had heard noblewomen in Spain had *duennas* who never let them out of their sight, and now I knew why. Was he not going to mention a possible foreign marriage to her?

'I told the queen,' he was saying, his large, square jaw dominating his profile as he walked around my girl, looking her over as if he would a filly to buy, 'that closer relations between us should be encouraged, even cultivated. What a joy to find I am related to such a delightful young woman and what sadness to hear there have been family troubles.'

I rolled my eyes. Was this some sort of trap or indirect inquisition? This man was deadly dangerous. He'd insisted, I'd heard; that Mary not pardon a thirteen-year-old apprentice who was to be burned at Smithfield for his faith, along with other common folk, a butcher and a barber. It was one thing to rid the country of those who had led a rebellion against her, but Their Majesties were alienating and angering the backbone of the nation. And I swear, speaking of burnings, I could scent the hiss of passion coming from the king each time he touched Elizabeth. I had expected harshness at the worst from him or disdain at the best, but not this – caresses and kisses.

I was even more angered when he closed first the door that he'd come in and then the one I'd been listening and peeking through.

'Did he treat you with the respect you are due as a royal sister-in-law?' I demanded the moment Elizabeth returned to her bedchamber.

'I can tell he's bored, Kat,' she whispered, gesturing me over to the open second-story window, much as her mother used to do when she did not want conversations overheard. 'Bored with waiting for an heir he is not sure is coming—'

'What?'

'Sh! Oh, the doctors and midwives and sooth-sayers claim so, but I can tell he's not sure.'

'The queen would not make that up!' I protested.

'Sh! She believes it – desperately. Now, this is all my reading between the lines, of course.'

'In English or Spanish or the language of love?'

'Were you eavesdropping? I used my wiles to get what I want, I admit I did.'

'But what *did* he want?'

'I warrant not only "my love," as he put it – oh,

do not look at me like that – he meant family love—'

'My green goat he did! I vow, he wants to wed you to someone where he can have access to your bed too.'

'He did mention a possible marriage, but I put that off. Kat, he promised we could leave as soon as Mary's child is born. He's leaving then too, though it grieves me it will be because he's stripped the treasury of funds and plans to lead good, stout English soldiers against France, which should be our ally against Spain – and not the other way around.'

And so, I saw my girl had learned to use her feminine wiles for political purpose. How and where had she learned such in prison and rural exile? Had it come through her blood from her mother? This was a far cry from the young woman who had nearly been seduced by Tom Seymour. I had thought she had much to learn but, evidently, so did I.

By the end of July, after putting off her heir's birth time, and again from May, Mary collapsed in hysteria and admitted she could not be with child. As relieved as I was for the country and Elizabeth, I pitied Her Majesty too, for I knew how painful it was to long for a child with a man one loved and never be able to bear one.

Then, too, Philip of Spain left England for a trip home, some said to see his mistress he had been kind enough not to bring with him for his honeymoon. Mary sent for her sister and, in the only ten minutes they had had together in years, told her that she would soon have her beloved husband back and indeed conceive a child next time. It was dropsy and belly swelling and the cessation of her menses that had deluded her this time, she claimed. But at least Elizabeth, her entourage and I were allowed to head for Hatfield, where a letter from my beloved John awaited me.

I read it with shaking hands, yearning for him so strongly that I sensed how Mary must have made herself sick, longing for a child, desperate for something she could not have. John wrote he was studying the classics and Italian art at the University of Padua, where he was training horses and continuing to write his book, *The Art of Riding*. He had been to Bologna and Venice and had bought me some books and 'pretty things.' They believed in *libertas scholastica* there, academic freedom. He was called an *ultramontana*, meaning a student who had come from beyond the Alps. He loved me greatly and missed me terribly – like a lovesick rustic, I kept kissing the page – and he bid me greet Her Grace for him and prayed the Lord God for our safety.

Beyond the Alps . . . pretty things . . . freedom . . . loved and missed me . . . safety . . .

I had held in my hopes and fears for him so long, I burst out in tears and fled outside, where Elizabeth came to comfort me as I had her so many times. We were in the privy garden when Sir Thomas Pope [a name I thought most appropriate for one sent from Catholic Mary], our latest gaoler, as Elizabeth called them, rode in with his wife and an entourage. It was another cruel reminder that I did not have freedom or safety or love, and mayhap never would.

# CHAPTER 18

HATFIELD HOUSE

*November 17, 1558*

From the depths of despair came deliverance for me, Elizabeth and England.

On the vast stage of national events, tragedy: King Philip squandered English funds and men in a foreign war and lost it, too, when Calais, the last English property on the Continent, fell to the French. How proud the previous monarchs of England had been to yet possess that European stronghold, a legacy of the powerful Plantagenet past. It was said that Queen Mary declared that if she died and they cut her open, they would find the word *Calais* incised upon her heart.

Philip returned to her for a brief time and another pregnancy was proclaimed, but people just shook their heads and grumbled. With Mary – some called her Bloody Mary now – seeing would be believing.

Elizabeth's entire household chaffed under the continued control of Thomas Pope and his wife,

Beatrice, as we had under other watchdogs all these years of waiting for events to fall our way. It gave me a new understanding of the term 'lady-in-waiting.' But in the autumn of 1558, great gifts from God began to rain upon us.

The first was in this way: Elizabeth and I, with several of her ladies – trailed, of course, by the ubiquitous Popes – took a brisk, late November walk on the grounds before Hatfield House. Our daily exercise helped us to manage the tensions and the tedium of our days.

Her Grace, like her sister, was somewhat near-sighted, though not as bad, so pointing, I told her, 'I see a messenger coming this way fast.'

'Dare we hope to hear another royal heir is a figment of disease and desperation?' she whispered.

We had heard that Mary was ailing sore, so I had hopes that someday the messenger would come to say she was on her deathbed and my girl should prepare herself to be queen. Mary had finally reinstated Elizabeth in the line of succession – though in line after, of course, any children she might bear Philip, who was by then King of Spain as well as England.

I shaded my eyes. Leaves were falling and blowing, but something about the rider's form and style on that big horse struck me, a definite command of the great beast and of himself and –

'John!' I cried. The steed's sharp hoofs threw gravel behind them like a cloud. 'It's John!'

Elizabeth gasped, but, lifting my skirts, I was

off, running. Yes, John. I was not dreaming. John had come home to me!

He called my name, once, twice, but I was too out of breath to answer. He looked so fine, his face sun-colored, his cloak flapping behind him like the wings of a great bird. Sturdy, broader-chested than I recalled. He slowed slightly, called out, 'My love!' and, with one arm, leaned down to snatch me up into the saddle before him.

My bottom bumped across his shin and knees, but I just held to him as we bounced along, managing a kiss that went from nose to chin until he reined in. I did not even heed the others when the Pope, as we called him behind his back, protested, 'You were not announced, sirrah!'

'Welcome back! Do you have news, my lord Ashley?' Elizabeth's clarion voice rang out, also ignoring the sputtering Pope as she grasped John's booted ankle.

'That I have returned to serve Your Grace and be a husband to my wife again!' John helped me slide to the ground, then dismounted and knelt at Elizabeth's feet. 'I returned in secret a few days ago and have been living at Cecil's house in Wimbledon,' he told her, 'but I could wait no longer to see you, Your Grace – or the stubborn woman who has long served you.'

She extended her hand to John, and he kissed it. My hands gripped hard together, joy rampaged through me. She tried to raise John, but he stayed down.

'I have more news,' he said. 'Her Majesty, your sister, is gravely ill, God rest her soul – despite it all.'

'I'll not have such talk, Lord Ashley!' the Pope interrupted again. ''Tis treason to talk such of the queen's dying. Now, everyone back inside and you, sirrah, with me.'

'He is my servant and friend,' Elizabeth said, rounding on the Pope, 'and he stays with me and Mistress Ashley. We will know our queen has left us only when she sends to me the coronation ring – she told me thus when I last saw her.'

That sobered Thomas Pope and me. Why had my girl not told me that? But if John was right, that Mary was truly, finally, going to depart this earth, then Elizabeth Tudor would no longer be my girl but England's queen.

That day I recall she had her way, keeping John with us. Even the Pope, who had been the bane of our existence for nigh on three years, backed off and bowed to her wishes. People – all but me – had begun to treat her differently of late. Hope for a new beginning was in the air, blowing the past away, just as the wind blew these leaves. We started back inside, the three of us walking together: John with one arm around my waist, the other holding his horse's reins; Elizabeth with her arm linked in mine and already peppering John with questions about his learning at the university.

But then, again, I heard more horses coming

and turned back to look up the lane again. 'Riders,' I said. 'A great cloud of them.'

'John,' Elizabeth said, 'give me a boost up on your horse. I want to be over there, under that biggest oak, should this be my time.'

My insides cartwheeled at the thought. That many riders, come clear to Hatfield, could only mean one thing. Were all our years of fearing, of waiting, over?

I thought she might ride out to meet them, but she did as she had said. She rode across the lawn to dismount under the massive oak where she and I had talked of many things, where I had given her her mother's ring. John and I hurried to stand behind her – the others came too, but at first I looked not at anyone but Elizabeth of England.

Bareheaded, her fur-trimmed cloak blowing in the brisk breeze, her cheeks burnished by the wind and excitement, she stood waiting for the men to dismount. Eleven of them, I quickly counted. And Cecil! Cecil was not only among them but seemed to lead them. I saw others of Queen Mary's Privy Council I recognized, some who had favored Elizabeth and some who had not. And tall and proud, intentionally slow in dismounting, sinfully handsome – dear Lord in heaven, it was Robin Dudley. We had heard that he had been released from the Tower and sent to France to fight for King Philip, who had told Mary she should pardon him, but we'd had no news of his whereabouts or well-being.

Our friend William Cecil nearly vaulted off his horse and went immediately to one knee, with Robin – all the men – uncovering their heads and going down too. John and I knelt behind her with the Popes on their knees farther back. Her red-gold hair glinting in a shaft of sudden sun, Elizabeth stood awaiting their words and her destiny.

'Your Grace – Your Majesty,' Cecil said, out of breath. He extended to her in his palm the onyx coronation ring that left the monarch's hand only upon death. For one moment, Elizabeth stared wide-eyed at it, not moving, mayhap not daring to believe.

'Your royal sister – I regret,' Cecil said, looking up and biting back a smile that lit only his eyes, 'has sadly departed this life, and left to you the Tudor throne and the realm of England, Scotland and Ireland.'

Blinking back tears, Elizabeth took the ring. Shaking, she thrust it on the fourth finger of her right hand. It was too big, but I knew this huge task that lay before her would never be too big for my girl – my queen.

'This,' she said in her lovely, clear voice, 'is the Lord's work, and it is marvelous in our eyes.'

I knew full well she was quoting the Bible, but I thought about that word *our*. It was the plural royal prerogative, but I believe, after all she and I and John had been through together, that *our* meant us, too.

★   ★   ★

Within several hours, while place seekers clear from London and English folk from nearby shires flocked to the gates of Hatfield to glimpse or petition their new queen, Elizabeth met with the members of her newly named, yet incomplete Council in the great hall at Hatfield. It was, I heard her announce to the lords in attendance, 'a place I find most dear, for it was here my royal parents used to entertain in their happy days.' I saw she wore not only the coronation ring on her right hand, but her mother's ring next to it.

First, Elizabeth declared three days of mourning for her sister, who they said had died of a stomach tumor and quartan fever after another false pregnancy. Secondly, she dismissed several Council members she knew would yet be true only to the former queen and her causes. Thirdly, the new queen named Sir William Cecil her principal secretary and chief counselor and bid him always give her honest advice, no matter the cost. I wrote her wise words down, of which I was so proud:

'This judgment I have of you, Cecil. That you will not be corrupted with any manner of gifts, and that you will be faithful to the state; and that without respect of my private will, you will give me that counsel which you think best; and if you shall know anything necessary to be declared to me of secrecy, you shall show it to myself only; and assure yourself I will not fail to keep taciturnity therein.'

I took those words to heart for myself, that

without respect of her private will, I would give her privy counsel I thought best. How was I to know that, though she had declared me her earthly mother, she might no longer heed me?

For she immediately ignored my first advice and named Robert Dudley, her Robin, Master of the Horse, a command that would keep him ever close to her. The annual salary for that post was fifteen hundred pounds annum with various benefits, unfortunately, I thought, including a suite of rooms at court. He would have servants of his own and could wear the coveted green and white Tudor livery. I heard murmurings that he was tainted by being the son of a traitor, but I had to admit he was a fine, handsome horseman, like my John.

I only hoped he would soon bring his rural wife Amy to court, because, without asking John or me to escort them, Elizabeth and Robin went riding alone in Hatfield park before we all headed for London. *Oh, well,* I tried to tell myself, *they have much in common and have both been deprived. It must, after all, remain only friendship. Surely, she has learned her lesson about married men in all she suffered – and I too – over Tom Seymour.*

Meanwhile, John and I were overwhelmed by the bounty of what the new twenty-five-year-old queen showered on us that day and shortly thereafter. I was named Mistress of the Robes and First Lady of the Bedchamber. Yes, once a servant, then a gentlewoman, Katherine Champernowne Ashley from the fringe of the bleak Devon moors was now declared a lady by my dear Elizabeth's command. I was to supervise the maids of honor, all from noble families.

I was also to oversee Her Majesty's – it took me months to use that term for her – wardrobe, which, despite the fact she wore her plain garb for now, soon vastly expanded so that we took over a huge building in Blackfriars in London to store the pieces of her many gorgeous, many-hued garments. I soon enough devised a logical system for their storage: sleeves and bodices hung by color and cost; farthingales and petticoats by fabrics and width, collars and cloaks and shoes – a daunting task, so I soon took on many helpers, but I am jumping ahead of my story.

Before we left Hatfield for London, Elizabeth named John the Master and Treasurer of Her Majesty's Jewels and Plate, ironically a lucrative appointment Thomas Cromwell had once held. It was a lifetime sinecure of much tradition and dignity with a salary of fifty pounds per annum and fourteen double dishes per day in the court bouche allotments – a lavish amount that allowed us to feed a retinue of servants and staff of our own. Free lodging at court included a lovely suite of apartments near the royal suite. The only thing that sat wrong with me was that we also had quarters (and John an office) in the Tower, but that was so he could visit to assess and protect gifts to the Crown as well as the royal jewels. And, of course, serving Elizabeth would entail my facing the Tower again – only under far finer circumstances than several times before. The moment we arrived in London, John began to prepare the coronation regalia, though that day was two months away.

He was also named Prime Gentleman of the Privy Chamber, while I was titled Chief Gentlewoman, so we had control of the domestic staff at whatever palace we visited with the queen. We had large stipends with those positions, too, and, better yet, lands that she had wanted to give me years ago now came into my possession: a house and acres in Dorset, properties at Abbotsbury and Milton, a manor at Osmington and the tenement of Chaldon, the rents of which would help to support us for the rest of our lives. From rags to riches, indeed, for both Elizabeth and me. I was a wealthy woman now and immediately sent two guards with a letter and pouch of coins for my father and his family in Devon.

And so, in slow procession, with both John and Robin Dudley riding behind her, the new queen's courtiers and household journeyed to London to await her rule and to plan for Mary's burial and Elizabeth's coronation, both in Westminster Abbey.

Even on the rural road, people went wild as she passed. I sometimes smiled with relief and joy, sometimes cried. How the good Lord had protected and blessed us. Free from fear at last!

Surely, only good times were to come to poor, ravaged England in this new age of Elizabeth.

## THE TOWER OF LONDON

*January 14, 1559*

Two months later, again London cheered their new queen as our cavalcade rode to the Tower, by tradition the place from which Elizabeth's coronation parade would set out toward Westminster the next day. John's eyes met mine as we rode in through the same Tower entry we had exited after our imprisonment there, the day we had first met Cecil. I thought of that earlier time I had been there with Queen Anne, a quarter of a century ago, before her parade and crowning. I prayed Elizabeth would feel no fear, but how foolish of me. She was all smiles, waving at her people from the pure white steed Robert Dudley had selected for her to ride.

But when the doors had closed London out and we all dismounted, I saw her pause and look around at the Tower green, where the scaffold had stood, at the palace that had been refurbished for her mother's coronation and had been both Anne's and Elizabeth's prison. But she went in and I hastened after her, with a quick kiss from John, while he stayed behind with Robert to see the horses were all led away and bedded down properly.

It was the fourteenth day of January, 1559. After our arrival in London two months ago, we had lodged first in huge Somerset House while Whitehall Palace was being prepared for her – Mary's old furniture carted away, the rooms aired, the garderobes cleaned, and the many peepholes found under arrases closed up. Elizabeth had told the workers, however, to leave the secret backstairs entrances her father had built at Whitehall and Hampton Court.

Then for Christmas, we had moved into a much renovated Whitehall. She was looking forward, she'd said, to visiting her many palaces and homes. Yet John and I missed Hatfield and Enfield Chase, for their coziness and comfort. May the Lord God forgive us, but of all the bounty of lands Her Grace had showered on us, how John and I wished she had given us Enfield above all else.

When we were settled in the Tower that winter afternoon, as daylight waned, Elizabeth said to me, 'I want to pray in St Peter in Chains Church here, and I've sent for John and Robin to go with us.'

'Yes, Your Grace,' I said and went to fetch cloaks for both of us. She evidently intended to take no one else, so I told her ladies – Robin's sister, Mary Sidney, had been newly appointed among them, and Elizabeth greatly favored her – that they would not be needed. They sighed with relief and went back to their chatting and roasting chestnuts, clustered by the fire, which hissed from time to time from snow spitting down the chimney.

I assessed Robert Dudley, her Robin, anew as he waited with John by the palace door to the central green of the Tower. [By the way, when we'd lodged two months earlier in the Tower for one night, Elizabeth had summoned Sir John Bedingfield, the constable who had been her gaoler there. She praised him for doing a good job to keep her close-confined while she was a prisoner and then promptly dismissed him.]

Robert Dudley was almost exactly Elizabeth's age, and I'd heard some call him 'The Gypsy' behind his back for his darker complexion than most Englishmen. Later, scandalmongers said the name was appropriate because he cast a spell on her. Always fashionably, almost fantastically attired, he was well featured with a neatly clipped reddish brown beard and mustache and heavy-lidded eyes, which made, I supposed, most ladies feel the impact of his charms. But his dark brown eyes were only on Elizabeth. As soon as she was crowned, I intended to remind her that being queen did not protect one's reputation when gadding about with married men – if I did not, John said he would.

Robert Dudley could not only ride and joust well, he was witty and learned, skilled at tennis and archery and dancing – how Elizabeth loved dancing with him – all of which flaunted his well-turned, muscular legs. Oh, yes, at age fifty-two, I could still realize what she felt for him. My John and I yet reveled in each other's arms and charms, and I could well recall those good old and bad old days when a man's physical wiles could quite turn my head. And like John – and Tom Seymour too, curse him – Robert reeked of masculinity and magnetism.

But Elizabeth was queen and had worked for years to rebuild her reputation after the Seymour debacle that almost ruined us both, so I assumed she would soon come to her senses. But already her courtiers – and Cecil, who did not trust Robert – lifted their brows as their maiden queen smiled at and tarried with the traitor's son whose wife was kept in the country.

But now, as the four of us headed for the church, it was a heady experience to see how the royal yeomen guards scrambled to open doors ahead of Elizabeth, doors we used to have to open for ourselves – or which were locked to hold us in. She was in a hurry now, perhaps so she would not change her mind to visit the site where her mother's abused body lay. I had to stretch my strides to keep up with her.

Outside, the crisp river breeze bucked against us, as if to hold us back. I fell in directly behind the queen, with John and Robert bringing up the rear. We blinked at the snow, and the winter wind curled into our clothes. Puffs of our breath blew behind us. No one spoke as we approached the small, squat building, the church of St Peter in Chains – so perfect a name, I thought, for a prison church.

John hastened to open one of the double doors. Some winter light filtered in through the window-panes to cast half shadows on the stone-flagged floor and bare altar holding a stone statue of the crucified Christ. A few effigies of knights and their ladies, frozen in perpetual prayer, stared heavenward above their tombs as we all started down the short aisle. Elizabeth stopped and said, without looking at us, 'Robin and John, please stay back to keep others from coming in. Kat, with me.'

Our skirts and cloaks rustled, and our footfalls echoed as we walked the aisle to the altar, before which sat four plain wooden benches, for the Tower yeomen guards sometimes worshipped here. We sat on the front one, side by side, not speaking until she said, not turning her head but staring straight ahead, 'I know her coffin – that arrow box – lies under the floor here. It has been twenty-two years since I have been this close to her – to her body, I mean – but I feel closer than ever to her in my head and heart. I yet cannot fathom how things have changed, the power and position that is mine. Have you had the nightmare of her since I've become queen?' she asked, turning to me at last.

'No, Your Grace. Not once.'

She jerked her gloved hand over to my lap to grasp mine. 'I neither. She is finally at rest, but she will always be with me, just as you must be. To be on my side in all things, Kat.'

I nearly brought up her foolish favoring of her Robin, but I held my tongue for now.

She went on in a rush, 'I'm going to take the Boleyn badge of the white falcon on the tree stump for my own to let them know my pride in my Boleyn heritage as well as Tudor. Of course, I honor her memory by appointing my Boleyn cousins, Catherine and Henry, to serve me and will advance them over the years.'

She was referring to the adult children of her deceased aunt Mary Boleyn, Anne's sister, the woman who had dared to wed the man she loved and had been exiled from court for it before I came to London. Elizabeth's sweet and charming cousin Catherine had been named one of her ladies I oversaw, and the queen greatly favored and relied upon her cousin Henry, who became Lord Hunsdon and served her well.

'That all pleases me, and it would have greatly pleased your mother,' I assured her.

'He's buried here, too, Tom Seymour.'

'Yes. Jane Grey, your cousin Queen Catherine Howard – others who made mistakes trusting or being ruled by the wrong men.'

She let out a rush of breath like a huge sigh. She was squeezing my hand so hard I thought to protest, but she said, 'It's different with me and Robin, Kat, no matter what you are thinking. Next to you, he's my dearest friend from the past, and he's going with me into the future.'

'Of course, you will need many strong men

around you, both men of rank and reputation. But—'

'Like Cecil and like John,' she interrupted. 'But Robin too.'

'Perhaps you should let his wife come to court to stop wagging tongues,' I dared.

She sighed again and let my hand go. 'She prefers the country. And besides, she's been ill.'

I held my breath as my mind raced. 'What kind of ill? Is it serious?'

'Of course, we hope not. Kat, we shall kneel and pray here for the parade and coronation.'

And for Amy Dudley's good health, I thought, as I got down on my knees beside her on the hard, cold stone floor. Elizabeth had vowed to me over the years she would never wed, so was Robert more or less safe for her to love, since he was wed? If something would happen to Amy, could the Council and the people accept him as a possible marital candidate? His family was still hated for being so arrogant to take the earldom of Northumberland, the first time non-nobles attained the ducal rank, though that title had died with Robert's sire.

My thoughts tumbled faster than did her whispered prayers. Privily, I knew she detested the idea of marriage, and, after Spanish Philip, England would have a hard time stomaching another foreign king. Still, Cecil and the Council were already adamant that Elizabeth consider royal suitors.

'Dearest Lord,' she whispered beside me, 'please protect my people and the kingdom as I take the crown of my father – and my mother.'

She prayed in whispers for a long time as my knees went numb but my heart overflowed with love for and pride in her. At her orders, John had planned for her to wear the ornate coronation crown King Henry had fashioned for her mother, one that would fit her head perfectly. Perfectly, as I prayed Elizabeth Tudor would rule her realm.

The main thoroughfare of London was awash with banners, pennants and brocade bunting on the new queen's recognition day. Despite the cold, in a canopied open litter, Elizabeth Tudor rode the adulation of her people through the swirls of their hurrahs. Down Fleet Street to where crowds poured into the Strand, she glittered in her gown and mantle of cloth of gold trimmed with ermine and gold lace.

Like a great tide came her red-coated gentlemen pensioners with ceremonial battle-axes, then squires, footmen and men on a thousand prancing horses. Behind her rode Robert Dudley, mounted on a charger and leading her horse, which was covered with golden cloth. John came next, before her ladies, including me, in decorated chariots, then members of her Privy Council, swept along in her broad wake.

The royal progress took all day, for the queen bade her cavalcade halt when someone in the crowd tendered an herbal nosegay or held up a baby. At certain sites proud citizens enacted play scenes, presented pageants and recitations, or sang madrigals. We were proffered food and drink – and privy closets to relieve ourselves – from time to time. Despite the constant pealing of church bells, the Queen's Majesty stood to make impromptu speeches. The crowd would hush to hear, then blast the wintry air with roars.

It was a wonderful day, although she and her Council faced the mess Mary had left – a devalued currency, the treasury bled dry, English towns full of vagrants and unpaid soldiers, and Catholic France and Spain covetous of her crown and country. [Prince Philip, the lecherous wretch, soon sent her an envoy asking for her hand in marriage, pledging to get her with child as he had not her sister!]

My favorite part was not even the lengthy coronation in the Abbey the next day, nor the fine banquet at which I sat at a front table with my John. Not even the moment when she was crowned and the bishop called out the traditional question to the great assemblage: 'Do you, good people of this realm of England, desire this royal person, Elizabeth Tudor, for your lawful, God-given queen?'

As if from one throat, they shouted, 'Aye! Aye!'

No, my favorite moment was when I realized – as she had come to learn too – the power of the common folk, the very backbone of England and

369

how much they adored their new queen. For, in her short procession from Westminster Hall to the Abbey, wearing her coronation robes, to the joyous sound of drums and the bells of London's churches, she trod a blue velvet carpet. I felt utter awe when I saw the crowd fall upon that carpet and tear off shreds for souvenirs, so great was their desire to have a memento of her, my Elizabeth, now crowned Queen of England.

# CHAPTER 19

GREENWICH PALACE

*Summer 1559*

The first summer Elizabeth was queen we lost her to a midsummer's madness. My thoughts assaulted by the romping music, watching couples turn and leap on the dance floor, I stood frowning in a corner of the great hall of Greenwich Palace.

My royal mistress screamed with delight each time Robert Dudley, her Robin, tossed her into the air and caught her again in the wild steps of the *volta*. Drums beat and sackbuts wailed the tune, one I knew her father had written years ago when his passion for Anne Boleyn was raging. But worse, I knew the words, and they boded ill like all else of late for the queen's reputation as she ignored her duties and spent time in the company of the man courtiers were coming to call her favorite:

*Pastime with good company*
*I love and shall until I die.*

*Grudge who likes, but none deny,*
*So God be pleased, thus live will I.*
*For my pastance:*
*Hunt, sing, and dance.*
*My heart is set!*
*All goodly sport*
*For my comfort.*
*Who shall me let?*

No words were sung now, but they haunted me nonetheless, just as dreams of the long-dead Anne had again. As Elizabeth's parents had displayed in their mad desires years ago, I had seen all the signs of such hectic blood in her and Robert. No one dared deny them their 'goodly sport,' though I knew, like her mother, Elizabeth still denied her body to the man she wanted. 'Who shall me let?' indeed, for anyone who spoke out against Her Grace and Robert's dalliance – riding, hunting, singing, dancing – was snubbed or sent away. King Henry, while wed, had lusted for the forbidden fruit of Anne Boleyn, and now their daughter wanted a wedded man.

John strode into the crowded, noisy hall in a huff, joined me in my corner and, raising his voice so I could hear him over the noise, blurted out, 'When I came to our chambers, a messenger from Her Grace was waiting for me. I've been banished again, and by another Tudor queen.'

'What? To where?'

'Only to Enfield, thank God. Supposedly in

service of her dear Robin to quarter forty extra head of horses there. She knows how much we love Enfield, and it's not far, but she wants me out of her way just as she did Cecil, because we don't approve of how she carries on with him and I told her so.'

'No one with a bit of sense approves. Even when I told her that 'tis said in the courts of Europe they are jesting that the Queen of England will wed her horse master, she didn't see the error of her ways. 'We are just good friends, Kat. We have so much in common, Kat. I am queen and deserve some happy times after all we have been through.' But when are you to return, my love?' I asked him.

'She will send someone to let me know.'

'How dare she keep you away! She's gone giddy. Are you sure she wasn't just jesting or threatening?'

'Hardly. I rue the day I taught her how to ride like the wind. This morning, when she and that man were going ahorse again with no guards – in other words, no chaperones – I told her it was not safe, not any safer than her sullied reputation when she bestows all that bounty on him. The right to export wool without a license, be damned! She's bending not only propriety for him but England's laws!'

'A pox on him!' I blurted, before I clapped my hand over my mouth. The smallpox had been rampant in London of late, a dread disease that took the lives of one fourth of the people it struck down and disfigured many of the rest. It was one of the reasons the court had removed to more rural palaces. 'I do not wish the pox, even on him,' I muttered, shaking my head, 'but what are we to do?'

'You must talk to her again. I know you've tried before, but this is crucial. You, above all others, have always been able to comfort yet confront her. Poor Cecil's no doubt at his wit's end up in Scotland. I just heard that he tried to have the Council appoint Dudley as ambassador to foreign courts, but 'someone' removed his name from the list. More than once I've heard Cecil say Robert Dudley would be better off in paradise than here.'

'Poor Cecil, conveniently sent away to parley with the Scots for who knows how long. Him, you – I'll be next, but you are right, my dear lord. My frowns and aside comments are not enough. I must pick my time, but I'll set her straight. Heaven's gates, you'd think our brilliant queen has forgotten the Seymour affair!'

Our gazes snared and held a moment, but he plunged on. 'Freedom and power too long denied has knocked her silly. And then there is that Boleyn blood.'

'Tudor blood, more like, to pin her attentions on someone who belongs to another. When did that ever stop her sire with all his mistresses, wedded or not? It is an unfair world that what is good for the gander is forbidden for the goose, but that is the way of it.'

'What queen has ever ruled alone? She needs a husband, but not this one.' He tugged me toward the doorway, along the back wall of the chamber and out into the corridor. Several young couples were in each other's arms there, leaning against the wainscoting or each other. I started to tell John that Elizabeth's laxity of decorum was running rampant, but he just swore under his breath and pulled me close for a devouring kiss.

The feeling that coursed through me at his touch and taste, as always, swamped my senses. Yes, I understood Elizabeth's heedless behavior to want a man so desperately that all caution – I prayed not a whole kingdom – could be cast to the winds.

That night, as usual, after the dancing and card playing and jesting, Elizabeth let Robert walk her through the presence chamber, then the privy chamber to the door of her bedchamber, where she always bid him good night, then went in with me and several of her ladies to be prepared for bed. Tonight, only I trailed them, for she had sent the others off a good hour ago and had sat in a window seat with him, washed by moonlight, giggling and whispering.

If I were to be alone with her tonight, it was, I told myself, the perfect time to talk to her. She'd expect me to remonstrate about her sending John away, but I would instead discuss her keeping Robert far too close.

At age fifty-three, my eyesight was not as sharp

as it used to be, but my ears were still good, and so I heard their fervent whispers.

'Bess, my sweetling, let me put you in bed tonight,' Robert was saying, his voice silky smooth. 'Kat won't tell.'

I bit my tongue to keep from scolding him.

'So, my Master of Horse would be master of my heart?' she parried, cleverly not answering his question.

'Master of your heart and beautiful body! I love and adore you, only you! If we were but country swain and milkmaid, we could openly love each other forever.'

I rolled my eyes. Such pretty words and a prettier face, I groused silently, as he seized her hand to lift it to his lips. I knew of his seductive ploy each night, though he always turned away from the queen's ladies. Just before he put his lips to the back of Her Grace's hand, as was proper, he smoothly turned it palm up and hotly, wetly kissed her there, his tongue darting back and forth to inflame her passions. The rogue must know how it affected her. She always left him dreamy-eyed and mooned about as we prepared her for bed, no doubt wishing that her Robin was divesting her of her garments and tucking her in and more.

Tonight, to my amazement, while the two yeomen guards at her door stood like stone statues, she said to him, 'My beloved country swain, you may kiss your milkmaid good night inside her door.'

From his avid look, you would have thought he had been awarded yet another rich bestowal. Last week, she'd given him a house not far from Richmond Palace at Kew and a larger allowance with it, not to mention she'd honored him with the title of Garter Knight. This – all of it – had to stop. How dare she risk all she had suffered and hoped for, all John and I had gone through for her!

When the two of them slipped inside the bedroom door and dared to start to close it on me, I stuck my hip in and pushed back at them. 'I am not leaving the queen unattended,' I said and bustled toward the bed so that they dared not follow that far. Robert frowned, but Elizabeth was so far gone she just ignored me. Recklessly, on she plunged to her destruction and—

He bent her back a bit, and the hot, open-mouthed kiss went on and on. I tried not to look, but the intensity of it shook me too. John and I used to kiss like that, and it always turned my bones to water and made me want him to just take me on the grass or floor or anywhere.

'I adore you, only you!' he told her again, evidently the theme of his song to her. It was one way, I thought, to set aside his wife without mentioning her. I wanted to scream at him to unhand the queen and get out, get back to his Amy. I recalled how I had witnessed the early morning romps when Tom Seymour invaded her bedchamber and teased and tickled her and how

I was greatly held to blame for it later and what it cost us both.

I intentionally banged the lid of the coffer at the foot of her bed up and down – *thud, bang*. Startled, they looked at me as if I had shot off a firearm. Though dazed, Elizabeth glared at me, but said, 'Best you be off until the morrow, Robin. We shall go riding just after dawn.'

'I won't sleep a wink this night but will dream of you,' he whispered in a raspy voice, and kissed her palm again, lingeringly – wetly.

After he went out, she leaned against the door and sighed.

'It's one thing,' I said, opening the coffer again to pull out a night rail for her, 'to go riding alone, but to be alone with him in your bedchamber . . .'

'I've told you a dozen times, I trust him.'

'Then do you trust others not to misunderstand and sully the reputation and character you worked years ago to rebuild after the Seymour catastrophe?'

'That was different.' She came over and turned her back to me so I could unlace her bodice.

'Oh, yes. That married rogue was named Tom and this one is Robin.'

She spun back to face me, hands on hips, her dreamy look replaced by her Tudor-temper countenance. Since she had become queen, she had shown a side of herself I had seldom seen. Even Robert had said she could go from goddess to guttersnipe in an instant and swear like a sailor – like both Tom Seymour and her royal father had.

'Hell's gates, Kat,' she cried, 'you are just upset I sent John away to cool his heels.'

'Robert Dudley is the one who needs to be sent away to cool another part of him besides his heels. Preferably sent to visit his wife once in a while.'

'They have naught in common. He is needed here as one of my advisers. A plague on it, I am not your girl but a woman grown, and queen here.'

'I have noticed. And how we have all yearned for that great gift from God. Now we must all protect that. Elizabeth – Your Majesty – I have lately had the dream about your mother again.'

Her eyes widened and her lower lip dropped. 'I – I have not. Why should you? I am safe now.'

'Was she safe as queen?'

'She was not queen in her own right, and I am.'

'You have said it is essential to keep the good-will of not only courtiers but commoners. You now have the opportunity to remain pure in your court and subjects' eyes, but you are squandering that, acting the wanton.'

For one moment I thought she would strike me, but I seized her upper arms hard and gave her a little shake. Other things had changed lately, for there was a greater gap between us. Power, as I had known for years and feared for her, did make a difference.

'I am not acting the wanton,' she told me, and tugged herself free. 'Of all people, I thought you would understand how much Robin means to me, even if Cecil and your lord cannot grasp it. And if you have that dream again, say to my mother that this man is to me as Thomas Wyatt the poet was to her: a lifelong love, but one I know I cannot really have. I am no dolthead on that account, and don't you act like one!'

Even when Cecil returned that autumn with a good treaty with Scotland and when John was recalled from Enfield, things did not improve. Scandalmongers now whispered terrible things: that Robert would poison his wife so that he could have the queen, that Elizabeth was with child by him. It was that which made me decide to risk scolding her again, for that very accusation about her illegitimate pregnancy had been bandied about in the Seymour scandal, and I could not bear her being dragged through the mud and mire again. She was blind to all but her dazzling love for her Robin. Even Cecil's threats to resign if she did not cast off Lord Robert Dudley did not change her willfulness.

But my burden to confront her again was taken from my hands by a horrible accident – or maybe not an accident. I recall the date well because it was September 8, 1560, the day after her twenty-seventh birthday. I was waiting for Robert and Her Grace to return from a ride in the great park at Windsor – also, hoping for a few words with John, who had managed to discreetly accompany them this time – when a man named Forester, one of Dudley's servants, rushed up to him when they dismounted.

'Yes, my man?' Robert said, turning to the tall, thin steward of his rural lands. Elizabeth leaned close to hear.

'My lord, I regret to inform you that there has been an accident. Your wife has fallen.'

'Fallen where? Is she all right?' I heard him ask.

'Fell down the staircase at Cumnor House, my lord, and broke her neck. She'd sent everyone out to a nearby fair and when they came back – dead, sir. Dead of the fall.'

Dead. Of the fall. I feared that my mistress, Queen of England, and her beloved Robin were about to take another kind of fall. Whispers, innuendos were abroad that the queen, too, had wished Robin's wife dead, so that they could wed. But now that it had come true, now that their – or at least his – desire had become dreadful reality, even though both of them were here and not in Oxfordshire when Amy fell, would he or Elizabeth herself be blamed? Not just for reckless passion this time, but for murder?

'You must send him away,' I told her that night after I had asked her other ladies to leave us. 'It's not enough that he gives her a fine funeral. Until it is all adjudicated, he must be close-confined.'

Elizabeth had feigned calm all day as she had ordered the court to go into mourning, as she had done business with Cecil at her side. But she had fallen too – fallen in everyone's eyes and fallen apart the moment the two of us were alone.

'I can't send him away,' she protested, blowing her nose while her eyes streamed tears. In her night rail and robe, she sat barefoot and cross-legged on the end of her bed while I stood next to it. 'That will make him look guilty, and he isn't.'

'Isn't guilty of being there where he could have done it, but —'

'Hell's teeth, do you think he's hired someone to rid himself of her? He's an honorable man! And how can I send someone to be close-confined who has been to the Tower – you, too, should know that. Amy was ailing with a lump in her breast, and it made her melancholy. She may have stumbled, or – God forbid – even taken her own life.'

'From being melancholy over and hearing rumors of her absent husband.'

'Leave off! If you care for me, leave off!'

'Because I care for you, I must speak.'

'He has begged me not to send him away or the jackals who are jealous of him – hate him and his family for being greedy upstarts and former traitors – will pick his bones. They are ravening jealous of how much I admire and care for him.'

'At least until there is a ruling on her death, he should go. After all, no one suspected of a crime is to be in the monarch's presence.'

'He's not suspected of a crime!' she shrilled. 'Not by me.'

'But he is by others. Yes, the Lord High God gave you this Tudor throne, but haven't you said you must rule by the love of your people?'

'This isn't like the Seymour scandal – that's what you're thinking again, isn't it? Seduction again? Well, it isn't. I have not allowed him the ultimate gift of my love. I do love him, yes, but I am not just – just taken in by his manly skills and wiles to surrender my body to him.'

'Elizabeth, he's been wed ten years and knows all the tricks. If you ever listened to me – one who's known you, loved you, gone to prison twice for you – listen now. You must harden your heart to him, or you'll go down with him. Even if he's declared innocent, people will talk, even as some dare to whisper now that you might be with child by him —'

'I said stop it!' she screamed. Before I knew she would move from her slumped posture on the bed, she reared up and slapped my cheek.

The sharp sound broke the sudden silence. My cheek stung and, more so, my heart. Tears crowded my eyes but did not fall. I cannot fathom what my expression looked like, but she gasped, scrambled off the bed and fell to her knees before me with her arms around my hips and her cheek pressed to my belly so it seemed my skirts would swallow her head.

'Kat, Kat, forgive me. I didn't mean – forgive me, forgive me, but I am so undone . . .'

I bit my lower lip and stood like stone as she babbled on, saying the same over and over.

'Get up, Your Majesty.' I finally found some words. 'You must not kneel to anyone.'

She stayed where she was. 'I can't do without you, Kat. You're right, I must distance myself from him, but I just – just can't face it. Cecil says the same. I can't, can't . . .'

I put my hands on her tousled head as if she were a child I would comfort or bless, and we stayed that way for a few moments as if we were both carved from marble.

'Oh, my Kat,' she said, slowly loosing me and getting to her feet, 'I see I wear not only a royal crown but a crown of thorns. Yes, I must send him away. I wanted him so much, but maybe now it's ruined. Amy couldn't keep us apart in life, but in death – her death day was almost on my birthday . . . Yes, I see what I must do. I'll write it out, his orders to go to his house at Kew—'

'Kew is not far. Not far enough from Richmond, where we are going on the morrow.'

'It will have to do,' she said, walking over to her writing desk, looking as if she were the one who had been struck, 'at least until the inquest – the hearing – provides a ruling to clear his name – and mine.'

Her pen scratched loudly across the paper. My heart still thudded hard. I had not moved from where she'd slapped me. Somehow, the world had changed, changed even more than when she was crowned, and I feared I could never call her my

384

lovey again, and certainly never again pretend in my heart that she was mine.

Finally but too late, the queen had realized the error of her passionate ways. The court, the country, even foreigners spoke of the scandal. Elizabeth's rival, Mary Stuart, now queen of France, was heard to say again, with a snicker, not only that the Queen of England would wed her horse master but that he had had his wife murdered to make room for her.

Any snippet of news from the coroner's inquest – which was soon to be examined by jurors – was bandied about everywhere. Though Amy had fallen down a flight of stairs and broken her neck, her cap had not been disturbed, so had someone straightened it before leaving or arranging the body? Her corpse bore no bruises. The staircase was not even steep enough for a fatal fall. And on and on.

Like everyone, I was shocked by it all, but even more shocked when the queen told me after we had been at Richmond Palace but one day, 'I am sending you to Kew to speak with Robin, to give him this poem I have written to explain our changed circumstances and to ask him outright if he had aught to do with her death.'

I just stared at her a moment, then blurted, 'Can you not send Cecil?'

'Cecil would be too harsh with him. I am sending you, and John is riding with you.'

'I'm to give him what poem?' I asked, recalling all too well the poem I had seen pinned to the bottom of the stool in Queen Anne's rooms when I was sent to carry a message from her to Cromwell. Indeed, what went around came around.

'Here,' she said, thrusting a piece of paper toward me. 'Besides the poem, I have written that, whatever the jury decides, things must be different between us. It is a message I thought you would like to give him.'

I took the parchment from her hand and saw she had addressed it formally to Robert Dudley, G.K., and had signed it Elizabeth R. That gave me hope. For now, at least, no more Robin and Bess. I skimmed the poem:

*The doubt of future foes exiles my present joy,*
*And wit me warm to shun such snares as threaten*
 *mine annoy;*
*For falsehood now doth flow, and subjects' faith*
 *doth ebb,*
*Which should not be if reason ruled or wisdom*
 *weaved the web.*
*But clouds of joys untried do cloak aspiring minds,*
*Which turn to rage of late repent by changed course*
 *of winds.*

It went on with other verses, but I recall them not. I nodded and went out to do for her – as oft I had before – a duty that I did not want.

With two horses, John and I went by royal barge from the Greenwich Palace water gate and then disembarked to ride the short distance to Dudley's small house at Kew on the edge of a huge dairy farm. 'Ah,' John said, sniffing the scent of distant cows and stables, 'good country air. At least at Enfield the prevailing breeze keeps that smell away. How I wish we could get away from all this to stay there for a while, just the two of us.'

I nodded as he helped me dismount. 'I, too, miss Enfield. Anywhere but here right now.'

I had somehow fancied Robert would greet us, but as the guard at the door – Robert was under restraint, which some called house arrest – let us in, I saw the place was dim and silent.

'Did you not announce us?' I asked the man. 'Was he told we were coming?'

'Aye, milady, milord. This way, by your leave.'

It was darker than a birthing chamber in the small house. Windows draped, a bit damp and musty. John pulled me behind him and even put his hand to his sword.

Our guide knocked once on a door, then again. 'Enter!' came the cry.

John peered in before he let me precede him. We had discussed that John would give me some space to speak with the man but not leave the room. Yet John stuck tight to my side as a shadowy figure rose from behind a large desk in the dim room.

'Lady Ashley,' came the distinctive voice, though

subdued now, 'welcome to my prison. Lord Ashley – how fare our two hundred and fifty charges in the royal stables?'

'Well, my lord. I am seeing that your favorites – horses – are well fed.'

'Ah, better than I am faring, for I've lost my appetite as much else. Sit, please, both of you. I was told of your visit.'

'Can we not let in some light and air?' I asked.

'Let in the light – well, yes, that is what the jurors are doing even now, are they not?' He walked to the window behind his desk and yanked the brocade curtains apart. Sunlight flooded the room; we all blinked. John took a chair against the wall, though hardly out of earshot. Perhaps he thought the man was unbalanced or dangerous, but I thought he only looked beaten, a mere shadow of his exuberant, confident self. His hair was unkempt, his usually immaculately trimmed beard shaggy. He wore a plain white shirt under a worn black leather jerkin, no fine fig of fashion today.

'Her Grace sends you this – it's a poem, my lord,' I said, taking a chair at the side of the desk while Robert dropped into the chair where he had been sitting. He reached for the paper not eagerly but warily and set it before him without opening it.

'Best read in private, I warrant,' he said. 'Is she casting me to the dogs?'

'Only a guilty ruling can do that, I suppose,' I said.

'Yes – I suppose. So, she sends her dear friend Kat Ashley to tell me what?'

'To ask if you know anything about your wife's demise or who might have wanted to harm her.'

'God as my judge,' he cried, slamming both fists into the desk top and leaping to his feet, 'does she suspect me too? Then I am doomed indeed!'

John stood when Robert did, but then, when Robert slumped down again, I heard John sit. I was tempted to rephrase the question, to soften it somehow, but this man was the cause of much pain and sorrow, whether or not he was somehow guilty of his wife's death.

'I had naught to do with Amy's death, obviously not directly, since I was at court, but not indirectly either. Please assure Her Grace of that.'

'I will.'

'Actually, I think, if it is ruled a murder, that it was more likely set up by my or the queen's enemies, who knew I – even she – might be blamed. My rivals at court who detest how far I have risen so fast in her goodwill, even the Catholics, who would like to have the queen dead in Amy's place.'

'That is, I suppose, a possibility.'

'And, Kat Ashley, there is another possibility,' he said, lowering his voice and leaning forward across the desk on his elbows. 'That someone who had been warning her, trying to turn her against me, someone with newfound possessions and power, might have hired someone to dispatch Amy so that I might be blamed – and make the queen back off from me. Perhaps someone who had a position to lose if Her Grace wedded me and made me her closest confidant. Perhaps someone who closely serves the queen but does truly not have her happiness at heart.'

My eyes widened. I feared my heart would pound out of my chest. I stammered, in a whisper so John would not pounce on the man, 'You – you are accusing me?'

'Or Cecil – or both. I know you detest me and want me gone. But accusing? Only pondering the possibilities, since you asked.'

'You are demented! Blame yourself for this mess, maybe blame the queen, but not me.' I rose and John strode over.

'On the other hand,' Robert went on, slumping back in his chair as if he'd said naught amiss, 'the fact that Amy insisted everyone else in the house go to the fair that day indicates she may have wanted to be alone to – to do the deed herself,' he said and his voice broke. 'She was in pain from the tumor in her breast. And, obviously, distraught to be living away from me, though I explained to her my destiny to help this queen, to earn the Dudleys' way back from my father's and my treason against Queen Mary and . . . hell, for all I know, Amy found the only way she could to keep me from the woman I will always love and mayhap now can never have!'

To my amazement, after that outburst, he broke

into sobs, though without tears. His shoulders heaved; like me a moment ago he could hardly catch his breath. Still, I feared, now that John must have realized what the man had said to me, that he might leap on his better and shake him until his teeth rattled. When John clenched his fists, I put one hand on his rock-hard arm to restrain him and told Robert, 'You may leave Cecil and me out of this spider's web you have slyly spun, or be damned to you!'

I tugged John away. We left Robert like that, bitter and shattered. I both pitied him and hated him. I did not mention to Elizabeth that he had insulted me, accused me and Cecil of so much as the possibility of arranging his wife's murder and his demise.

The next day the jurors ruled that Amy Robsart Dudley's death was *fatal mischance*, that is, accidental death. Robert would eventually be allowed back to court, but not, the queen vowed, as anyone but another adviser. I could only pray that my intelligent Elizabeth had learned her lesson. As a woman ruling alone, she could emulate neither her father nor her mother, but must tread her own, careful path through the pitfalls and snares of love.

# CHAPTER 20

WHITEHALL PALACE

*Autumn 1560*

Perhaps from guilt for her previous behavior, perhaps to forget Robert Dudley, the queen threw herself into hard work and a regimented daily routine, with me right behind her almost each step of the way. She seemed to need me differently now, as if she were young again and I were a comfort or security to her. It reminded me of the time she was just out of leading strings when she lost a small blue silk coverlet she fancied and was so sad until it was found.

Not only I but Cecil was hard-pressed to keep up with her energy. We were both relieved that Robert had not been welcomed back to court with open arms, though the queen had allowed him to return and still showed him every courtesy. Yet she avoided being alone with him as if he had the pox.

Each morning Elizabeth rose early and went for a fast walk that left her ladies stretching their strides and me breathless. Together, the two of us had a meager breakfast in her privy chamber, for she preferred not to eat in public unless there was a holiday or official banquet. Next, she tended to signing warrants and deeds, then oft presided over a meeting of her Privy Council. She was at odds with them and Parliament about marriage: even Cecil urged her to wed for the good of the kingdom.

'Look at this, Kat! Just look!' she cried one winter evening as she stormed into my withdrawing chamber, where I was resting and writing. She smacked down in front of me [right on top of a page of this very narrative of my life] a formal petition from Parliament, urging her to marry as soon as possible in order to safeguard the succession. 'How dare they?' she demanded, jabbing her index finger so hard up and down on the document that the hinged lid of the ring from her mother flew open and flopped up and down before she snapped it closed.

'They dare,' I told her, 'because they are to advise you, and they fear great upheaval if there is no legitimate Tudor heir.'

'Do you think I don't know that?' She began to pace, her skirts swishing and belling out. Since she was on her feet, I started to stand. 'Oh, Kat, do sit when I invade your own privy chamber. Since you are not remonstrating, shall I think you are on their side in this?'

'In an objective way only. Subjectively, I understand your fears and feelings.'

'If so, you are the only one! Tell me then – tell me the reasons I shall never wed, no matter how many of these pleas and petitions they send me now or forevermore.'

I put my quill on the table, sat back in my chair and said, 'Firstly, because you have seen women – queens, even – die in childbirth.'

'Granted. My kingdom needs me as much as I need it – my people. I shall remain a virgin in truth and in my people's eyes. I shall be wedded only to them. Secondly,' she went on, as if I did not answer her quickly enough, 'men conquer women when they couple. I vow, men like to be on top in all ways, and I cannot have that. Then, once they are sated, they move on. Can you deny it?'

'I cannot deny it with your own father, but . . .'

'But what? Did not you tell me your own father paid no heed that his second, younger wife could have done away with your mother?'

'Yes, but I was thinking about my husband. John—'

'Your lord is a rare man. Now, if I could find one like that, who is strong in his own right but lets me do what I must in the way of duty . . . one who coddles me and does not try to rein in or bridle me . . . Strange, is it not, that both John and Robin are so good with horses?'

My head jerked at that swift change of subjects. She had hardly breathed Robert Dudley's name to me since he'd been back to court. She shook her head as if to clear it and, pacing again, plunged on. 'Besides, I saw how painful marriage can be for reasons besides losing control of one's self, one's power. My sister loved King Philip with all her heart, and he could not wait to get her with child, only so he could leave her and return to his Spanish mistress. Mayhap all princes and kings are like that.'

She was flinging gestures now, walking in circles around me and the table. 'You were right that my own brother-in-law Philip wanted to seduce me that day we met and he looked me over as if I were a filly to buy. Worse, poor Mary would scream from her grave if she knew he quickly sued for my hand when she was gone. A necessary business, political business for a king and queen, that is what marriage is.'

I finally got a word in: 'My dearest, I do not like to hear you so bitter and jaded.'

'Realistic, more like. Kat, I want to rule alone. Only alone will I be safe. Robin thinks you speak against him and that's why I am publicly warm but privily cold to him, but I have tried to tell him no, that I am acting on my own and will never wed. Well, indeed, enough said.'

She reached over my shoulder, picked up the parliamentary petition and tore it top to bottom.

As for the rest of the queen's hectic, exacting schedule, in the afternoon and evening she filled her time with receptions for foreign visitors, conversing in official Latin or in whatever was their foreign tongue. I saw more than one continental ambassador's jaw drop in grudging admiration of the young, slender queen. Also, she spent extra hours, as she had not for years, practicing the lute or bending over the keys at her virginals. She drove herself hard, and I knew why. So it shocked me when she announced that she was going to elevate Robert Dudley to the peerage as Earl of Warwick, his father's forfeited title, and that anyone who cared to see her sign the papers in her presence chamber was welcome to attend.

'What's her game here?' Cecil asked John and me *sotto voce* as others filed in, whispering, where the queen was already seated at a desk she'd had carried into the center of the room. Robert, in elaborate peacock blue velvet doublet and hose, stood before her, preening as if he'd just inherited the entire kingdom.

'We are as taken aback as you,' I told Cecil.

'Has she hoodwinked us?' he muttered, almost to himself. 'She pretends to blow cold toward him but yet intends to have him so she must elevate him first? As the old adage says, 'Fickleness, thy name is wom—'

I frowned at him, but Mildred appeared and gave him a good elbow in the ribs which stopped him midword. 'I'll not hear such disparagement of strong women from you, my love,' she told him. 'Kat, how heartened I am to see you again,' she cried, and hugged me, then John.

The four of us stood near the doorway as the

queen began to read the petition aloud. The clusters of courtiers soon quieted. 'Ah,' she declared in a dramatic fashion, lifting the parchment with the wax and ribboned seal as if to gaze close quarters at it, 'papers for the earldom. And yet those in such lofty positions must be fully trustworthy and fully loyal. Were not your family once traitors against the Tudors, Lord Robert?'

Silence fell with a thud. Staring at her aghast, Robert cleared his throat. 'Your Majesty, I – Can you not just sign without publicly punishing me for things far past?'

'And not so far past. I fear this might be premature or even reckless, so at least I admit publicly when I have misstepped.'

Just as she had pounced in private on the parliamentary petition, she shredded the warrant, but with a little penknife from the desk, stabbing it, ripping it. With John, I fell back toward the door to the hall with Mildred while Cecil pushed his way forward.

'You'll not shame me so!' Robert roared at her.

'I'll do as I will,' she shouted back. 'Hell's gates, there will be but one ruler here, and it is this queen!'

Robert spun away and made for the door. Some stepped back from his path, others bumped his shoulder. He said nothing else to anyone but glared at me and muttered in as menacing a voice as I have ever heard, 'You put her up to this, and you will pay.'

★ ★ ★

Robert still hung about the fringes of the court, but he was seething. I avoided him, though John said he'd had words with him twice, and once Elizabeth in a snit sent John briefly away again for disparaging words against Dudley. 'I know how to calm all sorts of wild steeds but not Dudley or the queen,' John told me once.

But when he returned – I had not pleaded for him, but had said hardly a warm word to her – I could tell she rued her hasty, headstrong behavior. How grateful we were when Her Majesty named John to a position she knew would please us above all else: the grant of the offices of steward and ranger of the manor of Enfield, north of London in Essex. In short, whenever she excused us from court duties, we now had the right to live on the estate we both had loved best for years.

'For your love and loyalty to me, the both of you,' she told us as she presented us with the warrant for the titles and duties. For one moment, I wondered if she would rip it up as she had other documents of late, but I knew better. This was her love gift to us, proven by the fact she was letting me go with John for six precious weeks – August and part of September – when she oft said she could not bear to be parted from me.

She hugged us both in turn, then kissed me on both cheeks. 'I envy you a strong, happy marriage,' she told us, looking from one to the other. 'Yes, do not fuss or mourn for me, because I mean it. In you two, I see such exists. God forgive me, though I still love Robin and ever will, I must show him my love only in the ways of a monarch and not of a woman.'

Her dark eyes – Anne Boleyn's eyes – filled with tears, but she blinked them back. 'I shall think of you two riding the grounds and strolling in the meadows and – and so much more,' she said, and gave John's arm a playful punch. 'Go now and pack before I change my mind. I will see you both in summer progress when we all move to Hampton Court, for we must flee the vile pox in the city again this year.'

I could tell she was going to cry. She pushed us from the room and closed the door on us. And just as I could read her thoughts and temperament after all these years, John could read mine, for he said, 'No, you are not going back to comfort her. She has Mary Sidney, for she's never grown cold toward Robert's sister as she did him. Come on, now, or I shall sling you over my shoulder and ride off with you, just as I yearned to do the first time I beheld you in all that mire and mud, heading for King Henry's tent with Queen Anne's handkerchief. Come, now!'

I went. We had blessed, wonderful weeks. At our ages, both over half a century old, we enjoyed a second honeymoon. We loved each other, slept late and lolled about in various states of undress. We rode through the rich forests where oaks and beech turned to flaming crimsons and golds. Holding hands, we strolled Enfield's gardens and threw acorns in the moat, where we also sailed leaf boats.

John did his duties, we both worked on his book and I wrote more of my manuscript, now titled *My Life with the Tudors*. I remembered it was here at Enfield almost fifteen years before that Elizabeth and her brother Edward learned their royal sire was dead and the boy was king. That day I had stood up to Edward Seymour, the Lord Protector, telling him I had every right to comfort my Elizabeth.

Even the next September, 1562 it was, Her Grace sent us to Enfield, so it seemed it was our own. Yet in those dreamy days of love and beauty, for the first time in several years, I had my Anne Boleyn dream again. This time, she drifted not in through a window as before, but opened a dark door and emerged from its depths.

'Help her, save her,' came the whispered cry like sere autumn leaves shuffled by in the wind. 'Help my girl . . .'

As she turned away and started back toward the door, she beckoned to me. *One must follow a queen . . . obey a queen*, I thought. Yet, as ever in this dream, I could not move my feet. I was glad, for I did not want to follow her. What was down there? Deep blackness like a tomb? Was this a portent of my coming death?

I must have moaned or screamed, for I awakened with John holding me, rocking me. 'It's all right, all right,' he crooned. 'Not the old nightmare?'

'Yes – yes, something like it, but changed.'

'You've been missing Elizabeth. But in less than a week, we'll rejoin her at Hampton Court, just like last year, so let's enjoy this time, lest it doesn't come again.'

'But I – Queen Anne was gesturing me toward a dark door – down steps, I think. I'm not certain. Do you think she meant something dire will befall?'

'No, my dear love. A figment of the imagination, a night fear, that is all. Here, turn your back and let me hold you until you sleep again.'

I knew I was clutching at straws, but I had to keep talking. 'The dream probably changed because yesterday I was thinking how blessed we are to have doors opened for us, not like the old days at Hatfield or worse, when I was in the Fleet Prison or the Tower.'

'Brr!' he said, giving an intentional, dramatic shiver. 'If you mention that latter place again, I'll have nightmares too, and not because we were housed there once. I have a lot of work to do as Master of the Jewel House when we get back to London this fall,' he went on in an obvious attempt to take my mind off my fretting.

'Or not till winter, if the pox does not abate there soon, poor souls,' I said, and snuggled back against him. His beard stubble rasped against my naked shoulder when he kissed me there; that felt so good, so real, as my beloved man always had. 'Thank the Lord,' I added, 'the queen and court are safe in the country. It was just a dream, that's all.'

The very next day, during a driving rainstorm, a young lad, not even an official messenger, came riding in. I saw it was one of the newer grooms John had been teaching to train horses in the new way. He stood dripping and shivering before the hearth as John threw a blanket around him and thrust a mug of hot cider in his hand. My stomach cramped; in several days we were to join the queen and court at Hampton Court Palace for the rest of September.

'So, Geoff,' my lord said to him, 'I told you to come to me if you ever needed help, so what is it?'

'It's not that, but Lord Cecil sent me with this,' he said, extending a wrinkled, damp piece of parchment. 'Said he couldn't send a reg'lar man, lest he be missed by the Master of the Horse. The whole court – London too – is scairt to death. But Cecil asks did Lord Dudley's message reach you since you din't come? The queen's sore ill with fever and named him Lord Protector of the kingdom, if she don't live.'

'What?' John demanded. 'If she doesn't live? Do you mean Cecil or Dudley is Lord Protector, boy?'

'Dudley, milord. Not always in her right mind, Lord Cecil said, but the queen been calling for you, milady.'

I had gasped and clapped my hands over my

mouth, but John leaped to action. 'Chester!' he shouted for our house steward, who came bounding in. 'Send word for three horses to be saddled, Gentry, Devon and Orion. And find this lad some dry clothes and a fast meal. We are off for Hampton Court in a quarter of an hour. Kat, pack only what goes in six saddlebags, including an extra cloak and hood. We'll be drenched and mud spattered at best. Go, my love. We'll get to her in time, and you will help to heal her.'

The lad spoke again as I ran from the room. 'It's a risk to get too close to her. His lordship says she's caught the pox.'

The rest of that day and the early part of the next was a rain- and fear-swept blur for me. The roads were muck and mire, some almost impassable, but we pushed on, sometimes riding fetlock-deep through streams in ditches. Why had Robert Dudley's message not reached us? I prayed Her Grace would not think we had delayed or even stayed away for fear of catching the contagion. The pox! There were several kinds: the French pox, of course, which was a sexual disease, and the swinepox, which often struck children. But the smallpox disfigured and killed hundreds. Not the queen. Not my beloved Elizabeth.

When we reached the Thames, we hired a barge to row us upstream and paid dearly for it too. Not only was the going hard against the rain-swollen current, but the oarsmen had heard the queen had the pox and they wanted nothing to do with the area. They shoved off back downstream the moment we got our horses off their barge.

I knew I looked as horrible as I felt, exhausted, fearful, bereft. In Cecil's note to us he had said it was true that the queen had named Dudley as Lord Protector, should she be incapacitated or die.

Die! Not if my life depended on it.

Though I wanted to run straight for her suite upstairs, we stopped the first person we knew – I cannot recall to this day who it was – and asked the queen's condition. 'In extremis,' he said. 'Coming to a crisis and may die.'

Leaving the boy with the horses, we ran through the base court and clock court into fountain court nearest to the royal suite. Few people were about. John pulled me in a reception room to change our outer garments and wash our face and hands. We were soaked clear through, and my teeth were chattering from fear and chill.

'I'm going to her now,' I told John. 'They don't need to announce me.'

'Her bedchamber might be sealed.'

'I'll break down the door.'

We started along the corridor toward the main stairs but saw Robert Dudley coming down the large staircase, no doubt to greet us, even to escort us. He looked finely garbed, all in silver and black. I recall he seemed to have new high-topped

Spanish leather boots that creaked when he walked. He had an entourage of men behind him, but he held up his hand to keep them back and came over to us.

'How is she?' I demanded. 'We did not get your message. Surely, she hasn't taken a turn for the worse! I'm going to her now.'

'Impossible, Lady Ashley,' he told me. 'My sister Mary is tending her and has quite replaced you in her affections. The Privy Council awaits just outside her door to know if she survives the crisis. Only I and Cecil go in, I as Lord Protector, of course, so in effect, I am in charge here now.'

'I have heard she was calling for me,' I repeated, while John's strong arm about my waist propped me up. 'I am going to her.'

'I and the Council must deny you access to her person,' he said, frowning. Then his eyes lit, and his visage lifted. 'The tables are turned now, are they not?'

'You deceitful –' John began, before Robert cut him off.

'Both of you keep quiet and keep back. I cannot have someone near the queen who might continue to turn her against me. With you away, she has named me to inherit her throne. I have left word with the guards at her door that you are not to enter. Now I have business to attend to.'

He and his entourage swept off down the hall. I stood agape, my mind racing. 'He blames me for her turning against him – even though she's named him Protector.'

'In her delirium and fever, named the wretch thus.'

'But I must get to her somehow. For her sake, for mine – that is what Queen Anne was trying to tell me in the dream.'

'Go back into the room where we washed up, and I'll find Cecil. He'll gainsay that power-hungry seducer.'

'But what if you can't find him, or he must do what Robert says, or she – she takes a worse turn without me with her when I'm so close,' I insisted, my voice breaking on a sob.

He put me in the room and closed the door. For a moment I feared he'd locked me in, but it was only that the latch stuck when I checked it. Covering my head with my dry hood and cape, I took the single old cresset lamp which sputtered in the room and went back out into the corridor and then the courtyard. Now I knew what Anne's spirit had been telling me in the dream: 'Help my girl . . . save my girl . . .' and that gesturing toward the dark door.

Pelting raindrops drummed on the courtyard cobbles, but that suited me, as few were about in such weather, especially with the dread pox stalking all of us. Where was that door along here where ivy climbed, thicker now than years ago, thicker than that day my nine-year-old Elizabeth and her five-year-old brother Edward had found the door that led to the royal bedchamber? It had to be along here.

I ripped at a tendril, then a vine, pulling webs of yellowing ivy from the slick brick wall. Yes, here, the outline of the door with its recessed iron ring. When I first came to court, Queen Anne herself had told me there were secret passages here, built by Cardinal Wolsey himself, Thomas Cromwell's first wily master. But if it was bolted from inside, this effort was doomed.

I had a devil of a time trying to keep the lamp from sputtering out in the rain and yanking at the bolt with both hands until the door creaked and pulled outward. Amazingly, perhaps because it was unused and unknown – and quite overgrown now – it was unlocked, so I didn't have to use my penknife to lift the latch. That was a good sign, was it not? I swear that day I had a strength in my arms and back and legs that could have outdone John's might. Warm, slightly fetid air rushed at me as I pulled it open enough to squeeze in. After I had saved the wan light of the cresset lamp from the rain, a gust made it flicker, almost blew it out.

I pulled the creaking door shut behind me and looked about. The meager flame hardly lifted the blackness, as deep and dark as in my dream. What if, I thought, Elizabeth had told her Robert about this passage when they were courting? What if he or she had secured the door at the top of the stairs where it was hidden behind the arras in her bedchamber?

My face was wet from rain and sweat; each cobweb that laced itself to my skin seemed to stick. No matter. I had work to do, a battle to fight. If I could only get to her, surely I could stay. That damned Dudley, Lord Protector or not, could not stop my tending her.

I missed a stair and grabbed for the handrail, nearly tumbling backward. Amy Dudley had fallen down the stairs and died. No doubt Robert had resented her as he did me. But enough to have his wife killed?

I tried to recall how many flights I had raced up that day nearly twenty years ago to find the giggling, naughty Tudor children. I was out of breath so much more today than then. A splinter jabbed my hand from the crude rail. King Henry must have used this only in his youth, for his massive size and girth would have hindered him later. And Cromwell – did my old master Cromwell, who I damned but thanked for so much, ever use these stairs on his covert missions?

And then the strangest thing. A chill shivered down my spine and the hair at the back of my neck stood on end. The air turned icy cold. For one moment, I fancied I saw a woman ahead of me on the stairs, beckoning me on and up: a raven-haired woman with a crimson necklace on her slender neck. Anne! But I blinked and it was gone. An apparition or vestige of my dream?

I climbed yet another twisting flight and paused at the dim outline of a door I thought must be the one with entry to the royal bedchamber. Like the dim interior of this staircase shaft, it was laced over with spiderwebs and draperies of dust. I pressed my ear to it. Muffled voices. Someone intoning a prayer. I fumbled at the latch on this side of the door. Yes, I recalled it had a latch and not an iron ring.

I shoved, I heaved myself against it, banging my shoulder, then realized I must pull it inward, toward me. It moved easier than the downstairs door. The arras over it sucked slightly inward. Would someone see me and stop me? Let them try.

The hearth fire in the room burned low, the first thing I saw, but its brightness hurt my eyes. Several people – at least two doctors and Mary Sidney – bent over the queen's bed. A minister read from the Psalms, 'Yea, though I walk through the valley of the shadow of death, I will fear no evil, for Thou art with me . . .' *Dear Lord*, I thought, *those were the very words Anne Boleyn repeated as she walked toward her death on the scaffold.*

I was sorry I did not see Cecil in the room, but neither did I see Robert or anyone else who would try to stop me. As Robert had said, the Privy Council must be waiting outside.

I put down my lamp on the queen's writing table and approached the canopied, elevated bed where Elizabeth and I had talked so often until she fell asleep and I went away to my rest. Mary Sidney saw me first and blinked as if she'd seen a ghost. I prayed she would not summon her brother, that he had not ordered her to keep me from the queen.

'I was told you would not come back,' she said. Obviously exhausted with work and worry, she was dripping sweat, and her skin looked gray. 'I am so tired, Kat . . .'

I nodded and squeezed her shoulder, then took a step around her and beheld the queen unconscious. Yes, Elizabeth had the start of several pustules on her white face. I was shocked and horrified, but I could tell she breathed.

'I'm here now, Mary, so rest,' I said and climbed the mounting stool to edge my hips onto the bed.

'No, madam, she must be untouched, but only bathed and bled,' one of the doctors said. I saw he held a lancet and bleeding bowl at the ready.

'I am Katherine Ashley, her First Lady of the Bedchamber, and I have been with her for years. I have not seen you at court before.'

'They sent for special physicians when her own said she was beyond help. Lord Cecil has gone to fetch yet others, but you must unhand her.'

'I will touch her, and you will not bleed her,' I insisted, pushing his hand back. 'What has she been given to bring her fever down?'

'Boiled root of alkanet and wine, mixed with sweet butter and drunk with hot beer to drive forth the pox.'

'Well, it isn't working, is it, for she's popping out with them.'

'But that is the crisis, my lady, the saving or the losing of her.'

'Elizabeth, it's Kat. Your Kat is here, and you

410

are going to be all right. John and I came the minute we heard you were ill.'

'Here?' she whispered, but squeezed her eyelids tighter instead of opening them.

'Yes, yes, my dearest. I'm here.'

Using the warm, milky-looking water they had been bathing her with, I sponged her forehead and throat. 'Mother,' she whispered, 'I'm so happy you are here.'

We fought to keep the queen alive that night. I kept willing Elizabeth to be strong, to pull through. I murmured to her, reminding her of happy times, though she never responded.

Later, I know not what hour of those endless hours, Cecil appeared, with John at his elbow and a fuming Robert Dudley stalking in behind them. I nodded to John and Cecil but ignored them after that. Cecil had hauled in a little German man named Dr Burcote, who took over, despite the mutterings of the English physicians.

'Ve wrap her in dis scarlet cloth and build up de flames and put her right before da fire,' Dr Burcote said. 'She sveat out the red pox into dis scarlet cloth, a new cure, vorks vell. Ve need help lift her now,' he said, and Cecil and John appeared again to help us. Where Robert had gone I did not know or care.

We put her on cushions at the edge of the hearth. As heat blasted out from it, we all began to sweat. Still, dripping wet – if I had caught the fever, I still would not leave her – I sat next to her for hours, praying, holding her hand, talking to her. Twice more she called me Mother, once dazedly looking directly up into my face.

But indeed, in a way, I was her mother. Her real mother both in life and in death had told me to help her, to care for her, and so, risking my life, I did.

Her fever broke just at dawn, and we lifted her back into bed. 'Oh, Kat,' she murmured, squinting at me, 'you're back.'

Behind me, I could hear sighs of relief as John and Cecil said something, perhaps ordering Robert, who had returned, to leave the room and wait outside with the rest of the Council.

'I am so thirsty,' Elizabeth said.

'*Ja*, you survived the pox,' Dr Burcote told her. 'You vill not be too bad scarred, I think.'

'Scarred – scarred by too much, my Kat,' she whispered as Dr Burcote gave me a goblet of spiced wine to offer her. She drank greedily, and I thought she would sleep, but she asked, 'Where is Mary? She tended me too.'

For one crazed moment, I thought she was hallucinating again that not only her mother had tended her but her dead sister, Queen Mary. Then I realized she was asking about Robert Dudley's sister, her loyal and lovely friend, Mary Sidney. 'Resting,' I told her, 'as you must now.'

She gripped my hand weakly, nodded and slept.

★   ★   ★

Six days later, Elizabeth was sitting up in bed and feeding herself. I had not told her that her Robin, the man she had named Lord Protector of the realm, had tried to keep me from seeing her in her distress. He would probably convince her he was just worried for my safety. Perhaps I would not tat-tale to her because it was one way to keep the wretch in line over the coming years. Besides, he was grieved, as were we all, that Mary Sidney had caught the pox while nursing the queen. Mary had not died either, but the queen's savior, the strange little Dr Burcote whom Cecil had found, had pronounced that Mary, unlike her royal mistress, would be severely scarred for the rest of her life.

'Kat, I either want a mirror or you to tell me exactly how many marks are on my face,' Elizabeth said, her voice and testy tone back to normal. 'I've counted those on my arms and legs. You and Mary, Cecil and John – my little family – are the only ones I can trust to tell me the truth, even when I don't want to hear it. Well?'

No one had told her about Mary's tragedy yet. No setbacks, Dr Burcote had insisted. But I reckoned there would be many of those over the years, and, with Elizabeth as queen, many great leaps ahead for England, too. If she asked me about Mary, I would tell her the truth.

'I see one high on your forehead,' I said, leaning close to her and squinting, 'no, two – not very large scabs. One on your left cheek and one on your chin – that one a bit deep – but all of which, I warrant, we shall be able to cover with creams so that nothing looks amiss.'

'Thank you,' she said, and snagged my wrist. 'Kat, tell me true about something else the doctors won't. Mary Sidney – is she ill?'

'Yes, Your Grace. She will live, but the pox will leave her much worse off than you look.'

'Ah, beautiful Mary, and tending me,' she said, and tears tracked down her cheeks. 'Serving me – danger and destruction for her and how many others over the years? However she looks, I will never desert her, just as you have never deserted me. But there is something else before I go to comfort her. Something you must do for me.'

'Of course, Your Maj—'

'Besides not being hesitant to call me your lovey or your girl again, I mean.' She took her double-portrait ring from her finger easily for, as slender as she was, the disease had wasted her form even more. She touched the tiny spring, and we both peered down at the painted pictures of the queen as a toddler and the bold, brave Anne Boleyn.

'You knew both of us, served both of us, loved both of us through good times and bad,' she whispered, her eyes still running tears. 'She left me this ring, but she left it to you too.'

'Only as a keepsake for you. I wore it for years, remember?'

'You wore it for her and me, and I want you to do that now.'

She extended it to me and, when I didn't move, she pulled my hand closer and tried to put it on me.

'Your Grace – my lovey, my girl—'

'You cannot gainsay the queen, Kat.'

I had at least a brace of arguments, but I was so deeply touched. This brilliant and beautiful and brazen Tudor, by far the best of them all, had always touched me deeply, so any of my trials from her fearsome family were well worth the price.

'I shall wear it as a sign of – of all my times with the Tudors,' I promised as she put it on the finger next to my wedding ring, from the only other person I had loved so well in this life.

'Now then, I've much to do,' she said, throwing the covers off her legs and swiping at her wet cheeks. 'Please fetch my robe, for I must go to comfort Mary. That's where Dr Burcote's been, I warrant. I must be certain he is well rewarded for his good work – my dear Cecil too.'

She looked wan, weak and bedraggled, but as my girl stood on her own two feet and I wrapped a robe around her and combed the crown of her red-gold hair, she had never looked more a queen.

# AUTHOR'S NOTE

Readers are always interested to hear what happened to characters after the story itself ends, so a few odds and ends about that. Two years after she survived the pox that almost killed her, Elizabeth elevated Robert Dudley to the peerage as Earl of Leicester, rather than giving him the more coveted title Earl of Warwick. She also gave him Kenilworth Palace, which he enlarged and where he entertained her in later years. Robert was never far from the throne. When he died in 1588, I believe he was still the only man Elizabeth Tudor had deeply loved; she kept all his letters, which were found when she died. Robert remarried but had no children. His stepson became the Earl of Essex, also dear to the aging queen, but a man who, like Robert, caused her much heartache.

I note also that Elizabeth was always loyal to Mary Sidney, visiting her in her chosen retirement away from court. Although Mary usually remained a recluse because of her severe facial scarring from the pox, the queen kept a suite of rooms available for her and visited her privately when she agreed to visit the court.

As for William Cecil, Elizabeth always trusted him implicitly. She gave him increasingly powerful duties such as Lord Treasurer and elevated him to become Baron Burleigh. In his final illness, the queen visited him and fed him with her own hand. Although his heir Thomas by his first wife turned out to be a wastrel, his and Mildred's son, Robert, Earl of Salisbury, took over for Cecil as Elizabeth's chief secretary after Cecil's death in 1598. The Cecils traded Elizabeth's successor, King James I, some property to attain old Hatfield House, which they left standing, although they built a new manor there. It's a great place to visit. Until several years ago, they had propped up an old oak and claimed that it was under that tree Elizabeth learned that she was queen.

Should anyone wonder what happened to Tom Seymour and Katherine Parr's daughter, Mary, who had lost both her parents by age seven months, as in other Tudor records, there is some controversy. Some researchers claim she died shortly after her second birthday and was buried on the grounds of the Duchess of Suffolk, who had taken the child into her family. Others claim Mary survived and was taken to France with the Duchess of Suffolk to escape religious persecution under Queen Mary. Then again, controversy begins as to whether, after her return to England, she died of consumption at an early age or lived to wed Sir Edward Bushel, who served King James I.

Kat Ashley died in 1565; it was recorded that

417

her passing was 'deeply mourned by the queen.' John Ashley lived a good deal longer, dying in 1596 at a ripe old age. His book, *The Art of Riding*, was published and remained popular for several hundred years. As far as I can tell, even if John Ashley was not the first 'horse whisperer,' he was the first one to write in English about training horses with gentleness and patience. Unfortunately, his book is now out of print, or at least I could not locate a copy of it.

Also, a note on names: The Elizabethans are notorious for being inconsistent spellers. Spelling, including their own names, was not standardized, and one person might write his or her name various ways. This includes the greatest writer of the age, William Shakespeare/Shaxpere/Shagspear/Shakspere. While researching this novel, I also found the infinite variety of how to spell less famous names.

At various times I saw the maiden name of the main character in this book spelled Champernoun, Champernown, Champernon, and Champernowne. Although Katherine/Catherine spelled her own last name different ways, I have used the most common spelling of it, Champernowne, in Devon, the area of her birth.

The 'correct' spelling of Katherine Champernowne's married name is even harder to pin down. The big argument is between Ashley and Astley. In Mary M. Luke's excellent book, *A Crown for Elizabeth*, she notes that 'in correspondence of the period, Katherine Ashley is often referred to as Mrs Astley.' She goes on to explain that the owner of the Katherine Ashley portrait, Lady Marguerite Hastings, of Norfolk, England, claims that Astley was Katherine's actual last name. As Lady Hastings's husband was an Astley, she may have that on good family authority – or, as with some genealogies, it may be wishful thinking.

However, the Ashley pronunciation, and therefore spelling, seems most common among people, including Elizabeth Tudor, who obviously knew Katherine and her husband well. Queen Elizabeth (and no woman was better educated in the kingdom) spelled Katherine's married name with the *sh* rather than *st* sound. This includes a very important letter of 1549 in which the fifteen-year-old Elizabeth's spelling of the name of her beloved friend and governess was Kateryn Ashiley – but the *sh* sound and spelling are still there. So I will let the queen decide my *sh* or *st* dilemma and use Ashley.

Besides the variant spelling of words and names, there are other major challenges in Tudor era research. One is simply that, whatever excellent sources are consulted, 'facts' sometimes do not agree. If I can find three sources and two agree, I go with that. Other times, contradictions allow me to use what seems most logical. A small example: one reference claims that Queen Jane Seymour labored for three days to deliver her son,

Edward; another reference states two days. As she died shortly after the birth, I chose the three days, although that may not be valid. Another example: one source claims that John Ashley studied in Padua, Italy, during Mary's entire reign. Another says that by June 1555 Elizabeth 'had the Ashleys back.' And so it goes.

As for 'correct' dates, again research can be confusing. For example, their new year began on Lady Day, March 25, even though January 1 was called New Year's Day. This can throw things off, depending on who is recording what. Once again, I used dates I found in the majority of my references.

Another problem I faced while researching Katherine Champernowne Ashley is Kat's pedigree. In the Tudor world, where families and birth order and titles mattered a great deal, her family heritage is a contested mystery. The two main schools of thought both have drawbacks. Let me first outline these confusing, conflicting claims as simply as possible:

1. Some reputable sources claim that Katherine (or Catherine) Champernowne is the child of Sir John Champernowne of Dartington, Devon, and Margaret Courtenay. This family was, evidently, quite well-to-do. However, Sir John died in 1503 and Kat was probably born a bit later. Another reason these parents are

420

probably not hers is that in a letter to Thomas Cromwell in 1536, asking for funds to care for Elizabeth, Kateryn Champernon states that she would ask her father for financial help except that he 'has as much to do with the little living he has as any man.' [*Letters and Papers, Foreign and Domestic, of the Reign of Henry VIII*, vol. 11, p. 253, letter of October 10, 1536.] That is, her father is not a wealthy man and has worries of his own. So Kat's 'poor' father was living in 1536, and the wealthy Sir John was not.

2. The other front-runner for her father is Sir Philip Champernowne of Modbury, Devon. Married to Katherine Carew, he died in 1545, but he was also a well-to-do man, one the Crown had relied on to provide fighting men and funds. He had several manors and was one of the most powerful men in Devon. Just a few days before Kat's letter mentioned above, Sir Philip provided one hundred men for the king's forces against the northern rebels. Another caveat for Sir Philip being Kat's sire: There was another Katherine (older than Kat, later an ancestor of Sir Walter Raleigh) in that family. The same name in one brood for two children, unless the

older child was deceased, was highly unlikely.

3. There is also a third candidate for her father: Sir Edmund Carew. This theory claims Champernoun is Kat's early married name, but, again, Sir Edmund died before she wrote the Cromwell letter, and there is no proof she wed anyone but John Ashley.

So, perhaps one of the reasons Kat's life story has not been told before is because it is hard to get a handle on her beginnings. Those in the Philip of Modbury camp and in the Sir John of Dartington camp both claim that Jane (also called Joan) Champernowne is Kat's sister. Since Joan became Lady Denny, wed to a key court figure, Sir Anthony Denny, and a distant ancestor of Prince Charles, Diana, Princess of Wales, and Winston Churchill, it seems Joan's pedigree would be clear. But it is not. Those who claim Joan and Kat were sisters do so through assumptions, not proof.

In my research I have not found evidence they were sisters, although they do have the same maiden name and both come from Devonshire. (Devon was then *full* of Champernownes.) It is true both women were strong, evangelical Protestants, but many of that day were. Even when Joan took over Elizabeth's care at one point when Kat was dismissed, no one, including Elizabeth, who wrote several letters protesting Kat's removal, mentioned that one sister was taking over for the other, when that would have been an obvious time to do so.

To top off all this confusion, many of the Tudor-era Devonshire Champernownes named their children using the same names: Catherine/Katherine appears numerous times, as does Joan, Philip, etc. Because Kat comes to court as a gentlewoman and, apparently from a rather 'impoverished family,' as one source puts it, I agree with Bruce Clagett, who has researched Kat's pedigree for years (GEN-MEDIEVAL-L Archives online), that Kat 'may have belonged to an obscure younger branch of the family.' She was well educated but not well supported, and relied on her patron Cromwell's goodwill for years. And Cromwell was always out to serve King Henry and himself, the two most devious powers of that era.

Another note on confusing families: the Sir Philip Champernowne family of Modbury is listed in various sources as having different children. *Burke's Landed Gentry of Great Britain* includes John, Arthur, Elizabeth, Joan, Katherine and Francis, then a second Joan (and, finally – erroneously, I believe – our Kat). However, the online source www.fabpedigree.com lists only Arthur, Jane (Joan) and a Katherine. Yet another source lists Catherine, John, Arthur, Joan, Elizabeth and Frances. Of course, some of this confusion can be caused by the fact that many children died early. It is, at least, established that Joan, who married Sir Anthony Denny, is from this family, whether or not Robert Gamage was her husband before she wed Sir Anthony Denny.

All this to say, the more power to this remarkable woman if she came from an obscure, impoverished family.

About the double-portrait ring that Anne Boleyn gives Kat to keep for Elizabeth: such a ring exists, although with a more mature portrait of Elizabeth. During a 2003 research trip to England, I was able to view this ring with other items of Elizabeth's at the National Maritime Museum's Exhibition at Greenwich honoring the queen 400 years after her death. The ring has been dated circa 1575, because of the era of Elizabeth's portrait, but I like to think that it was entirely possible that Elizabeth had that updated to have pictures of two queens. I have read that the queen, among her many rings she changed frequently, always wore this one. (In my telling of the story, of course, the queen would have taken the ring back when Kat Ashley died.) The fact that Anne Boleyn's face was hidden allowed her to keep it close to her without others knowing that she honored her mother as she did her father. Despite the charges against Queen Anne and her shameful death, other proofs of Elizabeth's loyalty to the Boleyn side of her heritage abound.

It is difficult to assess the full impact Katherine

Ashley had on the life of Elizabeth Tudor. The bonds of affection between them were obvious, as seen in letters Elizabeth wrote to defend both Kat and John when they were arrested in her service. Because Kat was Elizabeth's mother figure, despite how she was fascinated by her birth mother, I like to think of Elizabeth as saying, 'Anne Boleyn gave me life, but Kat Ashley gave me love.' And Elizabeth did acknowledge in a letter that 'we are more bound to them that bringeth us up well than to our parents, for our parents do that which is natural to them – that is bringeth us into the world – but our bringers up are a cause to make us live well to do it.'

Anne's poem written before her death and the records of Kat's deposition in the Tower are factual. Also, the letters in the book and the poem to Robert Dudley are actually Elizabeth's. She wrote numerous poems, letters, prayers and speeches, which are set forth in an excellent reference, *Elizabeth I: Collected Works*, edited by Leah S. Marcus, Janel Mueller and Mary Beth Rose (University of Chicago Press, 2000).

Other books on the queen and her family well worth reading include *Henry VIII and His Court* by Neville Williams; *The Life and Times of Elizabeth I* by Neville Williams; *The Life of Elizabeth I* by Alison Weir; *A Crown for Elizabeth* by Mary M. Luke; *Elizabeth: The Struggle for the Throne* by David Starkey; and *All the Queen's Men* by Neville Williams. Obviously, there are numerous other biographies of key characters and other nonfiction books on Tudor England available. My bookshelves groan with them, and I delight in them.

*Karen Harper*